What Some Extra-Special Readers are Saying about
Three Weddings & a Giggle...

"Talk about a work of fiction! Liz assures me I'm her hero, but unlike this Hugh Osborne guy, I wouldn't be caught dead wearing a pair of bunny ears. I liked her story, though. You will, too."

BILL HIGGS, PH.D., HUSBAND OF LIZ CURTIS HIGGS

"I highly recommend that you buy this book. Not so much because it is well written and hilarious—though it certainly is!—but rather because the royalties will go toward that new nail gun I've had my eye on."

MATT PIZZUTI, HUSBAND OF CAROLYN ZANE

"I' ... ne of
th ... book
is ... ed, I
cr ... me
re ... njoy.
Y

Three Weddings and a Giggle

3 Novellas

Liz Curtis Higgs
Carolyn Zane
Karen Ball

Multnomah®Publishers *Sisters, Oregon*

THREE WEDDINGS & A GIGGLE
published by Multnomah Publishers, Inc.

"Fine Print" © 2001 by Liz Curtis Higgs
published in association with the literary agency of Sara A. Fortenberry

"Sweet Chariot" © 2001 by Carolyn Suzanne Pizzuti
published in association with the literary agency of Sara A. Fortenberry

"Bride on the Run" © 2001 by Karen M. Ball

International Standard Book Number: 1-57673-656-3

Cover image by Andrea Sperling/FPG International LLC
Cover image of mouse by Index Stock Imagery

Multnomah is a trademark of Multnomah Publishers, Inc., and is registered
at the U.S. Patent and Trademark office.
The colophon is a trademark of Multnomah Publishers, Inc.

Printed in the United States of America

For information:
Multnomah Publishers, Inc.•Post Office Box 1720•Sisters, Oregon 97759

Library of Congress Cataloging-in-Publication Data

Higgs, Liz Curtis.
    Three weddings & a giggle /c by Liz Curtis Higgs, Carolyn Zane, Karen Ball
        p.cm. ISBN 1-57673-656-3 (pbk.)
    1. Christian fiction, American. 2. Humorous stories, American. 3. Love
stories, American. 4. Weddings–Fiction. I. Title: Three weddings and a giggle.
II. Zane, Carolyn. III. Ball, Karen, 1957– IV. Title.
    PS3558.I36235 T48 2001   813'.54–dc21   00-012266

02 03 04 05 06—10 9 8 7 6 5 4

For my co-conspirators in fun, Karen and Carolyn—two crazy women who were among the first storytellers to read "Fine Print," my initial go at fiction in 1996. Bless you, sisters, for giving me the courage to go on…and on…and…

Liz

For Jeff and Elizabeth Kelley—one fun couple whom I adore not just because they were stupid enough to buy a thirty-year-old motor home with us on the spur of the moment, not pausing to question the asking price, or if the dumb thing even ran…but because they can still laugh about it, even after we found out the generator was toast, the appliances did not work, the walls were rotten, and the vehicle guzzled more fuel than the OPEC nations could supply. I love ya, man. Here's to years of camping together.

Carolyn

To Julee and Peggy, my heart-sisters—No one makes me laugh…and think…and ponder the deep things of life the way you two do. No one has ever had better (or more patient) friends. Here's to our nutty times together (Arkansas and the Turpentine Creek Wildlife Rehab center—how many people do you know who've been tinkled on by a tiger?; the Brookfield Zoo—oh, those crazy polar bears!; Borders for life's essentials: books, coffee, and talking; "Cracker Barrel!"; the death-defying hike up Table Rock; the zip line; "You be all right"; and so much more!).

Thanks for letting the kids inside come out to play with me.

I love you, dear ones.

Karen

Contents

Fine Print

Liz Curtis Higgs

Acknowledgments

Heartfelt hugs to…

Norma Blumenschine, former owner of Open Windows Bed & Breakfast in Suttons Bay, Michigan, for offering both enthusiastic feedback and the scrumptious recipe featured at the end of "Fine Print."

Jo Panter at Rainbow Bookstore in Traverse City, Michigan, for reading an early draft and making wise suggestions about local items of interest.

Elizabeth Jeffries, CSP, CPAE, of Louisville, Kentucky, for sharing valuable insights about speaking and consulting.

Betty and Jim Kennedy of B&J Printing in Jeffersonville, Indiana, for helping me get my facts straight about the printing business.

Bless you one and all for your "fine" contributions found here in "print"!

Liz

Prologue

The supply of good women far exceeds that of the men
who deserve them.

ROBERT GRAVES

regory.

Meghan DeWitt couldn't believe it was him.

Standing there, motionless, waiting to greet her as she strolled into the Concourse G waiting area.

Bigger than life and more handsome than ever.

The rat.

Meghan's heart landed somewhere around her ankles. She swallowed hard and tried to look nonchalant as she followed the deplaning passengers who were moving herdlike in the direction of Gregory's smiling face.

"Lord," Meghan whispered under her breath, "this isn't the least bit funny." She knew He was listening, though the still small voice was very still indeed this morning.

Gregory's face loomed closer.

It was him, all right, flashing that camera-perfect grin, every sandy brown hair in place. Mr. Nightly News, Greg Hammond, right there in the Detroit Metro Airport, a mere two feet away from the one woman on earth who secretly hoped he'd swallow his lapel microphone.

On camera.

Sometime between weather and sports.

Good thing this wasn't the *real* Gregory—only a cardboard version in a floor to ceiling advertising display. Slick, high-profile, and shallow.

Just like you-know-who.

Meghan was practically nose to nose with him before the idea came to her: If she had a black marker in her purse, she could draw a nice, ugly mustache on his three-foot-wide face.

The Channel 6 logo loomed behind him with one phrase emblazoned across the bottom: *The One You Can Depend On.*

"Oh, please." *Less funny by the minute, Lord.* Meghan touched the smooth surface of the display ad and bit her lower lip to keep from screaming. Or was it laughing?

When it involved Gregory, eventually it was both.

Two years earlier when they'd worked together in Columbus, the two of them had been engaged—the hunky six o'clock anchor and the lively brunette news reporter, a seen-about-town twosome that made the features section of the *Columbus Dispatch* on a regular basis.

Then Gregory entertained a solid offer from a major station in Detroit. The money was impressive, the time slot even more so, and the lure of a top-ten market proved too good to refuse.

"I'll get settled in while you put the finishing touches on our wedding plans," he'd purred, his chiseled smile exactly like the photo image at her fingertips. "Stick with me, Meg. The Motor City is only the beginning."

Gregory had promised her the world; Meghan had adored him too much to notice it wasn't his to give.

Within weeks, bright, educated, eager-to-please Meghan had said farewell to their peers at Channel 10 in Columbus and devoted every waking moment to creating a once-in-a-lifetime, call-*BRIDE*-magazine wedding. Invitations went out to throngs of friends from their postgraduate days at Ohio State University. Distant cousins and childhood classmates in postage-stamp towns across the Buckeye state circled May 1 on their social calendars.

"When I think of the hours I agonized over whether to serve green mints or yellow ones," Meghan fretted to herself, her eyes still trained on the two-dimensional object of her disdain.

In the end, there were no mints and there was no wedding. The four-hour drive from Columbus to Detroit every weekend put hundreds of miles on her Chevrolet, and even more on her heart. Little by little, so slowly that Meghan almost didn't notice, Greg began to distance himself from her.

Wrapped up in bridal lace and dinner linens—not to mention the five-speed blenders and silver-plated serving dishes pouring through her suburban Westerville door—Meghan was utterly unprepared for the phone call that came one April night.

"Meghan?" Gregory's voice sounded strained; not at all the smooth tones of a network-bound broadcaster. "We need to talk."

"Do what?" Meghan let loose a sleepy yawn. "I'll be up there tomorrow night, handsome. Let's talk then." She squinted at her alarm clock. "What time is it, anyway?"

"This…it can't wait until tomorrow night."

At the *Warning! Warning!* edge in his voice, she sat up straight in bed, feeling her skin grow warm. Flulike symptoms washed over her—hot, cold, hot, cold—and she pulled the covers up around her neck to keep from shivering.

Her voice was reduced to a froggy croak. "What's going on, Greg?"

Everything was going on—except the wedding. Greg stumbled through a half-baked, warmed-over story of new vistas and old regrets, repeating himself and adding pointless details. Even in the midst of her numbing pain, Meghan thought, *The man can't ad-lib to save his life. Without a TelePrompTer, he's toast.*

The messy narrative finally hit bottom when Gregory admitted he'd fallen in love with the technical director of Detroit's *News at Noon.*

"The tech director?!" A faint vision of Greg sharing kisses with a nameless beauty in a headset flitted through Meghan's barely-functional brain. "So, you'll be…marrying her? Instead?" The first tear slid down her cheek.

"I'm sorry, Meghan." He sounded almost sincere. "I should have told you sooner."

No, we should have married sooner. Skipped the wedding and eloped. Anything but this. Her shoulders sagged under the bedcovers. "Listen, I gotta go."

She eased the phone receiver down, numb to the core. *Now what, Lord?* She had no Plan B. Let alone C or D. What woman made a list of things to do "in case you're jilted"?

That left only one option: sob uncontrollably while eating a pint of Haagen-Dazs Chocolate Chocolate Fudge.

"This can't be happening," she moaned between bites. "It's April. I love April. How could my life be ruined in April?"

April was definitely ruined. May was shot to pieces, too.

Through the agonizing, embarrassing weeks that followed, Meghan didn't lay eyes on Greg. Had he walked through her door, he would've been clobbered by a flying punch bowl or plug-in lasagna dish as merchandise sailed through the air on a return trip to the Columbus department stores that had delivered them.

Meghan was fearless. She cancelled the flowers, paid off the musicians, and ate wedding cake for a month, all the while insisting she was thrilled to have her freedom back.

No one believed her, but they were smart enough not to say anything.

The only gift she couldn't bear to return was a dainty lace pillow, hand-embroidered with *Meghan and Greg* in navy and peach floss. It clashed with her decor, but the heart-shaped pillow made an excellent therapeutic device. She could toss it across the room, stomp on it, or thrash it against the wall and watch it bounce back for more.

Meghan sent the woman who'd stitched the pillow a generous check and a glowing thank-you note. "You've given me the one pleasure I'll never have this side of heaven—seeing Gregory Hammond crushed beneath my bedroom slipper, in danger of losing his stuffing."

Meghan pushed away the memories, stuffing her plane ticket back in her purse, when she felt a tap on her shoulder.

"Making a connection, ma'am?"

She stared at the perky, twenty-something flight attendant. *Ma'am?! Fine, great, just what I need on top of Gregory the Dependable.* Meghan sighed. "Traverse City, Michigan."

"Gate G-7." The young woman pointed across the concourse. "It leaves in ten minutes."

Meghan thanked her and hurried toward the gate, her carry-on bag careening along behind in a futile attempt to keep up with its owner. A seasoned traveler, Meghan packed light and never gave an airline the chance to route her luggage through, say, Poughkeepsie. Or Bora Bora.

She settled into an aisle seat and closed her eyes. Never mind Channel 10, Channel 6, or the rest of it. Things had turned out fine—in fact, better than she could ever have imagined.

Her new, Greg-free career as an executive speech coach had improved her confidence—and her bank account—considerably. She'd finally moved into her custom-designed Cape Cod last month, built half a block from the church that had been family to her all through her recovery process.

Furthermore, April had come and gone—twice—without a tear.

Meghan smiled as she reached for her briefcase. As long as the Gregorys of the world kept their distance, she was going to live happily ever after in cozy Westerville, Ohio.

All by her peaceful self.

One

There is but one pleasure in life equal to that of being called on to make an after-dinner speech, and that is not being called on to make one.

CHARLES DUDLEY WARNER

After Detroit Metro, the Cherry Capital Airport was a piece of cake.

Meghan steered her way through the milling crowd, finally planting herself near the Hertz counter and scanning the Traverse City visitors wandering past her.

"Look for a silver-haired fella in a plaid shirt," Roger Osborne had said in his warm, grandfatherly voice when they'd touched base by phone yesterday. She pictured the CEO of Osborne and Osborne Printing as a sixtyish Santa type, with intelligent eyes and a face filled with wrinkles. Undoubtedly, he was retiring from the daily grind and planning a new career on the lecture circuit. Why else would he need her coaching services?

Then she saw him: A tall, broad-shouldered man in a plaid sport shirt and tan slacks, looking a bit befuddled. *Bingo. Sixtyish. I was right. Dockers? Must be dress-down day at the office.*

He glanced up at last, and his frown eased into a hesitant grin. "Are you...Miss DeWitt?" Her hand disappeared in the warm grasp of his well-tanned fingers. "It is *Miss* DeWitt, yes?" His eyes were twinkling.

What a nice guy. She flashed her most professional smile. "So good to meet you, Mr. Osborne. I'm ready if you are."

He gathered up her luggage. "Carry-on bag, eh? Only enough for the two days, I see." His brow wrinkled for a moment, before he mumbled almost to himself, "No problem. Plenty of places to shop in Suttons Bay." Brightening, he waved her bag toward the door. "Right this way, young lady."

The *young lady* almost cancelled out the *ma'am* she'd heard in Detroit. *Almost.* And what was that business about shopping? She had more than enough clothes for two days. *Whatever.* Executives usually assumed it would take her a full week of coaching when, in fact, forty-eight hours was sufficient. He'd find that out soon enough.

Mr. Osborne held open the glass doors that ushered them back into the humid morning air and steered her toward the blue minivan with *O & O Printing* painted boldly across the side.

"Classy logo, Mr. Osborne." She slid into the front seat, anticipating the welcome chill of the air conditioner.

"Call me Mr. O. Everybody else does." The minivan started with a roar. "Hugh picked that out."

Hugh who? She buckled her seat belt and smoothed her skirt in place. "You say he picked out Mr. O?"

His hearty laugh bounced off the dashboard. "No, no! He picked out the company logo. Our employees picked 'Mr. O.' You'll be on a first name basis with the whole gang within a month."

"A *month?*"

His head snapped toward her. "D-did I say a month? No, I meant…ah, I meant a week. Well, that is to say, by the *weekend.*" He scratched his head, his cheeks ruddy. "Don't mind me, Miss DeWitt." The minivan headed out of the airport and turned left onto a busy road that hugged the bay. "Just sit back and enjoy the drive."

Poor man. Maybe the concept of a young, female coach unnerved him. She'd give him time to get comfortable with the idea by doing exactly as he suggested and taking in the scenery.

Meghan had visited bits and pieces of Michigan, but never the northwest corner. Majestic pines lined the road and high-end resort condos competed with mom-and-pop cabins for curb space. Between the evergreens, Meghan caught glimpses of Grand Traverse Bay, glistening in the morning light like a cool, blue-green sheet of glass.

"So." She turned toward the man behind the wheel, noticing his breathing was easier and his blush had faded. "You were telling me about O & O."

"Right. My father was 'Mr. Osborne.' Started the business sixty years ago with a handful of locals in the press room. Nobody thought he'd make it. Except Mother." His expression softened. "We have more than fifty employees now. Biggest year-round business in Suttons Bay, next to cherries and tourists. Dad brought me into the business when I was ten. Taught me everything from setting type to bidding a job. When it was my turn to run things, I became Mr. O."

"Oh."

"Hugh is just...Hugh."

"Who *is* Hugh?"

"Huh?"

"Hugh *who?*"

"Oh, *Hugh!*"

Were Abbott and Costello hiding in the backseat? Meghan swallowed a giggle. "Let me try again. Who is this Hugh person?"

"I thought you'd never ask." The grin spreading across Mr. O's face took twenty years off his features. Maybe more. "Hugh is my son, the heir-apparent of O & O Printing. He's your coaching assignment, Miss DeWitt."

What? "You mean you and I won't be working together?" She was genuinely disappointed. Even more, she was confused. One of her partners, Dan Ross, had filled out the client profile while she was in Denver last week. Her only conversation with Mr. O had been their brief phone chat yesterday. Had he even mentioned his son?

"I'm sorry I won't be coaching *you*," she said at last, and meant it. He was such a kind man, nothing like the hyper-driven CEOs and young Turks—or was it turkeys?—she usually coached.

"I'm sorry too, Miss DeWitt." He winked at her, then turned his eyes back toward the road. "My son is in for a real treat."

She smiled, temporarily distracted by the sunlight shimmering on the bay and a family of mallards paddling their way along the water's edge. "So, tell me about Hugh."

"He's a fine catch…er, *character*." He winced, then quickly continued. "A solid citizen of Suttons Bay. Respected by other business executives across the state, appreciated by his friends at church, and admired by every employee at O & O."

The man's proud-papa description warmed her heart. "Hugh sounds like a natural leader. I can't imagine he needs much help with his public-speaking skills."

"Hugh needs you, all right." His voice was so low, she wasn't sure if he meant her to hear him. He ran a hand through his thick silver hair. "Miss DeWitt—"

"Please, call me Meghan."

"Meghan, then. You deserve to know what you're getting yourself into here. My son has the worst case of stage fright you've ever seen. One on one, he could sell printing services to a dental hygienist while she's flossing his teeth. On the phone, he can wheel and deal like Monty Hall. And at our staff meetings, he has folks hanging on his every word, like a bunch of little birds waiting for a worm." He shook his head and sighed heavily. "Put Hugh on a platform with an audience, and he's a cotton-mouthed, sweaty-palmed, tongue-tied mess. Get the picture?"

"Clearer by the minute." Meghan smiled. She loved the nervous ones. Give her an executive who couldn't put a coherent sentence together while standing knock-kneed in front of a crowd, and she was in heaven. Two days with her, and they went from stammering card readers to silver-tongued orators.

Well, at the very least their knees stopped shaking.

Jotting down a few pertinent notes, she pressed for details. "What sort of speaking situations does Hugh find himself in?"

"Awful ones." Mr. O grimaced. "Hugh's the incoming president of the Traverse City Area Chamber of Commerce. First time they've ever honored a Suttons Bay business owner like that. Everybody loves my son except Mr. Microphone."

Meghan looked up from her notebook. "So, are we hoping to get him ready for a particular presentation?" She could read the bad news in his eyes. "It's soon, isn't it?"

"You don't miss much, Miss DeWitt." He studied her for a moment, then sighed heavily. "Three weeks. That's when he gives his presidential speech for the Chamber of Commerce banquet. Can you get his butterflies flying in formation by July 30?"

She laughed gently. "That's why you're paying me the big bucks, Mr. O. Don't worry. I handle fifty assignments like this every year. Hugh is in good hands." A companionable silence filled the van as they continued north along a two-lane road that meandered along the shoreline.

"Just so you'll know, Meghan, I've reserved a room for you at one of our local bed-and-breakfast spots. Open Windows, they call it. White picket fence, green shutters, view of the bay, candles in the windows." An elfin smile creased his face. "Your kind of place, I imagine."

He doesn't miss much either. "Can't wait to see it," she murmured.

As though on cue, the *Welcome to Suttons Bay* sign appeared. They turned away from the water and onto a heavily wooded side street, then pulled into the parking lot of a sprawling, one-story brick building displaying the familiar bold O & O logo.

Moments later, Mr. O ushered her down a paneled hallway and into a brightly lit office. Distracted by dozens of paper stock sample books littering the floor, she almost didn't see a man rising to his feet behind an expansive oak desk buried under a small mountain of file folders.

"Miss DeWitt?"

The first thing Meghan noticed was Hugh Osborne's height. Even the tallest pile of papers only reached his waist. Her gaze swept up the long row of shirt buttons to a collar unencumbered by a tie. Six-foot-three, easy. Muscular neck. Strong chin. *Is that a dimple in his cheek?* A charming, ear-to-ear smile that made her automatically smile back, and a face framed with dark brown wavy hair.

But it was the enormous pair of chocolate brown eyes, now trained on hers, that stopped Meghan's breath and sent her heart spinning in a merry dance.

She looked up at him and said the first thing that popped into her addled mind. "Hello…Huge!"

Huge?!

She tried desperately to recover, to act as if she hadn't just shoved her high heel down her throat, but there was no getting around her sizeable faux pas.

Hugh's rich, baritone laugh swirled around her. "I've heard that name before, believe me."

Mr. O patted her shoulder. "Don't fret, Meghan. It's time somebody cut him down to size." He pulled a chair out, nodded at her to sit down, then leaned over and said in a stage whisper, "He needs a lot of work, young lady. Don't let him give you too much trouble, hear?"

Two

I hear a sudden cry of pain! There is a rabbit in a snare.

JAMES STEPHENS

'm in serious trouble here.

Hugh watched the door close, leaving him alone with this small, dark-haired beauty gazing at him across his trash can of a desk.

He broke the awkward silence first. "Dad seems comfortable calling you Meghan. Is that your preference?"

She nodded slightly, her head tipped back as though regarding him. "I'd be very comfortable with Meghan. Shall I call you Hugh?"

Call me anything you like. He looked at the woman perched on the chair before him. *Does she know what a knockout she is? How could she not?* Her dark, straight hair brushed against her shoulders, thick as velvet. *Does it feel as smooth as it looks?* Rosy lips bloomed in the middle of ivory skin that was the color of rich cream. But those eyes! Pale blue, almost shocking, compared to the deep richness of her hair.

Those sparkling eyes were looking at him now. What was he supposed to be saying?

"Oh! Yes, call me Hugh. Hugh is fine." He flashed a grin he hoped would look casual and nonchalant, as though gorgeous women invaded his printing plant every day. "So, where do we start? Dad told you I'm hopeless, I suppose."

"Nothing of the sort."

Was that *her* version of a casual smile or was she hiding something? He shoved his hands into his pockets and waited for her to continue.

She tapped her notebook. "He did tell me that you have a major presentation coming up in a few weeks."

"Two weeks, five days, seven hours."

"You've been counting, I see. Stage fright is very common, Hugh, and usually has a definable source." Her voice was gentle, her expression compassionate. "Many successful people fear public speaking, so there's nothing to be embarrassed about. Can you put your finger on when your stage fright started?"

Hugh dropped down into his leather chair. *I can put my finger on it, all right.* His pulse was hammering away in his temple, his throat, his chest. "You'll think I'm certifiable."

She held up three fingers. "Scout's honor, I promise not to laugh. Tell me, Hugh. It will help me understand what you're going through."

He took a deep breath. "Third grade, Suttons Bay Elementary. I'm in the Easter pageant. The other kids are dressed up as eggs and chicks and jelly beans, but I'm the tallest kid in the class, so I have to be the Easter bunny."

The what?

Meghan mashed her top teeth into her bottom lip. She would not laugh. She would *not*. But she had to know. "Did you have a big, fuzzy white costume?"

He nodded. "With a fluffy white tail."

"Big ears?"

His long arms stretched above his head, creating imaginary ears of untold proportions. "Gargantuan. Big feet, too, but that wasn't the costume designer's fault."

"So what happened?"

"The auditorium was filled with screaming grade schoolers and their parents." He paused as if remembering. "Maybe it was the parents who were screaming. Anyway, on cue, I hopped out onto the stage—"

"And you forgot your lines!" Meghan blurted out, seeing his problem in an instant.

"No. I never got to my lines." Hugh wasn't smiling, which damped her enthusiasm in a hurry. "I hopped over to the microphone, opened my mouth to speak, and then…" He looked away, his lips pressed into a thin, hard line.

Bless his heart. She rose to her feet and moved closer to him in silent support as he continued, his voice noticeably tighter.

"And then I bent over to put down my Easter basket and promptly ripped a seam up the back of my costume, dropping the whole fluffy fiasco down around my ankles."

"Oh, Hugh!" Meghan slapped a hand over her mouth, but it was too late to stop the loud *whoop!* that slipped through her fingers.

I knew she'd laugh.

A familiar heaviness filled his chest. Whatever possessed him to tell her in the first place? So much for impressing the woman with his business savvy. *Go ahead, Osborne, just blurt it all out. Describe your first date, while you're at it. Make an even bigger fool of yourself.*

Meghan cleared her throat. "I am *so* sorry, Hugh. I didn't mean to laugh. Honest."

"Why shouldn't you laugh?" He sighed. "The audience did. Boy, did they laugh. There I stood, wearing nothing but my underwear and a pair of twenty-inch, pink-and-white bunny ears. I brought the house down. Unfortunately, my confidence went down along with it."

Meghan's hands met in a single clap of excitement. "You mean that experience is the sole reason you're scared to death of speaking?"

"Isn't that enough?" He shot out of the chair, feeling the vise in his chest clamp down tighter. "I can still hear them laughing, Miss DeWitt. Thirty years later."

"No wonder." Meghan's blue eyes held no judgment, only concern, as she stood and moved closer. "It certainly *is* reason enough to be leery of being on stage again. The good news is, you didn't fail as a *speaker,* your costume let you down." She winced. "Uh…what I mean is, you already possess great communication skills. You simply have one traumatic memory to put behind you. Have you ever talked with a counselor about it?"

A counselor? Great, now she thinks I'm a nutcase. He could feel his face growing warm. "I suppose you think I can exert a little willpower and make it go away?"

"Hugh, I never—"

"Well, it doesn't work that way!" He exhaled, forcing the pressure in his chest to ease up. "I've never told anyone about this. Heaven knows what compelled me to tell you, a total stranger."

"Heaven knows indeed." Her voice was gentle as she lightly touched his sleeve.

No doubt that soft hand resting on his arm was meant to calm him down. *Right?* His stomach did a slow cartwheel.

"Hugh, I'm not a stranger; I'm a coach." Her voice softened. "*Your* coach. This is precisely what I've been hired to do. What I'm *called* to do, in fact. I've helped dozens of executives work through this kind of thing."

He couldn't keep from grinning. "Oh? You've had lots of CEOs who hopped across stage with a bunny suit around their ankles?"

"Not exactly. But I've handled more than one case of stage fright." Meghan stepped closer still, lifting her chin. "Hugh, you need to know that I have a bachelor's degree in speech communications and an MBA from Ohio State. I did on-camera television news for four years in Columbus and have been coaching executives in public speaking for a decade."

Obviously she was trying to impress him.

Obviously, it's working.

Nor was she finished. "I have personally coached five senators and two governors; and my partners and I have worked with *Fortune 500* companies in twenty-seven states."

Meghan was almost standing toe to toe with him, close enough for him to feel a perceptible elevation in air temperature. Close enough to realize the woman barely reached the top of his shoulders.

Her voice grew softer, but no less determined sounding. "I know what I'm doing, Hugh. I can help you overcome this. On July 30, when you stand before your peers at the Chamber, you'll knock their socks off!"

He looked down at her, poised mere inches below his chin, intelligence and compassion pouring off her in waves, her blue eyes shining like liquid stars, her dark hair gleaming, her cheeks flushed with excitement, and he did the most natural thing in the world...

He backed up until he crashed into the bookcase behind his desk.

A dozen emotions churned around in his chest, clamoring for

attention. None of them had anything to do with his fear of the stage. No, this was another sort of fear altogether.

When he finally found his voice, it sounded hoarse and his breathing was uneven. "I have no doubt that you can do everything your brochure promises. Say the word, and we'll start."

Three

Why doesn't the fellow who says, "I'm no speechmaker," let it go at that instead of giving a demonstration?

KIN HUBBARD

*N*ot a bad start, Meghan decided, smiling back at Hugh.

Fifteen minutes into their session, she was precisely where she wanted to be: in charge. Yet another powerful executive had put his trust in her completely.

She took a deep breath and exhaled a silent prayer for wisdom. And insight. And the ability to concentrate. *It'd be easier, Lord, if Hugh weren't so handsome. Like old Gregory the Worst.*

"Hugh, if you're ready, then so am I." She held up her leather briefcase. "Why don't we find a clear spot on your desk?" Her eyes scanned the messy surface. *Could be a problem.*

"No problem." He wrapped his large hands around a stack of file folders and tossed the papers on the floor.

Meghan pressed her lips together to keep from chuckling. Once they had the speech challenge licked, he could definitely use some organizational skills. And where was his tie and jacket? *All in good time.*

"Now what?" Hugh dropped into his leather chair.

"Hugh, I'd like to start with—"

He jumped back up to his feet, sending his chair careening

toward the bookshelves. "Before we get rolling, have you ever worked with a client in the printing industry?"

Uh-oh. Where's this going? "Nooo, I haven't." Her skin grew uncomfortably warm as her credibility spiraled down the drain. *Shoulda done your homework on this one, Meg.* She squared her shoulders and said the only thing she could think of: "Shame on me for not knowing more about your business, Hugh."

"I can fix that. Why don't we take a walk through the press room before we do anything else?" He seemed pleased to have the upper hand again, striding toward the office door and grabbing a cellular phone off the credenza, then leading her down the hall toward an imposing metal door marked *Employees Only.*

"Two rules—" he swung open the door, then raised his voice over the din—"Don't be afraid to ask questions and don't touch anything."

The clack and clatter of machines in motion filled the air. Paper was stacked in haphazard piles around the room, and fumes from a dozen chemicals vied for her senses' attention. Award certificates and plaques—most of which were slightly askew—covered the walls.

She smiled and nodded as Hugh introduced her to one busy employee after another. "Here's Sheila. She handles electronic pre-press. That gray-haired guy is Pete, who makes our photopolymer plates. And this is Tina. She's a stripper."

"A...*what?*"

"A stripper." Hugh flashed a boyish grin. "She positions the negatives on flats. You know. She lays out a page for platemaking? We call it stripping."

Humph.

"Nice to meet you!" Meghan shouted in the woman's direction, then gave Hugh a pointed look. "You enjoyed that entirely too much."

"True." He stretched his grin another inch.

That dimple again.

Hugh guided her on a circuitous path through a dizzying array of machines that printed, folded, stuffed, and stapled. Inks of every hue sat in a jumble of pots on a shelf, cryptic numbers scribbled on their labels. Meghan took notes, asked questions, and tried to keep up with her client's detailed explanations of web-fed rotary presses, sheet-fed offset presses, and thermo-mechanical pulping.

Thirty minutes later, they were back in his office. If Hugh intended to thoroughly confuse her, he'd done a bang-up job.

She sank into a chair, rubbing her temples to ease the tension headache pounding behind her fingers. "Hugh, will knowing any of this help me turn you into a pro on the platform?"

"Absolutely not."

What? She looked up in time to catch a disarming wink.

"Truth is, Meghan, I needed to boost my confidence in what I *do* know before I'm forced to tackle something I *don't* know."

"I see." Their gazes held. One beat, then two.

Meghan moistened her suddenly dry lips. Truth was, she had a few confessions of her own which would never see the light of day.

Namely these: She appreciated his candor. She admired his expertise. She adored his dimple.

She was in deep trouble.

She hadn't felt such instant rapport and undeniable attraction to a man in years. Not since graduate school. Not since Gregory.

Meghan closed her eyes. Even the bright fluorescent lights added to the dull, throbbing ache in her head. "Do you have any aspirin?" she asked softly, squelching the temptation to whine.

"Better than that. I'll have aspirin, iced tea, and a chicken salad sandwich in here before you can spell magnetographic." She heard him make a quick phone call to put lunch in motion, then lean back in his chair. "Could be the chemicals, Meghan. That sodium hyposulfite is a killer. I avoid the darkroom like the plague."

She nodded once, moving her head as little as possible.

"Or could be the fact that you flew out of Columbus at the crack of dawn, probably had a bag of peanuts for breakfast…"

She held up her fingers. "Two bags."

"Right, and it's nearly two o'clock now. Way past lunchtime. Don't let me take advantage of you like that tomorrow."

Meghan opened her eyes and looked at him, imagining pale blue gazing into warm chocolate. "Hugh, you didn't take advantage of me. You took time to show me what makes you tick. This printing company is clearly very important to you."

A soft knock at the door announced the arrival of lunch. A young woman wheeled in an old metal typewriter table, draped with a checked cloth and covered with delicious-looking sandwiches, coleslaw, and tall iced teas. She parked the feast next to Meghan's chair.

"Help yourself, miss. You, too, Hugh." She leaned over and whispered in Meghan's ear, "I knew I'd never find room on his desk!" Giggling, she headed out the door, closing it behind her.

Hugh rolled his eyes. "I get no respect around here." He pulled up a chair to join her.

"Nothing could be further from the truth." Meghan eyed him across her sandwich. "Your employees not only respect you, they like you." *And no wonder.*

Hugh polished off an entire sandwich with surprising speed, then pulled a videotape out of a drawerful of clutter. "So, shall we have a working lunch?" He reached behind him to turn on a VCR, then slid the cassette into the machine. "This is a tape of a speech

I gave at our last employee awards banquet. You'll soon see what a tough job you have ahead of you."

He leaned over and added with a wink, "I want you to see this while your mouth is full so you can't say much."

Meghan smiled behind her sandwich. Mr. O was right: one on one, Hugh was a charmer. Sipping her tea to swallow an aspirin, Meghan leaned back to watch the small screen, keeping one eye on her client who was beginning to fidget in his seat, a thin sheen of sweat skimming his brow.

The color bars disappeared from the screen and there was Hugh, marching up the platform steps, his face the hue of the white caps on Lake Michigan. As the camera recorded every awful second, Hugh turned to the lectern, his hands fidgeting with a sheaf of papers that soon slipped from his grasp and floated over the edge of the stage like so many autumn leaves.

Meghan could hear the audience snickering in the back-ground, and her heart went out to the man. *Poor Hugh!* He was stumbling over words and mispronouncing names, never once looking at the audience. She'd seen men struggle on the platform before, but Hugh took the prize for Most Nervous.

She turned to find him looking at her rather than the video, and grasped for something positive to offer him. "Hugh, you… you have excellent posture." She stole another glance at the screen. "And that *tie!* That tie says something."

"What it says is that I have no taste." He laughed, relief in his expression, and snapped off the video. "Savannah picked it out for me."

A sudden sadness washed over her. Silly to have gotten her hopes up, of course, but still… "Savannah is your…wife, then?"

Hugh gave her a quizzical look. "My wife? Ah…no. I thought you knew."

"Knew?"

"Savannah is my daughter. My wife is…that is, Caroline died four years ago."

"Hugh, I'm sorry!" Meghan was stunned. And—she hated to admit it—relieved. *Bad, Meg!* Thoroughly chastising herself, she made sure the only thing showing on her face was genuine compassion. "How awful for your daughter."

He nodded slowly. "Savannah was seven. Six, when her mother was diagnosed with cancer. Savannah has such a sunny disposition, always cheerful, always cooking up offbeat things to amuse us. She entertained Caroline every waking minute. And then…after her mother was gone…"

"Savannah lost all her joy?"

Hugh looked up, a hesitant smile returning to his face. "On the contrary. Savannah made *me* her next cheer-up project. You'll see when you meet her at dinner tonight."

"I will?" Her heart did an odd little flip.

Dinner with a client? Careful, girl.

Hugh moved back to his chair behind the desk, which put more distance between them. "Dad will be joining us as well, of course."

"Of course." *Had he moved away on purpose?* Her heart flopped back in place. *Just as well.* Michigan men were trouble with a great big *T.*

Think business, Meg. With a great big B.

Business was the last thing on Hugh's mind as he watched Meghan pull a hefty notebook from her briefcase, and open it to the first page.

Smoothing her hands across the paper, she cleared her throat with a note of authority. "Let's begin with your upcoming presentation."

He grinned. *Let's begin with dinner.*

She pressed on, clearly a woman on a mission. "Have you gathered some ideas for the Chamber speech?"

"You bet." Hugh yanked a file folder from midstack and handed it to her. "Writing a speech is easy. *Delivering* it—"

"Will be easy, too." Meghan finished for him, opening the folder. "I promise, Hugh. You can do it."

He had to admit, her confidence was contagious. They bent their heads in tandem and spent the better part of an hour reviewing each section of the speech in detail. She seemed impressed with his outline, tossing out compliments like "well constructed" and "persuasive examples." Her command of her subject was impressive. *It isn't ego, either.* The woman knew what she was talking about. Caroline had always been sure of herself and her abilities, but this was different.

Meghan DeWitt was doing the impossible. Minute by minute, step by step, she was arming him with the weapons he needed to cut down a foe that had haunted him for decades. With her help, he was beginning to believe he might slay the dragon, once and for all.

Nearly three hours later, they were still huddled over the desk, discussing the value of maintaining eye contact with an audience. "See how much more effective it is when I look right into your eyes, rather than at your forehead?" Meghan was saying.

Hugh gazed back at her. *Effective doesn't begin to describe it.*

The centers of her blue eyes darkened. "And when I speak from my heart instead of my notes, don't you find my words more credible?"

Incredible is more like it. For the tenth time in as many minutes, his gaze drifted down to her lips.

Those lips formed into a beguiling smile. "Hugh Osborne, are you even listening to—"

"Well, now!" His father's unexpected greeting sent them both jumping back in their seats with guilt-tinged speed. "Been a productive afternoon, I see."

"Dad, you don't know the half of it." Hugh stood, rolling his shoulders to relieve the tension created by a lengthy session with a very appealing coach—who'd recovered nicely, he noticed.

Meghan offered his father a graceful thumbs-up. "He's an excellent student, Mr. O." The older man's face crinkled into a smile, which widened even further when she added, "The Chamber is in for quite a surprise."

"She's overstating our progress, Dad," Hugh protested, feeling a telltale wave of heat move up his neck. "We still have lots of rehearsing to do."

"And a whole day tomorrow to do it." Meghan glanced at her watch and stifled a yawn. "Hugh said something about us having dinner together?"

His dad suddenly launched into a coughing fit. Wheezing, even.

Alarmed, Hugh touched his shoulder. "Dad, are you okay?"

"I'm sorry," the man managed between gasps. "I think my annual summer cold has caught up with me."

Hugh stepped back, giving his father a quizzical look. "Your annual *what?*"

The wheezing continued with even more drama. "Sorry to disappoint you, son." The older man waved his hands in the air as if to keep any invisible germs from heading their direction. "Looks like you'll have to escort Meghan and Savannah to dinner without me."

Hugh shrugged. "Sure, Dad, but…"

His father headed for the hallway. The mysterious cough vanished every bit as abruptly. "Have a dish of cherry cobbler for me," he called over his shoulder, his voice smooth as old silk. "I'll see you both in the morning."

Hugh raised one eyebrow in Meghan's direction. "I think we've been stood up."

She laughed, snapping her leather briefcase shut. "As long as I get that cherry cobbler, I won't be one bit offended."

"We'll swing by the house and pick up Savannah, then. Be forewarned: She'll insist on a driving tour of Suttons Bay." He winked, motioning toward the door. "It'll take ten minutes, tops. But her commentary is charming."

Like you, Miss DeWitt. He led the way, grateful she couldn't see the size of the grin on his face. *Exactly like you: charming.*

Four

The lady doth protest too much, methinks.

SHAKESPEARE

o other word for it, the man was charming.

Disarming.

Alarming, she mentally added as she followed his broad back through the halls. *Why does this man affect me so?* She'd worked with hundreds of executives who were as handsome, intelligent, and personable as Hugh Osborne.

He was opening the door for her, flashing that dimple, surrounded now by the faint beginnings of a five o'clock shadow. *Well, maybe not as handsome.* She stepped into the bright afternoon sunshine. *If he'd close his eyes, I could concentrate.*

As if he'd eavesdropped on her thoughts, Hugh slipped on a dark pair of sunglasses. "Hope you brought some shades, Meghan. The bay can be blinding on a day like this."

She reached in her purse, shaking her head. *So much for that theory. He looks even more lethal in shades.* Climbing into the O & O minivan, she settled into her seat, wishing her mind would settle as well. *I can't let myself be attracted to this man, Lord. He's a client, he's in Michigan, and he's still in mourning.*

Not one of those arguments held water, and Meghan knew it. She'd have to come up with something better.

They turned left out of the parking lot, heading away from the bay, and Hugh began pointing out the sights. "Up ahead are the three public schools for Suttons Bay, built one right next to the other."

Tall pines lined both sides of the road, framing the empty schools with a dense, green border. "And Savannah goes to—?"

"Middle school. Starts there this fall." He sighed. "She'll miss being in the elementary building. Caroline taught third grade there."

"Oh." Meghan studied the sturdy brick walls and multipaned windows of Suttons Bay Elementary School. "My mother was a teacher, too. I had her for eighth grade English."

"English?"

She was her mother's daughter, all right. Would Hugh's daughter take after her dad? She'd know soon enough.

They passed a stately Catholic church and turned down an inviting street lined with mature maples, fir trees, and well-kept clapboard homes built a century earlier. "So," Hugh continued, "what's it like to have a mother teaching in your own school?"

"Awful." Meghan laughed. "And wonderful."

"Exactly what Savannah said." He slowed to a stop and pointed across the intersection. "That's our place."

Meghan's eyes opened wide at the enormous Victorian house that wrapped itself around the opposite corner. Twin gables, tastefully painted the color of café au lait, graced the front of the three-story home, which was trimmed in white with dark navy shutters. A deep, wooden porch stretched the full width of the house, then curved around an addition that extended into a quaint garden area along the side facing them. Ruffled white curtains hung in every window, and bright pink and white phlox tumbled along the walkways leading to several inviting entrances.

Meghan finally found her voice. "Hugh, it's exquisite! I've always lived in old houses—"

Until now. The spotless new Cape Cod she'd called home for the last two months was her reward for years of constantly repairing her crumbling 1860s cottage. *No more leaky roofs and antique plumbing for this girl!* she'd told herself when she sold it.

Now, gazing at a house that brought back warm memories of every old house she'd ever lived in, Meghan wasn't so sure. Her voice cracked slightly. "Lucky Savannah, to grow up in such a fine, old beauty."

Hugh tapped the horn. "Speaking of Savannah, she should be watching out the window for us." Within seconds, the wooden screen door flew open and a long-legged, ponytailed bundle of energy bounded toward them, waving with preteen enthusiasm, her braces gleaming out from a hundred-watt smile.

"What a welcoming committee," Meghan murmured, amazed to find her stomach tightening at the thought of meeting Hugh's daughter. Meghan wasn't sure why it mattered what Savannah thought of her, but it unquestionably did. "Look at that smile. Been quite a while since she's seen you?"

Hugh looked at his watch and chuckled. "Seven hours, give or take." The back door of the minivan slid open and a human dynamo landed in the backseat.

"Hi!" the young girl said breathlessly. "Who's this, Daddy?"

Meghan turned around and found herself smiling instantly at the pixie in the backseat—honey-colored hair swinging in a ponytail that sprang out of one side of her head, a round face circled in runaway curly wisps, those familiar dark brown eyes and expressive brows, a dash of freckles from a month in the sun, and an ear to ear grin.

"Savannah, this is Meghan DeWitt. She's a speech coach from the Columbus area."

"Sure!" Savannah nodded vigorously. "We've been to Columbus before."

Hugh smiled at her reflection in the rearview mirror. "Miss

DeWitt is in town for a couple of days to help your dad learn how to untie his tongue."

"Huh?" Savannah's face wrinkled into a delightful pout. "You speak just fine, Daddy."

"Not on stage I don't." Hugh put the van in gear. "Believe me, Miss DeWitt has a long day ahead of her tomorrow. Meanwhile, she's joining us for dinner at Hattie's restaurant downtown. Didn't Grandpa tell you?"

Meghan noticed a distinct blush heighten the color of Savannah's sunburned cheeks.

"Uhh…sort of. Anyway, I'm not hungry yet, Daddy. Can we drive around and show off Suttons Bay?"

Hugh shot a sideways, told-you-so glance at Meghan and turned down Madison Street toward the bay. "It's a deal, Vannah. Why don't you handle the tour guide patter?"

The job suited Savannah Osborne perfectly. Bubbling and bouncing in the backseat, she pointed out BG's Saddlery, Skrocki's Marine Supply, Muriel's Clothing with Distinction, and the village hall with the newly expanded public library next door. "Aren't the red British phone boxes cool? After we turn up Adams Street, we'll see the place that used to be my favorite one of all," Savannah promised.

Hugh sang out with her in unison: "Schneider's Chocolates!"

Savannah directed her father up one street, then down another, as she described her beloved town in colorful detail. Meghan noted the *1890* carved in stone above the Bay Theatre, and marveled at the restored exteriors and architectural gems.

Hugh steered the van down St. Joseph's again. "Now, to dinner. Savannah, that tour was a good deal longer than ten minutes."

Meghan's eyes met Hugh's. "And I loved every second of it. Do you suppose Hattie's serves cherry cobbler?"

Savannah gasped. "Are you kidding? They serve cherry everything in Michigan!" She jumped out of the van before her father
had turned the engine off and ushered them through the restaurant door, calling out greetings to every familiar face within
earshot.

The air-conditioned interior offered a refreshing welcome, as
did the soft leather cushions in the booths. Meghan leaned back
against them, feeling every minute of her long day. "I'll take anything seafood and the tallest iced tea they can pour."

Drinks were served, along with a crusty sourdough bread and
herb-seasoned butter. Hugh proceeded to eat everything in sight
while Savannah played her own version of twenty questions with
Meghan.

"Where'd you grow up?"

"Washington Court House, Ohio, a small town about twenty
miles south of Columbus. My dad was an accountant, and my
mother was a teacher at a school right across the street from our
house."

Savannah's eyes seemed to lose their sparkle. "Your mom
taught school, too?"

"She sure did. English, my favorite subject."

Savannah nodded and her grin returned. "Mine, too. Where'd
you go to college?"

Meghan briefly described her studies at Ohio State, obviously
garnering several gold stars from Savannah for her years in television news.

"Wow! Television, huh? Daddy, is she gonna teach you how to
be on TV?"

He laughed out loud, waving a piece of sourdough like a
protest flag. "No way. The Lord willing, that's a skill I'll never
need."

Meghan looked across at Hugh, and an unexpected surge of pride filled her heart. "You'd be wonderful on camera. It's much easier than facing hundreds of live bodies."

He shook his head. "Nice try, Miss DeWitt. You can keep your all-seeing camera lens. I'll be happy if I can survive facing five hundred live bodies at the Chamber dinner."

"Speaking of dinner," Savannah sang out, "here comes our Lake Michigan whitefish." Soon, the table was filled with the clatter of forks in motion. Discussions of plans for the summer ahead ensued, including picnics and boat rides and pilgrimages to the Old Mission Peninsula lighthouse.

"It's gonna be a great summer, Miss DeWitt." Savannah's ponytail bobbed up and down for emphasis. "Too bad you can't hang around for the weekend at least."

Meghan and Hugh both spoke at once.

"Well, I…"

"Savannah, she…"

They laughed and blushed in unison, then Hugh apologized. "Sorry, Vannah girl. Not this time." His gaze shifted from his daughter to her, and a question mark lingered in his words. "Meghan has important work to do in another fine American city, no doubt."

Is he eager to see me go? His steady gaze told her nothing. Meghan aimed her words toward Savannah. "Actually, I'm in the office Friday for a change. Tons of paperwork to do, as usual. Now, who said something about cherry cobbler?"

"Order me a dish, will ya?" The young girl was on her feet in an instant, her eyes darting toward the door, her voice rising to a squeak. "I gotta get something out of the van."

She was out the door before Hugh could toss her the keys. "She'll be back before long." He focused his brown eyes on

Meghan. "Quite a girl, my daughter."

Meghan glanced at the empty doorway. "Now there's an understatement. Funny, bright, and oh-so-personable." *Just like her dad.* She'd almost said it out loud.

"I think she likes you, Meghan." His tone was flat.

"You don't sound too happy about it." Hers was flatter still.

"It's not that." He bit down on his lower lip for a moment. "It's just been very hard for her to share me with other women."

"Other women?" Meghan stifled a laugh. "Hugh, she's eleven!"

"No, I mean women other than her mother."

"Oh." Her stomach sank to her knees. *Think, Meghan, think!* She chose her next words more carefully. "Have you…dated much since Caroline's death?"

"I wouldn't call it dating, exactly." He shifted his gaze to a spot just over her shoulder. "Marilyn was one of our clients. She started showing up with a lot more printing jobs than usual and we had lunch together once or twice."

"On a typewriter table?" Meghan asked, pressing her lips together to keep from laughing at his obvious discomfort.

"No. In this restaurant, actually." His gaze connected with hers again. "She sat right where you are."

Great. "She did?"

"Never went anywhere. The relationship, I mean. If you'd call it that." Hugh exhaled as if to sweep away even the memory of it. "Besides, I don't believe in mixing business with pleasure."

"Nor do I!" Meghan agreed, a little too quickly. A bit too forcefully.

Now Hugh was swallowing a smile. "The second woman I dated was a dear soul from our church. Sandy is the sweetest, kindest gal you'd ever want to meet. Cooks gourmet meals, grows her own herbs, lives in her garden all summer—"

"How nice." *I loathe the woman already.*

"And she makes cherry preserves, cans fresh tomatoes, sews her own clothes, makes quilts for the church—"

"No kidding." *A regular Proverbs 31 woman. I'm sunk.*

"You'd love her," Hugh insisted. "Everybody does, including me. But not…not that kind of love." A hint of color crossed his muscular neck. "Sandy's so *maternal*. She didn't want to marry me, she wanted to *adopt* me. A 4-H project without the blue ribbon."

Meghan couldn't stifle a less than ladylike hoot.

Hugh nodded. "It *was* laughable. Sad, too. Savannah didn't warm up to Marilyn *or* Sandy. In fact, my daughter did everything she could to sabotage our relationships before they ever got off the ground." He glanced down at his empty coffee cup. "She did us all a favor."

Meghan stared into the bottom of her cup as well, feeling every bit as empty. Clearly neither Hugh nor his daughter had any interest in inviting a new woman into their lives. *How foolish to have imagined anything else.* Better to know now, before she did something she'd later regret.

"So." She looked up and found him staring in the direction of the door. *He's already pulling away from me.* "Speaking of Savannah, where is she? Didn't she need the keys to the van?"

Hugh shrugged, still looking across the restaurant. "She'll be back in a minute. Probably ran into a friend. Savannah knows the whole town."

"Must run in the family." A worrisome knot in her stomach beginning to unravel. *It's better this way.* No pressure, no entanglements. By this time tomorrow night she'd be halfway home to Westerville, her life on track, her heart intact.

Fine Print

Savannah's heart was hammering in her throat as she darted across St. Joseph Avenue. What if Dad looked out the window and saw her heading for the phone box? What would she say? She couldn't tell him a lie—but she couldn't him the truth either. *No way!*

She ducked into the bright red booth, pulled the door closed behind her, and dug in her denim jumper pocket for the change she'd hidden there. Shoving coins into the slot, she dialed the number and prayed he'd be near the phone.

It rang only once before a familiar voice barked, "Osbornes."

"Gramp-O?"

"Who else, young lady?" Mr. O's voice softened into a smile. "And why the whisper?"

"Sorry!" She giggled, feeling her heart slow down a tiny bit.

"One question: Yes or no?"

Silence sang over the phone line. Finally, she stammered, "Gramp-O, I think she's a keeper."

"That's all I needed to know, honey. Now go eat your cherry cobbler before the ice cream melts. I'll take things from here."

Five

There's no such thing as chance; And what to us seems merest accident springs from the deepest source of destiny.

FRIEDRICH VON SCHILLER

ere it is!" Hugh congratulated himself for unearthing his coffee cup from the burgeoning stack of printing bids piled on his desk.

"And here you are," a female voice added.

To his delight—and he couldn't deny it, *delight* was the word for it—he looked up to find Meghan DeWitt leaning against the doorway, watching him.

Grinning.

"Morning!" was all he said, but his mind galloped on at a furious clip. *Those eyes!* Bluer than a cold north Michigan sky, yet warm and welcoming as a summer day.

Hmm. He stole a second glance, pretending to adjust the blinds. *Is that an "I'm interested" look or an "I find you amusing" look?* The woman was too intelligent, too complicated, to be reduced to a single mood or temperament. She was analytical *and* creative, funny *and* purposeful.

She was also beautiful. *Did she have to be beautiful, Lord?*

Precisely the kind of woman his father kept telling him was the perfect choice for his next wife. As if he was ready. As if he could risk...all that. *If I didn't know better, I'd think Dad arranged this whole coaching business, just so I'd meet Meghan DeWitt.*

Nah. Not Dad's style.

She slipped into a chair, pulling out file folders and notebooks. All business. "We've got a full day ahead, Hugh. Did you sleep well?"

"Like a log." A log rolling downhill at seventy miles an hour. "How 'bout you?"

"The B & B was perfect. Nice comfy bed, a lovely view of the bay over my peachy breakfast puff. I slept like a baby." The faint circles under her eyes suggested otherwise, but Hugh held his silence as Meghan assumed a wide-awake expression and pressed on. "I'd like to review your presentation outline once more and make some margin notes about where to stand, some body language tips. You know, staging."

Hugh did not know. "Staging? Don't I just stand behind a lectern and pray for the rapture?"

His heavenward glance was well-timed—a red light began flashing silently over his office door. "Arrgh. Trouble in the press room," he explained to her, already halfway across the room. "Sorry, Meghan. Be right back. I hope."

Meghan watched Hugh's broad back disappear out the door, then stared at the clock and groaned. *Now what?* She dug out her planning calendar and outlined her schedule for the following week, crossing out finished projects and jotting down new ones. Twenty minutes later, she inched Hugh's phone closer and made a few calls using her credit card, keeping one eye on her watch.

Where is that man?

Forty minutes later, with no sign of Hugh, she wandered down the hall, looking for the helpful secretary who'd served them lunch the day before. "Excuse me." Meghan rapped on her open door, noting the nameplate. "Kathleen, have you seen Hugh?"

"Didn't he tell you?" The secretary shook her head in mock annoyance. "Somebody accidentally dumped an entire box of paper clips in the gears of the film processor. He's been on the phone with our service guy, getting advice on how to get all the clips out without damaging the equipment."

"Does Hugh have to handle this kind of thing?" Meghan favored hands-on management, but this seemed a mite excessive.

"He's happier with the results if he does it himself," Kathleen admitted with a shrug.

Meghan laughed. "I'm exactly the same way. Tell him I'm ready to get back to work when he is. Meanwhile, I'll make a few more phone calls, if you don't mind."

"Help yourself."

But Meghan found Hugh back in his office, waiting for her. His sleeves were rolled up to reveal muscular, tanned forearms covered in grease and ink. A streak of dirt on his face added to her immediate impression of an overgrown little boy who'd played in a filthy garage against his mother's wishes.

His sky-wide grin made the picture complete.

"Sorry, Meghan." He didn't look the least bit sorry. Looked, in fact, pleased with himself. "We did it, finally. Got out all the paper clips. What a fiasco." He wiped a forearm across his brow, darkening his face with even more grime. "It'll put us behind half a day in production. Not much to be done about it, but I hated to keep you waiting so long."

"No problem." She liked the methods of this down-to-earth executive. Old Gregory couldn't have changed a typewriter ribbon, let alone taken an entire printing press apart.

"Woulda been back here ten minutes ago, but a bearing

dropped off a roller and fell down into our Heidelberg windmill press." Hugh shrugged. "Somebody had to fish it out."

Meghan laughed out loud. "So you volunteered?"

He was grinning again. "More or less. Give me a second to clean up."

He returned minutes later, wiping his hands with a towel that was now as black as his arms had been.

Meghan swallowed a giggle. Didn't men understand the concept of soap and water first, *then* towel? To make matters worse, he'd missed a long streak of grease along his chin.

Do I tell him?

She told him.

"Wha—? W-where?" he stammered, looking around for a mirror.

"Let me," she offered, taking the towel from his hands and reaching up to touch his face with it.

Uh-oh. Too close.

She could sense the warmth of him, the masculine scent of him. She could also feel a blush starting at her toes that would hit her cheeks any second now. *Oh Lord, whose idea was this?*

Meghan brushed the towel lightly across his strong jaw, succeeding in smearing the grease even more thoroughly. "So sorry," she murmured.

She was sure her cheeks now matched her lipstick: *Berries Jubilee.*

She wiped again, more firmly this time, and the grease smeared further across his face. The more she rubbed, the worse it got. Everything that was on the towel seemed to be transferring itself to his nicely sculpted face.

He saw the problem mirrored in her surprised eyes. "Am I beginning to look like a grease monkey?"

"Not quite. But if I smear some on the other side, you *could* run away with the circus as Hugo, the Clown Mechanic." She shook her head. "I'm making things worse here, Hugh."

"Not at all." His liquid brown eyes found hers. "You are most definitely making things better."

Please don't look at me like that.

He kept right on looking at her like that, only more so.

She blinked, but he didn't budge. Still looking. Still waiting for her to respond, while her mind—her heart—fought for a toehold.

Hugh was so kind, so smart, so nice, and sooo not married. *I can't put myself through this again, Lord. I can't. I won't!*

The still, small voice made a sudden, loud announcement: *Trust Me.*

Meghan gulped. She hadn't said a word, and Hugh's lips were stretching into a smile. *Oh, dear.* Had he heard her thoughts? Her prayers? Was desperation written all over her face? "Maybe another visit to the sink would help," she said faintly, backing up. Hugh took the hint and disappeared long enough for her to gather what was left of her wits and clear her head.

Her eyes bored through the acoustic tile above her as she directed her heart toward heaven. *Lord, did he have to be so good-looking? Couldn't You have found me some nice homely guy, the kind no other woman would look at twice?*

Not-at-all-homely Hugh returned in time to find her staring at the ceiling, transfixed. He stood next to her, looking up with an expectant expression. "Am I missing something up there?"

She turned in time to see him stifle a laugh. "Not at all." *Here we go, Lord.* "I was praying, actually."

"Really? Do you pray often?"

"All day." She looked at him for a reaction, but saw only affirmation in his eyes. "Not out loud, most of the time, but the Bible says to pray without ceasing, so…I do."

"No kidding. Me too. Lately, anyway." Hugh moved toward his seat and she followed suit.

"Lately?" It was plain there was more to the story. Some things were more important than work, she reminded herself, putting aside her notebooks and file folders.

Hugh sighed and leaned back in his chair. "After Caroline died, I decided that God didn't hear my prayers at all."

Meghan nodded. Hadn't she felt the same way after Gregory walked out of her life?

"So, I stopped praying for a short stretch there." He exhaled as though relieved to admit it. "Savannah got me back on track. See, I always pray with her before bedtime. One night, when it was her turn, she whispered, 'Dear Lord, please tell Daddy that You still love him and You're still listening. Maybe then he'll talk to You again.'"

"Oh my." Meghan blinked back an unexpected tear that threatened to sneak down her cheek. "'A little child shall lead them.'"

"Exactly. Savannah led me right back where I needed to be: on my knees." A gentle peace swirled around them and flowed into every corner, bathing the room with a warm sense of God's presence.

Meghan smiled, realizing she hadn't felt this relaxed in two days. *Two months is more like it.* Hugh Osborne was doing the impossible: slowing her down long enough to hear what silence sounded like.

It sounded like heaven.

The tug of too much work and too little time finally pulled her out of their shared reverie. "So—" she smiled and he matched it— "are you ready to take on the Chamber?" She gathered up her folders once more. "Just a dress rehearsal, of course."

"Do you want me to stand behind my desk, or should I find a mirror?"

She gasped in pretend horror. "Not in front of a mirror! After all, you'd never give a presentation to yourself."

"Nah, probably not." His dimple made an encore appearance. "Besides, I'd know all the punch lines."

"Right." Meghan laughed and moved next to him, pen in hand. "Okay, time to get down to business. I've marked your script. Let me show you what all these chicken scratches mean."

She explained her various notes about moving to the center of the stage for greater impact, focusing on one person at a time to deliver an important point, and planting his feet in one place rather than pacing back and forth.

"Meghan," he chided her lightly, "if I plant these big feet in one spot too long, I might send down roots."

"A tree isn't a bad metaphor," she agreed, deflecting his attention away from his size twelve loafers. "Use your height to your advantage on the platform, Hugh. Think of your arms as branches that stretch out to embrace the audience. See how easy this is?"

Easy does it, fella.

Hugh swallowed hard and watched as she swept her arms out in a graceful, unfolding motion. "In fact, at the point in your speech when you talk about—" she scanned his notes—"There it is: 'Reaching out as a community to welcome new business...' Right there, would you be comfortable stretching out your arms? The audience will feel your warmth and strength and leadership. It'd be so powerful. Can you handle it?"

Her arms were still open wide. Slowly, he spread his own arms out in a generous expanse, facing her, mirroring her embrace.

One step, and she'd be in my arms, Lord. Say the word.

Oh, my word.

Meghan's eyes widened. This wasn't happening. Maybe it *was* happening.

What's happening, Lord? A red light flashing above the doorway cut her thoughts short.

"Here we go again…" Hugh grimaced, dropping his arms to his side. "I'm truly sorry, Meghan. Why don't you have Kathleen order some lunch for us while I check on things in the press room? Shouldn't take but a second, I promise."

But it took much more than a second. It took most of the afternoon, with Hugh giving her progress reports through the day while she ate her lunch alone, then nibbled at part of his.

"What went wrong this time?" she asked him after the third long disappearance for the third mysterious accident.

"A malfunction in the double sheet detector." Her blank expression encouraged him to keep talking. "On the offset press, the sheets are separated by a vacuum, then each sheet is picked up by suction."

"So far, so good."

"Well, someone apparently changed the adjustment and the sheets started misfeeding two at a time."

"Like a paper jam in a copy machine." Meghan nodded, fully grasping the situation.

But Hugh was shaking his head. "No, not quite that easy. Those extra sheets got up in the rollers, so we had to shut down the whole press and take the rollers out one by one, clean them, and start the print run all over again."

"Uh-huh." When it came to machinery, she was clueless. "Have at it, Hugh. We'll still have some time to work on your

speech before I need to catch my 6:10 flight back to Columbus."
She winked at him playfully. "Or did you forget?"

He'd forgotten it completely.

Four hours from now she was going to walk out of his life.
Forever. His eyes sought hers. *Say it, Osborne. Don't be a wimp. Tell
her what you're thinking. Say it, man!*

"Meghan…would you consider staying…another day?" *There.*
He'd said it, and she hadn't even winced. She also wasn't looking
at him.

He watched Meghan flip through the pages of her calendar,
back and forth, back and forth, as though to prolong his agony.
Finally, she leaned back. "Well, what do you know? No appointments on Friday." Her gaze met his. "I suppose I could stay, if
Open Windows has room for me another night. Shall I call
them?"

"Yes!" Hugh coughed, realizing too late that he'd almost
shouted. "Great," he added more gently. "I'll get back to the press
room and see how things are coming along."

He paused in the doorway. Precisely as his speech coach had
instructed him, he focused on one person to deliver an important
point.

"I'm glad you're staying, Meghan." The power of his convic-
tion carried across the room, aimed straight at her heart. "You
won't be sorry."

Six

No one ever keeps a secret so well as a child.

VICTOR HUGO

Sorry, Gramp-O, but I'm not sure our plan is working." Savannah's ponytail tickled the side of her neck as she kneaded bread, pushing and pulling the sticky dough across the floured board.

Her grandfather regarded her over the top of his newspaper. "Not working? Now what makes you say that?"

"I dunno. Dad isn't all bubbly about her like he oughta be."

"Grown men don't bubble, Vannah girl." He wiggled his eyebrows. "It makes their hair fall out."

She giggled, then paused to stare pointedly at his bald spot. "Guess you bubbled once too often about Gramm-O, huh?"

He laughed, a warm, rolling kind of sound. "Sweetie, you couldn't be more right. I loved your grandmother with all my heart and she did indeed bubble me over. Remember, your daddy just met Miss DeWitt. Give him time. He'll bubble soon enough."

"But we don't *have* time!" She put her hands on her hips to emphasize her point, leaving two floury prints on her kelly green shorts. "We had all last summer with Sandy, and look how *that* ended up."

"And whose fault was that, I might ask?"

Savannah's shoulders drooped. "Okay, so I put those marbles

in her cherry pie." She stuck out her lip in a decided pout. "Sandy was too serious, Gramp-O. I wanted to see if she had a sense of humor."

"Humph." Her grandfather shook his head. "Probably did your father a favor there, even if we did spend months trying to bring them together."

"Well, how about what *you* did, telling Marilyn that Daddy wanted her business, then hiding her job tickets so the printing was never done on time?" *Gotcha there, Gramp-O.*

Her grandfather blushed. "Sorry, Vannah. I realized she wasn't a good fit either. But when I looked into getting a speech coach for your dad and saw Miss DeWitt's pretty face on that flyer, I knew she was worth a try." He grinned. "Definite bubble potential."

"She's smart, too."

"You're right there, sweetie. Sharp as a tack. And nice as they come." He rattled his newspaper with a decisive snap. "Yup, she's the one, Savannah."

"But it's her last day here! What if she won't stay?"

"She's staying all right."

Savannah peered at her grandfather. "How do you know for sure?"

"Kathleen just called." His grin was smug.

"I didn't know Daddy's secretary was in on this." Her chest tightened in a knot. What if Kathleen gave away their secret? What if her dad already *knew?*

Gramp-O didn't look the least bit worried as he folded up his newspaper. "We had to have somebody on the inside to give us reports, run interference for us, that kind of thing." He gave her a reassuring wink. "Everything is right on schedule. The paper-clip caper went like clockwork. Not a soul saw me drop them in there, and the film processor got a much-needed cleaning."

Whatever that is. "If you say so, Gramp-O."

He sighed with satisfaction. "That little twiddle on the double-sheet detector was even easier, not to mention a couple of calls to suppliers to cancel a paper order or two. Hugh was on the phone for an hour untangling that one." He grinned again. "A productive day, I'd say."

"I hope Daddy forgives us for all this." Savannah wrestled her bread dough into two pans, then covered them with a towel to let the yeast rise for an hour. "These loaves are for dinner tonight. Are you sure Miss DeWitt will be here?"

"Guaranteed, young lady. Open Windows has no room at the inn, so to speak." He chuckled at his own joke. "They're filled up through the weekend. Meghan doesn't know that yet, but she will. Won't be a room available for fifty miles in any direction." His wide smile revealed a whole set of laugh lines disguised as wrinkles. "I've already put clean sheets on the guest bed. She'll be stuck staying with us tonight."

"I think she likes our place, Gramp-O. She kept talking about growing up in old houses and how much she loved them." A lump lodged itself in her throat like a dry biscuit. "That will help, won't it?"

Her grandfather nestled his arms around her, squeezing tight. "Sweet Vannah, I think your brilliant father and your adorable self are all Miss DeWitt will need to convince her that Suttons Bay is her next home. For four years, I've asked the Lord to bring a bright, attractive, godly woman to Hugh's doorstep, and by jingo if He didn't do it. What do you say we watch Him work a little miracle here, okay?"

"With your help, Gramp-O."

He shrugged. "I do what I can. Suppose I finish whipping that guest room into shape while you pick fresh roses for the table and some tomatoes to go with those good-looking steaks in the fridge?"

Savannah skipped out the back door, her faith in their crazy scheme restored. She trusted her Grandfather Osborne with every bone in her body. If this really was God's idea, then getting her dad and Miss DeWitt together would be no problem.

"Hugh, we've got a problem." Meghan chewed on her lip, flipping back and forth through the yellow pages. "Not only is Open Windows full, but so is every B & B and hotel for miles around."

Hugh groaned, dragging a hand through his hair. "I should have thought of that. This is where most of Michigan comes to play in the summer. Let me call Dad and see if he has any suggestions."

As he reached in front of Meghan for the phone, the soft scent of her perfume tickled his nose. *Don't let her leave yet, Lord.* There had to be a hotel room somewhere. His father answered on the first ring, and Hugh explained the situation.

"Son, she's welcome to stay here. Won't be any problem at all."

"I don't know, Dad." Hugh hesitated, looking at Meghan's open expression. He cupped the phone in his hand and whispered to her, "How'd you feel about staying in our guest room? We really do have plenty of —"

"Perfect!" The minute the word left her crimson lips, her face turned a matching shade.

Well, I'll be.

Hugh made sure his voice didn't give away his own enthusiasm. "She says that's fine, Dad. Do you mind throwing some fresh sheets on the bed?"

His father coughed as if covering up something. "I'll see if I can get to it, son. What time shall we look for you two for dinner?"

"Be there in about an hour. And…thanks, Dad."

Hugh hung up the phone, never taking his eyes off the lovely woman settled in his chair. "I appreciate your flexibility, Meghan. We'll try and make you comfortable." *Even though you make me so uncomfortable I'm about to jump out of my skin!* How on God's green earth was he going to manage with her under his roof for twelve hours?

Meghan spread her notes across the desk. "We have just enough time to review the portion of your speech where you do the customer service example."

Hugh tried hard to concentrate on what she was saying, but her shiny mane of hair was swinging just beyond his reach. *And that perfume!* Utterly feminine, it put every nerve ending in his body on alert.

In two short days she'd stretched his mind and touched his heart and filled his soul to the brim with her compassion. But that perfume…that perfume was dangerous stuff. It stirred a place in him that all the Sandys and Marilyns of the world could never reach.

"Meghan—" he interrupted gently when she paused for a breath—"this day has worn me out. Mind if we call it quits and head home early?"

"Er…no!"

Why is she flustered? And blushing? He leaned back to get a better look.

"To be honest, Hugh, I'm having a hard time staying on task here myself. Give me two seconds to gather up my stuff and we'll go."

Kathleen popped her head inside the door. "Miss DeWitt? Your office is holding on line one."

With a groan, Meghan reached for the phone, murmuring

over her shoulder, "Sorry, Hugh. This shouldn't take a second."

He watched her listen, nod, and take furious notes for several minutes, repeating back information and asking for details. When she said with obvious amazement, "Mr. Osborne?" Hugh's curiosity kicked into high gear.

"What was that all about?" he asked when she hung up the phone still shaking her head.

"It's the craziest thing. That was one of my partners, Mike Gilbert. He received calls from *six* prospective clients today, all located in Michigan."

"Terrific!" Hugh grinned at her, surprised to find himself very proud of her business savvy.

"Guess who recommended my services to these six executives? A Mr. Osborne."

"Is that a fact?" Hugh was stunned. "I know *I* didn't…well, I mean I *would* have. Recommended you, that is…" *She thinks I did this. That I'm trying to keep her in Michigan.*

A stab of guilt sent him fumbling for a recovery. "I'd be happy to suggest your, uh, services to, ah…anybody…who needs to speak." His cheeks were on fire. "I mean, speak in front of people. You know, an audience." Frustrated, he exhaled and threw up his hands in surrender. "It must have been my father."

Meghan regarded him with gentle amusement as he regained his composure. For his part, Hugh didn't know whether to be pleased or perplexed. *What is Dad up to here?*

"He's very impressed with our progress, I know that," Hugh admitted. "Since he has cronies who own businesses all over the state, I'm not surprised he suggested they contact you. And *six* of them. The man has been busy."

"I intend to give him a big hug when I see him at dinner." Meghan closed her briefcase with a snap. "Lead the way, sir. I'm half starved. What's on the menu?"

"Steaks, and I'm grilling," he informed her as they headed for the van.

"Is that so?" She winked at him. "Well, even if you *didn't* recommend me to six executives, I still want to see your talents with a girl...I mean, *grill!*"

Meghan ducked her head and blushed furiously, while Hugh laughed at her verbal stumble. *Glad I'm not the only one who can't untangle my tongue today.*

"If I do say so myself, I'm a master chef when it comes to rib eyes." He opened the passenger door with a flourish. "Wait and see."

It was easy to see why the world came to Lake Michigan in July.

Reclining in the Osbornes' backyard, sipping iced tea, Meghan drank in the sights of a Leelanau County summer. The gardens around her were a riot of color. Petunias, snapdragons, and begonias were nestled between large, smooth stones made round by centuries of water flowing around them in the bay. Roses were everywhere—along a stone wall, climbing a Victorian gate—in hues of muted orange, dusty peach, and a buttery yellow.

The centerpiece of the backyard, though, was Hugh Osborne, standing guard over a red-domed grill, barbecue weaponry in hand, looking very intense. He poked at the steaks as if prodding them along, urging them to cook faster.

"How do you like yours done?" he called over to Meghan.

She peered at him across the top of her sunglasses. "Medium rare would be perfect, but anything is fine. Except burned to a crisp, of course."

He rolled his eyes then returned to his duties as Savannah bounded out the door, a basket of fresh bread in hand. "I made this just for you today!" she announced, clearly proud of herself.

Meghan dutifully peeked underneath the checkered tea towel to admire the girl's handiwork. "Mmm, smells delicious, Savannah. Do I have to wait until dinner to try a piece?"

"If Dad doesn't hurry up with those steaks, this bread *will* be dinner," the young girl muttered. "The table is all set. Why don't you come keep Gramp-O company? I'm sure Daddy will be along in a minute with the meat."

Meghan followed her in, taking one last look at Hugh's broad shoulders poised over the grill. He'd changed into a golf shirt and shorts, which made his tall, muscular form even more impressive. No doubt about it, of all the appealing views in the garden, he took the prize.

She found her place in the dining room at a round, oak pedestal table, much like her own in Westerville. It certainly suited this century-old home better than her brand-new Cape Cod. Maybe she'd made a mistake building her own home. The floor layout was convenient but had zero character. Not a nook or cranny in the place.

Her gaze traveled to each corner of the Osbornes' dining room, taking in the touches of antique lace, old woodwork, and clusters of family photos in handmade frames. The quaint, homey look wrapped around her like a quilt, warm and comforting.

Was this what Hugh liked, a place rooted in time?

She sighed, folding her napkin in her lap. All at once, her new house in Westerville seemed empty and cold.

Man, it's hot. Hugh wiped his damp forehead with the crook of his elbow. Was it warmer than usual tonight, or was it the grill?

Or the girl?

Hugh knew the answer. Meghan DeWitt was enough to make any man sweat.

He looked toward the dining room, wondering what they were finding to talk about. No doubt their old house looked like a cluttered mess to her. Didn't she say she had a new place? That was probably her style—clean, neat, new.

He swiped an arm across his forehead again and poked at the meat, sending a juicy stream sizzling across the charcoal. *Wait till she tastes these rib eyes.* All they needed was a puddle of steak sauce bubbling on top. He deposited his tools on the picnic table bench and strode purposefully toward the kitchen, trying to remember where he'd last seen the A-1. In the pantry? With the spices in the cabinets?

It shouldn't take him a second to find it.

"Wait a second!" Meghan lifted her head, listening. "What was that?"

Savannah's eyes were saucers as another tortured howl came from the general direction of the backyard.

Uh-oh. Meghan shot up from the table and headed for the screen door; Savannah and Mr. O were right behind her.

The sight that greeted them was grim indeed. Hugh's face was covered with black soot, flames were shooting up from the grill, and the charred remains of dinner were scattered across the lawn. A bottle of steak sauce oozed its contents onto his canvas shoes.

"Get the fire extinguisher!" Mr. O shouted, sending Savannah scurrying back into the house.

Meghan bit down on her lip so hard she could taste blood. No way was she going to laugh out loud, not this time. No way. *But he looks so ridiculous! Check out that expression. The man is ready to kill somebody with that barbecue fork!*

Savannah appeared and held out the extinguisher in her father's direction. "Do you need this, Daddy?"

"No!" He immediately lowered his voice. "Sorry, princess. The flames are finally dying down, now that they've consumed everything within striking distance. You can put that back under the sink. The fire's over and so's dinner."

Savannah and her grandfather slipped into the house to give the irate chef time to cool down, in more ways than one.

Hugh trained his eyes on Meghan. "Go ahead and say it." He tossed his utensils aside and stomped in her direction. "I've ruined our meal." Seconds later, he stopped in front of her, glaring, and shoved his hands in his pockets. "Well?"

Meghan didn't dare say a word and instead took her dinner napkin in hand and started wiping the soot off his face. "Now, this is a familiar scene," she whispered, pleased to see a slight twitch appear in the corner of his mouth. "Am I to spend all my days wiping dirt off your chin, Mr. Osborne?"

She stopped long enough to look up into his huge brown eyes, eyes that hinted at the smile about to grace his very handsome face.

"'All your days,' Miss DeWitt?" he echoed, finally grinning down at her. Only then did she realize the implication of her words.

"Oh! I didn't mean *all* as in…that is…"

He lightly touched one long, tan finger to her lips. "No need to explain yourself, Meghan." His voice was low, tender. "It seems I do need a keeper. Preferably one with a washcloth. And exceedingly blue eyes."

He slowly dropped his hand and wrapped his fingers around hers, never breaking his gaze, barely moving. The warmth of his touch brought her heart to a standstill, then sent it thumping wildly about her rib cage.

Thirty-six hours ago, this man was a total stranger. Now he was squeezing her hand, eyes locked with hers, breaking down her defenses with nothing more than a smile.

And one devastating dimple.

His voice was rough, rubbing her senses like sandpaper. "Are you ready to go inside?"

Yes. No. When had she ever been so undone by a mere mortal? She managed a half smile. "I guess so."

He steered her toward the door. "Pretty simple meal we're having tonight. Homemade bread and homegrown tomatoes. Suit you?"

Meghan swallowed the gargantuan lump in her throat. "I can't think of anything more delicious."

Seven

Freedom lies in being bold.

ROBERT FROST

"Ridiculous! I'm telling you, Meghan, this is nuts." Hugh stood alone on a raised platform in the dimly lit Governor's Hall of the Grand Traverse Resort. A wooden lectern was stationed to his right, and a sea of empty chairs filled the cavernous room.

"Trust me, you look like the Chamber president you were called to be." Meghan smiled her assurance. That morning over breakfast, she'd devised a plan to help Hugh rehearse his speech *and* tackle his stage fright. A forty-minute drive later, they were standing in the very place where Hugh would make his presentation.

His stellar presentation, if she had anything to do with it.

"Simply stand there and gaze over the entire room, corner to corner. I want you to imagine your precious Savannah sitting in every seat. That's how much this audience will love you."

Hugh sighed and threw his hands up in the air. "I'm working with a crazy person here."

Ignoring Hugh's diatribe, Meghan discussed sound and lighting requirements with the catering manager while Hugh practiced walking up and down the platform steps. She carefully observed him out of the corner of her eye, trying not to notice when he tripped.

"Very smooth!" she called out when he managed the wobbly steps twice in a row without stumbling over his long loafers. When the bright spotlights were finally arranged to her satisfaction, she focused her attention on the man edging near the back curtain.

"No you don't, Mr. President! This bunch is dying to hear what you have to say." She walked toward the platform, pointing his direction. "Plant your feet just to the right of the lectern—that's it. Now, look straight at me and let me hear your opening story."

She eased into a seat near the stage, eyes locked with his. His first words were barely audible, but as she smiled and nodded encouragement, his voice grew stronger and his expressions more animated. When he hit a transition point in the story, she called out, "Now, pretend Savannah is sitting on the other side and deliver the next part right to her."

Hugh followed her direction without argument, clearly grasping the method to her madness. Good thing, too, because it was working. Meghan walked Hugh through his presentation, story by story, point by point, until his mannerisms not only matched his words, but in fact, enhanced them in a naturally persuasive way.

Meghan could feel his confidence building right before her eyes. She beamed into the darkness of the empty ballroom as Hugh began moving farther away from his notes and closer to his imaginary audience, any traces of anxiety and nervousness disappearing like the faint trail of smoke from a candle extinguished at dawn.

Before she knew what was happening, Meghan brought both hands to her mouth to stifle an unexpected sob of joy. *The fear is gone! I can feel it, Lord. He's free!*

A jumble of emotions roared in her ears, the strongest of which finally burst forth the minute Hugh delivered the last words of his speech. "I am so proud of you!" Meghan ran to the edge of the platform, waving her arms exuberantly. "You have no idea how wonderful you sounded up there."

"This is only a rehearsal." Hugh slid his hands in his pockets, his eyes scanning the distant corners. "When the room is packed I'll be a nervous wreck. The whole speech will fly right out of my head, if not my hands."

She shook her head, still beaming with pride. "Nothing could be further from the truth. This is my area of expertise, remember? You were so confident. So sure of your material. So smooth in your delivery…"

Hugh held up his hands to stop the flow of praise, obviously embarrassed but genuinely pleased as well. "Okay, okay, I made it all the way through without fainting. I guess that *is* something."

"You did much better than that." She held out her hand with mock formality. "May I be the first to congratulate you, Mr. President?"

Instead of shaking her hand, he gave it a tug and brought her up on the riser with him, pulling her closer. "Meghan," he said, his voice suddenly husky. "Every bit of applause goes to you. I can't begin to tell you what a difference you've made. In so many ways."

His eyes enveloped her until she couldn't look anywhere else. Her heart was thundering so loudly she was sure Hugh could hear it. She watched, eyes widening, as he slowly lowered his gaze to her lips. Smiling ever so slightly, moving ever so smoothly, he eased his mouth in the same direction.

He was going to kiss her.

And she was going to let him.

Everything shifted into slow motion. Hugh's eyes darkened as his free hand caught her chin and gently lifted it up toward his. After what seemed like hours but could only have been the slightest pause, his warm lips barely brushed hers, just enough to send her heart plunging down to her toes and back up again at a dizzying speed.

Meghan closed her eyes to keep the world from careening out of control and breathed in the scent of him, clean as soap, warm as summer.

When his lips touched hers again, she was more than ready, kissing him back with tentative joy. Her mind was spinning, but her heart was surprisingly at peace. The rightness of it all was undeniable. And irresistable.

It was a brief kiss, but filled with promise. Even when their lips parted, it was a moment before Meghan's eyes fluttered open to find Hugh looking down at her, earnestly scanning her features.

She broke the silence with a whisper. "Hugh, I'm—"

A voice boomed from the back of the ballroom. "Will that be all, folks?"

Meghan jumped back with a guilty start. *How could I have forgotten the catering manager?* Then she giggled to herself. *Pretty easily, as a matter of fact.* "Yes, sir, we're ready to call it a day. Thanks for letting us practice."

"Not sure what you're rehearsing up there, but I hope you sell tickets," he called out amicably, turning off the stage lights and plunging Meghan and Hugh into semidarkness. "Call my office if you need anything else." His footsteps faded out the back door.

"I guess we're through." Meghan kept her tone bright, grateful for the dim lighting that hid her faint blush.

"On the contrary, Miss DeWitt, I think we're just getting started."

Hugh led her carefully across the stage and down the shaky steps—or was that *her* shaking? They moved through the ballroom, still hand in hand, until they reached the back door and Hugh turned to her, his eyes warm with affection.

"What do you think, Meghan?"

She took a deep breath, inhaling a prayer with it. "I think you are one of the bravest, finest men I've ever had the privilege of knowing."

"And…?"

"And your charm and good looks are eclipsed only by your incredible wit and razor-sharp mind."

"So?" he persisted, watching her every expression. "Enough about me, Meghan, what about you?"

"Me?" She gulped. "I'm scared silly."

"Of a kiss?"

"Of you. Of men. Of falling in love and getting hurt all over again. Of another Gregory-the-Not-So-Dependable, if you want to know the truth."

"Gregory the what?" Hugh shook his head, grinning. "I do want to know the truth. All the truth you're willing to share with me."

He lowered his face toward hers until their eyes were level. "Meghan DeWitt, I'm not entirely sure what happened on that stage a minute ago, but I know this much. I liked it. A lot. And I'd like to do it again, preferably very soon. If there's some good reason we shouldn't, I need you to share it with me right now over a Cornish pastie and a fistful of chaisins."

She wrinkled her nose. "Would those be food items?"

"Traverse City's finest." He guided her down the hallway and through the lobby toward his van. "We'll find a little Front Street eatery with a cozy booth and you can tell me all about old

Fine Print

what's-his-name-the-defendable."

"Dependable," she corrected him, sliding in the passenger seat. "Which he wasn't in the least."

Hugh shoved the keys in the ignition and the engine roared to life. She watched him out of the corner of her eye. *So far, your dependability quotient is impressive, big guy. So far.*

Hugh eased the van down the hill toward town, the magnificent blue waters of Grand Traverse Bay spread before them in the sparkling midday sun. Meghan sighed wistfully. "Is it always this beautiful here?"

"Sure. At least 364 days a year, anyway."

"What happens on the other day?"

"It dumps two hundred inches of snow." Hugh winked at her. "Most folks leave town and miss the whole thing."

"I couldn't possibly eat the whole thing." Meghan sank her teeth into her inaugural Cornish pastie and suddenly was willing to try. "What's *in* this?" she wanted to know, nibbling her way around the pastry pocket and trying not to let the contents dribble their way down her chin.

"Beef, potatoes, rutabaga, carrots, and heaven only knows what spices." Hugh downed his in a few big bites. "The wives of Cornish miners used to send their hubbies down into the mines with these in their backpacks."

"Mmm," was all Meghan could say.

"Those dried-up red things in your salad are chaisins." Hugh popped one in his mouth and offered her another.

"Chaisins?"

"That's what Mom always called 'em. Like raisins, only they're dried cherries. You know...Michigan? Cherries?"

73

"Got it." She bit in and discovered a delightfully chewy, sweet surprise. "Mmm," she said again, reaching for her salad fork.

Hugh seemed to be waiting for her to finish eating before bringing their discussion around to more vital matters. The minute Meghan set aside her napkin, he leaned toward her, elbows on either side of his empty plate, his chin cradled in his hands.

"So, Meghan. If you're ready to talk, I'm ready to listen."

The years—and tears—with Gregory unfolded in the restaurant's corner booth as Hugh nodded and listened intently, not offering commentary or asking questions, just listening. She was grateful for that, because once she began, she wanted to plow through and finish the tale before she lost her nerve.

Meghan talked, Hugh listened, through coffee and Italian ice and most of the drive up West Bay Shore Road toward home. "Now you know why I've never married," she concluded, weary of the whole subject. Dredging up so many painful memories had put her in a bit of a funk. She could feel her spirits sagging and a heaviness settling around her. *Hugh is a very nice guy, but he's still a man with the power to break my heart.*

As if he could read her thoughts, Hugh turned toward her when they pulled into the O & O parking lot. "Not all men are like that, Meghan."

"Maybe not. But men don't come with a money-back guarantee, now do they?" She hadn't meant to sound so flippant, even if it was the truth.

Hugh appraised her cooly. "Women don't either, you know. For Savannah's sake, I'd give anything to have Caroline back."

"And what about for *your* sake?" She regretted her words the minute they shot out of her mouth.

Hugh's eyes became narrow slits. "Of course I'd give anything to have Caroline back. She was my wife, and I loved her with all my heart."

Meghan, you fool! "I'm…sorry, Hugh." She reached for his arm, but he was already steering his tall frame in the direction of the office. She grabbed her briefcase and hurried after him. "Hugh, wait! I'm truly sorry."

He turned toward her and held open the door, his expression grim. "I know you weren't intentionally cruel, Meghan. You don't have it in you to be unkind." He sighed, regret filling his eyes. "It's still hard for me to accept the fact that Caroline is gone forever. Maybe I'm not as ready to try again as I thought."

With that he headed toward the press room without looking back, not knowing he'd slammed shut the door to her heart.

Eight

A hero is one who does what he can.

ROMAIN ROLLAND

*M*eghan stared at Hugh's office door, waiting for him to reappear. It seemed he'd found more important things to do elsewhere. *On purpose, no doubt.*

Killing time was not her strong suit. She jumped up, she paced, she sat down, she fretted. *Just get me home, Lord.* Her packed bags were already loaded in the van, and her rescheduled Northwest Airlines ticket for 6:35 that evening was in her purse. Hugh was as prepared for his Chamber speech as he'd ever be, so her work in Suttons Bay was finished.

Any hope of something happening with Hugh Osborne was finished, too.

Meghan eyed the VCR, wishing she could hit the rewind button and start her whole day over. *What came over me, Lord? Why did I run scared and say such a thing?* Maybe she needed a relationship coach the way Hugh needed a speech coach. If there were such a thing as "love fright," she was definitely suffering from it.

A plaid shirt and Dockers suddenly filled the doorway.

She straightened and turned toward him. "Mr. O," Meghan said fondly, grateful for his company. "How has your morning been?"

"Never mind my morning, young lady. What have you done to my son?"

Meghan almost choked. *How could he know? And how much did he know?* Mr. O was grinning broadly, confusing Meghan even further, so she stalled. "I'm...um, not sure what you're talking about."

He guffawed. "Nonsense. Somebody's gotten under Hugh's skin but good, and it's about time. That boy is stomping around here like a wild horse that's had his first taste of a bit and is mighty unhappy about the situation."

"I'm not in the horse breaking business, Mr. O." She felt her cheeks warming. "I think you have the wrong woman."

He looked at her as if for the first time, assesssing her at length and settling his kind gaze on her eyes. "No, Miss DeWitt, I think you are the perfect woman for the job. Confident. And feisty. I like that. So does Hugh, though he may not have discovered that about you yet."

"Oh, he discovered it," Meghan muttered under her breath. "Mr. Osborne, I don't think your son is ready for a relationship, with me or anyone else."

"Nonsense!" The word was more forceful this time. "Hugh doesn't know what he wants. That's why he needs a little help." He looked at his watch, then spun and headed for the hallway, calling over his shoulder, "Be patient with him, Meghan. Things have a way of working out."

Alone with her thoughts again, she paced the room, reviewing the events of the last three days and trying to sort out how she really felt about this widower from Michigan. Granted, he had everything she might be looking for in a man. *Be honest with yourself, Meghan—in a husband.* But who said she wanted that kind of upheaval in her life?

Hadn't she just bought a house?

A house can be sold.

Didn't the partnership need her full attention?

There are other kinds of partnerships, Meg. Does the phrase "husband and wife" ring any bells?

Sure, it rang bells. *Warning bells.* A phone ringing late one April night. And wedding bells that never rang at all.

Meghan plopped down in Hugh's desk chair and stared at the briefcase waiting patiently for her attention. *Work, honey. Get your mind off "what if?" and back on "what is."*

She was a speech consultant. It was time she behaved like one.

Dragging her leather-bound portfolio toward her with a decisive yank, she began organizing her summary report for Hugh, a service she provided to all her clients. On Monday she'd mail him a complete analysis of their coaching sessions, reviewing all the pertinent points, and giving him a reference tool for future presentations.

Should I include an evaluation of our kiss? Might give him a good laugh, and some perspective on it all. It happened sometimes. When clients and coaches worked so closely toward the same goal, a chaste congratulatory kiss wasn't utterly out of line.

That was hardly a congratulatory kiss. "I think we're just getting started" is what Hugh had said. The exact words, embroidered on the tattered edges of her poorly mended heart.

Without warning, the red light over Hugh's office door began flashing, and Meghan instinctively jumped to her feet. "Kathleen?" she called out, hurrying down the hall toward the secretary's office. She rounded the corner to find Hugh bent over Kathleen's desk. He looked over his shoulder, brown eyes directed at her, his composed expression undecipherable.

"There's an…um…emergency." Her voice and knees suddenly

resembled Jell-O. "Anyway, the red light is flashing."

"Now what?" Hugh sighed, clearly frustrated as he brushed past her. "Haven't we had enough accidents this week?"

Meghan watched Hugh disappear through the *Employees Only* door into the press room and fought the urge to follow him. If today's fiasco was anything like Thursday's, he could be in there for the rest of the afternoon.

She had no choice. She had to follow him.

She had to apologize before he walked out of her life and never gave her another chance to make amends.

Meghan reached for the door when it exploded open and a contingent of employees poured into the hallway, all shouting at once. She backed up, making way for the throng. Hugh was in the lead with several press operators in his wake and one very pale younger man from the bindery, whose hand was swathed in a bloody towel.

"Kathleen!" Hugh shouted above the commotion. "Call 911 and get Suttons Bay Ambulance over here, pronto. Then call Munson Medical and tell them they'll need a hand surgeon in the ER, stat. Tell them Hugh Osborne said so. Call Smitty's wife and tell her to meet us there."

Meghan felt the color drain from her face as she pressed against the wall, allowing room for the man they were calling Smitty as he made his way to a chair in Kathleen's office. His face was shades whiter than the towel wrapped around his left hand, now crimson with his blood. Smitty looked ready to faint at any moment, so Hugh wisely instructed him to lower his head between his knees and keep breathing.

"I'll get him some orange juice," Sheila offered.

"No!" Hugh countered. "He'll be in surgery within the hour. No food or liquids." He lowered his voice. "Help is on the way, buddy. These hand surgeons are the best in Michigan, so don't you worry. I'll be with you the whole time."

"What happened?" Meghan whispered to no one in particular.

"Smitty got his hand crushed in the cutter," Sheila said in a low voice, anxiously watching her coworker. "That Polar puts more than five thousand pounds per square inch on a clamp that you control with a foot pedal." She shuddered. "His finger is still attached, but not by much. Hope they can do something for him."

Feeling helpless, standing there and staring at the roomful of strangers, Meghan closed her eyes and did the only thing she could do. *Lord, You are the Great Physician and Your services are very much needed here today.*

She opened her eyes to find Mr. O hurrying toward her, anxiety and pain etched on his pale face. "Honest," he groaned softly. "I had nothing to do with this."

She looked at him, perplexed. "Of course you didn't, Mr. O! Don't worry, Hugh has everything under control."

Which he certainly did. The future CEO was the picture of grace under fire, answering questions, gently giving orders, and reassuring Smitty, who was looking more ill by the minute. Meghan had never seen Hugh so in command. Even his confidence on the platform that morning paled in comparison to this display of courage and quiet strength.

At last the EMS team appeared, stretcher and equipment in hand. The office emptied as the paramedics went about their business with speed and efficiency, wheeling Smitty toward the waiting ambulance, with Hugh right behind them.

"Kathleen, did you reach Gloria?"

The secretary nodded at Hugh. "She'll meet you at the door outside the emergency entrance. How are you getting back?"

Meghan saw her chance to be useful. "I'll drive Hugh's van, so he can bring it home later." Hugh looked at her in surprise, and Meghan shrugged. "My bags are in the back and I need to catch the plane from Traverse City anyway."

She hoped it sounded plausible, that he wouldn't see through her thinly veiled attempt to be alone with him, even if only for a few minutes, before she left northern Michigan for good.

Hugh had no time to analyze her motives. He tossed her the van keys as the small group gathered around the ambulance door. "Take 31 South to Division Street to West 7th. Munson Medical Center. Emergency entrance." He sent her a look of gratitude, then disappeared into the back of the waiting ambulance, all his attention directed toward the man on the stretcher.

"As it should be," Meghan whispered to herself, easing behind the wheel and starting the van. It would take every ounce of concentration to keep her mind on the road and off a certain fine printer who just took off with her heart tucked in his back pocket.

Meghan shoved her hand in her pocket, wrapping her fingers around the keys to Hugh's van. *Good. Still there.* On an afternoon like this, anything could happen.

The emergency area was jammed with the usual Friday afternoon hubbub of tourist mishaps and fender-bender patients. Meghan kept one eye on her watch and the other trained on Hugh as he moved about, firmly in control of the situation.

Smitty's wife, Gloria, seemed calm enough, thanks to Hugh's words of encouragement. Whenever a doctor appeared with a progress report, it was Hugh who nodded, took notes, and relayed the complex information to Gloria in person, then to the anxious O & O employees back in Suttons Bay by phone.

Meghan couldn't help but marvel at Hugh's leadership skills in such a critical situation. Obviously the months he attended to Caroline's medical needs had taught him well. Couple that with his own innate sense of how to take charge without taking over, and he was an impressive presence.

Gentle as a lamb, mighty as a lion. *Hugh's never looked more like You, Lord.*

Why hadn't she seen that before?

During a lull in the action, Hugh dropped into the seat next to her, clearly exhausted but still alert. "Your flight leaves soon, doesn't it?" He sighed, rubbing the nape of his neck, like his father did when he was under stress. "Let me take you over to the airport now, since Smitty will be in surgery for at least another thirty minutes. Plenty of time to get you safely headed back to Columbus."

Meghan nodded, not trusting herself to speak.

Hugh leaned toward her and tipped her trembling chin in his direction. His voice was as soft as a caress. "Meghan, are you okay?"

She nodded again, but the single tear sliding down her cheek said otherwise.

Hugh caught it with his fingertip. "Do you want to talk about it on the way to the airport?"

"Okay," she said in a shaky voice, standing up, not daring to look at him. As they walked in silence out to the van, she handed him the keys and they soon were rolling down Munson Avenue toward the Cherry Capital Airport, less than five miles away.

"Will they be able to repair Smitty's hand?" Meghan asked, doing her best to draw attention away from her own pain.

"I've seen worse damage done by that infernal cutter, but it'll be several weeks before he's back to work."

"You handled everything very smoothly, Hugh."

He shrugged. "I do what I can." Hugh regarded her carefully. "Mind if we talk about something a little closer to home?"

Meghan gulped. "Such as…?"

"Such as a memorable moment earlier today when I thought we were moving in a fairly interesting direction. Any thoughts on that?" His even tone said nothing. And everything.

"Honestly, Hugh, I don't know. I've never…gotten involved with a client before. It seems unethical, somehow."

"No problem. You're fired."

"Hugh!"

"Just teasing, Meghan." He reached over and gave her hand a gentle squeeze then quickly let go. "After all, the professional side of our relationship is finished. Whatever we paid for your consulting time, by the way, was worth it. I mean that. Dad was smart to recommend you to his buddies. You have an amazing ability."

"Right." She sighed. "An amazing ability to put my foot in my mouth and dance the two-step while I'm at it." She finally forced herself to turn toward him. "Hugh, I feel terrible about what I said about Caroline." She grimaced, turning back in time to see the large sign pointing them toward the airport. "On the platform, I'm the queen of self-control, but one on one, I could use a good coach myself."

"Apology accepted, incident forgotten." Hugh pulled up to the curb marked for departures and put the van in park. "I hate dropping you off like this, Meghan, but I really need to be…"

"At the hospital, of course." She held out both her hands and was grateful when he took them in his, giving them a warm squeeze. "Hugh, you've taught me a lot about overcoming fears."

"I haven't overcome them all," he murmured.

"Well…" Her voice had finally steadied. "Nor have I."

"Keep in touch, okay?"

She blinked hard to keep another telltale tear from giving her away, then leaned forward to put a hasty kiss on his cheek before pulling back completely and opening her door.

"I'll be thinking of you on the thirtieth!" Her voice sounded too cheerful and she knew it. "Knock their socks off, Hugh."

Carry-on in hand, she turned and practically ran toward the sliding door into the terminal, determined not to look back. Not with her eyes, and definitely not with her heart.

Nine

It was roses, roses all the way.

ROBERT BROWNING

Meghan had a deep, dark secret: She loved Mondays. Nothing thrilled her more than having a long, productive week stretched ahead of her, filled with appointments and opportunities to be useful. A busy calendar declared, "You are wanted by somebody!"

Right now, she needed to hear that.

This Monday was particularly welcome after a long, dreary, post-Michigan weekend during which she vacillated between being mad at herself, mad at Hugh, mad at Gregory, and mad at the world. She'd finally decided to deposit her anger on Gregory's doorstep—he'd never know the difference—and put the fiasco that was Michigan behind her.

Her secretary, Joan, popped her head around Meghan's office door. "Morning, boss. How was Michigan?"

"It was…an accident."

"What?"

Meghan laughed, a good cleansing laugh. "It was one accident after another, Joan. But only one of them was truly dangerous." *Okay, two of them. That kiss had three-alarm potential.* "The coaching went very well."

"I know that much." Joan stepped all the way into her office to reveal a single yellow rose in a tall stem vase. "This just arrived."

Meghan's stomach did a back spring. "Isn't that...lovely?"

Joan's hazel eyes twinkled. "Care to read me the card?"

Meghan opened the tiny envelope with fingers that refused to cooperate. She finally managed to pull out the florist's card and sent up a silent prayer as she glanced down at the message: *Sorry for the hurried good-bye. Thank you for everything—Hugh.*

Well. A nice thought...not overdone, a tad perfunctory.

"Here, you can read it." Meghan sighed, handing over the card. "What time is our partners' meeting?"

"The fellas want to get together at ten o'clock. I'll be bringing lunch in at noon." As the door closed silently behind Joan, Meghan stared at the single rose perched on her desk.

"Thanks," Meghan murmured absentmindedly. Flowers from a client were not unusual. Frankly, larger, more expensive floral arrangements were the norm. A huge, leafy ficus from a man in Toledo grew by her window, impervious to Joan's concerted efforts to kill it with overwatering, and a eucalyptus wreath graced the wall behind her desk, filling the room with its distinctive scent.

One rose must *mean* something, she decided. It was more personal than a big, business-size arrangement. A single stem hardly screamed "tax write-off." And it was yellow, like the ones on Hugh's dining room table the night their dinner went up in smoke. Was that intentional, or did the florist have more yellow roses on hand than anything else?

"This is silly." She grabbed the phone to begin her calls for the day. *It means the man is a tightwad. Get on with your day, Meghan old girl. Get on with your life.*

Tuesday arrived with a surprise in her morning mail: A hand-made card from Savannah. On the outside she'd drawn a surprisingly good picture of her father standing at a lectern, a chef's hat perched on his head and a barbecue tool in each hand. Inside was the carefully printed message: "Thanks for coming to Michigan and getting us all fired up for Dad's speech." It was signed, "Love, Savannah," and covered with kisses and hugs in preteen abandon.

Meghan sighed, feeling her eyes begin to moisten. *What a dear girl she is!* She deserved a wonderful mother. Should she send Savannah a thank you note for her thank you note? *Overkill. Better not.*

Still, it seemed so rude not to respond at all. *Bingo!* She would call her at home, thank her for the card, and ask how Smitty was doing. Surely that would be okay. Perfectly natural. Expected, even.

Meghan checked her Michigan notes for the number and punched it in the phone, surprised to feel a knot in her stomach. *What if Hugh is home? What if he answers the phone?* When Savannah sang out, "Hello, Osbornes!" the knot instantly unraveled.

"Hello, Savannah, this is Meghan DeWitt in Ohio. I got your beautiful card today and just wanted to say thanks."

Meghan could almost hear the young girl blushing over the phone. "You're welcome, Miss DeWitt."

"I also wanted to see how Smitty is doing."

"He came home from the hospital on Sunday. Dad says it'll be a while before they see him at work again, but we visited him yesterday and he looked pretty good." Savannah's voice flattened to a petulant whine. "His hand is all wrapped up, so we didn't even get to see the stitches or anything."

Meghan stiffled a giggle. How like curious Savannah to be disappointed! "Sure appreciate the update, sweetie. Please tell... everybody hello for me."

"Dad's upstairs. Want me to get him for you?"

"No!" Meghan's stomach knot returned with a vengeance. "No need to do that, Savannah. Give everybody my best, especially Smitty and Gloria, okay?"

When she hung up the phone, Meghan exhaled with relief. *Too close for comfort, that one.* She wouldn't risk calling again.

"Well, well, look what we have here." Joan stood in her doorway, another yellow rose in a bud vase. "If it's Tuesday, this must be roses, eh? Shall I put this next to the other one?"

"I guess so," Meghan said, wrinkling her brow. A mix-up by the florist, perhaps? If it had the same message, that would be the obvious explanation.

Joan waited expectantly while Meghan pulled out the card.

Oh. Different message: *Last week was very special, Meghan. Blessings—Hugh. Hmm.* Maybe she wouldn't read this one to her secretary.

"Thanks, Joan," was all she said, fingering the tiny card in her hand. *"Very special?" What kind of message was that?* Was it special professionally or personally? At least this note included her name. Didn't that make it more personal? And "very" special, now surely that meant something.

"For heaven's sake!" She tossed the card in her drawer with the other one. It meant he had leftover credit in his barter account with the florist. *Give it a rest, Meg.*

Wednesday dawned sunny and hot. Indeed, the path from the florist's to Meghan's office was heating up, as a third yellow rose

arrived with a decidedly more personal note: *Smitty is doing better.*
We miss you—Hugh.

They missed her, did they? Not half as much as she missed
them.

Enough of this!
She had to call.
No. I'm not calling.
One rose really didn't justify a phone call.
Of course, it's really three roses.
He might have had his secretary send them.
But surely he wrote the messages himself.
He expected her to call.
No, the last thing he expects is a phone call.
Notice, it said "we" miss you, a group thing.
He could be hiding something.
Should she call Savannah?
No.
Mr. O?
Never!
Her entire day ended on the same note: Sour.

Thursday was summer at its sweetest, blessedly cooler and not a
cloud in the blue Ohio sky. Meghan's desk was getting crowded
with yellow roses in bud vases, stretched four across the antique
cherry surface. The note this time was even more enigmatic: *Hope*
your week is going better than mine is—Hugh.

What does that mean? That he couldn't live without her? That
another box of paper clips fell in the prepress?

Oh, help.

❧

Friday morning, shock was one of a dozen emotions that fought for Meghan's attention when Joan walked in with Rose Number Five.

"Do you plan to tell me what's going on here?" her secretary demanded, gently but firmly. "I'm good friends with the florist, you know, and I can get the answer one way or the other." She grinned as Meghan slid down in her chair in defeat.

"It's like this, Joan. Remember Hugh Osborne, my Michigan client last week? He has a thing about yellow roses—"

"No, he has a thing about Meghan DeWitt." Joan grinned as she brought the newest addition to Meghan's rose collection to her desk. "As you were saying…"

"I don't know *what* I'm saying, or what he's saying either, for that matter." She straightened in her chair and reached for the card. "Maybe today's note will give me a clue." Meghan practically ripped open the envelope, praying for a clear word.

And she got one: *I'm miserable without you. Come spend the weekend with my family and let's talk. I'll meet your plane at 8:10 this evening. A ticket is waiting at the Northwest Airlines counter in Columbus for a 5:00 departure. Please say yes, Meghan—Your man in Michigan.*

It took three cards to contain the whole message, and three seconds to decide what she was going to do.

"Yes!"

Joan folded her arms over her chest. "I take it he's impressed with your coaching skills."

"Something like that." She pressed her hands on top of her head, as though to keep herself from flying apart at the seams. "Look, I'm going to need to block out my afternoon from two o'clock on. See if Peter can squeeze me in for a cut and style, and if Ellen has time to give me a manicure while I'm there, that'd be wonderful." She exhaled with a shaky sigh. "Do you mind making those calls for me, Joan? It's not exactly business."

"Are you kidding? I haven't seen you this happy in two years. Want me to polish your shoes? Hem your skirt? Whatever it takes to keep that grin on your face suits me." Joan was halfway out the door, and turned back. "I couldn't be happier for you, Miss DeWitt. Anything you need, say the word."

Meghan's day went forward in herky-jerky motion, sometimes going too quickly, other times slowing to a crawl. Every consultation by phone with her clients was an unmitigated disaster, since her mind was a million miles away—actually, one state away. She finally gave up trying to focus on business and started making lists of what she'd need to pack.

More than once, Meghan reached for the phone to call Hugh, just to say, "Yes, I'm coming!" or "Thanks, I'm anxious to see you, too!" *Nah. I'll wait until I see him face to face at the airport. Then I'll tell him how I feel.*

She gulped. *How do I feel?* Scared, of course. Excited. Nervous. Thrilled. Would he kiss her at the gate? *Undoubtedly.* A blush rushed up her neck at the very thought of it and she giggled like a teenager.

This is ridiculous!

Maybe so, but she was loving every glorious minute of it.

Her afternoon errands flowed smooth as silk. The drycleaners had her clothes ready, Peter gave her the best haircut she'd had in years, Ellen had time to turn her nails into Berries Jubilee and touch up her makeup besides, and the traffic on I-270 south toward the airport was miraculously light for a Friday afternoon.

Meghan knew the Lord was smiling down on her special day.

When she landed in Detroit, she had just enough time between connections to locate the lighted display ad with that bigger-than-life rodent, Gregory Hammond. Once she was certain no one was paying attention, Meghan slipped a black marker out of her purse and drew a huge handlebar moustache on Greg's unsuspecting face.

It took every bit of self-control she possessed not to laugh out loud as she hurried away, not feeling the least bit guilty. It was, after all, a washable marker. The ink would disappear without a trace, just like her painful memories of Gregory. Gone forever, leaving plenty of room for the happier memories she intended to collect in Suttons Bay this weekend.

Here I come, Hugh, whether you're ready or not!

Ten

Love is like war; easy to begin but very hard to stop.

H. L. MENCKEN

Meghan was not ready when the storm hit.

Halfway across Michigan, a thunderstorm center moved in, tossing her tiny commuter plane around the sky like a kite on a windy day. She gritted her teeth and begged the Lord for mercy, as passengers everywhere gawked out the oval windows at the relentless rain.

A spontaneous cheer rang out when the turboprop touched the runway in Traverse City. Meghan was so relieved to be on the ground, she didn't remember until she reached the cabin door that her umbrella was safely in her desk drawer in Westerville. To make matters worse, instead of using a jetway, the small plane offered slippery metal steps to the tarmac below, at which point she'd be forced to run for the terminal door and hope the elements were kind to her.

"Go ahead, miss!" the flight attendant shouted above the storm. "It's only a few yards to the terminal."

Meghan stared at the water-logged potholes below. My, wouldn't this rain do wonderful things to her new hairdo? She could see the *Traverse City Record-Eagle* headline now: Drowned Rat Poses as Speech Coach. Client Demands Towel with Refund.

Reminding herself that dear Hugh waited on the other side of the monsoon, Meghan balanced her overnight bag on her head and made a puddle-leaping dash for the terminal door. The rain-soaked wind blew her carefully combed pageboy in directions her stylist never dreamed of. Sheets of water poured down the slim skirt of her brand-new, cranberry red cotton dress. The pale pink stream of water running down her tanned legs did not bode well for this outfit's colorfast washability.

She headed up the stairwell toward the gate area. *Lord, give Hugh the grace to see past my horrible hair and soaking wet dress.* Maybe he'd be so delighted to see her he wouldn't even notice a few damp spots.

Okay, a *lot* of damp spots.

The Cherry Capital Airport was packed with other travelers in various stages of wet. Bedraggled mothers with toddlers dripping off their arms stood in puddles around the baggage claim carousel. Men in Bermuda shorts as slick as bathing suits watched for mud-caked golf bags to slither into view. At least she wasn't alone in her soggy predicament, Meghan thought, relieved.

A crack of thunder overhead made her jump, then laugh self-consciously. *Get a grip, Meg!* Her nerves were long past frayed—were in fact mere strings, tied around her fingers. *Please, Lord, let this weekend go smoothly.* The sooner she saw Hugh, the sooner she could relax and enjoy herself.

Craning her neck to see if she could spot him, Meghan instead caught a glimpse of herself in a mirrored poster and almost fainted.

The reflection staring back at her looked like the victim of a water balloon fight. Black hair was arranged willy nilly over her head in damp, dark clumps; makeup was smeared around her eyes, raccoon-like; her signature red lipstick had escaped its penciled borders.

Visions of Bozo danced in her dripping head.

Her new dress hadn't weathered the storm well, either. Wrinkles crawled from shoulder to knee and everywhere in between, shrinking both the hem and sleeves three inches, and giving her the overall appearance of a cranberry left in the bog one soggy day too many.

Meghan groaned aloud. *Hugh cannot*—cannot—*see me like this!* He'd leave her behind in the terminal like a piece of unclaimed baggage. Her eyes darted about for the nearest ladies' rest room. Spying one near the car rental counters, she made a beeline for it, praying Hugh didn't have her in sight yet, wherever he wa—

"Meghan?"

No mistaking that voice, not two feet behind her. She turned slowly, forcing herself to smile like a beauty queen, preparing herself to see a grown man faint. "Hello, Hugh."

The surprise on his face told her all she needed to know.

"Pretty bad, huh?" She hoped he'd offer a reassuring word so she could breathe again.

Now the look on his face moved to shock, even confusion. Finally, he seemed to find his voice. "Are you, uh…coaching someone in the area?"

Am I what? This weekend wasn't about coaching, it was about courting! She tried to sound casual, but the panic in her voice gave her away. "Hugh, you know I'm not coaching." Any minute, he'd wink and—*Why is he staring at me like that?* "You see I…I got your…you know, all your notes…"

His brow wrinkled. "My notes?"

"And the roses. And…the plane ticket?" Her throat closed in a tight knot. *Please nod, Hugh. Smile. Frown. Something!*

"Roses." He looked up at the ceiling as though to sort things out in his mind. "Uhhh…you mean the rose I sent you on Monday?"

Meghan finally took a breath, gulping air like a relay swimmer. "Right! The one on Monday." She laughed in relief. Hugh was smiling back, but a strained, still hesitant-looking smile, so Meghan barreled on. "And the Tuesday rose, and the Wednesday rose, and the—"

"There must be some mistake," he said faintly, shaking his head. "I sent only one rose, Meghan. Right after you left. Called the florist Saturday morning from the house."

"One? One rose?" Staring at his much-too-serious face, Meghan felt every drop of joy drain out the bottom of her soggy shoes.

"I'm very sorry." Hugh looked sincere. And bewildered.

She backed up against the mirrored wall, feeling dizzy with disbelief. *What is happening here, Lord? Help this make sense!* She licked her lips, the only dry part of her body. "Hugh, I'm confused. I had one beautiful yellow rose delivered every day this week, by the same florist, with a different note each day. From you."

"You're kidding."

Slumped over, she shook her head. "Only a crazy woman would kid about such a thing."

"You don't happen to have those notes on you, do you?"

"Have *what?*" Bristling, she straightened. "You don't believe me, do you?"

He held up his hands. "Of *course* I believe you. I just thought if I could read them it might help me understand what's happened here. Do you remember what the notes said?"

Do I remember? She'd memorized them word for word and written them on the tablet of her heart for safekeeping.

Did she remember?

"I dunno," she mumbled. "Something about how you enjoyed having me here."

"And I did enjoy it." Hugh reached out to pat her arm, then seemed to think better of it. His voice grew low and reassuring, the tone one might use when speaking to a child. "Is that why you came to Traverse City, because of the roses?"

"Nooo!" Her wail startled him. Almost as much as it startled her.

"That's *not* why I came!"

She threw her hands in the air, waving them like a banshee. "I came because the last note said—and I quote—'I'm miserable without you. Come spend the weekend with my family and let's talk.'"

Meghan was choking on every word, struggling but determined to continue. "It said, 'I'll meet your plane at 8:10 this evening. A ticket is waiting at the Northwest Airlines counter in Columbus for a 5:00 departure. Please say yes, Meghan.'"

She was sobbing now, putting aside any pretense of poise or sophistication. "It was s-signed, 'Y-your man in Michigan.'"

Hugh was clearly dumbfounded, his mouth gaping open, his eyebrows tied in a knot. "Could it have been a different man in Michigan?"

Her wail returned, only louder. *"Nooo!"*

"Um…no, I guess not." He slapped his hands against his sides, the picture of a man in dire straights. "Meghan, I'm as sorry as I can be, but I didn't send those other four notes. That last line…well, that's not my style, that's something Dad would say."

Dad.

Hugh froze, mentally sifting through the activities of the past week. *Surely not.* His father couldn't have, wouldn't have come up with such a foolhardy scheme for bringing him back together with Meghan. *Surely not, Dad.*

But what other explanation could there be? Meghan was too confident and straightforward to play such games. *Meghan.* He looked at her—clothes dripping, eyes red, nose running. *Poor Meghan.* He had to do something and fast.

"Look, I'm not sure what's going on, but I know this much: You need a hot bath and dry clothes. And probably some dinner."

He could barely hear her whisper, "I just want to go home." She sniffed, sounding like a homesick third grader at Scout camp, and dragged herself toward the Northwest counter, leaving him no choice but to pick up her dripping bags and follow her.

The ticket agent was sympathetic to Meghan's plea to fly home to Columbus on the next possible flight. "But that wouldn't be until tomorrow morning, miss. And since your departure was supposed to be Sunday evening, it will mean a significantly higher fare to change the ticket to a Saturday return."

"How significant?" Meghan croaked. The ticket agent showed them the amount. Significant.

Hugh was feeling responsible for Meghan's misery, even though he knew it wasn't his fault. He hadn't sent those notes, had he? *No way.* He didn't tell Kathleen to do such a thing, did he? Nah, his secretary would never have written anything as hokey as "Your man in Michigan."

It had his dad's fingerprints all over it. *Wait till I give him a piece of my mind…*

Hugh finally took decisive action. "Miss, we'll leave the ticket as is with the Sunday evening departure, no problem." He gently pulled Meghan away from the ticket counter and eased her toward an empty chair near the pay phone. "You wait here while I check with Dad and Savannah. They'll be delighted to have you stay the weekend." *In fact, they're probably expecting it.* "Okay? Just give me a minute."

Hugh punched in the number, not sure what he was going to say to his father. *Better on the phone than in person.* In person he might have to deck him. A man doesn't deck his dad, even if he deserved it. *The old codger.*

His father answered the phone on the first ring. "Osbornes."

"Dad, I'm at the airport."

"Anybody…uh…with you?"

"You know very well who is with me." Hugh didn't even try to hide his anger. "When you left that message for me to pick up an 'old friend' at the airport, you might have mentioned whose 'friend' it was." Hugh fought to keep his volume down, spitting out words between his teeth, wringing the phone cord for all it was worth.

"Stop fighting it, son. You care for the woman. You might as well admit it."

"I *what?*" He dropped his voice to a low growl. "My feelings are *none* of your business, Dad. You have embarrassed Meghan beyond belief. Did you even think about how she might feel when she got here?"

His father sounded contrite. "Son, I counted on you to be Mr. Smooth and handle it. Act happy to see her, like it was your idea."

"It's too late for all that." Hugh rubbed the nape of his neck. "Look. I assume the guest room is ready for her."

"Of course. Got water boiling on the stove for her favorite Earl Grey tea."

"Well, you better brew a big pot, Dad, because the woman is soaked to the skin. We'll be home in thirty minutes. And, Dad? This discussion is far from over."

Hugh hung up the phone, proud of himself for not slamming down the receiver. *How could Dad have done such a thing?* He bent down toward Meghan, huddled in the chair, obviously frozen from the air conditioning. "Let's head for Suttons Bay. This lame-brained idea was Dad's. Playing matchmaker, I guess."

"I'm sorry, Hugh."

Sorry? After all she'd been through, *she* was sorry? He bent down until they were eye to eye, and slipped his hands around hers.

"I'm the one who's sorry, Meghan. And Dad is the one who should be apologizing. I intend to remind him of that all weekend long." He paused and massaged her damp hands. "How are you feeling?"

She eyed him through still-soggy clumps of hair. "Do you really want to know?"

He nodded.

"Foolish, unwanted, and unwelcome. And wet."

Pulling her to her feet, he wrapped her in his arms and rested his chin on her head. He could feel her teeth chatter and wished he'd brought a blanket. *Get real, Osborne. Who drags a blanket to the airport in July?*

Without a jacket or sweater on hand, Hugh warmed her the only way he could: with his words.

He slid his chin across her forehead and down her cheek until his lips touched her ear. "You are wanted," he whispered. "And you are welcome, and you are hardly a fool."

I'm the fool for letting you go in the first place.

But he couldn't bring himself to tell her that. Not here. Not now. Not like this. He could only press her small form against his chest and ask himself for the hundredth time that week: *What is it about this woman that drives me crazy?*

Eleven

Lord, what fools these mortals be!

SHAKESPEARE

he drive up West Bay Shore Road was blessedly brief. Meghan nodded out for a few minutes, nestled in a blanket Hugh had found in the back of the van. When she woke up, they were pulling in the driveway off Park Street with Savannah bounding out to greet them like an enthusiastic puppy.

"Hi, Daddy!"

The girl's countenance fell when she saw Meghan's bedraggled appearance and resigned expression. "Hello, Miss DeWitt. I'm… I'm glad you're here."

"Thanks." Meghan couldn't think of anything else to say. The young girl's disappointment was so obvious Meghan did the only thing she could. She held out her arms for a hug.

Savannah let out a little wounded moan and fell, sobbing, into Meghan's lap. "I'm…so…*sorry!*" she said between sobs. "We…we didn't mean…we just wanted you to…stay."

"I know, sweetie, I know," Meghan murmured, still sitting in the van. She rubbed Savannah's slim back, trying to comfort the girl.

Bless her heart. Meghan held back her own tears by sheer willpower, not wanting Savannah to feel even worse. Finally she took the girl gently by the shoulders and pulled back to look her in the eye. "Did you have anything to do with this cockamamy plot?" Meghan's voice was stern, but she knew her grin gave her away.

Savannah nodded and sniffed. "I ran the notes to the florist every day. The clerk had Dad's credit card number and all, so we kept sending the same thing with a new note." She finally met Meghan's gaze. "Did you…like the yellow roses?"

Meghan hugged her tight. "I loved every one of them, no matter who sent them." She shot a sideways glance at Hugh. "Next time, sign *your* name, Savannah. I'd be just as tickled to get flowers from you."

Savannah pulled back, clearly relieved. When she disappeared through the back door, Meghan noticed Mr. O standing there, brown eyes as sad as a hound dog's.

He took a few steps closer to her, then stopped. His bottom lip was trembling as he spoke. "Meghan, I sure do hope you can forgive us for this. We didn't think about anything but getting you back to Suttons Bay. The box of clips in the prepress, the double paper jam, the cancelled shipments—"

Hugh exploded. "*You* did that stuff? Dad, what were you *thinking?*"

The older man shrugged. "I was thinking about one thing: keeping Miss DeWitt here as long as possible. I…well, we *both* owe you two an apology."

Oh, you dear soul. She stood and walked toward the older man, her hands outstretched. Taking his hands in hers, she couldn't help but notice how much like Hugh's they were—large, masculine, strong.

Good hands that belonged to a good man.

"Mr. O, I know your heart is set on finding a wife for Hugh and a mother for Savannah."

He hung his head and nodded. "Guess Osborne men aren't as complicated as we think we are."

She stole a glance at Hugh, who regarded them both with an odd mix of anger and amusement. "You meant well, I know that," she continued. "But Hugh and I are adults and fully capable of finding our own partners for life, in our own ways."

It sounded so right, so safe. Then why did it feel so wrong?

Mr. O shrugged. "If you say so, Meghan. This whole thing wasn't my idea anyway. It was God's."

Hugh jumped into the conversation with both big feet. *"God's idea?"*

"That's right." Mr. O squared his shoulders. "For years, I've prayed for a woman who could match you, toe to toe, in talent, brains, wit, faith, and pure stubbornness. When I saw Meghan's picture, God whispered, 'She's the one.' Who am I to argue with Him? The Lord steered me to your mother in much the same way, and we had a grand life together, wouldn't you say?"

"No denying that, Dad."

"You have a long life ahead of you, Hugh. Meghan was right: It's time Savannah had a mother. And you need a wife." Mr. O paused, slapping a suddenly red-faced Hugh on the back. "No need to get embarrassed, son. Meghan's been around the block, she knows how this works."

Around the...? Her eyes widened. *Trust me, I've never seen this street before in my life.*

Sobering, Mr. O leaned toward Hugh and lowered his voice to a hoarse whisper. "Caroline would want this, you know."

Hugh merely nodded, though Meghan didn't miss the sheen of tears in his dark eyes as he shifted his gaze toward the distant bay. She strained to hear his answer, wondering if it would echo her own.

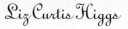

"Dad, I want to be sure it's what I want. And what Meghan wants."

Her heart collapsed like a forgotten balloon. *Don't you know, Hugh? What I want is time.*

She swallowed hard when the truth hit her. *What I want is you.*

"Time to head for the orchard, you two!" Savannah sang out, grabbing an empty pail before dashing through the back door.

Meghan gulped down the last of her morning coffee while Hugh dug in his pockets for his keys. After a sleepless night in the guest room, worrying about how the weekend might unfold, she needed every ounce of caffeine she could get. It still wasn't clear if Hugh was happy to have her company or not. The sooner she figured that out, the better.

The weather, at least, offered a warm welcome. As she followed Hugh outside, heading for the van, her senses were awakened by glorious blue skies and summer breezes washed clean by the rain. Savannah, who'd admitted over breakfast that she'd been plotting all week to keep them busy through Sunday, was waiting for them in the backseat of the vehicle, her braces gleaming, a map spread across her narrow lap, a picnic basket perched by her side.

Hugh had been quiet over breakfast. Polite, friendly…and distant. He looked at her now, a little longer than necessary. Offering a silent prayer, she flashed her warmest smile, hoping it said what she felt: *I'm glad to be here.*

He smiled back, broader than before.

He's glad too.

Meghan took a full breath for the first time in twelve hours.

And Hugh, on cue, exhaled. "Where to, Vannah girl?"

"Old Mission Peninsula," she crowed, launching the trio on a full day of adventures. Meghan's first u-pick-it experience at a local cherry farm had them stuffing their faces and dripping with sticky, sweet juice.

Hugh suggested a cherry-pit spitting contest. Meghan politely declined, then spit one at his back, just to see if she could do it.

She could.

Later that day they traveled up the narrow, eighteen-mile peninsula that separated Grand Traverse into east and west bays. The breathtaking drive was surprisingly hilly. At many points, Meghan could see both arms of the bay as she gazed over the cherry, apple, and pear orchards on either side of the road. Old farmhouses dotted the landscape, along with acres of grapevines, fruit stands shaped like big cherries, and an occasional church, pointing its spire into the splendid Michigan sky.

Old Mission Lighthouse was waiting for them at the peninsula's point. They visited the cabin moved there by the historical society, admired the lighthouse, and stomped around in the sand. Hugh pointed out Suttons Bay across the west arm of the bay, water that matched the sky except where sailboats added a burst of color on the azure surface.

"My, I could live here," Meghan sighed without pretense. Hugh's inquisitive look sent her scrambling. "I mean, *you* must love living here! Wonderful place. Don't you think?"

I don't know what to think.

Hugh watched Meghan cavort across the sandy peninsula beach with Savannah at her heels like a loyal beagle. Meghan was already a vital part of their lives, like a missing puzzle piece that had landed in place, a perfect fit.

She wasn't Caroline, though. Not even a little.

Maybe that's good. He could start all over, without stubbing his toe over memories that refused to go away.

She was more driven than Caroline, more business minded.

Less dependent on him, less malleable.

More like me. He grinned at that. She might share some of his traits, but she was still uniquely Meghan.

His grin stretched further. *And all woman.*

"What are you grinning about, Osborne?" she demanded, running up to him, out of breath, with Savannah tagging along by her side. "Is it the hair sticking straight up or the soggy pant legs?"

"I've seen both before," he reminded her with a nonchalant shrug, then ducked when she swatted a sand-covered hand in his direction.

Lord, I need some direction here.

Meghan spread their picnic blanket across the sand, then claimed a spot next to the basket and divided the spoils among them. Egg salad sandwich for her, cheese for Savannah, sliced ham for Hugh.

It felt so natural, so *right,* to be sharing a meal this way. Nothing awkward, no sense of being left out of their father-daughter circle.

Relax, Meg. Stop asking "Is he the one?"

If he were the one, she would know soon enough.

If he weren't, she would know that as well.

Only time would tell. And only the Lord knew the answer. She would simply wait and see what unfolded.

The hours flew by like the gulls overhead, airy and grace-filled. Meghan found a secret pleasure in watching Hugh play the role of stern papa one second, prankish schoolboy the next. Fathering suited Hugh. Would Greg have been this comfortable with kids?

In the fading light of sunset, Meghan watched them cavort along the shoreline, Hugh sporting the picnic blanket like a cape, Savannah in close pursuit, her eyes filled with joy and adoration.

Me too, young lady. Meghan laughed for the sheer pleasure of hearing it. *Me too.*

Within the hour, they were packed up and headed toward home. They'd stayed on the peninsula late enough that the sun sneaked out of sight behind the Leelanau hills, leaving only twinkling stars and a sliver of a moon to light their way back across the narrow road to Traverse City. Savannah fell asleep in the backseat, snoring lightly, her ponytail hanging out one side of the blanket, her sand-covered sneakers poking out the other.

Meghan studied Hugh's daughter in the companionable silence. *She does need a mother, Lord. I have no idea if I could be worthy of such a task, but I could try.* She swallowed hard. *Do You want me to try? Was Hugh's father right about us?*

Lately, it seemed Meghan had only questions for God. Her prayers had always been filled with praises and thanks and concern for others. These days, though, every prayer started with "why" or "how" and ended with a question mark.

She broke the silence with a single, soft word. "Hugh?"

He leaned slightly in her direction, keeping both eyes on the road, both hands on the wheel. "What is it?"

"It's…it's…"

"Us."

"Right."

"What's next?"

"What do you want to be next?"

"You brought it up."

"No, *you* did."

"Did what, Meghan?"

"Asked 'what's next!'"

"Well, you haven't answered me yet!" He laughed, then lowered his voice when Savannah stirred in the backseat. "I only know that I love being with you."

"You do?" She wrinkled her nose, as though not quite convinced. "Even if being with me for the weekend wasn't your idea?"

"On the contrary, it was a great idea. It just occurred to my dad first, that's all."

Her laugh was like tinkling bells. "Good save, Hugh. Now… what were you saying you loved?"

"I love how you make me feel more capable than I ever imagined. I love how you show every person around you that they're important and cared for. I love your faith, your strength, and your confidence. A pretty impressive résumé, I'd say."

She leaned over and wiggled her eyebrows in the darkness. "You haven't said a thing about my ruby red lips or my pearly white teeth or my bright blue eyes or my silky black hair. Get with the program, Hugh. That Song of Solomon material is the way to a woman's heart."

Hugh suddenly pulled over and turned off the ignition. He leaned his back against the van door and regarded her in the faint moonlight, his eyes black in the darkness.

Meghan's heart skipped a beat, then two. "Did I say something wrong?"

"Wrong? Not at all. You couldn't be more right. I've been thinking about what a wonderful person you are, when in fact, it's the woman in you that turns me inside out."

"Ohh."

"Yes, I do love your ruby red lips." He leaned forward. "Loved kissing them once." His muscular arms pulled her toward him. "Make that twice."

Hugh found her lips in the shadows and kissed her thoroughly. She pressed her hands against his chest, at first to keep him from getting too close and then—*ah, the shameful truth of it!*—to keep him from getting away.

Releasing her only far enough to gaze into her eyes, he continued with his careful evalution of her attributes. "Your blue eyes are a wonder of nature, like sky and ice and sea, all wrapped up in two beautiful circles, filled with light."

"I think those circles are leaking," Meghan whispered with a sniff.

He lightly touched her hair with his hands, sending tiny shivers down her back. "And your hair." Hugh ran his hands through it, closing his eyes. "I've lost sleep thinking about how your hair would feel in my hands."

Meghan's own eyes drifted shut. *I know exactly how it feels. Wonderful.* If she weren't careful, she'd start purring.

"Your turn," Hugh whispered.

She looked up at him through half-closed lids, so relaxed that her words were as slurred as her brain. "My turn to pet your hair?" A moment later, her eyes popped open. "I mean, my turn to…what?"

"Tell me what you think of me, Meghan DeWitt. I feel like I'm out here on a limb all by myself."

"I'll join you out there then, with pleasure." She pulled back to look at him as carefully as he'd gazed at her. "I love your honesty, love your compassion, your fine mind, and your business wizardry."

"And…?"

"What else is there?" She gave him a wide-eyed, innocent

stare. When he looked like he might kiss her again, she gulped and plunged on. "And, I like your…"

"'Love' is the word we're using here, Meghan."

"Ah…right. I *love* your wavy brown hair and how it curls down under your collar." She twisted a lock of it in her finger and drew small circles on the nape of his muscular neck.

Hugh suddenly looked drugged.

"And I love your chocolate brown eyes that look more delicious than the real thing. Especially when they look at me like that."

Oh, especially then. She shivered in the eighty-degree heat.

"Meghan." He gently pulled her hand from his neck and held it in his. "The truth is, I'm falling in love with every bit of your beautiful self. I'm just not sure what to do next. My business, my family, my life is in Michigan."

She nodded. *Exactly.* "And mine is in Ohio. Our company is in a growth mode and I just built a new house. Plus, I…I like being single."

"You do?" Hugh peered at her intently. "You've got to be kidding. I despise it. Marriage with a wonderful woman is heaven on earth. When I think of the joy that Caroline and I shared, I feel so empty realizing it's gone forever."

Meghan sat back on her side of the van so she could give him a bit of breathing space. "Hugh, you've never really told me what happened."

He sighed again. "Lymphosarcoma. Cancer of the lymph glands." Hugh's voice was so low, Meghan strained to hear his next words. "By the time we realized it, she had tumors everywhere. Caroline was a tiny woman to begin with, but to see her shrink away to nothing…" He turned toward the window, as if the sight of moonlight on the bay would make the terrible memory of those last days disappear into the black night. "She was only thirty-four."

"My age." Meghan whispered, finding it difficult to swallow the lump in her throat. *Don't let me cry, Lord, not now!* She could feel tears gathering in her eyes, and quickly brushed them away, mortified to find Hugh watching her every move.

"Sorry," she added with a timid smile.

"Never apologize for tears, Meghan. I cried buckets of them after the funeral. Maybe that's why marriage scares me half to death."

"More than public speaking?" she teased gently.

"Much more." He found her other hand in the darkness and brought them both to his lips, caressing them with kisses until she thought she might faint. "You are the first woman God has brought my way who has made me even consider marriage again."

Her heart turned a slow somersault. "Uh, Hugh?" She gulped. "That thing I said about enjoying singleness? Forget I ever mentioned it." She laughed, brushing his sandpaper cheek with her hand, feeling him smiling beneath her fingers. "It's a bald-faced lie, one I've been telling myself for years. I loathe being alone. With the right man, marriage would be divine."

"Am I the right man?"

She tugged his hands toward her and lifted them to her lips, pressing a kiss into the warm center of each palm. "I think you could be. Where do we go from here?"

His gaze rested on hers. "I was hoping you'd move to Michigan. To come with me and be my bride."

"Hugh." She groaned, feeling a deep wound inside her split open. *It's happening again.* A successful man was asking her to leave her career, her friends, her life, for the mysteries of

Michigan. *Not again, Lord! Not that kind of risk. Not even for Hugh.*

She pushed open the van door and stumbled out into the muggy night, needing air, needing time.

Hugh was beside her in an instant. "Meghan, are you ill? I've never proposed to a woman who got violently sick at the very idea of it."

She shot him a sideways glance. "How many other women have you proposed to?"

"One."

"Caroline, you mean."

"That's right." His expression was grim. "She said yes."

Meghan stared hard at the bay, at the orchards, at the distant moon, anything to avoid eye contact. "I said yes once too, Hugh, and it almost destroyed me." She couldn't stop the bitter memories that crowded her thoughts and seeped into her words. "I'm not certain I can let that kind of hope grow in me again."

He stepped in front of her, blocking her view of anything but him, and looked at her with eyes that flared with angry amber sparks. "Meghan, I am *not* Greg Hammond."

She looked away, her cheeks hot. "I know that, but—"

"But you expect it! You think if you pull up your roots and come to Michigan that I'll leave you for...for..."

"Sandy, the Proverbs 31 woman?"

"Whoever! The point is, you don't trust me."

"No, Hugh. I don't trust *myself*. I don't trust my judgment when it comes to men." She groaned, flailing her arms in the dark. *How did it come to this?* "Look, in the business world, I'm a big success. In love, I'm a...loser."

"Losing is what this weekend is all about, then."

Hugh stormed around to his side of the van, climbed behind the wheel, and flung her door open. "Get in. I'm tired of being compared to the one man who played you for a fool."

She spun in his direction. "Hugh, I'm not comparing you…"

But she was, and she knew it. Worst of all, *he* knew it. Steadying herself, she climbed inside the van and pulled her door shut, being careful not to slam it. Enough damage had been done tonight. *Too much.*

He started the van, grinding the transmission as he shoved the gear shift in place. "Tomorrow you can take the first plane back to Columbus and decide how you want to spend the rest of your life. I intend to spend mine with someone who trusts me."

Twelve

*Woman begins by resisting a man's advances and
ends by blocking his retreat.*

OSCAR WILDE

eghan faced the hard, cold truth: She hated Mondays. Nothing burdened her more than having a long, stressful week stretched ahead of her, filled with appointments and opportunities. A busy calendar declared, "No man will give me the time of day, so I might as well work."

Right now, she didn't need to hear that.

How had Hugh put it? *"Losing is what this weekend is all about"*? The man did have a knack for hitting the nail right on the head.

Sunday had been a complete disaster. Hugh had disappeared by the time she woke up. Mr. O thought he'd gone to the early service at church, then over to Lake Leelanau to get in some fishing before the tourists showed up. Savannah and her grandfather left for the second worship service while Meghan waited around for Hugh to reappear, trying to read, trying to work, trying not to cry.

Finally she gave up, called a cab, and caught an earlier flight home, slamming her new front door with a satisfied bang.

If Hugh Osborne wants me, he can by golly come to Ohio.

She glanced at her watch. Ten o'clock Monday morning and

nary a rose in sight. Meghan gathered her notes and appointment book and dragged herself into the firm's small conference room for their weekly partners' meeting, tossing her things unceremoniously on the table.

"Meghan?" Her two partners, Mike and Dan, looked at her in amazement. They'd never seen her depressed before. Tired, argumentative, stressed out, maybe; but this was a new Meghan and she knew it was not an improvement.

Mike ventured a smile. "Is...uh...everything okay?"

"Why do people keep asking me that?" she growled. "Everything is fine. Let's get our client scheduling set up for the rest of the year, shall we? I have work to do."

The two men exchanged worried glances and buried their heads in their calendars, comparing notes on which clients were already penciled in, and which needed to be added to their schedules by year's end.

"Meghan, I gotta tell you, you made an incredible impression on this Osborne guy in Suttons Bay," Dan announced, obviously watching to see if this news brightened her spirits.

It did not.

"That's the *senior* Mr. Osborne," she clarified. "Roger, the father, is the one who made all those helpful referrals. The actual client was Hugh." *Humph.* "The son."

"I see," Mike agreed, though Meghan was sure he saw nothing at all. "Anyway, between his recommendations and several others, we have more than twenty appointments to schedule in Michigan alone. Each one will take two days to a full week."

Out of the corner of her eye, she watched him motion to Dan for support while she stared out the window.

"So—" Dan chimed in—"what we were thinking is, perhaps you could set up a temporary office in Michigan and handle all these clients yourself, Meghan. The savings in time and travel would more than offset the cost of an inexpensive studio apartment. With your laptop and cell phone, you'll be up and running in a day."

Mike added with obvious enthusiasm, "If this works as well as we think it will, Michigan could be the first permanent branch office for Gilbert, DeWitt, and Ross—with you as director of operations, of course."

Meghan may not have been looking at her partners, but she heard every word of their "good news/bad news" announcement. Expanding their business into Michigan was more than good; it was terrific. But if Hugh found out and decided she was—*heaven forbid!*—pursuing him, it would be more than bad; it would be terrible.

Then again, who said Hugh had to find out? Michigan was a big state, right?

She tried to look relaxed. Unconcerned. "So…did you have a specific location in mind?"

Mike slowly nodded, studying a mitten-shaped map of Michigan. "Based on the calls we've been receiving, I'd say somewhere between Lansing and the Upper Peninsula should work. The ideal place would be Traverse City."

"Absolutely not!" Meghan hadn't known until this very moment that she could sound like a banshee.

"What's the problem with Traverse City?" Dan was obviously losing patience with her. "Weren't you just there? I hear it's a great place."

Yeah, a great place to lose your heart.

Hiding from Hugh would be out of the question now. The minute she started working with his father's friends, Hugh would hear it through the grapevine.

Unless I tell him myself first.

Mike was saying something about scouting out locations as she shook her head and brought herself back into focus.

"Meghan, why don't you take a two-week swing around the mitten and report back to us? Make it a working vacation. Wherever you want to operate from in Michigan is fine with us. Okay?"

"Okay." She forced a smile. "Sorry, guys, it was a rough weekend. Let's nail these dates down through December, then I'll pack for a long stretch on the road."

After I make a certain phone call.

She mapped out her travel calendar through December, one eye on her planner, the other on the silent phone across the room.

Calling him was risky, no question. He might laugh. Hang up. Leave her feeling like the biggest fool in two states.

Which is the bigger risk, Meg? Losing face? Or losing Hugh?

Forget saving face. She would call him. Tell him precisely how the deal came down. Assure him that it was all strictly business. That she would just as easily have moved to any of the other forty-eight states, that Michigan held no special place in her heart whatsoever, that—

Liar, liar, skirts on fire.

She would call him. She would tell him. "Hugh, I'm moving to Michigan."

Would he gloat? Men always gloated when a woman seemed willing to follow them to the ends of the earth.

But Lord, I am willing.

That was the truth of it.

She didn't care if he gloated. She didn't care if he smirked. She might not go all the way to earth's end, but she was willing to go to Michigan.

And not just for business.

For love.

Say the word, Meg. "Love." Atta girl, you can do it. Love, love, love.

Meghan's day was now toast. She fidgeted through the rest of the meeting then dashed back to her office to place a very important phone call to O & O Printing.

She cradled the phone in her hands, planning what she would say, how she would act. She would be very calm. Smooth and professional. She'd simply tell him exactly how the branch office idea came about and see how he reacted. He was a businessman, he'd get it.

No.

She would not hide behind her schedule book. She would tell him the truth. *Hugh, I care for you, and God has provided a way for me to come to Michigan.* If she could think it, then she could say it out loud.

So she did. Eleven times.

It was starting to sound natural.

Meghan pressed the numbers that would connect her to O & O and listened to the phone ring. And ring. Finally the front desk answered, at which point she chickened out and asked for Kathleen.

"Hugh Osborne's office."

"Kathleen!" Meghan exhaled in relief. "Meghan DeWitt here. Is Hugh busy this morning?"

"I'm sure he's busy somewhere, but not here."

The hairs on the back of her neck stood up. "What do you mean?"

"Let me check his schedule book." Kathleen was gone for several very long minutes, then finally picked up the phone again. "I found it. Sorry it took forever. You know how his desk is." She chuckled. "He flew out at 7:30 this morning and it looks like he's in…hmm, Ohio somewhere."

"*Ohio?*" Meghan fought back a shriek. "Uh…*where* in Ohio, exactly?"

"Boy, this handwriting is almost illegible. Looks like he jotted this down right before he left town. Let's see." Another pregnant pause. "Could it be…Columbus?"

"It could be." Meghan was barely breathing. Out of the corner of her eye, Meghan noticed someone standing in the doorway. Curious, she glanced over and nearly dropped the phone.

Hugh!

She abruptly hung up and stared at the man who filled her doorway as surely as he filled her heart.

He was dressed in a suit. Had she ever seen him in a suit? Had she ever seen anything more handsome? He was sporting a dozen yellow roses and one very smug smile.

Hugh spoke first, which was ideal, since she was numb from the lips down.

"That wasn't by any chance my secretary?" He stepped into the room, closing the door softly behind him. "Looks like I'll have to apologize for your hasty good-bye. Did she tell you what the nature of this business trip happens to be?"

Meghan shook her head in stupefied silence, grateful to have any movement back at all.

"Then let me be the first to tell you the news, Miss DeWitt. I am absolutely crazy about you and have no intention of letting you walk out of my life." He added in a softer tone, "Unless you want that, of course."

She shook her head again and remained glued to her desk chair.

"Good." The man exuded confidence and charm. In the back of her mind, Meghan realized that she'd been part of that refining process. My, but she'd done a bang-up job.

Hugh moved toward her now. "I'd like to suggest a merger of our…uh, mutual…um…"

"A—what?" she asked faintly, finding her voice at last.

"That is to say, a collaborative effort toward…well…" He shrugged his shoulders and flashed her a lopsided grin. "Meghan DeWitt, will you marry me?"

"Yes!" She jumped to her feet and yanked the roses out of his hands, standing on tiptoe to throw her arms around his neck. "Yes," she repeated, whispering this time and gazing into his delicious chocolate eyes.

When he bent down to kiss her, she was already moving in his direction. This, their third kiss, was by far the most noteworthy to date. Everything inside her turned to music. She sensed a sweet singing in her bones, a melodic hum that wound its way through every inch of her.

Hugh finally broke the kiss, though clearly reluctant to do so. He had something on his mind, Meghan could tell, so she perched on the edge of her desk while he took a deep breath and reached in his suit pocket for a small notepad covered with penciled notations.

"Now, there are a lot of complicated details to work out," he began, consulting his notes. "With O & O in Michigan, it will be harder for me to work from Columbus, but by no means impossible. That's why they make fax machines, right?"

Meghan nodded, starting to lose feeling again in her limbs. *What is he saying?*

"So, assuming we…uh…put this all together in the next thirty days, Savannah can begin the school year in Westerville." He looked up from his notes. "From all reports, an excellent school system. And you have a church you love, yes?"

She couldn't even nod at this point.

"Meghan, blink if you're with me. Twice for 'yes.'"

She blinked. Twice. She was with him, all right. *He's coming to Ohio! He's willing to give up everything...for me!*

Meanwhile, Hugh was on a strategic planning roll. "Dad thinks he can sell the house in Suttons Bay very quickly during the tourist season, and then he'll find a nice condo with a bay view—"

"Hugh!" Her voice came back all at once. "Stop the presses!"

"Stop the what?" His eyes took on a cagey gleam. "Don't you know those words strike terror in a printer's heart?"

She smiled broadly. "Suttons Bay is about to become the first branch office of Gilbert, DeWitt, and Ross."

"You're kidding." Hugh stared at his notepad as though this vital bit of information were scribbled there somewhere. "When did that happen?"

"About sixty seconds ago." She stretched up and kissed the look of utter astonishment off his face. "In fact, my two weeks of vacation begin today and I'm spending them in Michigan."

His eyes widened further. "And when did you find *that* out?"

A sly smile stole across her face. "About twenty minutes ago. Come meet my partners."

Meghan guided Hugh through the small group of offices, doing a one-sentence introduction of each coworker, while they and Hugh gawked at one another in disbelief.

Except for Joan, who jumped up and gave him a big hug. "I'd know him anywhere." She winked at Meghan. "'Your man in Michigan!'"

Meghan announced to no one in particular that her vacation was effective immediately and followed Hugh out the door, roses in tow, headed home to pack for a nice long visit to northwestern Michigan.

When they pulled into her driveway, she watched his face take in the new house, the freshly seeded lawn, the just-planted shrubbery.

"Meghan, are you sure?" He shook his head, doubt darkening his features for the first time that morning. "Our house is old and the neighborhood is—"

"Perfect." She leaned over and kissed his neck, delighting in the clean, masculine scent that was altogether Hugh. "Joan informed me she already has a realtor ready to list it."

"But it's your *house*."

"True." Her steps slowed as they walked toward the brightly painted front door. "But it's not my home."

"Is that right?" He spun her around and gathered her in his arms, kissing her forehead, then her cheek, then her chin, before whispering in her ear, "Then where's home?"

"Right here," she sighed, as he pulled her closer still and sought her mouth with his. *Right here.*

Thirteen

Tell a man he is brave, and you help him to become so.

THOMAS CARLYLE

*M*onday, July 30.

Meghan was finding it hard to breathe. *You'd think I was the one speaking tonight.* Except she seldom got nervous before she spoke.

No, it was Hugh's performance that chilled her hands and glued her tongue to the roof of her mouth. Her man—and her skills as a coach—would both take the stage that night, and she wanted every one of those five hundred people to see Hugh the way she saw him: as a hero.

Mr. O sat on her left, looking dapper in a new suit purchased for the occasion and chosen by her. "No plaid shirt?" Meghan whispered in his ear, then watched a pink tinge decorate his bald spot. "You look very handsome, Mr. O. It's easy to see where Hugh gets his good looks."

Savannah sat on her right, a vision of youthful beauty. Meghan had tamed the young girl's curly locks with half a dozen ribbons and found the perfect dress in vibrant peach to complement Vannah's summer tan and pixie brown eyes, which were sparkling with anticipation.

"Here he comes!" Savannah squealed, as her father emerged from a back stage curtain and made his way to the head table on the low riser along with his Chamber associates.

Meghan blushed, remembering the morning when he pulled her onto that very riser for their first kiss. Could it really have been a mere two weeks ago? He looked devastatingly handsome under the lights, his hair carefully combed, his dark suit and colorful tie the ideal choice for the evening.

Of course. She'd picked them out, too.

While the three of them sat there in the audience, too nervous to eat a single bite, Hugh was laughing and chatting with his peers at the head table on the platform, dining with obvious delight, cool as a cucumber.

"Daddy looks awfully calm," Savannah observed, obviously concerned. "Shouldn't his hands be shaking or something? What if he's okay now, but freezes when they introduce him?"

The girl was wise beyond her years. That was precisely the scenario that had haunted Meghan's nightmares the last two days. Hugh was almost too relaxed. *Lord, please don't let my hero fall off his white horse in front of five hundred people.*

Glasses were clinking as the executive director stepped to the lectern to begin the festivities. After endless introductions and awards, the moment of truth finally came.

Hugh moved smoothly to the lectern, picked up the microphone, and immediately stepped to the side, just as Meghan had taught him.

He certainly looks confident…

He began his opening story and was getting to the punch line when his eyes found her in the audience and he stumbled over the next few words, producing only a ripple of laughter instead of the big response they'd hoped for.

The still small voice shouted in Meghan's ear: *He needs you!*

She sat up as straight and tall as she could, prayed with all her might, and allowed God's love to pour through her eyes and flow to the platform in waves.

I love you! I love you! I love you!

She let her eyes communicate it so loudly she expected the front row to turn around in their seats.

I'm with you, Hugh. You can do it!

All at once he smiled, bathing the stage with the glow of it, and dove into his next story, which captured the crowd's attention almost instantly. Meghan did not relax her concentration for a single moment, but kept directing her prayers toward the platform.

Hugh was nearing the close of his presentation. By now the audience was clasped in the palm of his hand, laughing one moment, wiping away tears the next, as Hugh told story after story of his own business successes and failures.

Suddenly, he paused and reached underneath the lectern, as though searching for something. Meghan's mouth went dry. *What's going on?* Had he tucked his notes under there and lost his place?

"In closing, may I share the one experience that, more than any other, has shaped my professional career to date?" He took a deep breath and Meghan took it right along with him.

"Third grade, Suttons Bay Elementary. I'm in the Easter pageant. The other kids are dressed up as eggs and chicks and jelly beans, but I'm the tallest kid in the class, so I have to be…the Easter bunny."

Meghan's eyes almost popped out of her head. *The bunny story! He's going to tell them the bunny story!*

And he did, every hilarious, outrageous, embarrassing minute of it. The audience was in hysterics, identifying with him every painful step of the way and celebrating his victory right along with him.

Meghan was speechless with joy, watching a miracle unfold before her.

Hugh hadn't merely overcome his fear. He had mastered it.

"And so, my friends," he concluded, "to take us through the next year, I've chosen a theme that captures the spirit of Traverse City, a place where people from everywhere gather to have fun. I think we owe them a promise."

Hugh pulled out a pair of giant, two-foot bunny ears and slipped them on his handsome head, a winsome grin spreading across his features. "Let's tell America that we plan to *Keep Traverse City Hopping*. Won't you join me?"

With that, he hopped down from the platform and began shaking one hand after another as the crowd leaped to their collective feet, applauding wildly.

"Wow!" Savannah finally let go of the breath she'd been holding all night. "Did you know Daddy would be that good?"

"No, sweetie, I didn't. But the Lord knew." Meghan winked at her, brushing away her tears. "Let's hop down front and give him a hero's welcome, shall we?"

Meghan pressed toward the stage, Savannah firmly in tow. It felt so right, this young girl's hand in hers. *Family!* The thought of it still overwhelmed her—soon she would stand next to Hugh at the altar, Mr. O on one side, Savannah on the other.

Family!

When Hugh spotted them, his smile turned up two more notches. "Meghan, Vannah! Come rescue me!"

The throng of well-wishers parted enough for them to squeeze through, and they found themselves wrapped in Hugh's bear-sized hug, everyone talking at once.

"Daddy, I'm so proud!"

"Hugh, you were incredible!"

He shook his head, then planted a kiss on Savannah's freckled nose. "No, it's my *family* that's incredible. You were up here with me, I could feel it. And you…" Hugh gathered Meghan snugly against him. His voice was low in his throat, thick with emotion. "You're the best partner a man could ever want."

"In business?" she teased, hugging him back.

His lips brushed her hair. "And pleasure," he whispered.

Meghan blushed to her roots. "And…ah…family?"

She felt him smiling against her forehead. "Most definitely family, my future Mrs. Osborne. Most definitely."

Leaning back to return his smile, she waved toward the empty platform. "Now that this little hurdle is behind us, are we ready to discuss a wedding date?"

He shrugged. "I like April."

April? Not April!

"April is out," she informed him. "So is May." No way was she going to give this man time to change his mind. *No way.* She offered him a vampish grin. "I'm not sure I can wait that long, handsome. How 'bout something sooner, like October?"

"October? Well, well." He tightened his embrace, ignoring the amused onlookers crowding around them, then lowered his voice. "I like a woman who knows what she wants. A big wedding?"

"No!" She blanched at the mere mention of it. A woman never forgets eating her entire wedding cake. "We're talking a small ceremony, Hugh. You, me, Savannah, your dad, your minister." She held up five fingers. "Very small. Work for you?"

"Works for me," he murmured, then bent to capture her lips in a breath-stealing, toe-curling kiss.

"This is not working!" Meghan tossed her veil on the couch and avoided looking over at the anxious fluttering of her mother's hands rescuing the gossamer mess.

The wedding was one hour away. *One hour!* And her veil still didn't look like it belonged on her head. Her new tea-length dress in white satin and lace was lovely, the ideal choice for a warm October day. Her new shoes were a perfect match—and comfortable, of all things.

The veil, however, was not quite new. It was instead a pricey leftover from two Aprils ago, the only thing she'd salvaged "just in case" she ever needed such a thing.

This morning, she definitely needed it. Meghan stared at the beaded headpiece and mountains of netting in her mother's hands. Was there such a thing as too much tulle?

The veil wasn't her only challenge; the guest list had expanded a bit. Okay, more than a bit…a *bunch*. Seventy-five people would be planted all over the Osbornes' lawn and gardens. That had meant renting a tent in case it rained—which it wouldn't dare, but she had to be ready. It meant a caterer and musicians and a whole long list of concerns that five people would never have required.

Though she really had no choice.

"You are *not* getting married without your father and me in the front row," her mother had informed her back in August in a tone that brooked no argument. Many of Hugh's employees had felt the same way. And his friends from the Chamber. And his church. And half of Suttons Bay.

One by one, they were starting to arrive.

And Meghan was starting to fall apart.

"No tears, dear," her mother cautioned, touching a tissue to the corner of each eye. "They'll ruin your pretty makeup."

Meghan groaned and slipped the veil on her head once more. *There.* She stared at her image in the Osborne's guest room mirror. Like it or not, she had to admit the veil complemented the dress perfectly.

It was the right size, the right style, the right color, the right length.

And all wrong.

The reason why hit her like a bolt of lightning, leaving her mouth gaping and her hands clammy. *Because you bought it for Greg.* Because two springs ago she'd envisioned him—over and over—lifting that veil to kiss his blushing bride, the new Mrs. Gregory Hammond.

Well! She snatched the veil off her head. Greg was *not* on the invitation list for this wedding, nor would he cast even a tulle-thin shadow on the life-changing ceremony ahead.

"But it's nice," her mother reminded her, shaking her head.

"And it's history!" Meghan shouted with glee, wrestling with the fluffy tulle until it tore in two. *There!* She felt better immediately, though her mother looked as though she might faint dead away.

"Child, the wedding starts in an hour!" Her mother's voice rose to an anguished pitch. "Where are you going to find—?"

"Not to worry." Meghan flashed her first genuine smile of the morning. "The problem is solved." Ducking past her wide-eyed mother, she opened the bedroom door and called out, "Sa-van-nah! Are you almost ready?"

Halfway down the hall, a door cracked open and a freckle-covered face popped into view. "I've been ready since breakfast!" Savannah took a tentative step into the hallway.

"And you look adorable," Meghan assured her, taking in the charming pastel dress and beribboned hat. "Could you do me a huge favor, sweetie?" When Savannah nodded, eager to help, Meghan waved the girl over and whispered her instructions, sending her off with money and a prayer.

She'd ruled out her first idea—a pair of bunny ears—knowing

her mother would boycott the wedding before she'd let her wear them. This was a better solution; a gentle peace offering to her new family.

If Savannah could find them and get back in time.

And that's a mighty big if.

When she returned to the guest room, her mother greeted her with eyebrows raised. "And?"

"All taken care of." Meghan donned her most confident smile. "Help me get my hairstyle back in order, will you, Mom? That silly old veil turned my hair into a rat's nest." She offered her bewildered mother a comb and a reassuring wink. "Everything will be fine. You'll see what I mean, the minute Savannah gets back here."

"Here comes the bride!"

Hugh heard the crowd's murmur rise to a crescendo, and felt his own heart take flight with it. Meghan would join him in the garden any minute. *Finally.*

To think he'd suggested April! It had taken every ounce of self-control God gave him to keep his hands to himself and his mind on things above for the last three months, counting the long days and the endless nights, holding Meghan at arm's length until they were husband and wife.

Not tonight, Lord. Tonight she's all mine.

Hugh grinned at the thought, then exhaled, looking at his watch for the umpteenth time. He hadn't been allowed to see her, of course. Tradition, her mother insisted.

Would she be wearing white? A long gown? A short dress? *A pair of white painter's pants are fine with me, woman—just show up!*

And then she did.

And took his breath clean away.

His bride stood before him, separated by an expanse of lawn filled with smiling friends and weeping family members. A string quartet he'd barely noticed took their cue as Savannah pulled a long, narrow carpet of white across the grass with one hand while tossing rose petals with the other, her head held high, her grin a thing of youthful beauty.

But it was the beauty behind his daughter that claimed every bit of his attention now.

Meghan.

She began moving toward him, her graceful steps falling in time to the familiar strains from Lohengrin that filled the air, her father by her side. Everyone and everything else faded from view except the woman who grew closer to his heart with each step.

Her dress was white, though the details were blurry. He only knew that it fit her like a silk glove.

Her lips were crimson, as delicious-looking as Michigan cherries. Soon enough, he'd taste them and see.

Her eyes were iridescent, strikingly blue even from this distance. He couldn't help but notice they were trained on him. *Good thing.* He would share her with no one this day.

Her hair was swept up off her neck, gathered in a knot of curls on top. Tucked inside those curls were flowers. Were they...?

They were. *Roses. Yellow roses.*

He gazed into her eyes when she reached his side, praying his love for her was written all over his face, exactly as her love for him was etched all over hers.

"I thought you'd never get here," he whispered, tucking her hand in the crook of his elbow as her father stepped to the side, eyes moist.

"I hope it was worth the wait," she whispered back, turning

with him toward the minister who stood before them, smiling patiently, Bible in hand.

Hugh's gaze left hers only long enough to take in the fragrant roses in her hair. "You are definitely worth waiting for, Meghan." He lowered his eyes to hers once more, and lowered his voice so that she alone would hear his heart, "I'm grateful you waited for me."

Dear One:

What a joy it was to spend a few sunny weeks in Suttons Bay, Michigan, with Meghan, Hugh…and *you!* Watching people overcome their fears by exercising faith always warms our hearts, doesn't it?

My hubby, Bill, is right in his "endorsement" at the front of the book—he's nothing like Hugh Osborne (except for the messy desk). And no way do I resemble the petite, dark-haired Miss DeWitt, although I *have* delivered many a speech on camera and on stage. But a speech *coach?* Not this girl!

Our courtship was a bit longer than Meg and Hugh's, and it not only ended with a big wedding, but also *started* with one. As a still-single woman in my early thirties at the time, I was none too excited about sitting alone at yet another wedding, watching the church fill up like the animals filing into the ark—two by two—while I whined, "Where's *my* giraffe?"

Even more daunting was the prospect of being surrounded by a group of giggling eight-year-old girls at the tossing of the bridal bouquet while the spectators hollered, "Throw to Liz! Throw to Liz!"

That particular wedding, however, had two things going for it: (1) I knew both the bride and the groom, and rejoiced in how much they loved one another and the Lord. And (2) the woman getting married was named "Liz."

How handy! I could take her vows with her.

When the minister said, "Do you, Liz, take Doug?" I nodded and whispered, "I do." I didn't, of course, take Doug, who safely left the sanctuary with his blushing bride. But repeating all the vows certainly did put me in the mood for marriage.

At the ceremony's end, I scanned the whole sea of pairs and found a spare a few pews back. *Hmmm.* A distinguished-looking guy, all by himself? Stag on a Saturday night? No ring on his hand? Gotta be single.

The best part of all? He was smiling at me.

I marched toward him, extending the right hand of fellowship. "Welcome to our church!" I sang out.

"Oh, do you attend here?"

I smiled from ear to ear. "I do!"

Eight months later on March 14, 1986, I said those words again. So did Bill. We've been celebrating ever since.

Some love stories take longer to tell than ours, or the one you've read here in *Fine Print*. But whatever the length of the courtship—short story, novella, or epic novel—it's the happy ending that matters most.

For a virtual visit to Suttons Bay, visit my Scrapbook at *www.LizCurtisHiggs.com*. I'm also honored when readers take time to drop me a line, and love to keep in touch twice a year through my free newsletter. For the latest issue, please write me directly at: Liz Curtis Higgs, P.O. Box 43577, Louisville, KY 40253-0577.

Until next time…you are a blessing!

OUR WEDDING DAY   TODAY

Bloom-and-Shine Peach/Blueberry Puff Pancake

This is truly a yummy way to start the day!

Ingredients:

Non-stick pan spray

3 Tablespoons margarine, melted

1/2 cup canned peach pie filling (apple pie filling would work, too)

3/4 cup fresh berries—whole blueberries, raspberries, or strawberries (quartered)

6 large eggs

1-1/4 cup flour (all-purpose)

1-1/2 cup milk

1 Tablespoon sugar

1/2 teaspoon almond extract

Preheat oven to 400 degrees.

Spray 6 glass ramekins (small, individual 7 oz. baking dishes) thoroughly with pan spray.

Pour an even amount of melted margarine into the bottom of each one—1-1/2 teaspoons per ramekin. Cut peach slices in the filling into smaller pieces, then spoon pie filling and berries equally into the 6 ramekins.

In blender, combine eggs, flour, milk, sugar, and almond flavoring, then blend on high for 30 seconds. Pour mixture evenly into 6 ramekins (to 3/4 full).

Bake at 400 degrees for 25 minutes until puffed and golden.

Remove from oven (warning! hot!) and serve immediately in baking dish. Top with maple syrup, if desired.

Giggles!

Good Marriage Rule #47

Marriage pays great dividends—as long as you pay plenty of interest.

A Dinner to Remember

A June bride loved collecting the recipes featured on a local radio station each Saturday morning. One Saturday, she had to go out, so she asked her new husband to copy the radio recipe that morning.

The husband did his best, but somehow tuned in two stations at once. One was broadcasting the recipe his new bride wanted, but the other? Morning exercises.

When the bride returned home, this is what her proud husband handed her:

1. Hands on hips, place one cup of flour on shoulders, raise knees, curl toes, and wash roughly in one-half cup of milk.
2. Count to four, raising and lowering legs, and wash two hardboiled eggs in a sieve. Repeat six times.
3. Inhale one-half teaspoon of baking powder, one cup of flour, then breathe naturally. Exhale and sift.
4. Jump to your feet and bend whites of eggs backward and forward.
5. Arms overhead, raise the cooked egg in flour and, counting to four, make stiff dough.
6. Lie flat in flour and roll into marbles the size of walnuts.
7. Hop to straddle in boiling water, but do not boil at a gallop. After ten minutes, remove and wipe with a dry towel.

8. Breath deeply. Dress in warm flannels and serve with fish soup.

The Secrets to Success

"I have learned that only two things are necessary to keep one's wife happy. First, let her think she is having her way. Second, let her have it."

Lyndon B. Johnson

The Truth and Nothing But?

Woman to marriage counselor: "That's my side of the story. Now, let me tell you his."

Explain That!

Little Johnny was seated next to his mother at a wedding. When the bride and groom were standing at the front of the church, he tugged on his mother's sleeve and asked, "Mommy, why is the girl wearing white?"

His mother smiled down at him. "The bride always wears white because it's a happy color and this is the happiest day of her life."

Johnny absorbed that, then tugged again. "Well then, why is the boy wearing black?"

The Best of Intentions

Marrying for better or for worse is good; marrying for good is better.

Sweet Chariot

Carolyn Zane

$\mathcal{P}rologue$

olks who knew the widow Eunice A. Kelley liked to say that her middle initial stood for *Adventure*. That's why it surprised no one when, on her sixty-fifth birthday, Eunice took a hot-air balloon ride with her best friend, Opal Dinsmore, also a widow.

Unfortunately, Opal suffered from acrophobia.

Once they were airborne, Opal panicked and had to hunker down on the floor of the balloon's basket with her head between her knees. Eyes closed, poor Opal prayed the entire time for the wretched ride's swift conclusion.

But Eunice…well now, Eunice couldn't stop squealing with delight.

For her seventieth birthday, Eunice dragged Opal along for a bungee jumping spree from the top of a crane in their hometown, Tacoma, Washington. Considering her tendency to panic, Opal wasn't stupid enough to jump, but she sure took enough pictures of the devil-may-care Eunice flopping around by the ankles to fill a whole album.

Skydiving was the next natural step for Eunice and so, to celebrate her seventy-fifth birthday, she bought herself some lessons and took the plunge. Opal recorded this momentous occasion on videotape—from the safety of the plane's cockpit, of course.

Eunice was fond of saying that, since she'd passed the standard life expectancy of seventy-four years for women, nearly six years ago, she was living on borrowed time. And, since borrowed time was twice as valuable as regular time, it had better be packed with joie de vivre.

And so, as Eunice approached her eightieth birthday, she was in the mood to splurge.

One

ake Kelley flopped down next to his grandmother on her overstuffed, floral print sofa and accepted the glass of iced tea she offered. He'd spent the better part of that Sunday afternoon at the duplex she shared with Opal, tilling their garden patch and pruning the jungle that passed for landscaping. He was bushed, but it was a good bushed. Nothing like a little physical exercise to work out the kinks.

Eunice hunched over the coffee table, loaded a small plate full of her freshly baked cookies, and pressed it into his hands. "You're looking tired, honey." She peered up into his face. "You have dark circles under your eyes."

Jake grunted. "This last month has been a killer. I've had to pull a bunch of overseas flights this month."

"Can they do that to you?"

"Sure. When they don't have enough healthy pilots they can. Somebody has to fly the plane."

"That doesn't seem fair. When do you get some vacation time?"

"I'm on a two-week layover starting yesterday." Lolling his head on the back of the sofa toward his grandmother, Jake tucked his chin and smiled down at her. "I have nothing more pressing on my schedule than beating your yard back into shape. That, and laying around the pool at my apartment and catching some zees."

A maternal sound of approval issued from somewhere deep in

her throat. "Good boy. I hope you've made time for a little fun, too. Maybe you could go out on a date."

"Now don't go fixing me up with some daughter of some friend of a friend. I hate that."

Eunice pulled an expression of studied innocence. "Would I do that to you?"

Jake rolled his eyes as he sampled an oatmeal cookie. Every time he had more than a day or two away from the airlines, Eunice was always fixing him up with somebody or other. He wouldn't have minded quite so much if she didn't have such lousy taste in women. Self-absorbed, ladder-climbing, corporate mogul power rangers, every last one of 'em. Didn't anyone know how to bake a pie anymore? Call him old-fashioned, but he wanted to wear the pants in his future marriage.

"Yes, you would do that to me. Gran, don't waste your time this layover, huh? I'm exhausted. I just wanna veg."

Eunice shook her head. "I don't understand you. I'd think a smart, handsome, professional airline pilot such as yourself would be happily married and giving me several great-grandbabies to spoil by now."

Jake threw back his head and laughed. "Give me a break, will ya? I'm not *that* old."

Eunice pursed her lips. "Well, being that you're pushing thirty, you're not getting any younger, either. You really need to start thinking about settling down. Jake, my darling, I've been praying for you every day on this matter."

"Oh, boy."

She ignored his pained look. "Surely the good Lord will send the perfect girl into your life sooner or later."

"Well, good. Now that you've asked God to take over, *you* can stop playing matchmaker and relax, huh?" Lifting his glass to his lips, Jake took a long pull on his tea and, regarding the woman who'd raised his father, attempted to change the subject. "So, Gran, what have you been up to while I've been gone?" At nearly eighty years old, she was still such a bundle of energy. He got tired just hearing about one of her typical days.

Eunice brightened. "I thought you'd never ask. You know, my eightieth birthday is just around the corner."

"Uh-oh. What now?" Jake reached for another cookie.

"Well, just this morning before you got here to fiddle around in my yard, Opal and I purchased a motor home."

Jake stopped chewing midcookie and stared. "Come again?"

"'Thirty-one feet of pure vacation magic,'" she quoted and, reaching for the advertisement she'd found in that morning's paper, jabbed a gnarled finger at the classified section. Though Jake was seated on the sofa not two feet away, Eunice's throbbing falsetto pulsed with a giddy note that no doubt had the neighborhood canine faction burying their heads in agony.

"'*Looking for adventure?'*" Eunice winked at Jake. "That's me and Opal, all right. Always looking for adventure." Eagerly, she continued to read. "'*Look no further. 1972 Camptime motor home, mint cond. fr sale. $4,500 firm.'*" Her brow knit in consternation. "Firm what?" she muttered, then shrugged. "'*Perfect for fun-loving retired couple on the go.'*" Eunice patted Jake's arm. "That's Opal and me."

Jake gawked at her in disbelief.

"Says here, *low mi*. Whatever that means." Eunice harrumphed. "Can't figure some of this code. Wish they'd just say what they mean in these goofy ads."

"Low mileage," Jake supplied, his jaw still hanging.

"Well, now, that's wonderful." Eunice continued to read. "'*Drvs like drm.'*"

"Drvs like drm?" Drives like...what? A dormitory, no doubt.

Jake was still too stunned to comment.

"Whatever, whatever. Surely we can figure out what they are talking about if we put our heads together. Listen to this! '*31 ft of pure vacation magic. A/C.*' Hmm. A...C... Must mean abundant cupboards or something."

"Air conditioning—"

"'*Clst spc. Fl bth, chm tlt, loaded kitn includes mcrowv, dbl ovn and more. Needs TLC. Call now before this beauty is snapped up. Owner desperate to sell due to death in family.*'" Eunice beamed at Jake. "Doesn't it sound marvelous?"

"I'm assuming you're not referring to the death in the family." Jake pressed his palms to his eyes and rubbed.

"Jake, darling, I can see by the look on your face that you have doubts. But honey, don't worry. Opal and I prayed about it before we called, and miracle of miracles, it was still available! A nice man in Seattle says I can wire him some money first thing in the morning, right before Opal and I leave to pick it up. I can hardly wait!" She twittered with excitement.

"You're planning on picking this thing up yourselves?" Jake was thunderstruck. What would Eunice think of next?

"Sure! Right now, it's in storage in Montana—"

"*Montana?*"

"Yes, on a ranch there. We figure it's about an eight- to ten-hour drive from here. Opal and I are leaving first thing in the morning to go pick it up."

"Just the two of you?"

"Of course."

"Are you *crazy?*" Jake sprang to his feet, stepped over the coffee table, and plowing his hands through his hair, began to pace. "Gran, you've had some wacky ideas in your life, but this takes the cake. There is no way that you and Opal are going to drive from here to Montana and pick up a motor home—that you have bought, sight unseen, I might add—by yourselves!"

Eunice dismissed his concerns with a wave of her hand. "Jake, my dear, you are always such a killjoy."

"Yeah—" he stopped and, spinning around, squinted at her— "I'm a real party pooper all right, wanting to keep you and your buddy, Opal, around for a few more years. Try to remember that you are nearly eighty and not eighteen for once, will you?"

For the better part of an hour, Jake ranted and raved about the problems he foresaw with their ill-planned scheme. He pointed out the dangers for two elderly women, out in the middle of nowhere. He brought up the fact that Eunice knew nothing about driving a rig that size, let alone maintaining it. He wore tracks in her carpeting as he paced, but for all of his warnings and common sense, he could see that he was making absolutely no headway with his hardheaded grandmother.

When he'd finally run out of steam, Eunice bestowed him with a tolerant smile. "Jake, darling. I gave the man my word. So as much as I thank you for your concern, please, dear, butt out of my business."

Head still spinning, Jake tried to reconcile—as he lathered up a sweat mowing Eunice's lawn a short while later—how on earth he'd allowed yet another blissful, uncomplicated respite from work to be taken over by his grandmother's wacky plans. Luckily, the roar of the mower obscured his disgruntled mutterings. Somehow he'd agreed to charter a plane first thing in the morning—on his day off, for crying in the night—to fly Eunice and Opal to Montana. He could only hope that they would take one look at the old pig, demand their money back, and hop back on the plane and come home with him. A 1972 Camptime motor home, for pity's sake. He'd never heard of a Camptime motor home. Good grief, the stupid thing was nearly as old as he was.

Lexie Dinsmore—her face puckered into a wad of consternation—studied the classified ad that her grandmother, Opal, had asked her to read. As was her habit on Sunday afternoons, Lexie had stopped by Opal's cheerful, cluttered kitchen for a quick cup of coffee. Seated together at the dinette set in the bay window, Lexie glanced up from the newspaper, shot Opal a bright smile that she hoped belied her anxiety, then focused once again on the ad. She cleared her throat.

"Let me get this straight, Nanna. You say that you and Eunice *bought* this motor home? Earlier today?"

"Yes, honey. Well, Eunice actually did the buying with our joint vacation account, but she made me see the beauty of it."

"That figures." Though Lexie liked her grandmother's best friend, she knew Eunice Kelley could be a loose cannon at times.

Clasping her arthritic hands around her coffee cup, Opal fairly wriggled with anticipation. "Now that we've gone ahead and bought the motor home, I can hardly wait to see it!"

Slack jawed, Lexie stared at her grandmother. "You haven't *seen* it yet?"

"Why, no. It's in storage in Montana right now. We are leaving to go pick it up tomorrow."

"*What?*" Springing to her feet, Lexie strode to the window and, clutching the wooden sash, tried to hide her agitation from her grandmother. Opal tended to be easily discouraged, and Lexie didn't want to dampen her enthusiasm for life, but really! A thirty-one-foot motor home? Were they *crazy?*

As Lexie clutched her grandmother's kitchen window, she took some deep, cleansing breaths.

This beautiful Sunday afternoon was her favorite kind of day in Tacoma. Unusually warm and clear for early May, sunlight streamed through the giant fir trees in the front yard Nanna shared with Eunice, and sent dappled shadows sprawling across the old porch. Colorful flowers blooming in brick planters that flanked the steps heralded the advancing season. Off in the distance, the voices of children frolicking in the street mingled with the occasional bark of a dog. A lawn mower's rumbling hum underscored these sounds of spring.

As the rumble grew louder, Lexie could see Eunice's hunky grandson just outside, mowing the lawn.

What was his name again? Jack or Joe or something like that. He was a pilot. That much she knew. That, and the fact that he looked enough like Kevin Costner to be his younger brother.

Anyway, she didn't like him. Not that she could put her finger on the reason. Perhaps it was because he was kind of arrogant. Oh, he was friendly enough. But he always wore such a pained expression whenever Eunice would drag him over to Opal's apartment to make light conversation on the odd occasion that she and he were at the duplex at the same time. Luckily his flight schedule prevented him from being there on most Sunday afternoons.

Lexie's sigh fogged the windowpane and, for a moment, she watched Jim or John or what's-his-name's lanky stride crisscross back and forth over the yard. Muscles bulging, he dragged the noisy old mower around various trees and bushes, making tidy rows of grass clippings. If he weren't such an egomaniac, she'd be tempted to offer her services and help him rake. But the look on his face was formidable, as usual. Besides, she had much bigger problems on her mind than Eunice's stuck-up grandson's chores.

Absently she wondered if he knew what his dotty grandmother was up to. Not that he was the type to care about more than his rugged reflection.

Pushing herself off the sash, Lexie turned to face Opal. "Nanna, I can't let you and Eunice drive all the way to Montana to pick up a thirty-plus-year-old motor home by yourselves. It would be, well, Nanna, plainly speaking, it would be suicide. Why, it's eight hours to Montana! Or more! Can you change a tire?"

"Well, I…"

"What about engine problems? Have you ever driven anything that big before?"

"No, but Eunice's grandso—"

"What about your night blindness? What about operating this thing? The appliances in a motor home run on propane! There are switches and knobs and dials involved here. Nanna, I mean no disrespect, but you can't even set the clock on your VCR!" The lost-little-child look on her grandmother's face tore at Lexie's heart, but *honestly*. Someone had to be the voice of reason. "How on earth are you going to get this…this…*thing* home?"

"Well, we are goin—"

"You don't even have a cell phone, Nanna! What about the weirdos out there?"

"Yes, you see—"

As if on cue, Lexie's own cell phone rang from the depths of her voluminous purse and she held a finger up to Opal. "Hold that thought." Taking a deep breath, she dug out her phone, flipped it open, and became all business. "This is Lexie Dinsmore, how may I help you? Oh, hi Maude. Number 568? Yes, that's the Cascade highway property number in this morning's paper. Right. No, I'm here at my grandmother's house, so I don't have my files handy." Lexie glanced at her watch. "I could probably show it to them in about an hour...."

As Lexie spoke, her eyes fell to the ad for the motor home, and then darted to Opal's rather crestfallen expression. Rats. She'd gone and burst her grandmother's bubble. Now she felt like a first-class heel.

Inhaling deeply, Lexie filled her lungs and made a quick decision. She'd probably blow a bajillion dollars in commission, but who cared? Nothing was more important than Opal's safety. And why be a realtor with flexible hours if one couldn't be flexible now and again?

"Listen, Maude—" Lexie turned her attention back to her assistant—"call them back and tell them I can't show that property today. In fact, I'm going to have to be out of the office for the next few days on a family emergency. I'll call you later tonight and explain everything and go over my appointments with you and stuff. I don't know exactly. I'll probably be back before the end of the week. Sure. And we can always keep in touch by phone. I'll have my laptop and files with me, so I shouldn't miss a beat. Good. Okay. I'll call you later. Bye."

Lexie snapped her phone shut and smiled at Opal. "I'm heading home to pack. What time are we leaving in the morning?"

"You're coming too? Oh my soul, how wonderful!" Opal fairly vibrated with joy. "Well then, I guess you should be here at 6 A.M."

"Six it is, then."

"Good, because that's when Eunice's grandson, Jake—"

Jake! That was the doof's name. Again, Lexie's phone jangled. "Oops, that's for me." Tucking her phone between her shoulder and ear, she blew her grandmother some kisses and whispered as she backed out of the kitchen and headed for the door, "Bye, Nanna. I'll see you at six." Then, donning her business persona, she spoke into the phone, and headed out of the duplex. "Lexie Dinsmore. How may I help you?"

She had to cover her ear in order to hear above the roar of the lawn mower. "Maude? Can you say that again? I'm having trouble hearing—" Lips pursed, she watched Eunice's grandson as he dragged the stinky, smoke-belching mower over to where she stood and deliberately roared back and forth past the porch.

"Hang on a second, Maude," she shouted, then scowled and waved him away with her arm, encouraging him to buzz off.

He gleefully ignored her.

"MAUDE! I'LL HAVE TO CALL YOU BACK!" With that, she tossed her phone into her purse, strode to her car, hopped in, gunned the engine and—to give vent to the smoke that she was sure poured from her ears—burned a little rubber as she pulled onto the street.

Yes, indeedy. One good thing about this vacation with Opal; she could enjoy her grandmother's company without fear of running into Jake…or Jerk…or *whatever* he answered to.

That was something, anyway. For reasons that she'd never be able to fathom as she drove home that afternoon, Lexie knew that though skipping work and traipsing off to Montana in search of a motor home with two little old ladies was one of the nuttiest things she'd ever done, it was also the right thing.

Opal's thousand-watt smile had only cemented the feeling.

Two

At promptly 5:45 the following morning, Lexie pulled up to the curb in front of Opal's place. Struggling out of her car, she hoisted her duffel bag, her laptop computer, her briefcase, and her purse into her arms and slammed the car door with the heel of her shoe.

She yawned, her mouth stretching wide, her eyes squeezing shut, her back arching beneath her load. It was far too early for her blood. Hopefully, Opal had a nice, strong pot of coffee on. She was desperate for some caffeine—and maybe a couple of toothpicks to prop her eyes open.

As Lexie sleepwalked to Opal's front door, she roused herself enough to notice Eunice's studly grandson moving through the shadows over in the driveway. What was *he* doing here at this hour of the morning? And why were he and Eunice stowing those suitcases into the back of his SUV?

Still staring, Lexie stumbled up the steps to the top of the porch where Opal—saint that she was—waited with a fresh cup of coffee. After kissing Opal's time-weathered cheek, Lexie shucked her luggage onto the porch floor and, with a grateful sigh, took the proffered steaming cup of java. Lips puckered, she blew into her cup and frowned her dismay over the rim.

"Eunice's grandson is coming with us?" She kept her voice low so as not to be overheard.

"Yes, dear. Isn't that nice?"

"Nice? Oh, puhleeze, Nanna. What do we need *him* for? I'm perfectly capable of getting us to and from Montana." Over her shoulder, Lexie peered between the porch posts into the morning twilight. She watched what's-his-name's bulging muscles in grudging fascination as he loaded Eunice's baggage into his rig. Feeling peevish, she mumbled into her mug, "He probably thinks I'm not capable. Chauvinist."

"Actually, dear, I don't think Jake even knew you were coming with us. I didn't have a chance to tell him after you left. But I don't think he'll mind."

"You mean you knew he was coming yesterday?"

"Well, yes. I tried to tell you, but your phone kept ringing—"

Opal smiled as, once again, Lexie's purse began to ring from the depths of the pile at her feet.

Disgruntled, Lexie bent over and searched out her phone. Had she known Eunice's self-important, patronizing boob of a grandson was coming along, she'd have stayed home. But it was too late to back out now. She'd promised Opal she was going and had already spent half the night filling her coworkers and clients in on her plans. Her grandmother was really looking forward to their time together. And, to be honest, so was she.

Too bad old snootie-patootie would be there to throw a monkey wrench into the works.

Once she'd discovered her phone, Lexie tucked it between her shoulder and cheek. She tossed her hair over her shoulder and donned her professional facade.

"Lexie Dinsmore here. How may I help you?"

As she made mental notes of Maude's litany of last-minute questions, beefcake Jake bounded up the porch steps to assist Opal with her things.

Lexie's shoulders drooped. Somehow his mere pearly-toothed,

too-handsome-for-his-own-good presence sucked out any joy she may have felt over this adventure with her grandmother.

A sudden tension headache assaulted a spot between Jake's eyes as he stuffed the ton of luggage the three women had packed into the back of his jeep. Pots, pans, baking gear, bedding, computer, briefcase…everything but the kitchen sink. This stuff would never fit into the plane's tiny hold. And now Gran had even made sure that he had a date for this trip.

It figured.

He began to unload some of the boxes. Some of these things could be purchased in Montana.

He cast a wary glance at Lexie as she yammered to some business associate on her cell phone. Another power-hungry executive…just like the other women Eunice had foisted upon him in the past.

Not his type.

Something about her, he couldn't pinpoint it exactly…she just turned him off. Perhaps it was the polished, professional persona. Or maybe it was the platinum blond hair in the trendy style and the subtle scent of expensive perfume. For crying in the night. Here it was, not yet six in the morning, and she looked gussied up enough in those designer duds of hers to have just stepped off the cover of *Cosmo*.

And, he…well, he was unshaven and had jammed a baseball cap backward on his head to keep from having to comb his hair. The fact that he'd showered and brushed his teeth was more than he usually did on a day off.

No doubt about it: he and Ms. All Business were from different planets.

"What's the deal, Gran?" Jake jerked a thumb in Lexie's direction. "You didn't invite her along for one of your harebrained matchmaking schemes, did you?"

Eunice—who had for the last fifteen minutes been hovering about under his feet, directing his every move and clucking at him to be careful—paused and looked up at him. "No, dear. Seems she thinks Opal and I are as incompetent as you do. She decided to come after you demanded we take you along."

Jake glanced back at Lexie. "Is that right?"

He didn't buy it. Her presence smacked of Gran's meddling. Yep. Gran had tried to get him to notice Opal's upwardly mobile granddaughter before. He'd simply nipped her efforts in the bud. No use starting something he had no intention of finishing. Especially with a friend of the family.

From where she stood on the porch, Lexie flashed her teeth at him—and he couldn't be sure if she was smiling or trying to communicate her disdain. Certainly, there was something phony about her too-bright smile. Ah, well. Who cared? Like the rest of Gran's blind dates, she was no concern of his.

"Let's go," he barked, herding Eunice and Opal into their seats and giving Lexie the high sign to get it in gear. "Let's get this show on the road."

After an interminable flight in a twin engine Cessna that had Lexie's hair standing on end, they landed at a small airport in the middle of nowhere, Montana. Still green around the gills from something Jake referred to as minor turbulence, Lexie clutched Opal's arm, and they both wobbled after him and Eunice to the car rental area. Though sorely tempted, Lexie resisted the urge to fall to the ground, kiss the earth, and thank God for sparing her life. The bouncing approach to the landing strip had sorely jangled her nerves. She could tell that Opal had fared no better.

Jake, on the other hand, had been grinning like a fool, clearly loving every spine-tingling minute of their flight from Tacoma. As had Eunice. He'd probably hit every air pocket in the sky on purpose, the show-off. Never would she be able to understand how anyone could fly for enjoyment, let alone for a career. The fact that the rakish Jake lived most of his life thousands of feet above the ground only increased her suspicion of him.

However, much as she hated to admit it, she had admired the way he'd handled the plane. He was the consummate professional in the air. Calm, unflappable, confident.

Even so, she'd been at his mercy quite enough that morning. If he drove anything like he flew, she preferred to be in the driver's seat. Her stomach was in no shape for another wild ride. After they'd made arrangements to hold the chartered plane at the rural airport for at least a week—if need be—and rented the only remaining van the rental company offered, a hideous hot pink number, Lexie held her hand out to Jake for the keys.

"I'll drive."

He closed his fist around the keys and shoved them into the pocket of his snug jeans. Rocking back on his heels, he tucked his thumbs in his belt loops and smiled down at her in a condescending manner that had Lexie's blood suddenly perking in irritation. "No, that's okay. I'll drive."

Arms folded across her chest, Lexie's stare was icy, her words clipped. "But you drove on the way over."

"I flew. Big difference."

"Yeah, right. Come on. Give me the keys. I want to drive."

"Tell you what. I'll drive now, you fly us home."

A telltale flush crawled from her neck to her cheeks. Lexie

resisted the childish urge to slug him in his steel-belted-radial guts. This man was positively infuriating.

"Fine." Lips tight, she grabbed Opal's arm and stalked toward the van, muttering under her breath all the while. The gray thunderclouds that gathered against the horizon were the perfect complement to her foul mood.

Once they'd loaded the metallic, shocking pink minivan with the supplies they'd brought, they set off on what Lexie felt sure was a wild lemon chase. Eunice and Opal opted to sit in the back so that they could chat, which forced Lexie into the front with Jake. He tossed the map into her lap and, with that roguish grin that she was really beginning to hate, suggested she navigate.

Despite the evident tension in the air, Lexie did her best to keep up the facade of happiness with this debacle simply because her grandmother was so very excited. With any luck, Jake would have the consideration to play along.

As they pulled out of the airport's parking lot and followed the exit signs to the main road, Jake shot an expectant look at Lexie. "Which way?" His too polite tone set her teeth to grinding.

Lexie fumbled with the map, her gaze searching for the directions that Eunice had scribbled in the margin. "Uh…let's see…the airport is…over…no, that can't be right. According to this, we should be…I…hmm…Rural Route One intersects with…"

Jake exhaled noisily and rotated his head. His impatience was palpable. He made a show of adjusting the rearview mirror.

"I'm waiting." Though his voice was a study in patience, he drummed his fingers on the steering wheel.

"Give me a second, will you?"

Jake sighed and stared out the window.

"This is such a beautiful van, is it not?" Opal warbled from the backseat, waxing enthusiastic about the mind-blowing pink upholstery and paint job. "Weren't we lucky to get the only van they had left?"

Under his breath, Jake muttered unintelligible comments about girlie mobiles and Barbie cars.

"Perhaps we might consider this color for the motor home," Eunice agreed.

"Now there's an idea! We could make some curtains to match."

Jake grunted.

"That sounds nice, Nanna," Lexie mused, running her fingertips over the coordinates on the map. After a confused moment, she turned the map upside down and started over.

Jake allowed his head to thud back against the headrest and motioned for the cars that waited behind them to go around. "Have you figured out where we are going yet?"

"I'm working on it."

Rolling his head to the side, Jake shot a pointed look at the map. "Any day now."

Lexie tightened her grip—wishing she were doing so on his neck rather than on the map. "Turn left. Just…go east."

"Are you sure?"

"No."

"Then why are we going east?"

Lexie glared at him. "Because you seem to need any old direction more than you need the correct one, and east is as good as any."

His lips twitched, and Lexie could see a glimmer of humor light his eyes. "East it is, then." With that, they pulled out onto the highway and began speeding down the road.

Lexie narrowed her eyes at the speedometer. He certainly wasn't leaving her much margin for error at this speed. Clearly oblivious to the tension in the front seat, Eunice and Opal's chatter was animated and nonstop.

Jake pulled in behind a semitruck and set the cruise control. "Are you sure we're headed in the right direction?"

Lexie shrugged, still scrutinizing the map. "I think so. According to Eunice's notes, we follow this road east until it intersects with Rural Route One. Then we head north for about fifty miles until we come to a small town. From there, it's about an hour drive on some back roads to another small town. The motor home is at a place about a half hour beyond the town called the 'Flying Horse Ranch.'"

"Sounds simple enough."

Her voice dripped with sarcasm. "Yeah. Right."

"Are you always this cheerful in the morning?"

"Are you always this patient?"

"Touché."

Lexie bit her lip to keep from smiling. She wouldn't give his inflated ego the satisfaction.

"So." He draped a wrist over the top of the steering wheel and spoke in a confidential tone. "What do you think of this whole motor home thing?"

"I think this is crazy."

"Yep. I know how you feel."

"How do you know what I feel?" Her laughter was brittle. "You have never given me the time of day, so I can't imagine you know much about how I feel."

An insensitive cad such as himself couldn't begin to know how she worried over Opal. The odd Sunday that Eunice prodded him to offer a civil hello, he'd acted so put out that Lexie had been tempted to apologize for her existence. And now he pretended to know how she felt? Bah.

"Admit it. You don't know anything about me." She watched the unfamiliar Montana landscape blur by out the window. A heavy raindrop splattered against the windshield, and then another, the perfect symbols for the day. Her phone rang, and she was grateful for the distraction.

"Lexie Dinsmore here. How may I help you?"

"Oh, yeah." Jake muttered under his breath as he checked traffic and changed lanes. "I know you all right."

Lexie ended their conversation by nodding and turning her back on him.

The same way he'd ended the few conversations they'd had in the past.

For the next hour, while Lexie hammered out details on a property deal on the phone with someone called Maude, Jake continued to head east. In the backseat, Eunice and Opal dozed, their heads bobbing and swaying to the road's rough terrain. As the gas gauge began to dip and his stomach to rumble, Jake felt his patience wearing thin.

"Hey." He nudged Lexie's elbow, upsetting her impromptu desk. "It's been an hour. Are we still headed in the right direction?"

A beleaguered expression on her face, Lexie slapped her hand over the mouthpiece of her cell phone and stared at him. "How should *I* know? I've never been here before." Lips back to the phone, she went on with her business call.

"I thought you said something about hitting Rural Route One about fifty miles down this road."

Lexie instructed Maude to hang on a second. "That's not what I said. I said we go to Rural Route One, and then go fifty miles north. Have we passed the intersection for Rural Route One, yet?"

"How should *I* know?" he mimicked.

"Have you been paying attention?"

"That's *your* job. You're the navigator."

"Oh, for the love of…" To Maude, she issued a clipped good-bye and, tossing her phone on the hot pink dash, wrestled the map out from under her pile of folders and paperwork. "What's the next exit number? That should give us some clue."

Jake shrugged. "One sixty-five."

"One sixty-five!"

"Why? What's wrong with that?"

"Nothing, if you want to go to North Dakota."

"What?" Jake grabbed the bill of his cap and twisted it back and forth on his head. "How could you let this happen?"

"I didn't let anything happen. You're driving."

"Well, if you would put the phone down long enough to pay attention to the map this would never have happened."

"You want to read the map? *Here!*" In a childish fit, Lexie smashed the map into a wad and flung it at him.

"Oh, that's mature."

In the backseat, Eunice and Opal stirred.

"What's the matter?" Eunice rubbed the sleep from her eyes and hauled herself forward, peering into the war zone that was the front seat.

Jaw jutting, Lexie stared out the window. "We're lost."

"Oh dear. Jake, honey, pull over."

"What for?"

A sound of disgust rumbled from deep within Lexie's throat. "How typical of a man not to want to pull over and ask directions."

Jake stared at her, then gestured to the desolate landscape that yawned beyond the hood of their minivan. "There is *nobody* to *ask!*"

Eunice tsked. "Aren't you forgetting the Lord?" Thrusting her age-spotted and shaking hands into the front seat, she gripped Jake and Lexie's shoulders and began to pray for the path to be made clear.

Opal, as was her habit, murmured in agreement.

Four and a half short hours later, Eunice's prayer was finally answered, and Jake almost wished it hadn't been. If they were still lost, they wouldn't have had to face the dismal sight set before them at the Flying Horse Ranch.

"This is not good." Lexie gripped the dash to keep from hitting her head on the ceiling as they jounced down the deeply rutted driveway.

In the backseat, Opal and Eunice were flopping about, clutching each other, giddy with anticipation.

Jake shifted down and slowed to a crawl. This whole fiasco just got worse by the minute. Where were the flying horses on this...ranch? If the broken-down, crow-bait nag that stared at them from the edge of the road through its one good eye was any indication of the horse flesh on this so-called ranch, they were in trouble.

"Still wanna drive?" he muttered, navigating around a pothole that looked as if it could have swallowed the hideous minivan without a trace. He knew his sarcasm was unmistakable and his attitude despicable, but he couldn't help himself.

"No, thanks. I'd rather fly us home. Now."

The grim look on her face had him smiling in spite of everything.

Slowly he pulled to a stop in the only area not covered with something rusted or rotten and surveyed the house and grounds that had to have been used as a movie set for *Deliverance.*

"There it is!" Eunice spotted the motor home parked out behind the falling-down barn, and pecked at the glass of her window.

Then her bewildered gaze, along with everyone else's in the van, traveled the landscape. All mouths hung slack with wonder.

Chickens and pigs wandered loose about the homestead as the existing barbed-wire fence lay in curly ribbons on the ground between rotted posts. Abandoned cars and washing machines littered almost every available square foot of the property. The shanty, clinging precariously to a muddy river's bank, was filled with grimy, curious children, who peered at them through broken windowpanes.

"Oh my." Opal tsked and offered a tentative wave at the children. "Poor things. No wonder they needed the money so badly. Eunice—" she tugged on her friend's arm—"I'm so glad we bought this motor home. I can see the hand of the Lord in this transaction."

"Amen," Eunice murmured.

Jake shifted into reverse and gunned the engine. "It's not too late, ladies. We can be back in Tacoma by nightfall."

Lexie scowled at him. "We've made it this far. Let's at least look at the—" her eyes drifted to the decrepit motor home—"the, uh, thing there."

A heavy stench—something animal, something rotten, something burned—seeped into the van through the air filtration system.

Jake lifted and dropped a shoulder. She had a point. Might as well take a peek and make two elderly ladies happy. Perhaps the grim reality would dissuade them. A little barnyard odor never killed anybody. He opened his door and swung his legs into a mud puddle that threatened to suck his boot right off his foot. At least he hoped it was mud. The smell was unbelievable.

Before he had a chance to warn them, Opal and Eunice struggled out of the backseat, eager to begin the transaction. The ooze that enveloped their pumps and stockings seemed not to daunt them from their mission. Fingertips fluttering and hands outstretched, each gripped one of Jake's arms, and the three of them picked their way to higher ground. Her face puckered with revulsion, Lexie disembarked from the passenger side and hippity-hopped after them.

A mean looking critter that Jake guessed to be somewhere between thirty and eighty in age, staggered out of the shack followed by a half dozen raggedy kids.

Jake swallowed and took a step in front of the women to shield them. From what, exactly, he wasn't sure.

"Hello there." He nodded at the belching, scratching, partially toothed man whose filthy overalls, unshaven jowls, and tangled hair made a defiant fashion statement. Perhaps the stench wasn't coming from the barnyard after all.

"You must be Mr. Percival Jenkins," Eunice said, peeping around Jake's arm. "I declare, it's a pleasure to meet up with you and your kin." Noticing Jake's puzzled frown, she whispered up at him. "Let's try to speak his language, dear."

"Yeah?" Percival's furry brows seesawed. "What do you want?"

The ever-plucky Eunice stepped forward and extended her hand. "We are here to pick up the motor home?"

"Oh?" Suspicion drew Percival's rubbery brow into a straight line, and he made no move except to stare at them.

Eunice pulled the ad out of her purse and read aloud, "The 1972 Camptime motor home? Drvs like drm? Needs TLC?"

From where he stood, Jake could see a chicken come flapping out of the Camptime's interior. "Needs TNT if you ask me," he muttered under his breath.

Percival spat a long stream of tobacco juice. "Yeah?"

"I believe your brother...a Mr. Jethrow Jenkins of Seattle handled the transaction for you?"

A pithy stream of expletives exploded from between Percival's tar-stained lips.

Obviously disgusted, Lexie asserted herself, stepping up to the plate, best business foot forward. "I assume you were not appraised of this transaction?"

Percival simply stared.

Lexie forged ahead. "The ad states that you were eager to sell due to a death in the family?"

Jake grimaced. "My guess is the only death in the family was the motor home," he groused, then he took a step toward Percival that was meant to intimidate. Nobody was going to con his grandmother. Not while he was on duty. "Listen, bub, we have a bill of sale here." He reached for Eunice's purse and after some impatient rummaging, produced the receipt and the key ring. "So we're just going to pick up our merchandise and leave."

For several tense moments that had everyone's hearts doing the foxtrot, Percival continued to stare. His brows were furrowed, his eyes narrowed, and his lips a hard slash above his boxy jaw. From some dark place deep within, a feral growl emanated. Jake couldn't help but wonder if ax murderer was among the skills listed on Percival's résumé.

After a moment, Percival spat another blackish stream, then, seeming to come to terms with reality, commanded the kids to clear their stuff out of their bedroom. "The city man has come to take the motor home away."

Eunice and Opal wore horrified expressions that they were taking the veritable roof from over the children's heads.

Lexie's phone chose that moment to ring, so—with a comforting pat to Opal's arm—she moved off to settle herself at the nearest washing machine to conduct business.

Jake had no such sympathy for Percival and his kids. Good old Percival was getting far more money than the disgusting heap was worth, of that he was sure. Not wanting to spend another moment in this godforsaken neck of the woods, he assisted Eunice and Opal across the mosquito-infested paddock, around the falling-down barn, to the motor home for the initial inspection.

After several false starts and some backfiring that had everyone ducking for cover, Jake finally got the old engine started. Meanwhile, the kids unloaded their soiled bed linens and meager personal possessions and dragged them into the shack.

Eunice and Opal watched these proceedings with tears in their eyes.

Jake could only shake his head. For the love of Mike! For the forty-five hundred dollars the Jenkins family was getting for this garbage scow, Percival could no doubt rustle up several more broken-down motor homes, give each of the kids their own room. Eunice and Opal should feel good about that.

Once Jake was satisfied the engine would carry them at least to the end of the driveway, he hopped outside. Backing up so that he could take in the whole picture, he stared agog at his grandmother's latest purchase.

Lexie came up to stand beside him, a similar expression gracing her face.

They exchanged glances that said without words, *"This thing is HUGE! It's ugly. It's…"*

"Where in thunder are they going to park it?" Jake thrust his fingers under the bill of his cap and rubbed.

Lexie shook her head. "I vote the city dump."

"At least we agree on that much."

"Careful there." Lexie grinned at him for the first time since he'd laid eyes on her. She was pretty when she smiled. "You're starting to agree with me."

He gave his head a dubious shake, but he couldn't hold back an answering grin.

Finally, after profuse apologies to Percival on the part of Eunice and Opal for robbing the children of their home, Jake and the three ladies were on their way.

"Wanna drive?" Jake held the motor home keys out to Lexie.

"Oh, no thanks." Her sardonic tone was intentional. "No, no, no. You made it clear that you are the driver in this group. I'll follow you in the stunning hot pink number. You know, the one with the comfortable seats and the heater that works." She batted her eyes and tossed him a saucy grin.

"Very funny." His words were clipped, but the humor that flashed in his eyes belied his foul mood.

He really wasn't that bad, when he smiled. Unfortunately, those instances were rare. "What now?"

"Uh, well, how about if we meet in Tuttlesville in—" he shot a glance at his wrist—"say, twenty minutes. If we're lucky."

Jake and Lexie agreed to backtrack to the nearest town and so, after waving good-bye to Percival's motley crew, they bobbed and bounced down the driveway, a fetching caravan made up of one disintegrating motor home and one flamboyant family car.

Without too much effort, and much to everyone's surprise, they arrived at Tuttlesville, alive and unhurt. There they unloaded the minivan into the motor home, turned the minivan in at the only car rental depot in town, gassed the motor home, then grabbed something hot for dinner and a few groceries for the trip home.

Most unfortunately, before they could get out of town, Eunice and Opal spotted a sporting goods store.

Within mere minutes they had the motor home outfitted with enough fishing and camping type gear to satisfy the needs of a small army platoon. Since only a fraction of these new purchases would fit inside the motor home, Jake had to lash a good deal of it to the roof with bungee cords.

Once he was satisfied that it would all stay in place, they were on their way once again.

Just as the ad promised, the motor home drove like a dream.

A bad dream.

A bad dream complete with nerve-jangling backfirings and noxious fumes filled with carbon monoxide. And it continued to perform in such a manner until they'd headed out on a back road on the shortcut that Eunice promised would shave hundreds of miles off their journey.

That was when the bad dream became a bona fide nightmare.

Three

A good twenty minutes outside Tuttlesville, Lexie was the first to smell smoke.

"Just somebody's campfire." Jake was too busy wrestling the giant steering wheel around yet another tight curve to take her fretting seriously.

"No…no, it's more than that."

"Maybe it's chicken manure."

"No. *Smoke.* I smell smoke."

"Maybe it's smoked manure."

"Very funny."

"And highly possible."

Lexie's chuckle was nervous. Not wanting to alarm the grandmothers who were seated at the dining table on the greasy, orange plaid cushions, making plans for redecoration, she untied the rope they'd rigged for her safety belt and moved through the motor home, sniffing.

She smelled mold in the cupboards. She smelled mildew in the sink. She smelled wet dog in the corner. The stove was cool, but smelled of rotten grease. Everything else smelled of stale cigarette smoke. But above and beyond that Lexie was sure—as she sniffed her way to the bathroom—she smelled smoke. Fresh smoke. The kind that signified fire.

The source of the smoke wasn't immediately apparent when

she opened the bathroom door. But when she lifted the toilet lid and flames shot out, the mystery was solved.

Lexie shrieked and stumbled out of the bathroom. Arms waving, she wobbled down the narrow corridor, screaming as she went. "Fire! *Fire!* The toilet is on *fire!*"

Not needing to be told twice, Jake jerked the wheel, and bumping the giant motor home over to the shoulder, they all abandoned ship.

Jake was exhausted and cranky as a bear after having single-handedly battled the flames that threatened to reduce the motor home into a pile of smoldering charcoal briquettes. Not, of course, that it would have made much difference in the looks of the old heap, but it would have made it somewhat more difficult to get back to a town. According to his best guess—being that the odometer didn't work—they were probably at least ten to twenty miles from anything that remotely resembled civilization.

The sky was still leaden with rain clouds, and off in the distance a coyote howled. A heavy feeling of foreboding settled in his gut, and Jake had to wonder if this is how the Donnor party felt during their journey.

Near as he could figure—as he lay on the ground peering up at the underbelly of the old motor home—the rusty tailpipe had fallen off somewhere along the way and the exhaust fumes had gone right up the plumbing where they superheated the toilet, which eventually caught fire. Trouble was, the propane tanks were located right in front of the exhaust system. Without a new tailpipe, they were a rolling bomb waiting to go off. Vexed beyond belief, Jake wriggled out from under the motor home, then climbed back up inside to search for something that could help him jury-rig a tailpipe. They just needed to limp along far enough to get to a garage.

"Great." He spat the word as if it were a curse as he rummaged through the cupboards in a futile search for some kind of metal pipe. "This is just...*great."*

"Don't worry." Lexie's smile was smug. "I'll simply call AAA."

"Whatever." He didn't have time to praise Her Majesty for remembering to lug her office along. "I'll be under the bathroom, trying to rig an exhaust pipe while you—" he pointed to the map she held—"work your navigational magic on AAA."

Lexie stuck out her tongue.

As he hunted for a length of pipe and the toolbox he'd decided at the last minute to bring, Jake couldn't help but notice that the motor home had an odd smell, aside from that of charbroiled toilet. It was a dank smell. Damp. Musty. Like...dry rot, perhaps? Well, without further research, Jake couldn't be sure, but a smell like that was always bad news.

At long last, he found his toolbox and—after a little more hunting—an old, steel vacuum-cleaner hose, and headed back out to work on the tailpipe problem.

As far as Eunice and Opal were concerned, this was the perfect opportunity to have a picnic. They were in an excited, festive mood. The toilet fire was simply a little setback. A bit of excitement to tell the other seniors about down at the senior center upon their return. No big deal. After all, they'd gone into this prayerfully. All would be well. The Lord was with them. Giddy as schoolgirls, they sorted through the myriad boxes of newly purchased kitchen paraphernalia and began to prepare a feast.

From the back of the motor home, Lexie's scream rang out. "My phone! It's *gone!* And...my *purse!*" Sounds of her frantic rummaging through her luggage underscored her shrieks. *"What?* What on earth? Ohhh...I'll bet...Oh no! That *creep!* Percival and his…his…merry little band of artful dodgers *stole my purse!* And my *phone! And…and my computer!*"

Unable to help himself, Jake—a grin tugging at the corners of his mouth—dropped his tools, poked his head inside and tsked. "Oh, now that's too bad."

He was smug until Lexie discovered that the satchel that contained his wallet was missing as well.

Jake spun on his heel and stormed back outside, brandishing his vacuum-hose-cum-tailpipe as he went. Jaw muscles grim and twitching, he ranted about thieving lowlifes and gullible women and being stranded in the middle of nowhere with no money or identification. Jake was more determined than ever to fix this rolling landfill and get back to civilization—even if it meant he had to get behind the dumb thing and push. The sooner the better.

Eunice called out to him as he elbow-walked his way through the mud into position beneath the bathroom plumbing.

"Now, don't worry, Jake, dear. I'm sure we'll all be just fine. Opal and I still have our purses and our mad money is pinned to our brassieres. And we have plenty of food. We won't starve."

Jake could only grunt. It was either that or kill something.

After a knuckle-scraping, head-banging, half-hour-long exercise in frustration, he finally had a pretty credible semblance of a tailpipe back in place.

"Soup's on!" Eunice yodeled out the door. "We've got tuna on whole wheat and fruit salad. Come on, Jake. You can finish fiddling around under there after supper."

Jake snorted. Gran made it sound like it would be a treat that he could enjoy, but only if he was a good boy and cleaned his plate.

Once the eclectic group of both happy and unhappy campers assembled around the chipped and stained wood-look Formica tabletop, Eunice lead them in prayer over the food. And while she was at it, she laid her hands on the motor home wall at her back and asked the Lord for healing.

After their impromptu supper, amazingly enough, the motor home started right up and purred like a kitten. An asthmatic kitten to be sure, but Lexie wasn't going to complain. They were finally moving again and that's all that counted. Rather than turning back toward Tuttlesville, Eunice suggested they forge ahead. It would be much quicker this way, she assured them all. Jake apparently didn't have an opinion one way or another, since he agreed.

Eunice and Opal were in rare form, encouraging Lexie and Jake to sing camp songs as they rumbled down the winding road.

"And if the devil doesn't like it he can sit on a tack…sit on a tack! Sit on a tack!" Eunice warbled along with Opal. "Come on, kids. Sing with us. Stop looking so gloomy. The Lord is with us. You can relax."

Though Lexie knew the Lord was no doubt with them, the last thing she could do was relax. Not until her computer and files were back in her possession and her credit cards had been canceled. Seated next to Jake in the sticky, slightly damp passenger seat, Lexie stared through the cracks in the vast windshield and watched the shadows begin to lengthen. Soon it would be dark. Hopefully they could find civilization before too long. Her gaze darted over her shoulder to the caterwauling grandmas in the back. They were so cute. So happy. So…naive.

The sudden bouncing change in terrain under the wheels had her turning to look at Jake.

"What's wrong?"

"I'm pulling off to the side of the road."

"Why?"

Jake reached through the massive steering wheel and tapped at the temperature gage. "If this thing is even halfway accurate, she's running hot. You can tell by the steam that's beginning to rise from under the hood. This is as good a place as any to make camp."

"Make...*camp?*"

"Yeah. We gotta sit tight for the night. Give the engine a chance to cool off."

"But we've only driven a few hours! And we've been crawling at a snail's pace!"

"And we're lucky we've made it this far, if you ask me."

"*What?*" Agitated, Lexie twisted in her seat and wrung her hands. She peered past his stony expression and out the window. "You want to camp *here?* In *Weirdoland?* We're sitting ducks out here, for heaven's sake! We'll be murdered in our sleep for sure."

By this time, Opal and Eunice had stopped singing and were listening to the conversation up front.

Jake sighed. "Don't be so dramatic. I'm not exactly looking forward to staying out here myself, but we have no choice."

"But what about my credit cards? My business deals? Everything! We can't camp here! We have to get to a town! I have to talk to the police!" Much to her consternation, there was an emotional tremor in her voice that she couldn't control.

"I'm doing my best, Lexie."

Not wanting him to see the tears that hovered at her lashes, Lexie stood and strode down the narrow corridor to the area just behind the bathroom that converted into a sleeping area. Though she would rather die than admit it, she knew Jake was right. And as much as his arrogant, know-it-all attitude irritated her, she was very glad he was there. She couldn't imagine being out here in the middle of nowhere with just Eunice and Opal.

Emotions warred in her stomach, tying knot after knot, until Lexie feared she might be sick. Exhausted, she sank onto the soggy, lumpy, rotting mattress and buried her head in her hands. Just as she was gearing up for a good, soul-cleansing cry, something furry scurried past her feet and into a hole beneath the bed.

A bloodcurdling scream followed, and though Lexie couldn't be sure, she thought maybe it had come from her own throat.

Shaking like an autumn leaf in a tornado, she leapt to her feet and tore back the mattress. There she found not just one, but several nests of mice. Recoiling, she staggered backward, screaming all the while.

"*Aaaauuuugggghhh! Moooouuusssse!* No, *Miiiice! Lots of MICE!*"

Without stopping to think, Jake set the brake, jumped to his feet and flew down the tiny hallway till he reached Lexie.

"What's the matter?"

Apparently too traumatized to explain, Lexie leapt into his arms, screaming, freaking, clutching.

He pried her fingers out of his ears, his nose, his mouth, his hair. "Le…le…lex…*Lexie!* Owww! For pity's sake, woman! You're choking me!"

"Auuggghhh!" Still hysterical, she resisted every attempt he made to set her on her own two feet. There was no way she was letting go.

Her arms wound fiercely around his head, blinding him. The two of them careened around the interior of the motor home, banking off the paneled walls in a fashion that would have made a pool shark proud. Finally, their combined weight was too much for the rotten bathroom wall, and they landed in a heap amid a shower of splinters.

"Uh-oh." Jake closed his eyes for a moment, then opened them again to survey the damage through Lexie's fingers.

Still clutching him for dear life as they rolled about on the floor, Lexie closed her eyes in fear. "What now? Rats?"

"Worse."

"W-w-worse?"

"Yep." He sighed. "Dry rot." He pulled her hands away from his eyes and peered up into the now-exposed ceiling. "Lots…and lots of dry rot."

Eunice and Opal, who had come running, clapped their hands over their mouths in shock.

Jake, seeing their crestfallen expressions, tried to smile. "Maybe," he offered hopefully, "it can be fixed?"

Once again, Eunice and Opal laid their hands on the motor home and prayed a quick and earnest prayer for healing. Eunice's reverent amen reverberated in the ensuing silence, and then she smiled at Jake. "Of course, it can be fixed, my dear. With the good Lord, nothing is impossible."

Jake stared in admiration at Eunice. Now *there* was some serious faith.

Four

That night—after the mice had been cleared away and the rotten bathroom wall replaced with a blanket—Lexie and the grandmothers prepared for bed as Jake prowled around outside, battening down the hatches.

There was a profusion of boxes strapped to the roof—not to mention the fishing poles and lawn chairs and life preservers and heaven only knew what—that he needed to check. The air had the decided smell of rain, so he tightened the bungee cords that held the tarp in place. The last thing they needed was a rain storm. The tiny tarp would never keep everything dry.

Meanwhile, back inside the motor home, Lexie blew up the inflatable air mattresses. Eunice handed out sleeping bags and pillows. In the galley kitchen, since all of the appliances were out of order, Opal put together a festive bedtime repast that required no cooking.

Her head swimming with dizziness from inflating their beds, Lexie admitted to Opal and Eunice that she was glad Jake decided to pull over and get some rest. She was exhausted.

When Jake had come in and they'd finished eating, everyone wordlessly retreated to their makeshift beds. Opal and Eunice shared the double bed in the tiny room at the back of the motor home. Lexie chose to bunk in the overhead compartment above the driver's seat and Jake took to the hall floor with his sleeping bag, just below.

As Lexie lay in her uncomfortable bed, breathing in the dank, fetid air, she imagined she could hear wild animals prowling about just outside, looking for food. Human food. Or worse, humans as food.

Or maybe it was Percival and the kids, come to take the money pinned to Opal's brassiere. Or maybe some chainsaw-wielding relative of Percival's... Her imagination running wild, Lexie crushed her fists to her lips and muttered a quick prayer for peace and protection. Then she wriggled to the edge of her bed and peered through the shadows. Jake's lumpy form was wedged between cabinets in the corridor below. Funny how the sight calmed her nerves.

"Pssst."

Silence.

"Pssssssssssssssst."

Jake grunted and rolled onto his back. "Yeah?"

"You awake?" She kept her voice low so as not to disturb the peacefully snoring faction in the back.

"Am now."

"Oh."

"What?"

"Well, nothing, really."

"Okay then, good night." With another grunt, Jake buried his head in his pillow and sighed.

"Good night." Lexie now hung over the edge, her hair dangling down to the driver's seat. "I...I was just wondering when you thought we might reach a phone."

"Phone?"

"Yeah, so I can call work."

"Your work means that much to you, huh?"

"You make that sound like an insult."

"I do?" Jake yawned and stretched. "Well, if the shoe fits…"

Lexie was incensed. "What's wrong with caring about my clients?"

"Nothing, I guess."

"What do you mean, you guess?"

"Well, if you put your work ahead of your family, then I guess it's wrong."

"Hey, if I put my work ahead of my family, do you think I'd be here?"

It was silent for a moment before Jake's chuckle rumbled forth from deep in his chest. "I have to admit, you do have a point."

Lexie cupped her smiling cheeks in her palms. He had a nice laugh. When he wasn't busy being snooty and judgmental. "Aren't you worried about your wallet?"

"I don't know. A little."

"Only a little?"

"What good is worry going to do?"

"It must do some good. Nothing I worry about ever happens."

Again Jake chuckled and, turning on his side, propped himself up on an elbow and looked at her through the moonglow that filtered through the windshield. "So let me see if I've got this straight. Since you're worrying, the bears that are lurking around the door won't come in and eat us after all?"

To keep from waking the grandmothers, she muffled her laughter with her sleeping bag. "How did you know I was worried about that?"

"Like I told you, I know you better than you think."

"You make that sound like an insult too."

"Not necessarily."

A heady smile bloomed across her lips in the dark. She was beginning to grow on him. She could tell. Ever since they'd crashed through the bathroom wall together and she'd screamed in his ear and cried in his neck, he'd been a little easier to live with. More sympathetic. Understanding. He'd even loaned his handkerchief to help mop her smudged mascara. Then he'd helped her to her feet, inspected her arms and legs for cuts and bruises, and doctored the ones he'd found. He had gentle hands. And lazily hooded eyes that could jump-start a cardiac patient.

He wasn't so bad, she decided. Perhaps her first impression of him had been a little premature.

"I admit, I do worry too much. I wish I had your grandmother's deep, unwavering faith."

"Me too." The raspy sound of Jake scratching the whiskers at his jaw filtered through the darkness. "Takes practice, I think. That's why I like hanging around her. She's a good influence."

"Umm." Lexie smiled. Perhaps he was beginning to grow on her just the tiniest bit, too. "I know what you mean. That's why I visit my grandmother every Sunday." She rubbed her eyes and yawned. "I'll have to make a note in my day planner: 'Get more faith.'"

Jake chuckled. "Get some for me while you're at it. I'm afraid we're gonna need it."

Lexie groaned. "So, what's the game plan for tomorrow? Any idea how far we'll be able to go?" Always good to have one's ducks in a row. Hadn't that been a part of Lexie's secret to success? "Think we'll make it home?"

"Home? No way. To a town? Maybe."

"You're kidding, right?"

"Nope. We can only go as far as the old engine will allow. She's running so hot that I couldn't begin to hazard a guess about how long it will take us to get home."

Lexie groaned. "I hope not more than a week. I told everyone I'd be back by then."

"Hey, if it takes that long, I'm sending up a flare." He gave his chest a lazy rub with his fingertips. "If we have any flares, that is... Must be some in that pile of supplies that Gran bought. Anyway, guess we'll just have to play it by ear." Again, Jake yawned and, after giving his pillow a thorough thrashing, burrowed further into his sleeping bag.

"Oh. Well. Okay."

Playing it by ear was not her forte. She wanted to know exactly when she would be home so that she could begin making appointments.

His yawn was contagious, and Lexie found herself following suit. Once again, she reflected as her eyes grew heavy with fatigue, she was glad that Jake was there. If not for his solid, comforting presence, she would no doubt lay awake all night long worrying about lions and tigers and bears...and...oh...my...

As she drifted off to sleep, Lexie contemplated Opal and Eunice's unwavering faith. If only her own relationship with God were as rock solid.

The next morning, they breakfasted on home-baked pastries that they'd unearthed from one of Eunice's tins. Then Jake spent some time trying to figure out the plumbing problems in the bathroom so that they could all take a makeshift shower with the water in the reserve tank.

Fortunately, the fire and the broken wall did not affect the shower enclosure.

Unfortunately, the only thing to pour out of the shower nozzle was rust. To make matters worse, the toilet was melted and the sink didn't work. So, after a quick trip to the woods to take care of pressing business, they did the best they could with a towel and a bottle of water to make themselves presentable, and hit the road once again.

Jake drove, Lexie navigated, and Eunice and Opal played canasta at the table in the back.

It took about three hours for Lexie to became frustrated and bored with the snail's pace. More than once, she leaned over Jake's armrest and checked the speedometer, then gave her watch a disgruntled glance. She could saunter past the motor home at this rate. So far, the only good thing about the trip was that it hadn't rained yet. But judging by the darkening sky, it would. It was just a matter of when.

"Can't you go any faster?"

"Not on a hill like this. Any faster and I'm afraid she'll overheat. See that steep grade just ahead? I'm saving all our power just to make it to the top of that. Hopefully, it won't be long before we crest the hill. We can pick up speed on the slope down and gain some time."

"Feels like we've only gone about ten feet since we left this morning."

Jake chuckled. "That's only an illusion. Actually we've probably gone at least twenty."

"Funny." She grinned in spite of herself. Then out of sheer boredom, she turned to him for some light conversation. *Anything* to help pass the time. "As a commercial pilot, you must be used to living life out of a suitcase."

"I don't know how 'used' to it I am. It's just a fact of life. To be honest, I love my job, but I love being home more. I'm a bit of a homebody, actually. Drives my grandmother crazy."

Hunky was a homebody?

Last week that would have surprised Lexie more than it did today. Last week, she'd have thought he had a flight attendant in every port…airport…whatever. Today, she was beginning to see that there was a lot more to Jake Kelley than met the eye.

"Why does it drive her crazy that you like to stay home?"

"Because she wants me out and about, hopefully at a church social with her, meeting Mrs. Right. Unfortunately, the women she singles out for me are the kind I could never settle down with."

"Oh." Lexie chuckled. "I hear you. My grandmother does the same thing. Last time she set me up with a Trekkie. Spent the entire evening reminiscing about the glory days of the Enterprise and watching him act out the action scenes from his favorite episodes."

A slow grin crept across Jake's mouth and he stared at her, giving her the oddest sense…as if he felt he'd suddenly found a kindred spirit. "That's almost as bad as my date with the interior designer. The first thing she did was throw my La-Z-Boy away and scatter these little smelly grass clippings and pine cones—"

"Potpourri," Lexie supplied.

"Right, right, she stuck that stuff everywhere, I'm still vacuuming." He was so incensed that Lexie had to laugh. "I *love* my La-Z-Boy. It's one of the reasons I look forward to coming home."

"Then you should have it."

"You got that straight." Jake took his eyes off the road to shoot her an appreciative grin, and she felt her armor melt a little.

The guy wasn't half bad. In small doses, of course.

She smiled back, and their gazes flashed together…and held. In that moment, Lexie felt a connection of sorts forge between them. Nothing earth-shattering, just…nice.

Quite nice, in fact.

She shivered and told herself it was because the heater didn't work. But that wasn't the cause, and she knew it.

Jake turned his face back to the road, and Lexie allowed her gaze to travel his profile. He was handsome when he wasn't sneering. Really handsome. Thick brown hair, soulful eyes, square jaw, chiseled lips that currently bore a rakish curve. Her heart hauled off and gave her ribs a vicious thumping. Why hadn't she noticed how appealing his smile was before now?

Probably because he'd never smiled at her before now.

Lexie blinked and forced her gaze back out the window. She was only feeling companionable because of this predicament. It certainly wasn't because they had anything in common. Hardly. She squirmed in her seat—and nearly jumped when her stomach growled.

Knock it off, Dinsmore! She shook her head. Her sudden and completely idiotic attraction to a man who was wholly unsuitable made her peckish. She wondered if her grandmother had packed any chips or cookies or something. "You hungry?"

Jake pointed to the steam that billowed out from under the hood. "We'll need to stop once we get over this hill and let her cool down. It'd be a great time to eat lunch."

Her stomach growled again and heat filled Lexie's cheeks. With any luck, Jake couldn't hear these rumblings above the roaring, backfiring engine. "Great. I could really use a sandwich. Why don't I fix us something to eat now, so that it'll be ready when we stop?"

"Good idea. I'm starved."

After she'd extracted herself from her safety rope, Lexie stumbled down the corridor. "I'm making lunch."

"Let us help," Opal offered.

"No. You two stay put. I can handle it."

"But we don't mind."

"Nanna, this road is far too curvy and steep for you two to be wandering around in here. I'll make the sandwiches." Lexie could just see the broken hips and not a doctor in sight for miles.

"You'll find sandwich makings and chips in the overhead compartments," Eunice called as Lexie wobbled past them and to the kitchen galley. "I have juice, egg salad, and tuna salad in the cooler. Though heaven only knows how 'cool' it is anymore. But I'd imagine it's all right if there is still some ice in there."

"Okay. Hang tight," Lexie instructed, more to herself than to the elderly women, "and leave the cooking to me."

"Fine, dear," Opal said.

Lexie spread her legs wide for balance and, gripping the countertop with one hand, proceeded to explore the overhead compartments with the other. As Jake careened around corners and chugged up the seemingly endless hill, Lexie staggered about like a drunken sailor.

Must be some special knack to cooking in a moving motor home, she mused. A knack she did not have. For it seemed that no matter how careful she was, the contents of every cupboard she opened slid out and tumbled to the countertop. Some even hit her on the head, bringing tears to her eyes and loud complaints to her lips.

"Jake!" She gripped a cabinet handle with one hand and rubbed what was sure to be a lump on her forehead with the other.

"What?"

"Could you maybe not jerk around the curves that way?"

"What?"

"What do you mean, what?" She blinked at the stars that danced before her eyes. "I'm trying to make lunch without slipping into a coma, that's what."

"Let us help, dear," Opal warbled and attempted to stand.

"No, Nanna! Sit!"

When Jake swung around another hairpin curve, Lexie lost her footing. The cabinet door snapped off in her hand and she took it with her as she slid down the corridor toward the back of the motor home.

"Jaaaaake!"

"What?"

"Puhleezzze! The curves!"

"First you tell me to put the pedal to the metal for civilization," he groused, "and when I do, you're all mad. Will you make up your mind?"

Lexie rolled her eyes. So much for their soul connection.

"Ufff." A loaf of bread skittered across the countertop and thumped the back of her head. "Help!"

"Are you all right, dear?" Opal laid down her cards and strained to see what Lexie was up to. Her cards slid off the table and fluttered to the floor.

"Jake, honey." Eunice clutched Opal's arm for dear life as the old engine chugged and gasped and misfired around another steep turn in the bumpy road. The grade had increased dramatically and the force had them all sliding toward the rear. "We were all wondering if you could smooth out your driving just a wee bit?"

"What?" Jake hissed through his teeth. He was standing on the accelerator and playing tug-of-war with the wheel.

Lexie made the mistake of hauling herself to her knees and peering out the window. The sight left her dizzy and breathless. They'd just emerged from a thick stand of trees, and the terrifying view was now clear. On her side of the motor home, a sheer cliff loomed just beyond the narrow shoulder. Several hundred feet below, a silver thread divided the canyon walls. It took a moment before Lexie realized the tiny thread was a river. Panic pushed her heart into her throat. She hoped Jake knew how to fly this thing.

"Uh, Jake?" Lexie dropped back to her hands and knees and crawled away from the window.

"*What?*"

"Why don't we just stop for a while?"

"No way. If I do, we'll lose so much momentum that we'll never make it to the top of this hill. Trust me on this, we *don't* want to get out and hike. Just do the best you can for a couple more minutes, then it will be smooth sailing."

"Smooth sailing. Right." She supposed that's how one could look at a free fall over a cliff in a 1972 Camptime motor home. Her giggle, even to her own ears, was borderline hysterical. With great concentration, Lexie was finally able to grip the counter and haul herself back up to her feet. Perhaps preparing lunch would take her mind off her fear.

After a moment's practice, she began to get her sea legs. If she used the cupboard door that she'd torn from it's hinges as a weight, the paper plates stayed on the counter. She made a clean spot to spread slices of bread and begin slathering them with mayonnaise. Next came the tuna fish concoction, but with each hairpin curve, more seemed to end up on the floor than on the bread. Just as she was getting the hang of swaying—and spreading—with the turns, the potato chips jumped ship and scattered over the floor.

Lexie looked at the filthy strip of carpet and groaned. Those were her favorite kind of chips. And she was starving. As she stared in dismay at the carnage, the pickles began to taxi down the counter for takeoff. Clutching the sink for balance, Lexie strained to catch them before they leaped to their death. But it was hopeless. The pungent smell of pickle brine blended with the Mountain Lilac carpet freshener Opal had sprinkled over the dank carpet and sent Lexie's gag reflex into overdrive.

The steep incline created the perfect atmosphere for an avalanche. Soon Lexie was diving for soda bottles and trying to hold the refrigerator door shut with her free foot.

"Ouch! Jaaa-eee-aake! Uff! Could...you...please...! Ooowww!"

As Jake crested the hill and began a rapid descent around yet another sharp curve, a five-pound bag of flour sailed out of the now doorless cupboard and exploded over Lexie's feet. Trust Eunice to think of baking supplies.

"Jake!"

"WHAT?" His tone made it clear that he was in no mood for conversation as he grappled with the wheel and pumped at the brake pedal with his booted foot.

As Lexie looked past his shoulder and out the windshield, she could see by the harrowing decline that lay ahead that now was not the time to bother him. "Oh...nothing."

Pots and pans and tins of cookies pummeled her as she struggled to secure the cabinet doors against the shifting loads. For as long as she could, Lexie fought the valiant fight to save their supplies.

But alas, gravity was against her.

Five

nce they'd reached the bottom of the hill, the engine died of its own volition. Left with no choice, Jake jockeyed the massive machine over onto a wide spot on the shoulder of the road and set the brake. Great plumes of steam belched forth from under the hood. It would be a while before he could get close enough to inspect the damage. However, he didn't need to look under the hood to know that steam like this meant trouble.

Behind him, he could feel Lexie grip the back of his seat and drag herself to her feet. Her eyes were two burning coals in a sea of white flour and the pink slash of her mouth was twisted in shock and dismay.

He had to bite his lip to keep from laughing. She looked like something the cat dragged in—and then dragged back out again.

"Well, this is a fine kettle of fish!" She gave her flour-coated clothes a futile dusting and her tuna-caked hair a smoothing pat. "Everyone, careful of the glass shards." She waved her hand at the slop on the floor behind her and then proceeded to sneeze five times in a row.

Jake unfastened his seat belt, and ducking his head, emerged from the driver's compartment. He couldn't believe the carnage that lay beyond. It looked as if a bomb had gone off in the galley. So much for a picnic lunch. Again, the humor of this ridiculous situation threatened his composure.

In stunned silence, Eunice and Opal scooted out of the orange plaid booth where they'd been riding. They moved up next to Jake to stare through the windshield at the alarming clouds issuing from the engine.

In an effort to comfort the grandmothers, Jake draped his arms around their shoulders and bowed his head as they prayed. At this point, he could only hope the good Lord was listening, because it would take a miracle to get this old bucket of bolts up and running again. Even with a good engine, he still had to solve the little problem of their location. The map had stopped making sense miles ago. Without proper provisions and a good engine...well, any pilot worth his salt knew the possibilities could be grim.

After the last amen was murmured, Lexie planted her hands on her hips and began to issue orders.

"Nanna, you and Eunice sit down over here and stay out of the way." Her clipped tone brooked no argument. She grabbed a broom and—following Jake outside to the engine that was now spouting more steam than Old Faithful—thrust it at his chest. "Here. Since you were the Evil-Knieval-wannabe behind the wheel, you can help."

Jaw dropping, Jake jerked his thumb at the hissing and spitting engine. "You act like I did this on purpose."

Lexie took a step toward him, her foul mood making her brave. Eunice and Opal were watching them through the windshield. "We asked you to take it easy!"

"And I told you I *couldn't*. If I had, we'd still be on the other side of that mountain!"

"Big deal. I'd like to know where in blue blazes you think we are now!"

"You're the navigator, you tell me!"

"Oh yeah, blame the navigator. Like I forced you to go swerving up that hill. Thanks to you, we have no edible food left!"

"I wasn't the one who opened all the doors and let it escape!"

"It didn't jump out of the cabinets all by itself, you know." Arms gesticulating wildly, Lexie waved at the desolate stretch of road that disappeared into the thick forest ahead. "We'll probably starve to death out here in the middle of nowhere."

Jake stared at her for a moment as her eyes sparkled with anger and indignation. Frown lines crinkled in the flour between her delicate brows. She was such a mess. Food had spattered her silk blouse and designer jeans, and her usually perfect hair looked like a squirrel had been nesting there. And without plumbing, there was no way for her to clean up.

He had to bite his tongue to keep from laughing out loud. "Oh, come on now, Lexie. Where is that faith you're supposed to be working on?" He squinted at her.

She blew a raspberry at him, and that was his undoing.

Jake could hold back no longer. Thigh-slapping belly laughter grabbed hold of him and he roared with glee at the cloudy sky. Oh, but it felt great to laugh.

Lexie stared uncertainly at him and took a step back, which made Jake only laugh harder. He wrapped his arms around his middle to keep his guts from bursting out. It was all too much. The food on the floor, the food on Lexie, the steaming engine, the rotten walls, the mice, Percival Jenkins, the fact that they were so lost it would take a boy scout with two compasses to help them find the end of their noses…

Man. He hadn't laughed this hard in years. It made the whole trip worthwhile.

His gales of laughter must have been contagious, because the flour at the corners of Lexie's mouth cracked as a smile tugged at her lips.

Soon, they were both howling.

Jake dropped to his knees, and Lexie joined him on the ground. They gasped for air, wheezing and snorting and hooting and rolling in the grass till the tears streamed down their cheeks. The stress that had kept them at odds vaporized like so much engine steam.

After a while their laughter began to subside, and Lexie reached out and tapped Jake's arm.

"Hmm?" He rolled onto his side to face her and couldn't believe how appealing she was, even covered in flour. He resisted the insane urge to stroke the sides of her cheek. Her mouth. To lean forward, just a fraction, and kiss those full, rosy lips.

"Too bad you're not a Trekkie. You could have Scottie beam us up."

He pretended to pout. "I want my La-Z-Boy."

"Maybe we could fashion one out of sticks and pine cones."

"Now there's an idea! And then we could eat it when we run out of Gran's baked goods."

Lexie rolled over to her stomach, plucked a blade of grass, and tucked it in the corner of her mouth. "I need a shower."

"I don't know. I think you look kind of cute all covered with goo." Finally, he gave in to his impulse and reached out to touch her cheek. "Yummy."

"You're delirious."

She batted at his hand, but he twined his fingers with hers and wouldn't let go. He chalked the familiar gesture up to the beginnings of a truce. But deep inside he knew there was more to it than that. Though he'd been acquainted with Lexie for years, it was only now that he was beginning to know her. And darned if what his grandmother had always told him wasn't true: Lexie was special.

"No, I'm not delirious. But I am feeling surprisingly good, all things considered."

It was hard to tell, her being covered in flour and all, but he had the feeling she was blushing and it endeared her to him even more.

"Me too," she murmured. "All things considered."

Inside the motor home, Opal and Eunice looked at each other and shook their heads, unsure as to whether this was a good or bad sign. They simply shrugged and began to put together a meager lunch from what was left of the supplies. At least the kids weren't fighting.

And for that, they were thankful.

"Interesting—" Eunice mused as she slapped cold cuts on whole wheat—"how those two seem to be getting along."

"Very." Opal nodded and shot streams of mustard over the meat.

"You don't suppose…"

"Now, Eunice, don't go and push your luck. They have nothing in common. I know this, because Lexie tells me every Sunday."

"True." Eunice glanced out the window. "Jake has made that clear more than once. But still…"

"Eunice." Opal's voice held warning.

"Oh, all right. I'll leave them alone. But I don't suppose a little prayer would hurt."

Opal smiled. "Surely not. And while we're at it, we must thank the Lord for our bounty."

"And for this magical adventure."

Together they bowed their heads.

❧

"Hey! Hey!"

Jake peered out from under the hood where he'd been working on the engine.

"Hey, Jake!" Huffing and puffing, Lexie stumbled out of the woods. There were twigs in her hair and smudges of dirt and long, pinkish scratches on her arms. She held the ends of her now-torn blouse out in front of her, cradling a pile of something that leaked. His heart suddenly in his throat, Jake could only hope that she hadn't been mauled by some kind of wild animal. As much as he was loathe to admit it to his grandmother, he was becoming fond of Lexie Dinsmore. There was something vulnerable beneath that business facade that he found very appealing.

He dropped his tools and broke into a run, meeting her at the edge of the woods.

"Look, Jake!" Her face beamed. "Berries! There are tons of some kind of blueberry bushes back in there. We can have these with our lunch."

Jake peered into the pile. Sure enough, she had a bunch of berries. And they were blue. But they weren't blueberries. Blueberries wouldn't be blue for months. He had no idea what these were, but he doubted they were edible. "Well, way to go, sport," he praised.

She ducked her head at his words. "And that's not all I found in there." As she limped toward the motor home door, he noted that her fancy Italian leather shoes would never be the same. "There's a creek back in there. Even if we can't drink it, at least we can clean up. I'll just go give these berries to Nanna and—"

She tripped over a root, stumbled, and dropped the berries, crushing them as she righted herself. "Ohhhhh…*esshhh.*"

He rushed to her side, where she stood next to the motor home, staring at the ground. Her expression was one of pure despondence.

"Hey, now. Don't worry about that. I'm sure we still have plenty of food to eat. Gran packed enough stuff to feed an army." He gripped her elbows and helped her around the slippery mash. She had to clutch his shirt to maintain her balance.

Something flipped over in his stomach as he held her arms and looked into her large, baby blues. She blinked at the tears that pooled near her lashes. She was tired. And dirty. And out of her element. But she was being a terrific sport. He admired her pluck.

He resisted the crazy urge to kiss the tip of her nose.

"But I wanted fresh berries." Her tone was as plaintive as a little girl's.

His heart melted toward her yet another notch and he set her away from him before he gave into one of his nutty impulses of late and embarrassed them both.

"How about if I buy you a piece of berry pie when we get back to civilization?"

If they got back to civilization. He only hoped they wouldn't have to survive on those berries she'd found.

With a heartfelt sigh, she pushed her hair out of her face and gave him a tremulous smile. "That sounds heavenly. Thanks. You're…sweet."

"Nah." She thought he was sweet? His chest swelled and he suddenly felt as if he could taxi the motor home down the road and fly them all back to Washington state. He was superman.

"I'm…just, uh—" she gestured to the door behind her—"I'm just going to change into a swimsuit and head down to the river to clean up." As an afterthought she added, "Wanna come?"

Lexie in a swimsuit? Nobody had to ask him twice. "I'm right behind you." He didn't even try to deny that though the thought of a spit bath was welcome, it was the excuse to spend time with Lexie that held the greatest appeal.

It was decided that they would eat their lunch down at the water's edge. But first, everyone was dying to get cleaned up. The sun broke through the clouds, taking the chill out of the air. Unfortunately, it did nothing for the temperature of the water.

Jake watched with a grin as Lexie picked her way into the icy stream, squealing and gasping all the way. Violent shivers wracked her body for a while, so he waded in next to her and rubbed at the goose flesh on her arms with his hands. Much to his pleasure, she didn't seem to mind the familiar gesture, and in fact, encouraged it when, teeth chattering, she leaned against him, clutching his shirt in her hands.

Mmm. He could stand here in this frigid water—losing feeling in his feet, his toes turning bright blue—for days, just so she stood with him, tugging on his shirt and smiling up at him this way. Yeah. She was definitely worming her way into his heart.

He darted a narrow gaze at Eunice. She was hunched over a picnic basket, unloading the sandwiches she and Opal had scraped together, seemingly not watching them at all. Even so, he was still convinced that she'd somehow managed to get Lexie here in some wacky matchmaking scheme or another. Not that it mattered at this point. He was already sold on Lexie. She was, he was discovering, nothing like the other women Eunice had foisted upon him over the years.

Lexie was complex.

Independent, yet loving and family oriented. Spunky and feisty, yet funny and quick to laugh. And, he had to admit—

though he'd never tell Lexie—he was glad Percival stole her phone. She was a lot of fun when she didn't have that stupid thing glued to her head.

Reluctantly he stopped rubbing her arms, and with a lingering pat on her back, moved to the bank to gather his shaving supplies. While he shaved, he covertly watched Lexie wash her thick, gorgeous head of hair. He wondered why he'd never noticed how natural her beauty was before this trip.

Maybe because you never really bothered to look beneath the glamour girl facade?

Maybe. When Eunice pushed him toward a woman, he usually went blind to her attributes.

After a refreshing cleanup session—where even Eunice and Opal shucked their stockings and waded into the zippy water—Jake joined the women on a blanket near the shore and ate lunch. Some cold cuts, the plastic bottle of mustard, a loaf of bread, a box of crackers, and some slightly bruised fruit had survived the hill and made a pretty decent meal. Opal had been able to salvage more food than they'd thought possible. Even so, thanks to the loss of many supplies, they would need to find a grocery store. Soon.

Since this stream afforded running water and Jake still had some tinkering to do on the engine, they decided to camp there for yet another night.

Lexie groaned at this idea, but was far more relaxed at this news than she'd been yesterday.

Of course, she was still the tinniest bit crabby. "At ten miles a day, we should be back in Washington state by fall."

"You wanna drive?" Jake offered, teasing.

"No, no. You're doing fine. Really fine."

"Still wish I hadn't come along?" He hated himself for fishing, but he wanted to know if she'd changed her tune about him. The way he had about her.

Lexie looked askance at him, then her lips pulled into a coy curve that had Jake's pulse shifting gears.

"I suppose if I admit that I'm glad you're here, you'll hold it over my head."

"Maybe."

"Then maybe I'm glad you're here."

Six

*N*o one slept very well that night.

Shortly after midnight, the clouds finally let loose and it rained. Not just a garden-variety spring shower, Lexie thought as she peered out the drizzling window-pane into the soggy world beyond. This was more of a monsoon. The kind of rain that made her glad Eunice had insisted on buying that life raft.

It wasn't simply the incessant pounding of rain on the roof and the shrill howl of the wind that had kept Lexie, and from what she could tell, the others, from sleeping soundly. No, it was because they all were forced to sleep sitting up in the orange plaid booth as it was the only area in the entire motor home that didn't leak like a run-over garden hose.

When Lexie finally woke from the fitful doze that she'd managed in the wee hours of the morning, she discovered, much to her chagrin, that she had been sleeping on Jake's shoulder. And she'd been drooling. To make matters worse, he'd been watching.

An amused, almost endearing smile graced his sensual lips.

When she'd noticed the puddle she'd left on his bulging bicep, she'd wanted to die. She could only hope that the straw pile on her head that passed for hair hid the crimson spots of mortification in her cheeks. Without a blow dryer and her usual beauty regime, Lexie was sure she looked a fright.

Jake, of course, was quite the opposite. He looked debonair

with his tousled hair and whisker-shadowed jaw. She'd always known that he was handsome, but merciful heavens. Even after sleeping bolt upright with a grandmother on one arm and a patch of drool on the other, he was a sight for sore eyes. Funny how he just seemed to get better looking with every passing hour. And nicer. After all, how many guys would give up much needed vacation time to escort two little old ladies across country in a motor home?

Lexie gave her head a little shake. Sleep deprivation was doing strange things to her brain. Deciding that she would be better off not sitting quite so close to Jake, she got up to rummage through the cupboards for breakfast makings.

After peanut butter and jelly sandwiches, they hit the road once again. All things considered, Lexie thought, their little group was in remarkably jolly spirits. The pendulum of doom seemed to have swung in the opposite direction. Jake had done something magical to jury-rig the engine. The motor home was, for once, living up to what the ad had boasted and driving like a dream.

And so—though it was raining both inside and out—Lexie was enjoying herself. She even had to admit that she didn't miss her phone all that much. Who knew life cut off from society could be so relaxing? It took a little adjustment, of course, but once she accepted the idea that there was nothing she could do about her predicament, she was fine. Especially since Jake was there to take her mind off her troubles.

As they traveled the primitive back roads that Eunice promised would lead home in record time, Lexie and Jake teased and flirted and discussed a vast array of subject matter from politics to religion, from their memories of the past to their dreams for the future. Lexie was shocked at how much they agreed on just about everything. Who'd have thought that the arrogant flyboy next door would be someone with whom she'd have so much in common?

"Coffee?" Lexie held up a thermos and an empty mug. She'd brewed a crude batch in a pot over their open fire, using a paper bag as a filter. It wasn't much, but it was hot and strong.

Jake cast her a grateful smile. "Yes. Please."

"Black?"

"Yup."

"Good, 'cuz the sugar and cream are stuck to the carpet."

He laughed. "You're pretty clever, making coffee this way."

"I was a girl scout."

"Really? Me too!"

"I bet you were an ugly one."

Jake rolled his eyes. "I was a *scout,* too. A boy scout."

"Well then, between the two of us, we should be able to live through this experience."

"Actually, I dropped out before we got to the wilderness badge."

"Rats. Me too."

"Bummer."

He didn't look bummed out at all. He looked cheerful. Content. She studied the set of his mouth and the little crinkles at the corners of his eyes. Happy, even. He glanced at her and winked. A flirtatious wink. Her heart fluttered. He was enjoying being with her.

Just as she was enjoying being with him. Very much. Too much, probably. And it wasn't simply because he agreed with her on so many things that she found him so appealing. As they talked, Lexie discovered a sweet, family-oriented side of his personality that she very much admired. Like her own father, Jake was a good, God-fearing man. Hardworking, honest, caring.

And so capable. Something about him instilled Lexie with amazing confidence, given the nutty situation which they found themselves in. Come what may, she felt they would be all right as long as Jake was there. Yes, everything was progressing nicely as they crested the summit of yet another hill and began a rapid descent toward the timberline. Eunice and Opal were singing "She'll be comin' round the mountain" for the dozenth time in the back.

It wasn't until Jake unrolled his window and reached into the pouring rain, around the windshield, to pull a twig off the wiper—and the wiper broke off in his hand—that Lexie began to suspect the luck pendulum was swinging back.

In fact, from the look of things, the pendulum had turned into a wrecking ball.

"Oh, for the love of—" Jake stared in disgust at the windshield wiper he held for a moment before he tossed it over his shoulder. His knuckles whitened as he put a death grip on the steering wheel and pumped at the brakes.

"Jake, can you see?" Fear crowded into Lexie's throat. Water sluiced over the roof and across the windshield in great rippling sheets. Even with the wiper blade still working on Lexie's side, visibility was nil.

"No."

"That's not good, is it?"

Slowly, Jake turned to stare at her.

"Okay, dumb question."

He snapped his head back to the windshield and squinted through the waterfall. "I'm gonna have to pull over. This is ridiculous. Can you tell me if there is a wide spot on the shoulder?

Preferably a flat spot. This hill is no good."

Lexie strained forward, her eyes darting about for an area to pull safely off the road. "Uh, no. No flat spot."

"Never mind."

"Never mind? Why never mind?"

Jaw grim, brow furrowed, Jake stabbed at the brakes for all he was worth. "Well, even if there were a place to pull over, I probably couldn't stop."

"No?" The word came out in a tinny squeak. She swallowed past the dry lump in her throat. "Why?"

"Brakes don't seem to be responding well."

"But they are responding a little?" She crossed her fingers.

"No."

"But you said they were not responding *well*. Not they're not responding at *all*."

The muscles worked in his jaw. "I was trying not to scare you."

"Didn't work. I'm scared."

Lexie could see that they were still a ways from the bottom of this hill and heaven only knew what loomed ahead.

"What are you going to do?" Casting a covert peek over her shoulder, Lexie checked to see if their grandmothers were listening.

They were.

"Pray the steering doesn't go out."

Eunice and Opal bowed their heads.

"Okay, now you're really scaring me."

"Sorry." Jake hunched over the steering wheel, his eyes focused on a small, dry spot in the windshield that afforded a bit of visibility.

"What's wrong with the brakes?" Lexie whispered, not wanting to break his concentration.

"For crying out loud, Lexie, how should I know?"

She shrugged. He always seemed so in command. Like he knew everything.

He grunted and gave the brake pedal a vicious pumping. "The load must be too heavy for these old, wet brakes at this angle."

She wrung her hands. Another glance over her shoulder told Lexie that the grandmothers were still praying. She bowed her head and joined them.

Everyone was silent.

They were picking up speed.

The scenic view of the forest became a blur as they bumped rapidly down the road. Lexie tightened her safety rope, and the grandmothers followed suit. Beads of sweat popped out on Jake's brow. There were no cars in front of them and none approaching, but that could change.

In the galley, pots and pans rattled, bottles clinked, and a few items that were not strapped in began to roll. Opal's spare glasses, Eunice's Bible, and a couple cans of soda all skittered down the hall and landed with a thud in the back of Jake and Lexie's seats. The high-pitched whistle of wind screaming through various cracks grew higher.

Lexie crammed her fists beneath her chin and began another fervent prayer. This time, she repented for not having repented in a while. Then she begged the Lord to spare the lives of Eunice, Opal, and Jake. She thanked God for her life, as it had been good. She hadn't had the chance to do the husband, kid, and pet thing, but hey, that was her fault. She'd been far too wrapped up in her work.

She regretted it, though. After all, on her dying day—which most likely would be today—she doubted that she'd look back and say to herself, 'Golly, I sure wish I'd sold a few more pieces of property.' Tears sprang into her eyes as she grieved over the husband and kids and dog that she would never know.

She swiped at her eyes. She was digressing.

"Lord," she whispered, "if you spare my life, I'd just like to let you know that I finally think I'm ready to find a relationship and settle down. This trip has taught me so much, Lord, and I—"

"Uh, I hate to cut you off there," Jake said, his voice filled with all the strain she was feeling, "especially since you're praying and all, but I need you to tell me if I'm seeing what I think I'm seeing."

"What are you seeing?" Hands as a shield above her eyes, Lexie scanned the view ahead.

"That spot up there in the middle of the road—would that be a tunnel?"

Lexie focused on the spot. "Uh, sure looks like it. Wait. There's a sign."

"What's it say?"

"It says 'Tunnel height, twelve feet. Taller vehicles use truck route.'"

"What truck route?"

"Doesn't say. Could it be that road?"

"What road?"

"That one! That one right there…right there…the road that you are passing…that we just passed."

"Uh-oh." Jake was sweating bullets now. He stomped on the brakes and pulled on the wheel, as if that could reign in the old horse.

"'Uh-oh'?" Lexie stared at him. "Are we in trouble?"

"Not if we are under twelve feet high," he grunted. "Put your seat belt on, and get ready to duck. *Eunice! Opal!* Get down under the table and stay there!"

"Under the table? But why—?" The old voices were throbbing with alarm.

"Just do it!" Veins stood out on Jake's neck.

Eunice and Opal, recognizing the urgency in his tone, did what they were told. Lexie reached over and gave Jake a pat of encouragement just before she tucked her head between her knees.

And just before the interior of the motor home went black.

Seven

As long as Lexie lived, she would never forget the horrendous scraping of metal against concrete. The popping and crashing noises that accompanied them on their journey through the tunnel were deafening. And now, as the motor home burst into the stark light of day and hurtled down the hillside, she had to marvel that they were alive at all. For it looked almost as if a giant, rusty can opener had removed the roof of the motor home and flung it to the four howling winds.

To Lexie, the descent to the bottom of the mountain seemed endless, but in fact probably only took a matter of minutes. Despite the calamity, Jake—good pilot that he was—kept his cool. Like a bronc buster in a rodeo for big rigs, he battled the steering wheel, hanging on to the bouncing, bucking machine for dear life and shouting words of encouragement to the failing brakes.

If anyone could get them out of this situation in one piece, Lexie knew Jake could.

However, in those uncertain minutes—with her head cradled between her knees—her life flashed before her eyes.

And she didn't like what she saw.

Teeth rattling, Lexie clasped her hands together and made a vow. A vow to both herself and to God, to get her priorities straight. A vow to stop and smell the roses and the coffee and even the disgusting mold and mildew in the motor home. Life was far too short. Far too precious. And here she was, squandering it on paperwork and pencil pushing and the pursuit of material gain and a happiness that was forever elusive. If they lived through this ordeal, she would turn over a new leaf.

Immediately.

Lexie would never know how he did it, but Jake finally reached the bottom of the hill and—finding a treeless, gentle slope—swerved off the road and made a perfect four-point emergency landing. After bouncing over a stump here and a boulder there, they eventually came to a stop in the middle of an open field. But not before they left a long and depressing trail of debris behind them.

The giant bundle of camp chairs, fishing poles, and other miscellaneous supplies that Jake had lashed so securely to the rotten roof between the air conditioning units, had exploded when they'd hit the tunnel. The bungee cords that held the bundle in place had peeled the rotten roof—air conditioners and all—off the motor home on impact.

For the first few minutes after they'd bumped to a stop, Lexie sat in stunned silence, staring at Jake, too shell-shocked to move. Then, realizing that they were still in Montana and not in heaven, she crawled back to the orange plaid booth and helped Eunice and Opal out from under the table. Amazingly, they were both unharmed.

The three women staggered to the door and followed Jake outside. The whipping wind tore at the grandmothers' skirts and blew Lexie's hair across her face, making it difficult to see.

It was raining like a car wash now, and the wind and rain were merciless as they inspected the damage. And there was plenty of damage to inspect.

If the motor home had been a pile of junk before, it was a

busted-up, soaking-wet pile of junk now.

A lump lodged in Lexie's throat when she noticed Eunice and Opal clutching each other by the arms and looking at their thirty-one feet of vacation magic in dismay.

Apparently Jake noticed too, because it was then that he lost his cool. Eyes burning with fury, he plowed his fingers through his rain-soaked hair and vented his rage at the leaky heavens.

"Of all the low-down…conniving…thieving…selling this pile of *junk* to two little old ladies…when I get my hands on that clown…" Fists swinging, he shouted until he went hoarse. As he kicked the giant, rubbery tires and punched the motor home's walls, he reminded Lexie of a wounded rooster in a cock fight with the chicken coop.

Eunice and Opal moved off to huddle under a nearby tree. Clutching each other against the elements, they began to pray.

Even though Jake had murder in his eye, Lexie wasn't afraid. She understood his frustration. He had every right to blow off a little steam. Jake had carried the bulk of the responsibility for this fiasco of a trip from the moment they'd left and he'd done an admirable job.

She only wished she could help somehow. For a long while, she simply stood and watched him vent. Then, as he began to wind down, she took a step forward and placed a hand on his shoulder.

"At least the bad smell is getting aired out," she ventured, hoping to assuage his foul mood.

Jake stopped in his tracks and peered at her over his shoulder. A violent shake of his head had rain spraying in all directions.

She ignored his glacial gaze and bestowed upon him a tentative smile. "And another advantage would be that the, uh, carpet is no doubt getting a good rinsing."

A muscle twitched in his jaw. Then, grudgingly, the sparks in his eyes began to twinkle.

"If all else fails, I think it will make a dandy swimming pool." She wiped at the rain that sluiced over her forehead and into her eyes. "Probably be ready for a swim meet by the end of the day, if this keeps up. Too bad we didn't think to bring a stopwatch."

A smile tugged at the corners of his mouth, and returning his smile, Lexie slipped her arm around his waist and nestled into his side.

"You did a really good job, keeping us alive. I never could have gotten us this far. You're a hero."

Jake snorted. "Perhaps it has escaped your notice that we lost the roof?"

"Hey, you saved us, and that's what really counts. And—" she tilted her head and looked him straight in the eyes—"in answer to your earlier question, I'm really, really glad you're here."

Gaze warm, he wrapped his arms around her and pulled her close. "Me too."

Lexie lay her cheek against his chest and listened to the comforting beat of his heart. It was so good to be alive.

Never before had she realized how wonderful it was to simply be alive. From this moment forward, she would live life in the here and now. She would make a conscious effort to enjoy the beautiful things that each precious moment had to offer.

Like basking in the glow of Jake's warmth, his wonderful laughter, and the wonderful feel of his arm around her shoulders.

"Opal, look!" Eunice nudged her buddy as she murmured her last amen and opened her eyes. The tree under which Opal and Eunice stood was doing precious little to shelter them—their

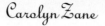

soggy dresses clung to their legs and the wind tugged at their hair-pins.

Opal peered after Eunice's bony finger. "Heavens to Betsy, will you look at them! Think he's going to kiss her?"

"I have a ten spot in my brassiere that says he will."

"You're on."

They clasped hands and shook.

"When?" Eunice wanted to know in her typically blunt fashion.

"Soon. Mark my words. I can feel 'em gearing up for the big clinch. Puts me in mind of Howard and me, back when we were sparking behind the big red barn."

Eunice snorted. "Jump into the new millennium, Opal. Nobody uses words like 'sparking' anymore."

"Well, what do you call it?"

"I think the term today is 'going steady.'"

"Really, Eunice, aren't they a little long in the tooth for 'going steady'?"

"Look what pot is calling the kettle black."

Opal clutched Eunice's arm for balance as they braved the storm back to the motor home. "Eunice Kelley, are you saying I'm old?"

Their laughter was swallowed by the howling winds as they walked. "If the support hose fit, Opal, old girl. If the support hose fit."

To shield them all from the elements, Jake stretched some plastic sheeting above the galley kitchen. He would worry about a makeshift roof later. For now, they at least had an area to prepare a meager lunch and to wait for the rain to subside.

While they crowded in front of the sink and ate what was left of the apples and cookies, Eunice and Opal praised him for his quick thinking and grace under fire.

Embarrassed, Jake waved a hand. He didn't think he'd done anything all that special. A real hero would have demanded that they hightail it from Percival's place in the Barbie car.

"I mean it. That was a wonderful thing you did back there, Jake." Opal looked at him with fondness.

Eunice agreed. "We are all still alive. And for that, my dear one, we are truly grateful."

Jake thought their praises were nice, but it was Lexie's admiring smile that had him standing up just a little straighter.

"In fact," Eunice continued, "why don't we take a moment to thank our heavenly Father for our good fortune?"

Dumbfounded, Jake stared at his grandmother. Trust Eunice to take life's lemons and make a blasted lemon meringue pie. "*Good* fortune?"

"Why yes." A minxish expression pushed at the creases in her time-weathered face. "I always wanted a convertible."

The lump in his throat caused his chuckle to come out in a strangled fashion. He bunched his shoulders and let them drop. He guessed he was feeling pretty thankful himself. For his life. For the ladies' lives.

For Lexie.

He took Eunice's hand in one hand and Lexie's hand in the other and when they'd all bowed their heads, he led them in a heartfelt prayer of thanksgiving.

The rest of that afternoon was spent getting reorganized. Jake pulled what was left of the motor home under a stand of trees at the far edge of the field to afford it some protection from the elements.

When the rain finally stopped, they all hiked back up the hill and tried to salvage what they could of the camping gear and other accoutrements that had flown off with the roof.

While they worked, Jake offered Eunice some suggestions about how they might be able to repair the old roof without spending an arm and a leg. Eunice and Opal were, per usual, optimistic. The sooner they could get the old girl seaworthy, the sooner they could set out on another vacation, they said.

As much as it stupefied him, they were still pleased with their purchase and were enjoying their adventure. While he untangled a fishing pole from a branch in a tree, Jake reflected on what Lexie had said about the grandmothers' mind-boggling faith in God.

Here they were in the middle of nowhere, their little vacation investment was blowing up in front of their eyes. Everything that could go wrong had, and yet…they were happy.

Lexie was right. With faith like that, life's little annoyances seemed inconsequential in the scheme of things. He wondered if it took eighty years to learn that.

Hopefully not.

After all, Lexie seemed to have changed her tune and was having a great time. He watched her as she walked ahead of him, a fetching silhouette in the patch of sunshine that had finally burst through the cloud cover. In spite of their harrowing trip through the tunnel, she too seemed to be having a good time.

While they strolled along searching the ditch for debris, he listened to them all making jokes about the sporty new look for the motor home. Wouldn't the neighbors be green with envy, they wondered, and giggled about camping under the stars.

What was it with these nutty women? But even as the thought formed, a warmth filled his heart and a smile nudged his mouth.

A poignant feeling that he couldn't quite pinpoint suddenly

assailed him, filling him with an intense yearning. For what, he wasn't sure…but he had a suspicion it might have something to do with needing roots. Family. And, as he and Lexie had discussed, a deeper relationship with Jesus and a strong sense of spirituality that had been eluding him in his fast-paced, workday life. He was beginning to see that he possessed the very qualities that he abhorred in the women he'd dated.

Too much focus on self and career and not enough on the here and now, on what was really important. How had he not noticed that about himself before today? Maybe it took being stranded out in the middle of nowhere, away from the control tower and his flight schedule to reassess what was really important to him.

On the other hand, maybe it took a beautiful woman who appealed to him on a hundred different levels. He'd have been in far worse shape without her wacky sense of humor and sweet smile. Yes. Without Lexie, he'd have lost it miles ago.

He watched as she dragged a lawn chair off the road and set it up for his grandmother. She was so thoughtful. So tenderhearted. So…doggone cute. She giggled at something Eunice said, then bent to kiss the woman's cheek. Seeming to sense his gaze, Lexie glanced up. Across the camp area, they communicated silently with their eyes, saying things they wouldn't dream of saying out loud at this point in their relationship. Jake took a deep breath and slowly let it out. A smile started deep in his belly and flared upward to settle across his mouth.

Slowly, Lexie responded in kind, and they stood there, smiling stupidly at each other, for an inordinately long time. Thank God he hadn't given in to his original impulse and demanded that she stay home. Life was just so much less lonely with Lexie around.

When they'd finished retrieving what they could of their possessions, Jake built a campfire out of a store-bought log, some big chunks of the rotten bathroom wall and a few branches he found in the woods. For supper, Eunice and Opal cracked open the remaining two cans of chili and found some saltine crackers in a tin. Lexie added a sliced banana to a can of fruit cocktail. For desert, it was chocolate bars and instant coffee. It wasn't much for a hungry party of four, but it would have to do.

While Eunice and Opal cleaned up, Lexie came over and sat down on the cooler next to Jake. She picked a stick up off the ground.

He could feel the warmth radiating from her body and unable to resist, he leaned closer and nudged her. "Hi."

Her smile was bashful. "Hi." She nudged back, then gestured at the map he held. "Any idea where we are?" The embers of their dying campfire swirled and glowed red when she poked them with her stick.

"Yep."

"Really?" She looked at him in awe.

"I think so." After a thorough study of the map, Jake figured he might have their location pretty well pinned down. "If my calculations are correct, we're only about ten miles from a little town." He handed her the map and reaching across her lap, pointed out the various roads. "See? I think we're about…here. The tunnel is what finally helped me get my bearings. This whole area that's shaded green? That's where we've been driving—in a big circle—for the last three days."

"Why is it shaded green?"

"It's national forest service wilderness area."

A girlish smile brought out the dimples at the corners of her mouth. "Eunice's shortcut?"

"Eunice's shortcut."

"That would account for the lack of traffic in these parts."

Jake grinned and nodded. "Most likely. And this map isn't too detailed in this area. No wonder we got lost."

As she leaned over to focus on the map, he caught the subtle scent of wood smoke and the floral shampoo she'd used to wash her hair in the stream. His mouth went suddenly dry and he cleared his throat. "This, uh, would be the tunnel, and over here is the closest town—right here. See? The terrain on that ten-mile stretch looks relatively flat. I figure the brake system will probably work well enough to get us there in one piece."

A small frown of worry marred Lexie's brow. "Are you sure?"

"Reasonably. It's true the brakes are shot. Obviously they can't take a steep grade. But they seem to do well enough on level ground. I tested 'em out when I parked her under the trees and they worked fine. I think we'll make it to town. I wouldn't take a chance if I didn't think so."

"I trust your judgment."

The way she was looking at him, with the firelight dancing on her cheeks, had Jake's pulse roaring in his ears. Feeling suddenly like a kid back in high school, he glanced at his shoes and shrugged. "Yeah. Well. Thanks."

"Eunice and Opal want to camp here tonight."

He sighed. "I know."

"I'd kill for a steak and a hot shower. Think we could talk 'em into it?"

"I wish." With a groan, Jake leaned forward and propped his elbows on his knees. He glanced at his watch. "It's gonna be dark in about half an hour. As much as I hate to say it, I think driving the motor home at night, the way it is now, would be suicide. I know it sounds nuts, but I think we should stay put until day-light. Especially since we're not familiar with the roads." He tucked his chin into his shoulder and looked askance at her. "I thought about trying to hitch a ride to town and coming back with help, but considering the lack of traffic in these parts, my odds don't seem too good. Besides, I don't like the idea of leaving you women out here all by yourselves in the dark, even for a short time."

Lexie shivered. "Please don't."

Jake grinned. "Still afraid of the bears?"

"Of course I'm afraid." She glanced around as if one might be lurking nearby as they spoke. "But I'm more afraid of hitchhiking. Especially in this neck of the woods. I think you're right. We should just sit tight till morning." Lexie pointed at the sky with her stick. The clouds were dissipating and the sunset glowed red on the western horizon. "Looks like we'll be dry enough."

He nodded. "We can only hope."

Jake stretched the tarp over the gaping hole where the motor home roof had been. Then he secured it with the remaining bungee cords and an assortment of ropes that included a clothes-line and an extension cord. The interior of the motor home had air dried, and their sleeping bags and clothing had dried by the fire. Before long, it was pitch dark outside.

After several rousing games of gin rummy by firelight, every-one was ready to call it a night.

Once more, Eunice and Opal took the bed in the back of the motor home. Lexie crawled into her bed above the cab, and Jake tried to find a comfortable spot on the floor.

No such luck.

He tossed and turned and thrashed about, but it seemed that no matter what position he chose, he was miserable. Maybe a little conversation with Lexie would take his mind off his knotted shoulders and the pain that throbbed in his temples.

"Pssst."

"Hmm?" Lexie flopped over the edge of her bed, her silky hair shining in the moonlight.

He fought the urge to reach up and see if it was as soft as it looked. "Just wondered if you could sleep."

"No."

"Why not?"

"The tarp keeps rattling in the breeze. It's like trying to sleep under a flock of flapping birds."

Jake chuckled. "I could trade you places, if you want."

"And sleep on the floor with the mice? No thanks."

There was a smile in her voice that warmed his blood. "The mice aren't so bad. I think they're keeping me warm."

"Ah. Lucky mice."

Jake's heart skipped a beat. Was she flirting with him or just making conversation? Not sure what she meant by that comment, he chose to play it safe and changed the subject. He sure wished he could see her face. "I think Eunice and Opal passed out the minute their heads hit the pillow. I can hear them both sawing logs back there."

"It's been a pretty exciting day. They're probably beat."

"I think they are just relaxed. With God on their side, I think it would take more than a runaway motor home to ruffle their feathers."

"I think maybe you're right. Don't you just love the way they lay their hands on the motor home and pray for healing?" Lexie giggled. "I want to be just like them when I grow up."

"Me too. Of course, without the support hose and stuff…"

The low tones of her mirth warmed his blood.

The position in which he was laying was causing his arms to

fall asleep. He pushed himself to a seated position against the kitchen cabinets and settled in for a good chat.

"I really mean it." Lexie went on. "I want the kind of happiness Nanna has had in her life. And I know I won't get it by working myself into an early grave."

"Amen to that."

"You been working too hard?"

"Way."

"Same for me." Lexie sighed. "It's ridiculous. In five years, this is the first vacation I've taken. And I only took it under duress."

"Really?"

"Yeah. I was worried about Nanna, so I insisted on coming along."

"You mean Eunice didn't…"

"Didn't what?"

Jake ran his hand over his face and chuckled. "All this time I thought you came along because Gran invited you to be my date."

"Your…*date?*" Lexie flopped back on her mattress and laughed. "You thought I was here as your date? That's a riot."

Wounded, Jake sat up. "Why is that so funny?"

"For one thing, you hate my guts."

"I don't hate your guts. I never hated your guts."

"Okay. I'll rephrase. Until recently, you didn't give a rip about my guts."

"Hey. I've seen the light. Now I happen to be very fond of your guts."

Lexie stopped laughing and dropped over the edge of her bed and peered through the moonlight into his eyes. Without the roof to filter the light, Jake could see her face quite clearly. And it was oh, so beautiful.

His central nervous system shut down.

"Really?" she whispered.

"Really—" he whispered back and drew himself to his knees—"and all the rest of you, for that matter." He touched her nose.

She reached out and gently pushed at his forehead. "You're just saying that because you're stuck out here in the middle of nowhere with me and are afraid of being murdered in your bed by Opal's scary granddaughter."

He knee-walked a tad closer, bringing himself within a foot of her face as she dangled from the overhead bunk. "You don't scare me." He chuckled. "Anymore."

"And I don't think you're a pompous poop. Anymore."

They laughed and hovered within twelve inches of each other, neither one backing into the relative comfort of their personal spaces. Unable to resist, Jake reached forward and ran his fingers through the shiny strands of her hair. As he'd known it would be, it was soft, tantalizing. Like the woman herself.

Lexie went still and, in the dim light, he could see her eyes flashing, searching his for meaning.

"They—" he gestured over his shoulder to the sleeping compartment that contained the two older women—"have a bet." Even though the grandmothers were asleep and snoring, he kept his voice as low as possible.

"A bet? About what?"

"Us."

"Us? Uh-oh. Is this going to embarrass me?"

"I don't know." He grinned. "I overheard them talking earlier. They bet—" Laughter welled and he suddenly felt silly.

"What?"

"Nothing."

"C'mon. What?" Her low laughter gave him courage.

"They bet that I'm going to kiss you."

Her eyes grew round. "They said that? To each other? Out loud?"

"Yep."

"Why, those little…those little…"

"Matchmakers?"

"Yes!" A tiny smile pushed at her cheeks. "And just when is this kiss supposed to take place?"

"According to my grandmother, soon."

"How soon?"

"That…would be up to you."

"Oh." Lexie gripped the back of the driver's seat and strained a bit closer. "Well. In that case, how does right now strike you?"

Eight

ake's heart did a full gainer with a half twist, and for the first time since high school, he found himself shaking at the idea of kissing a girl. He had to clear his throat before he could make a sound. "Strikes me fine."

"Good. 'Cause I hate to procrastinate. Nanna always says, 'Never put off till tomorrow, what you can do today.'"

"Smart woman."

Lexie grinned. "Me or Nanna?"

"Both." Raising his hands he cupped her cheeks in his palms. "Only problem with this plan is—" *What was he, some kind of idiot pointing out problems at a time like this?*— "They, uh, won't be able to settle their bet."

"Then I guess you'll just have to kiss me again. When they're watching. Consider this a practice round."

"I could do that," Jake murmured against her lips. "I could certainly do that."

He kissed Lexie good night. Several times. And it was during the last, lingering kiss that he knew he was a goner. She was like no other woman he'd ever met. Dated. Kissed. Lexie was one of a kind, and he'd be a fool to let her go.

She clung to his neck as he stood.

"Good night," he whispered against her cheek.

"Yes. It is."

He kissed the palm of the hand that had been resting against his chest, then ducked into the relative safety of his sleeping bag. It wasn't until a long time after Lexie's soft breathing became regular that he was finally able to drift off into dreams of trailers and smiling grandmothers and kisses that made him feel as though he could fly.

The following morning, Lexie stretched languidly in her sleeping bag and yawned. She'd been having such a beautiful dream, about Jake, and kissing Jake, and sitting in the moonlight with…

She froze. That was no dream. She brought her hands to her mouth and touched her lips. He'd really kissed her.

From what she could see between the cracks as a light spring breeze lifted and dropped the tarp that was tied over her bed, it promised to be a nice day. No, a fabulous day. The dark clouds had rolled back, and the deep, blue Montana sky was breathtaking. And Jake had kissed her. Even though it was still early in the morning, the temperature was already rising, along with her spirits.

Today they would find civilization.

Lexie pondered that notion with mixed emotions.

It would be more than wonderful to sleep in her own bed again and shampoo her hair under the hot spray of her shower. Even so, she was surprised to find that she was going to miss being on the road with Eunice and Opal, and, most especially, Jake.

It was too bad. The trip was ending just as she was really getting to know him. And admire him. And…care for him.

She traced a hole in the tarp with her fingertip. Would he think her too presumptuous if she called him once they got home? It was hard to tell with Jake. He was an old-fashioned kind of guy. If he wanted to go out with her, he would call.

But what if he didn't?

"Hi."

Startled, Lexie rolled over to discover Jake standing at the edge of her bed, his handsome grin mere inches from her face. She pushed her tangled hair back out of her eyes. "Oh! Uh, hi there!"

She scrambled back away from him and hoped that the sandman hadn't been too generous that night. Half hiding behind her pillow, she wished that he'd go away until after she'd brushed her teeth, washed her face, and applied some makeup.

"And how are you this morning?" His grin was familiar. The kind of grin two people exchanged when they'd spent part of the previous evening sharing an intimate moment.

"I'm fine," she squeaked.

"Looks like it's gonna be a nice day today."

"Mmm," she agreed through tight lips. Anything to protect him from her undoubted halitosis.

He leaned forward and propped his elbows on her bed. Lexie peeped at him from behind the hem of her sleeping bag and tried to look nonchalant. But it was hard. Have mercy, he was handsome first thing in the morning. It wasn't fair.

"I was thinking if we left right away, I'd take us all out to breakfast. My treat." Lexie's pulse surged. He looked so boyish and hopeful, standing there, smiling. Even in her state of dishevelment, the way he was looking at her made her feel special. Beautiful.

"You're going to need your wallet for that, big spender." She couldn't resist teasing him.

His face fell. "Oh. Right. Dumb idea."

"No, no. Not dumb!" In fact it was the best idea she'd heard all week. "I bet Eunice and Nanna would float you a loan."

"True. They do know where I live."

"Then let's get this show on the road. I can't think of anything I'd rather do than go out to breakfast." Realizing what she'd just said, she laughed and backpedaled a bit. "Okay, there are some things I'd rather do."

His smile was knowing. "Good. Then it's a date."

"What's a date?"

With a jaunty nod, he pushed away from the edge of her bed, and whistling a happy tune, swung outside the motor home door and began to make preparations to go. "Hey, Jake! A date to do what?" Was he talking about breakfast or another kiss? No answer. Didn't matter. She was spending time with Jake and that was enough. "It's a date." Lexie repeated the words to herself, her heart thrumming with joy at his words. So what if the date included their grandmothers? They had to start somewhere.

Yes indeed, it was shaping up to be a glorious day. As she wrestled her way out of her sleeping bag, Lexie had a feeling that all their troubles were behind them. They had to be. After all, what else could go wrong?

"I don't believe this." Jake groaned and tapped on the console behind the steering wheel.

"What?"

"This can't be happening."

"What?" Wringing her hands, Lexie leaned toward Jake and strained to see what he was talking about.

They'd only traveled about a mile that morning in the topless motor home, and already the engine was coughing and chugging in a most alarming fashion. Their speed had slowed from an unhealthy twenty miles per hour to a downright sickly five miles per hour. Odd, considering Jake was practically pushing the accelerator through the rotten floorboards.

"Jake, please. Tell me what's wrong."

Grabbing the bill of his ball cap, he savagely twisted it back and forth on his head. His words fired from between his lips like bullets. "I should have known."

"Known what? What is it you should have known?"

The knitting needles that had been cheerfully clicking away behind them fell silent.

Jake exhaled long and slow. "I think we're out of gas."

Lexie's gasp was echoed by the grandmothers.

He flipped a switch marked "reserve tank" back and forth. "Reserve tank must be empty too." He beat on the dash with his fist. When that didn't accomplish anything productive, he punched the steering wheel and took Percival's name in vain for good measure.

"Out of gas?" Lexie felt the muscles in the back of her neck begin to bunch. "How can that be? We filled up before we left Tuttlesville."

He turned his baleful gaze on her. "Obviously, the fuel gage is stuck. And since this barge guzzles more fuel than a 747..." he let her draw her own conclusion as he coasted over onto the shoulder.

"What are we going to do?"

"*We* are not going to do anything. *I* am going to hitch a ride into town and get some gas." Twisting in his seat, he looked over his shoulder at the grandmothers. "Gran, you and Opal might want to get your mad money out of your...uh...your place where you keep your mad money—" he gestured to his chest—"there." With that last edict, he ripped off his safety belt and swung out of the driver's seat.

Before he could leave, Eunice stopped him. "Honey, come here a minute."

Jake moved back to the orange plaid booth. "What can I do for you, Gran?"

"You can give us your hands and let us ask the good Lord to place a hedge of protection over you."

Jake glanced back at Lexie, his smile tender. "I'd love that."

They laid their hands on his arms and prayed for his safety. When they'd finished, he leaned over the tabletop and kissed them each on the cheek.

After rummaging through her brassiere and purse, Eunice withdrew a small wad of cash and several credit cards and pressed them into his hand. "Here's what's left of our mad money, honey. Don't spend it all in one place."

"I won't. Gotta save some to take all you dolls out to breakfast."

Their girlish twitterings at his teasing words caused a lump to form in Lexie's throat. She followed him and clutched his arm just as he was poised to jump out of the motor home.

"Jake, do you really think hitching is such a good idea?" She hated the idea of him leaving them. But truth be told, she feared more for his safety than for their own.

He leaped from the motor home, then placing his hands on her hips, assisted Lexie to the ground. He swung her around to face him, seeming to sense her anxiety. His voice was gentle, as was his gaze.

"Hey, don't worry. I'll be back before you know it." Reaching out, he brushed a strand of hair out of her eyes and let his fingers linger on her cheek.

They stood and looked at each other for a long, electric moment. Unspoken messages of something that was becoming more than just a passing attraction flashed between them. Overhead, birds chirped. A light breeze stirred the newly budding branches of a nearby stand of trees. The air was pure and fresh and smelled of sunlight and yesterday's cleansing spring rains.

Lexie's entire being was charged with awareness and she knew these images would be forever imprinted on her brain. Slowly, she allowed her grip to slide from his bicep and down his arm. It felt as if some giant, clumsy butterflies crashed about in her stomach as he grasped her hand and then, drawing her forward, kissed her on the temple.

"You'll be fine," he whispered. "I have faith."

"But what about you?" Lexie felt like blubbering. Silly tears pricked her eyes, and she blinked, forcing them back. His free arm circled her waist and she leaned into his embrace, loving the feel of his solid chest beneath her cheek.

"I'll be fine too. Eunice and Opal prayed for me, remember?"

She sniffed, then grinned. "Right. Of course you'll be fine. I have faith too, you know."

An echoing grin captured his lips, and just as he pressed his wonderful smile to her own, a rusty old pickup truck came chugging down the road toward them.

Rats! Lexie shot a peevish look at the rattletrap Chevy loaded with what looked to be several of Percival's less savory relatives. *Talk about lousy timing.* The only truck to pass for eons and it had to pick this very moment to intrude.

She sighed as Jake dropped his hands from around her waist and thrust his thumb into the air.

The truck slowed to a stop in front of them. There were two men in the cab of the truck and two in the bed. Only the driver was awake and he seemed a little rummy. If the stench of alcohol that fouled the air immediately surrounding the truck was anything to go by, he and his buddies were just now coming home from an all-night binge.

"Need a ride into town?" His slurred words had an affable enough quality, but that didn't make Lexie feel any better. The driver closed one eye—probably to block out the dual images that swam before him.

Lexie quailed and gripped the placket of Jake's shirt with shaking fists. "No!"

Jake took an eager step forward, unintentionally dragging her along with him as he went. "Yes!" He stopped and shot her a befuddled glance. "No?"

"No!" she hissed, still clutching his shirt and stumbling at his side. "Going with them would be insane."

Jake gave his head a tolerant shake. "Oh, come on."

"Oh, come on? *Oh, come on?*" She was at a loss for more convincing prose. Trust a man to ignore the extreme danger of a situation. Especially an air-cowboy like Jake. "Don't go. I'm serious. Please, Jake. Please, oh, please, oh, please. I don't want you to go with them. They're scary. I think I saw one of them on America's Most Wanted."

Jake's chuckle had a parental quality that made Lexie want to scream. "Honey, we can't wait here all day for another car to come by."

"We won't have to wait all day." Had he just called her *honey?*

"How do you know?"

"I have faith?" Her voice was high and tinny.

Jake laughed. "I'm glad to hear it. Put it to good use and pray for me. I have a feeling I'm going to need it."

Percival's lookalike was growing bored. "Well, are ya comin' or not?" He gunned the engine and briefly roused the boys in the back.

Jake nodded. "I'm coming."

"Come on then. You can ride up front with me 'n' Duke here."

"Okay." To Lexie he muttered, "I can drive if he falls asleep."

"That's not funny."

"Sorry." Suddenly Jake grabbed Lexie and gave her a quick kiss on the lips—but brief or not, it turned her knees to mush. He turned to leave, then stopped short. "Lexie?"

"Hmm?"

Covering her hands with his, he began to pry her fingers from his placket. "My shirt?"

"Yes?" Her head was still reeling from the soft pressure of his lips against hers. Why was he yammering on about his clothes at a time like this?

His smile was spine tingling. "I want to take it with me?"

"Oh!" She gave a nervous giggle. "Of course."

In less time than it took to squeeze her hand, Jake had shoved the snoring Duke to an upright position, wedged in beside him, and was waving good-bye. Duke's head flopped against Jake's shoulder, but Jake seemed not to notice, for, as they pulled away, he only had eyes for Lexie.

"Bye." She whispered the word around the thickness in her throat, as she watched him disappear in a cloud of dust. "Honey."

Nine

As hour passed into endless hour, Lexie began to pace at the side of the road. A watched pot never boiled, she knew, but she couldn't help but stare down the road, hoping to catch a glimpse of Jake. Over the course of the morning, several vehicles had rumbled by. Each time, Lexie's heart leaped into her throat, then plunged into her shoes when she realized Jake had not yet returned.

Lunchtime came and went. Eunice and Opal tempted her with the remaining can of applesauce, but she couldn't eat.

She couldn't swallow.

Fear closed its icy fingers around her throat as visions of Jake lying somewhere in a ditch, broken and bleeding, tormented her. How, she wondered, as she chewed the polish off her thumbnail, could Opal and Eunice nap at a time like this?

Even though she knew the answer to that, it still astounded her. They had prayed for God's protection. They had done their part. They trusted God to do his. No matter what the outcome, Opal and Eunice knew that God was in control. That was something Lexie knew she had yet to come to terms with. But knowing that didn't stop her from staring down the road, as though by doing so she had some control over Jake's return. As though by sheer will, she could cause him to appear.

"How are you doing, honey?" Opal hovered at her shoulder.

Lexie knew her smile was wan. "Worried."

"That's natural, but certainly not necessary."

"I know. Worrying never accomplishes anything."

"That's true enough, too. But I don't want you to worry, because Jake is fine. Eunice and I prepared his way through prayer. God is with him. With such a traveling companion, what could possibly happen that God can't fix?"

"You really believe that, don't you?"

"Of course."

Tears of some nebulous emotion pooled against Lexie's lower lashes. "How?"

"Faith is a process, child. A process one begins by simply asking the good Lord for it. It's a gift, freely given if one is seeking."

"Do you really think that someday I could have a faith as strong as yours?"

"Honey." Opal patted her back and chuckled. "With your perseverance, you'll have twice my faith and more."

Lexie blinked back the tears and pasted a broad smile on her face. "Come on, Nanna. Let's go play some rummy."

"Now that's the spirit!"

With a heavy sigh, Lexie decided that she was doing no good and she might as well let God take over. It took a Herculean effort, but she tore her eyes from the horizon and forced herself to go inside the motor home.

There, she crawled into the orange plaid booth, and as midday gave way to afternoon, Lexie prayed for Jake's safety and for an unwavering faith. Just like Nanna's.

As Lexie lay, her cheek stuck to the woodlook Formica tabletop, her eyes scrunched tightly shut, her fists clutched beneath her chin, Jake's voice penetrated her muzzy brain from far, far away.

He was calling…calling…*Eunice…Opal…Lexie…*

He was in trouble. Terrible, terrible trouble. He needed her.

No, no. Please, Jake. Don't walk toward the light! I still need you here!

Yes, she noted with some vague satisfaction. She needed him. Wanted to be with him. More than anything. He couldn't leave her here, just as they were getting acquainted. Just when she thought there might be some hope of a relationship with him. *Come back, Jake!*

"Lexie? Where are you?"

I'm here, Jake! Fight to stay with us, Jake!

"Lexie? I'm back."

Startled, she tore her cheek away from the tabletop and sat bolt upright. Confusion clouded her thoughts. Had she been sleeping? It sounded like Jake was calling from somewhere outside.

She scrambled from the orange plaid seat and stumbled out of the motor home. Head turning, eyes darting, she searched for him. As she reached the edge of the road, she spotted him coming toward her, carrying a gas can, and looking about as harried as any human being could look. Off in the distance, the truck that had picked him up rattled back down the road.

A joy she'd never known before crowded into Lexie's throat at the sight of Jake's tall, strong form striding toward her. Her emotions got the better of her and, as tears of happiness and relief spilled down her cheeks, she broke into a run. When she reached him, she threw herself into his arms, nearly knocking him and the gas can over in her exuberance.

Face pressed into his neck, she blubbered, laughing and crying at the same time. "Oh, thank God you're back! I prayed and prayed and prayed some more."

Jake grinned, the lines in his face easing with his own relief.

He dropped the gas can, gathered her into his embrace, and rocked her back and forth.

"I'm so glad you're safe. I was so worried. When you didn't come back and didn't come back and...oh, I didn't know what to think. All those guys were so drunk and there you were—"

"Hey, hey, hey." Jake pulled back slightly and, cupping her cheeks in the palms of his hands, looked into her eyes. "Shh." His breath tickled her lips. "I'm fine. Really."

"Ohh."

The tiny lines at the corners of his eyes forked and he brought his nose to hers. "But thank you for praying for me. And...caring."

"I do. Care."

"Me too."

For a long moment, they held one another, drinking each other in with their eyes. Time seemed suspended as they stood there in the middle of the road in the middle of nowhere and realized they were in the middle of beginning to fall.

Fall in need. In want. In like.

In...love.

Ever so slowly, Jake brought his lips to hers, and Lexie clutched his arms to keep from falling down. Their sigh was simultaneous and filled with longing. Lexie stood on tiptoe, reveling in his gentle touch, her heart fluttering beneath her breast. His whiskers rasped pleasantly against the soft skin of her cheeks as he lifted his mouth from hers and rained a trail of tiny kisses along the edge of her cheek.

"Umm." Her eyes drifted shut and she arched back in his arms to give him better access to the side of her jaw. "I'm really, really glad you're back."

His chuckle rumbled pleasantly in her ear. "I'm really, really glad to be back."

"We should probably get out of the middle of the road." Lexie lifted her arms, and looping them around his neck, nuzzled his cheek with her nose.

"Yeah." He made no move to leave.

Neither did she.

A short while later, Lexie hovered over Jake's shoulder as he poured the gas he'd bought into the motor home. The relief in her voice was evident as she chattered a mile a minute about faith and fear and the fear of faith. Her sigh was lighter than air, and Jake had never enjoyed listening to anyone quite so much.

"I was beginning to think you might have been kidnapped by Duke and the gang, you were gone so long."

Tucking his chin, Jake peered over his shoulder at her and grinned. "Sorry about that. Actually, the ride to town was pretty uneventful, aside from Duke's loud snoring in my ear. You'll be happy to know that we are only about four miles away from the airport."

"You're kidding."

"Nope. Eunice got us there after all. We took the deserted route, but it's all going to work out fine in the long run. I found a little restaurant and a motel, then used Eunice's credit card to reserve us each a room. Then I went to the airport and let them know I'd be picking up the plane we chartered in the morning, about a week earlier than I'd planned."

A shadow of melancholy crossed Lexie's face. "What about the motor home?"

Jake finished filling the tank and screwed the gas cap back into place. "We can't drive it home in this condition. The airport agreed to let us park it in their lot until we figure out what to do about it. We can cover it with plastic and hope for the best until then." Hands on thighs, he pushed himself to a standing position.

He took a step toward Lexie and pulled her into his arms. Oh, it was good to hold her. He'd never before experienced this wonderful feeling of coming home when he held a woman.

"You know—" she ran her hands around his waist, locking her fingers at the small of his back—"I'm really glad we're going home, but somehow I'm going to miss all this. I know it sounds weird, but I'm almost sad it's over."

Jake drew her close and pressed her head against his heart. He knew exactly how she felt.

"You know," he said, "we could do this again someday."

She gazed up at him, her eyes shining. "Really? You mean it?"

"Well, we'd need to put a roof on the motor home, of course."

"Of course."

"And we'd need to get the brakes done…and the plumbing fixed…and the wiring repaired, and—"

"Are you sure you want to do this?" Lexie interrupted, laughing.

"If you promise to come with me, yes."

"I promise."

"I'll hold you to that promise."

"How about if you just hold me?"

Jake buried his nose in her neck and inhaled the floral scent that was uniquely Lexie. "Deal."

Opal and Eunice, having heard voices, were watching their grandchildren out the motor home window.

"You know, Eunice, all these years, and it never once dawned on me to try to get these two together."

Eunice shook her head in wonder. "I did once, but I let it go when they didn't seem interested. Lord knows I've tried with plenty of other nice girls. Jake can be so stubborn, I'd all but given up."

"Let go and let God, as they say."

"Amen to that."

"You owe me ten dollars."

"For what?"

"Look there." Opal pointed out the window. "They're kissing."

"And so they are. I knew it. But I'm afraid it is *you*, my dear, who owe *me* ten dollars."

"What? That's *not* the agreement."

"It most certainly was!"

"Was not!"

"Was too!"

Opal sighed. Arguing with Eunice was always fruitless. "Eunice, do you suppose that we are having all this trouble because the Lord doesn't really want us camping in a motor home?"

Eunice's shrug was philosophical. "Perhaps. Maybe owning the motor home was more about them than us."

"Maybe."

"Perhaps we should look into a nice timeshare condo at a resort somewhere. Do a little parasailing out over the ocean…"

Opal shook her head. "Here we go again."

Ten

ne year later, on another lovely spring day in
Tacoma, Eunice A. Kelley and Opal Dinsmore, best
friends and neighbors, became shirttail in-laws. And
they couldn't have been more delighted.

The beautiful ceremony that united their grandchildren in
holy matrimony had concluded only moments before. Lexie and
Jake were now standing on the church steps beneath a shower of
birdseed, gazing at each other with adoration.

With much puffing and exclamation, the elderly women battled
their way through the crowds to stand beside the young couple.
Eyes misty, Eunice tugged on the sleeve of Jake's tuxedo jacket.
Upon capturing his attention away from his bride, she pressed a
set of keys into his hand.

"Sweetheart," she began, breathless with excitement and exer-
tion, "Opal and I wanted to give you a very special wedding gift."

Jake lifted a teasing brow. "Keys?"

Eunice batted his arm and laughed. "And not just any old
keys, you old poop." She pointed out to the street.

Jake's and Lexie's gaze traveled to the spot she indicated and,
gasping in unison, they rushed down the steps to the sidewalk.
For there, parked at the curb in front of the church, festooned
with balloons, streamers, and a string of tin cans clinging to the
back bumper, was the motor home.

"Honey," Eunice exclaimed in glee, "are you just going to stand there staring all day or are you going to carry your bride over the threshold?"

Laughing, happier than he'd ever been in his life, Jake swept Lexie into his arms, and much to the crowd's delight, lifted her into the motor home. Once inside, they were amazed at the changes that had taken place over the last twelve months. The old girl sported a new roof, bathroom walls, carpet, curtains, and cushions. The plumbing worked, as did the electricity, and the engine roared to life at the turn of Jake's new key.

Jake smiled at his new bride, loving the way she looked perched on the passenger seat—a seat fully equipped this time with a state-of-the-art seat belt. "Shall we take if for a spin, Mrs. Kelley?"

Her answering smile was a thing of beauty. "I can't think of anything I'd like better, Mr. Kelley."

Giddy at the prospect of a new adventure, Jake pulled away from the curb and waved to the last of their wedding guests as they headed down the street.

In the passenger side rearview mirror, Lexie could see Eunice and Opal clutching each other and waving wildly.

"Where to?" Jake wondered as they wove through town toward the open road.

"How about the Flying Horse Ranch?"

Jake grinned. "I was hoping you'd say that."

"I think Opal and Eunice would be glad to see the kids get their bedroom back, especially now that Percival is out of jail and trying hard to change his ways."

"Um-hmm. And I can charter a plane from Tuttlesville to Seattle and from there…well, I was thinking Hawaii to check on

Gran's new timeshare condo." He pointed at the set of keys that dangled from the ignition. "One of these is labeled Maui."

"Mmm. Maybe we could go on that parasailing trip that Eunice said was so great."

"That sounds like fun."

As Lexie snapped her seat belt over the voluminous skirts of her wedding dress, she sighed. "You know, Jake, I'm going to miss the motor home. I learned more about myself in the few days we traveled together than I learned in a lifetime of work days."

"True. But don't despair. I have a feeling we'll be learning a great deal about ourselves in the coming week."

"Why is that?"

"Well, Gran didn't go into too much detail, but she did mention that her condo—the one she bought sight-unseen from the newspaper I might add—needed a little…uh, TLC."

"Uh-oh." Lexie groaned, then laughed. "Well, I'm in the mood for a little tender loving care. How about you?"

Jake caught her hand in his and brought her fingertips to his lips. "A lifetime's worth."

Dear Reader:

My wedding day, July 22, 1978, was probably the hottest day on record in the delightful town of Silverton, Oregon. It was around 103 degrees in the shade and we picked the blistering hour of 2 P.M. for our ceremony to begin. My face was beet red, and the makeup meant to hide this fact had slid off my face before I even began my trip down the aisle.

My husband, Matt, was also barbecued to perfection in his polyester suit and his stylish afro hairdo. I wanted nothing more than to rip off my wedding dress, but not for the usual reasons a bride dallies in this fantasy. No, I wanted to run through the sprinkler, as the air conditioning in the church was on the fritz. Unfortunately for me, there was no time for such folderol. Too bad, as I believe my husband would have joined me.

Being college students in the late seventies, our priority was not a lavish wedding. I wore a Gunny Sax dress that my mother forced me to buy (I wanted a new winter coat). My mother-in-law harvested her rose garden for the occasion, and my father twisted the arm of a family friend to act as photographer. The reception was a makeshift cake and ice cream affair in the church basement, and when the time came to throw the bouquet, my father-in-law—having been a veteran of the college football team—intercepted the pass, much to the dismay of all the single girls present. I think a couple of them are still chasing him…

When the reception was over, my new husband and I left the church in separate cars. Honestly. I rode with the maid of honor, and he, with the best man to my mom and dad's house, where we opened our presents and feasted on a dinner catered by my dad.

To one who didn't know, this dubious beginning would have pointed to a dubious future together. And at times, I must admit, we've hit our share of bumps in the road. But now, after nearly twenty-three years, I can honestly say I would do it all again. In a heartbeat. Perhaps, I'd make a few style changes and move the ceremony to a less tropical time of day, but I'd marry the man all over again. God knew, even if I didn't, at the tender young age of twenty, that Matt was the perfect man for me. He was then. He is now. Every day I thank God for blessing me with this wonderful husband and father to our daughters, one of whom, I might add, was born on our wedding day. Not THE wedding day, for heaven's sake, but sixteen years later, July 22, 1994. I couldn't think of a nicer day for her to be born.

Wishing you all the love I have stumbled upon,

Burrito Casserole

This recipe is guaranteed to be the first one eaten at a potluck. I love it because it's easy and it freezes beautifully. Great to take on those camping trips in the motor home (provided the oven works).

Ingredients:

1 1/2 lb. to 2 lbs. hamburger
3 cloves of minced garlic
1 pkg. taco seasoning mix
1 large can chili (or some of Karen's chili from page 401, yum yum!)
2 cans refried beans
1 can diced Ortega green chilis
1 can diced olives
1 pkg. flour tortillas
1 to 2 lbs of medium cheddar cheese, grated

In a skillet, brown hamburger with minced garlic and taco seasoning. When the meat is browned, mix in chili, 1 can refried beans, green chilies, olives. Set aside.

In nine-by-thirteen-inch baking dish, smear some beans on the bottom of the dish, then make layers in the following order: (1) tortillas, (2) beans and meat mix, (3) cheese. Continue in this order till dish is filled, then top with layer of cheese. Bake at 350 degrees for 45 minutes or until cheese is bubbly.

Excellent when served with rice and a salad.

Giggles

Just Rewards

One afternoon, Christopher's father picked him up early from school to take Chris to a dental appointment. Knowing that the parts for the school play were supposed to be posted today, the father asked his son if he had gotten a part.

Christopher enthusiastically announced that indeed he had gotten a part. "I play a man who's been married for twenty years."

"That's great, son. Keep up the good work, and before you know it, they'll be giving you a speaking part."

No Wife of Mine!

Husband to wife: "Look, you just stick to your cooking and cleaning and laundry and carpooling and parenting. No wife of *mine* is going to go to work!"

The Best Husband of All

"An archaeologist is the best husband a woman can have; the older she gets, the more interested he is in her."

Agatha Christie

Who Needs Britannica?

Ad seen in newspaper recently: For sale by owner: complete set of Encyclopedia Britannica. 45 volumes. Excellent condition. $1,000 or best offer. No longer needed. Got married last week. Husband knows everything.

The Art of Conversation

The real art of conversation is not only to say the right thing at the right place, but to leave unsaid the wrong thing at the tempting moment.

Dorothy Nevill

Makes Sense!

Bobby was thrilled to be a part of his sister's wedding. His mother and sister explained very clearly what his duties were: to walk down the aisle with the ring on pillow, then present the ring to the groom.

The big day came, and when it was time for Bobby to head down the aisle, he did so happily. But everyone was puzzled when the little boy took two steps, then turned to those beside him and growled in his fiercest voice, then two more steps and more growls. So he went, eliciting giggles and titters, until he reached the groom, face beaming.

After the ceremony, Bobby's mother asked him what he'd been doing, and with a huge smile the little boy replied, "I was being the Ring Bear!"

Bride on
the Run

Karen Ball

One

*T*wenty feet.

No, maybe twenty-five. Okay, thirty at the most. Thirty more feet to climb down. Couldn't take more than ten minutes.

Even less time if the rose trellis gave way.

Ten minutes at the most, then she'd be free.

"For the *love* of heaven! Alexandria Anastasia Wingate, would you kindly remove your foot from me hand."

Alex glanced down, shooting her lifelong friend and one-time nanny an apologetic grin. "Oops."

"Oops, indeed."

Leave it to Birdy to make a snort sound dignified. The older woman reached up to push Alex's white-slippered foot off her hand and back onto the trellis they both were hanging from. "Yer slippers may be soft as velvet, m'dear, but I'd prefer you watch where ye're stepping, *if* ye don't mind. I've little need of yer dainty footprint on my poor, arthritic knuckles."

Alex shot Birdy another look and had to bite her lip to keep from laughing.

Bertilda Hiffenstone was, ever and always, the picture of decorum. There she was, dressed in an elegant though understated summer suit, a small, veiled hat perched atop her tidy, every-hair-in-its-place bun. The fact that she was dangling from a rose trellis a good thirty feet above solid ground didn't lessen the impression she gave of all that was prim and proper.

Well, not much, anyway.

What *did* mar the image somewhat was the wriggling ball of fur tucked inside Birdy's jacket.

"Dusty, you behave!" Alex scolded, knowing even as she spoke it was hopeless. The terrier's clear displeasure was no surprise. Like most silkies, Dusty was utterly convinced that she was both the focus and the commander of every event that came into her tiny, furry life. She wanted to be front and center, directing everyone and everything with sharp, concise yaps. To that end, she kept scrambling out from under Birdy's tightly buttoned jacket, her dainty head stopping only when it came in contact with Birdy's firm chin.

"Get back in there, ye wretched rodent!" Birdy hissed, shoving Dusty back in place.

Oh, Alex thought with a grin, *if only I had a camera.* She'd love to preserve this scene for posterity. Ah well, picture or no picture, she'd have her memories. And her imagination for embellishment...

Oh yes, she'd be able to tease Birdy about this escapade for a very long time.

Provided, of course, they made it to solid ground alive.

Alex's fingers clutched at the trellis, and she leaned forward to rest a moment. As she did so, she drew in the fragrance of the roses growing all around her. Each bloom was a picture of manicured perfection—gloriously full, richly colored, and delightfully fragrant.

But then, her father wouldn't have had it any other way.

No, if there was one thing Charleston Franklin Wingate demanded in life—and, of course, that he got—it was perfection. In everything.

Alex shifted on the trellis, remembering how the house had looked that morning. White bows and garlands, hand formed from the finest silk, had been draped over doorways and windows, waiting to welcome visitors to the spacious, marble entryway of the Wingate estate. Glorious bouquets of spring blossoms adorned hallway tables; rose petals blushing in the softest hues of pink, peach, and yellow were strategically sprinkled here and there, just so, across tables, floors, rugs, and walkways.

The house, the grounds, the gardens where the wedding was to be held…it was all exactly as her father had ordered. The picture of perfection.

He accepted nothing less. Not ever.

Except, of course, where his daughter was concerned.

"Alexandria…please!"

Alex peered down at Birdy through the layers of gauze that kept falling over her face. Darn! Why hadn't she at least left the veil in her room when she crawled out the window?

"Will you stop *squirmin'*, gel?" Birdy's Canadian inflections were never more evident than when she was under pressure. And since Alex loved the sound of Birdy's accent—the woman was as purely "Avonlea" as they came—she'd made a point from her earliest years of keeping Birdy under one pressure or another.

Of course, that meant Alex was generally under pressure as well.

Like now.

Clutching at the trellis with one hand, Alex swept the cascading veil back off her face. "I'd love to stop squirming, but this isn't easy, you know! This cursed dress is going to be the death of me!" She emphasized the words with a kick at the hem of her long, white dress.

An action she immediately regretted. True, the kick knocked

her dress out of her way. Unfortunately, it carried enough *oomph* to jerk her other foot off its less-than-firm perch on the wooden trellis.

With a yelp, Alex grabbed at her perch, gripping it for all she was worth as her feet pedaled thin air, seeking a foothold.

Birdy, of course, was no help whatsoever. With a high-pitched *"Eek!"* she swatted at Alex's airborne feet with one hand while pulling herself firmly against the trellis with the other.

"Birdy! For the love of—!" Her comment was cut off with relief when one foot finally connected with something solid.

"Oooh! Get *off* me head, ye silly nit!"

Catching her balance for one precious second, Alex slid her other foot onto the wood of the trellis, then did as Birdy so graciously requested. Alex hung there a moment, catching her breath, commanding her heartbeat to return to a normal rate.

"Really, Alexandria! Was that necessary?"

She shot a look down to Birdy—a hot retort on her lips—and promptly lost what little composure she'd regained.

Birdy's once-stylish little hat was now mashed down on her head, the veil all askew. As for the dear woman's bun of hair…well, apparently Alex's scrambling feet had scrambled Birdy's graying, chestnut hair as well. *Rat's nest* was far too kind a term.

The woman looked a total fright.

Oh, my kingdom *for a camera!* Alex bit her lips fiercely. Giving in to her laughter would only make matters worse. Far worse. And for a painfully long time. If there was one thing Birdy could not endure it was being laughed at.

Alex shifted her hold on the trellis and they continued their descent. "Birdy, I'm so sorry. I…well, it's this dratted dress. It keeps getting in my way."

"Oh, and I suppose ye think I've got it easier, then?" Birdy pushed her hat out of her eyes and blew at the dangling veil with a frustrated puff. "At least all you have to deal with is a weddin' dress. I've got this ridiculous beast of yours to manage, thank you very much."

As though on cue, the aforementioned "beast" chose that moment to pop out from under Birdy's jacket and give her trellis-clutching mistress a sound dressing-down.

Birdy's pointed glare only tickled Alex's funny bone that much more, and she lost the battle she'd been fighting with self-restraint. At her gale of giggles, Birdy pressed her thin lips even thinner and shook her head.

"Yer as hopeless as yer beastie, dear." So saying, the angular woman made a small hop backward and landed, at last, on firm ground with a soft *plop*. "Thanks be to heaven," she intoned, straightening her clothes.

As Alex stepped down to join her, Birdy lightly tapped the still-yapping Dusty on the bridge of her indignant nose. "Hush up, ye mongrel! Or I swear it's fricasseed beastie we'll be having for dinner."

"Birdy!"

She met Alex's look, utterly unrepentant. "Oh, away with yer outrage, my gel. It's an empty threat and ye know it."

Alex slipped her arm about Birdy's strong, albeit bony, shoulders. "Left your recipe for fricassee in your room again, did you, dear?"

Birdy's lips twitched as she fell into step alongside Alex. "Indeed, I did." She cast a sideways glance at Alex, and the tender regard Alex saw in those brown eyes completely belied Birdy's next words: "On a table, right next to my better judgment and sanity."

"Ah no, Birdy, my love—" Alex looped her elbow with Birdy's—"You lost those years ago." She smiled, hoping her gratitude showed in her eyes. For all that Birdy had been, her nanny as a child and her companion as an adult, agreeing to climb out a three-story window and clamber down a rose trellis was going above and beyond the call of duty.

Way above and beyond.

"Twenty-nine years ago, to be exact." Alex squeezed her friend's arm. "And I, for one, am awfully glad."

Birdy patted Alex's hand, looking inordinately pleased at the comment. But her words were as brusque as always. "And so ye should be, my gel. For it takes someone completely dotty to go along with this mad scheme of yours." She brushed at her clothes as they started walking. "Really, Alexandria, was the prospect of marrying so terrible?"

"No, not marriage itself," Alex said with a grunt as she gathered the long, sheer train of her dress in both her arms. "This thing might be a bride's dream for the wedding," she muttered, "but it's a pain in the neck for making a getaway."

Birdy's arched look spoke volumes.

"I know, I know, I should have made up my mind sooner."

"Ye did cut it a bit close, dear. I mean, really! An hour before yer wedding…ye couldn't have said something sooner?"

Alex tugged on the material, bunching it into as small a wad as she could, then stepped out. "I did! I told Daddy this morning at breakfast—"

Her friend snorted. "Oh, *much* better, of course."

"Birdy, you know as well as I do when Daddy's got his mind set on something, he's impossible to sway. I did tell him I wasn't going through with the marriage. And then when I put my foot down this morning…" She jerked her dress free from a twig that snagged it as she went past. "Well, you know how that ended."

Indeed, everyone in the three neighboring counties probably knew how that ended. Her father had exploded, telling her in no uncertain terms that she *was* getting married and she *would* be happy about it.

A gentle touch on her arm pulled her from her unhappy thoughts. Birdy's gaze was compassionate. "I know, child. Ye're only doing what you have to. Yer father just doesn't understand that you can't go against what's right just because he says so." She patted Alex's arm. "But don't you worry. God will honor the stand ye're takin'. And He'll help yer father understand."

Alex couldn't stop the laugh that escaped her at that, and she linked her arm with Birdy's. "Bertilda Hiffenstone, you never cease to amaze me! Imagine, after all these years, finding out you believe in miracles."

Birdy's indulgent chuckle warmed Alex's weary heart. If only she and her father communicated as well. If only they shared the same respect for one another that she and Birdy had developed.

But Alex's father was too busy being in charge to listen to much of anyone. Too busy telling everyone where to be and what to do. And most everyone he bellowed at hopped.

Most everyone but Alex. From her earliest days she'd butted heads with her father. He'd wanted a sweet, angelic little girl— what he got was an inveterate adventurer. No tree was too tall, no attic too dusty, no shed too dark to keep Alex out of it. Her father insisted she be dressed in frilly dresses, that she have her hair tied back with velvety ribbons...but nary a day went by that she didn't show up for dinner, soiled and tattered, hair going every which way because she'd used the ribbons for something far more important than hair—like tying sticks together to make a sword.

And then there was her bent for wounded things. She was

always dragging something home to be cared for, be it animal or human. Broken limbs and broken hearts, they seemed to be her specialty. Birdy and her mother said it was because God had blessed her with a tender heart.

Her father, on the other hand, often muttered something about a soft head. Clearly, Alex was not the little girl her father had dreamed of. He didn't understand her at all.

For years he'd urged her to take her place in society, to fill the role to which she'd been born—mainly to marry well and make her family look good. But Alex would just shake her head.

"I'm waiting on God, Daddy. He'll show me where I belong… and who I belong with." She'd said it a time after time; and each time, he'd give her that pained, tolerant look. She'd thought after all these years he was accepting it, that he believed as she did, that God was in control.

She'd been wrong.

When Alex's twenty-ninth birthday arrived last August and she was, as her father so succinctly put it, "Miserably devoid of prospects for marriage," he'd shown her just how wrong she was. "You need a husband, my girl," he said. "The right kind of husband."

"Daddy, God—"

"Seems to be otherwise involved, my dear. But don't worry, Daddy's on it."

Was he ever. In less than a month, he'd found the perfect suitor—to his mind at least. Oh, Shelton was all right. Shelton Everett III, to be exact, the eldest son of a wealthy business associate of her father's. Tall, well-built, proven in business and society, Shelton was, in her father's opinion, the perfect merger on every front, personal and business.

Alex had done everything she could to stall them both, but

finally, at the largest party of the social season, her father asked everyone for their attention. Alex had stood with the others, never suspecting what was coming—not even when Shelton and her father stood in front of everyone together. No, it hadn't been until her father announced, with much delight, that Shelton had asked for Alex's hand in marriage, that she realized what had happened.

She'd gotten engaged—and she hadn't even had anything to do with it.

She should have been firm. Should have simply laughed it off and said it wasn't true, but she couldn't. She just couldn't bear humiliating her father and Shelton in front of everyone.

And so it had progressed, all the while Alex trying to get her father to listen to her. And this morning she'd realized he never would. So she'd sat there, staring at her eggs Benedict, then finally blurted it out.

"I don't love him, Father."

Her father had pinned her with a look over the *Wall Street Journal*. "Indeed? A bit late to decide that, isn't it?"

"I know. I should have told you before now, but…well, you were so pleased by it all. So certain it was right, but it's not. Not for me."

He stared at her, not even noticing that his *Journal* was sagging into his cereal bowl. His look told her he couldn't believe his ears—but she didn't stop there.

"I can't get married today."

He blinked.

"Daddy?"

Her pulse raced. *Say something, Daddy. Anything…*

"Are you out of your *mind?*"

Well, okay. Anything but that. "I wish I could do this…that I could be what you want me to be—"

"All I want you to be is happy."

The sadness in her heart must have shown in her face because he flinched. "No, Daddy, you want me to be like you. To think and feel the way you do. But I don't. I...I can't. I don't know where I belong, what I'm supposed to do. God hasn't made that clear yet. All He's told me is...to wait."

He opened his mouth to argue, but she held up a hand to halt his words.

"Daddy, I tried. I really did. But this is wrong."

"Wrong? Wrong to want you married, cared for?"

"Wrong to ask me to go against what I know is right. What I know God is telling me to do—"

He leaned back in his chair. "God has far more important concerns than whether or not you marry Shelton."

"But that's just it, Daddy." She'd fought against the tears then. "He cares about my obedience, and marrying Shelton would be an act of disobedience to Him—"

"What about obedience to me?" His tone was curt. Cold, even. "What about that, Alexandria? What does your precious Bible say about obeying your father?"

"Daddy—"

"Come on, Alexandria. You're always so quick to quote verses at me."

She gripped her hands together in her lap. "'Anyone who loves his father or mother more than me is not worthy of me.'"

The quiet words hung there, suspended in the silence—and then outrage filled her father's face. "I *beg* your pardon?"

With a miserable sigh, she repeated it: "'Anyone who loves his father or mother more than me is not worthy of me.'"

"You're making that up. The Bible says children are to obey their parents. I read that myself—"

She gave him a knowing look—he hadn't picked up a Bible in years—and he at least had the grace to falter.

"Well…once. A while back."

Alex sighed.

"Okay, a *long* while back. But whether it was yesterday or more than ten years ago, I don't think the Bible has changed."

He gave her a glare she knew all too well—it was the look he usually reserved for employees just before they got the boot; the one that said he'd reached the end of his tolerance. Pointing to the stairs, he issued his final word on the subject. "You, young lady, will hie yourself to your room, put on that dress that cost me a small fortune, and prepare yourself to *get married!*"

It was no use to argue, she knew that. Pushing back her chair, she rose.

He watched her, jamming his fists into his pockets. "It's for the best, Alexandria. Trust me."

She didn't respond. She merely gave him one long look, then turned and walked from the room.

Ten minutes later, she and Birdy were out the window and on their way down the trellis.

"No sign of the coppers."

The hushed whisper pulled Alex from her thoughts, and she looked at Birdy. "The…what?"

Birdy slanted a grin at Alex from her hiding place behind a manicured shrub. "You know, the coppers. The police. Or, in this case, the gardeners and chauffeurs."

Alex shook her head, and Birdy waggled her eyebrows, her thin lips pulled back in a playful smile. "Just tryin' to get into the spirit of things, m'dear."

Alex batted at her friend. Someday they were all going to laugh about this.

At least, she certainly hoped so…

A quick glance told her they were almost to the garage. A relieved sigh started somewhere down in Alex's toes and surged through her every fiber.

They'd escaped.

Almost.

As they finally crossed the driveway to the garage, Alex cast a quick glance at her watch. Just past 10:30. They wouldn't start looking for her for at least another ten, maybe fifteen minutes. They wouldn't know for sure that she was gone for close to thirty minutes.

By then, they'd be well on their way. To where, exactly, she had no clue…

She reached out to take Dusty from Birdy, who was looking tested to the limits of her patience by the dog's continual whining and squirming. "That's enough!" Alex hissed into the dog's perked ear, and with a sniff remarkably reminiscent of Birdy at her most deeply offended, Dusty fell silent.

"I don't suppose ye thought to bring yer car keys, did ye?"

Alex grinned at her friend. "As a matter of fact, I didn't."

Birdy cast a baleful glance to the skies. "Heaven preserve us, I should have kno—"

"I brought yours." Alex let the keys dangle from her fingers.

Birdy reached out to take the keys, studying them carefully. "Mine? Whatever for? Yer father's got a veritable fleet of luxury vehicles from which to choose. Why would ye want to take my old clattertrap of a car?"

"Because it's yours. Which means Father can't call the police and accuse me of stealing it, now can he?"

"What about your own car? The title's in your name, isn't it?"

"Not that that would keep him from reporting it stolen."

"Well, he could do the same with my car, couldn't he?"

Alex grinned. "Sure, but your car is considerably less notice-able than mine. Think about it. Bright red sports cars with per-sonalized plates don't exactly blend into traffic, certainly not as well as your car does."

An admiring glimmer stole into Birdy's gaze, and she nodded slowly. "Truth enough in that, child. Well thought out. Perhaps this mad scheme of yours will work after all."

"Of course it will," Alex said, sweeping past Birdy and opening the door to the garage, not letting even the slightest bit of her apprehension seep into her tone. "I wouldn't have it any other way."

"Indeed, but a perfect plan for what? Heartache, if you ask me."

Alex ignored her, which was hard to do with Birdy practically walking on her heels.

"Please, Alexandria, won't you reconsider? Go back inside. Speak to yer father. He'll listen to ye. I know he wi—"

"He won't." At her quiet words, Birdy fell into a miserable silence. Alex hesitated, then turned to lay a tender hand on her friend's shoulder. "I tried, Birdy. You know I tried. But Father is set on this marriage, and I can't go through with it."

Thin brows arched over Birdy's troubled, brown eyes, perplexity painfully evident in her expression. "But why not, gel? Shelton seems a perfectly respectable young man. The eldest son of one of the finest families in the state. He has good business sense, he's reasonably good-looking, refined, and quite taken with you from all evidences. What possible reason could you have for not—"

"I don't love him."

Birdy paused. Opened her mouth, then closed it again. Finally, she nodded. "Well. Yes, that would pose a bit of a problem."

"And I'm not supposed to get married." She looked down at her wedding dress and a choked laugh escaped her. How had she ever let things get this far? "Not yet, anyway. I'm supposed to wait. On God."

As Alex had known she would, Birdy understood. The woman was well grounded in her faith in God. "Well, then, there's no choice, is there? One simply doesn't argue with the good Lord when He's made His wishes clear."

Grateful tears sprang to Alex's eyes as Birdy turned and marched forward, bypassing the line of sleek, new vehicles and going to unlock the door of her own faithful brown, '75, four-door Chevy Impala. Opening the door, she swept out an inviting arm.

"Come along, then, Alexandria. Your chariot awaits."

Two

The sky was just starting to take on that late evening haze, giving a hint that the sun was seriously considering its initial descent toward the horizon, when Alex pulled the car into a parking lot smack-dab in the middle of nowhere.

She had no idea where they were. All she knew was that they were someplace far away from home. Very far, considering that they'd been driving for nearly seven hours.

Once in the car and on their way, Birdy had asked where they were going. At Alex's shrug, she'd nodded. "North, then."

"North?" Alex slanted a glance at her. "Why north?"

"Ye'll see soon enough, gel." She waved her hand at the windshield. "To the freeway with ye."

They took turns driving and, as Alex studied the atlas, she began to understand. By the time they'd followed the winding road across the state line into Oregon, Alex thought Birdy was a genius.

Her father would never think to look for them here! He'd most likely assume she'd head for a friend's house or to the nearest luxury hotel. But there was no way he'd expect to find her here, in the middle of mountains and tall evergreens, where one drove for miles without seeing a house or town.

Alex leaned back in the driver's seat and stretched, then swept her shoulder-length hair up and off her neck. As much as she liked having thick hair, it could sit pretty heavy on the neck when she was bone tired.

Speaking of tired….she glanced over at Birdy's snoozing form. She was so grateful her friend had come along. It hadn't been easy for the older woman. Running away just wasn't Birdy's style.

"Stand yer ground, child, and face the furies," had been her counsel to Alex for as long as she could recall. But even Birdy had finally seen there was no other recourse, not when Charleston Franklin Wingate was set on something. "C. F." his business associates called him, for "Charge Forward" Wingate.

"Control Freak" was more like it, Alex thought with a disheartened sigh. She didn't like defying her father, she never had. If only he'd try to understand her…try to understand that Alex wasn't able to just "fit in" where he thought she should. She had to do what God wanted, and that was one thing:

Wait.

That was the sense she got every time she prayed about her future, about finding a place where she fit in, where she could be of use, where she made a real difference in something. For someone.

It wasn't so much about falling in love. She wasn't so young and naïve as to think there was a Mr. Perfect out there and only in finding him would she be happy. No, the Bible was clear on that count: the source of real happiness was God and nothing else. In fact, had Alex felt God was calling her to remain single, she would have done so, joyfully.

But there was a longing deep within her…a certainty that God wasn't calling her to a single life; He was simply calling her to be patient.

To wait on Him.

She'd read all she could find in the Bible on love and marriage, and she'd been drawn, over and over, to the Song of Songs. The beauty shown there—the love and passion between bride and bridegroom—always stirred her heart.

"Awake, my beloved, and come away."

How her heart longed to hear such a call from a man who loved her as wholly as the man in Song of Solomon loved the young maiden.

"You are so beautiful, my beloved. So perfect in every way...How sweet is your love, my treasure, my bride."

Just reading the words took Alex's breath away. That was what she wanted, that kind of connection, that kind of joining between hearts and spirits. She would wait for love that would last, no matter what, because it was grounded in God rather than in books and fairy tales and "happily ever after."

She wouldn't marry until she heard, deep in her heart, that call: "Awake, my beloved, and come away."

For the past several years she'd read Song of Solomon over and over, until she echoed the young bride's request that God would not "awaken love until the time is right."

She'd hoped that would happen with Shelton. She certainly liked him well enough. But her hope had been more for her father than for herself, and today...well...she just knew. She'd been wrong to think she could go through with it. She'd gone against what she knew was God's call and as a result she'd hurt people.

I've got a lot to make up for, Lord. How, exactly, she would do so was a bit beyond her at the moment. It was difficult to make up with someone who most likely wasn't even speaking to you.

I should have held to what I knew was right. You said to wait. I should have done so, no matter what. But I wanted to make Daddy happy...

A muffled sob caught in her throat at that: Happy? Her father was anything but, now. She stared up at the ceiling of the car, imagining what her father must have thought…must have felt…when he realized she wasn't there to walk down the aisle.

Frustrated. Flouted. Furious. Hurt. Humiliated…

All of the above.

Sadly, the one thing her father *wasn't* was less determined to bend Alex to his will. That much had been evident when Alex tried to pay for their gas. Her debit card, her numerous credit cards—all refused.

"Reported stolen," Alex heard one clerk hiss to another as she dug in her purse for cash. "Didja get her license plate number?"

Alex had decided there and then as she raced to her car and squealed the tires getting out of there—an action that had Birdy up in arms until Alex explained—that she had no choice. She had to find someplace to hide. Someplace to think…to find a way to help her father understand.

Thank heaven she thought to grab her stash of mad money. It wasn't a lot, but it would keep them going for a few weeks, anyway. After that…

She closed her eyes. *What happens after that, Lord?*

She couldn't hold back the small smile when the same answer she'd been receiving all along floated through her heart and mind: *Wait on Me.*

Well, she thought with a sigh, at least God was consistent.

There was a weathered sign near the front door of the small, wooden building in front of them, and Alex leaned forward to read it. Large, hand-painted letters declared, "Granny's Place— Open 24 Hours. Home Cookin', Served with a Smile."

Sounds good, Alex thought, fighting back the weariness that sat on her spirit like an oversized anvil. *I could use some home cooking. And a smile.*

They'd pulled off the freeway a little over an hour ago. Birdy had decided on their destination: a small dot on the map called Applegate. They'd wound their way through several towns, each smaller than the last. Alex had wanted to stop at one of the restaurants in the last town they'd gone through—a quaint-looking, historic community—but Birdy shook her head.

"Best not stop, child. This place has the look of a tourist town. Too many people coming through here. Possibly even the authorities, and you know your father will have them looking for you. We'd do better to find some little spot somewhere a bit more remote."

Alex peered out the windshield again. Remote, eh? Well, this place certainly fit the bill. She reached over to nudge Birdy's shoulder. "Wakey, wakey, sleepyhead. Time for dinner."

The older woman roused with a start, sitting up and looking about in alarm. "Where on earth are we, child?" She peered through the car window, the picture of suspicion. "Good heavens, you surely don't intend us to enter that…that…"

"It's called a restaurant, Birdy."

"Restaurant, my Aunt Fanny! A rum house, more likely."

Alex fixed her with a stare. "You wanted remote, didn't you? Well, that's what you got. And it's the first café I've seen for the last thirty minutes. I'm hungry, I'm tired, and I'm not driving another inch without some coffee."

Birdy clutched the handle of her purse, her hands gripping and releasing. "We'll probably be accosted and murdered the very moment we go inside."

"So long as they let me get something to eat," Alex muttered, opening the car door and stepping out into the cool, clear mountain air. She leaned down to peer in at Birdy. "Tell you what, bring Dusty along. She'll protect us."

Birdy slid from the car, a gently snoring Dusty cradled in her arms. "Hmm. More likely she'll end up one of their—" she peered at a sign in the window, which sported a picture of a giant hotdog dripping juices and heaven-only-knows what else, and enunciated with clear precision—"mmm, Super-Duper-Lose-*Yer*-Uppers, Jimmy-Jumbo, Hot-Dogs-to-Die-For."

Her arched brows spoke volumes, but Alex just laughed and led the way.

Once inside, though, Alex felt a momentary flash of alarm. There were a surprising number of people there, and every single one of them—from the wide-eyed waitress behind the counter to the booth full of big, hairy brutes sporting leather jackets, studded boots, and foot-long beards—seemed to be staring right at Alex, eyes wide, mouths gaping.

She swallowed, forcing a cheery greeting to her lips, but before she could say a word, Birdy jumped in front of her, brandishing the suddenly awake and yapping Dusty, looking for all the world like a linebacker protecting a quarterback with a bad knee.

"Stay back, all of ye!" Birdy demanded in a strangled voice, and for a moment the silence in the small establishment was so profound it almost made Alex's head hurt.

Then the largest of the leather-clad bruisers leaned back in his booth, crossed his thick arms across a massive chest, and drawled, "Well now, little lady, no need to be testy." He cocked his head, stroking his beard, a slight smile tipping his lips. "But you cain't perzakly be surprised when folks stare at ya, now can ya? I mean, ain't often we have a doo-dadded-up, livin', breathin' Cinder-elly-type bride come walztin' in, asking for the dinner special."

"Oh!" Alex's hand flew to her mouth. How could she have forgotten she was still wearing her wedding dress? Realizing the picture she and her erstwhile protectors must make, she couldn't help but laugh. "No, sir," she said to the man over Birdy's stiff shoulder, "you're absolutely right. We shouldn't be surprised at all."

The tension in the room eased, and as Alex grabbed Birdy's shoulders and dragged her to a booth, the behemoth motioned to a waitress. "Gladys, fetch our lovely bride and her bodyguard here some brew, on me." He glanced at Dusty, his lips twitching. "And you might bring some water and a bone fer their...uh...dog." He cast a sideways grin at his companions. "Leastways, I *think* it's a dog."

Alex laughed and plucked Dusty from Birdy's hands. "She's a dog, all right." She plopped down on the wide seat of the booth, hugging the wriggling terrier and offering the man a friendly smile. "And please don't say anything about her size. She doesn't know she's...uh...well..."

"Height challenged?" the man offered, his grin growing a notch wider.

Alex nodded. "Precisely. She thinks she's at least as tall as a Doberman." She gave Dusty a tender scratch behind the ears.

"Well, gotta love a critter that don't accept its limitations." The man inclined his head to Alex, then his gaze shifted and he frowned slightly. Alex looked to find Birdy, lips pressed together, wiping down the duct-taped vinyl of the seat with a napkin.

"Hey there, sunshine," Alex's newfound friend called out. "If'n you don't care for that seat, I got a nice clean one right next to me."

Alex barely managed to restrain a hoot of laughter as Birdy shot the man a glare. But before Bertilda could reply, she was bumped into the booth by a stout waitress, who nailed her with a well-aimed hip as she set silverware, glasses of water, and menus before them.

"Take a load off, honey," the waitress said, pouring them each a steaming cup of coffee that looked—and smelled—strong enough to strip paint. The woman's smooth-skinned face was broad and kind. Perched on one cheek, where women ages ago might have worn a beauty spot, was a small tattoo of a rose. Every time the waitress smiled, the rose dipped and danced, as though overflowing with the same gaiety that spilled from the woman's eyes. "Now, you two just study them-there menus, and I'll be back in a tail-shake to take your order."

Alex sat, biting her lips, first watching the woman saunter away, then watching Birdy's face turn at least a dozen shades of purple.

"See, Birdy? Completely safe here, just like I said," Alex managed around the laughter that nearly choked her.

"Completely in*sane* here, if ye ask me," Birdy muttered as she reached out to open the menu. "Best do as we've been instructed by the…*tattooed* lady…and study *them-there* menus."

Alex aimed a kick at her under the table. "Bertilda Hiffenstone, you are an insufferable snob, you know that?"

Birdy waved her hand in Alex's face, brushing her words aside like gnats. "No time to discuss such banalities, my dear gel. After all, we've but a 'tail-shake' to discover the delicacies offered us." She cast a glance to the ceiling. "Merciful heaven, help us. Grant that the food be at the very least sanitary." She gave a sniff. "Edible would be far too much to ask, I'm sure."

Alex lifted the ceramic coffee mug to her lips and took a cautious sip. Her eyes widened. "This is good," she said to the waitress, who had just returned to their table.

"Don't sound so amazed, darlin'. We're famous 'round these parts for our coffee. Everyone knows Granny makes her brew same way she likes her men: strong, rich, and full-bodied." The woman's grin was almost as outrageous as her words. "So, ladies, what's your pleasure?"

"Where, exactly," Birdy spoke slowly and clearly, the way one would to someone who was very young—or very dense—"are these…um, parts?"

"Why, this here is the booming metropolis of Redemption."

"Metropolis?" Birdy's tone was as arch as her pencil-thin brows.

"Yes, ma'am. After all, we've got the only restaurant, gas station, and fruit stand for miles around. Used to have a bar here not too long ago, but now it's just us. You might even say we're the county seat 'round these parts. A regular hub of activity."

"Centrally located, I'm sure, between the area penal institution and the local rum shop."

Alex kicked at Birdy under the table, but the waitress wasn't the least bit fazed. In fact, she just grinned and slapped Birdy on the arm. "That's real purty how you do that."

Recoiling as though a cockroach had just jumped onto her arm, Birdy yelped, "I *beg* your pardon?"

"You know, make your *r*s sound like that, all rolled out so nice and purty, like a fancy red carpet. Sounds real educated. Just like a preacher we used to have. Held meetings over at Bubba's Big Boys' Bar." Her expression fairly dripped with sympathy as she shook her head. "Weren't nearly as smart as he sounded, though. You'd a thought from all them fancy sounding words he used he'd a known better." She smiled at them. "Now, what can I get for you ladies."

Alex and Birdy stared, first at each other, then back to the waitress.

"Well?" Birdy demanded.

The woman gave her a blank stare, then nodded. "Oh, you

want to know the specials? Okeydokey, they're—"

"My dear woman, you simply can*not* say such a leading thing as you have about the minister and…and *leave* us hanging like this! It's most cruel."

"Oh, that!" A cheeky grin eased its way onto the waitress's round face. "Why, he shoulda known better'n to try using dynamite for church candles."

"Dynamite?" Birdy's face went white, and Alex wondered if she might actually swoon. Birdy would never faint; swooning was *much* more her style. "What possible rationale could the proprietors of the bar have for keeping dynamite?"

"Oh, that's simple. Fishin'."

Birdy blinked. "Fishing?"

"Well, sure. Ain't no one could pitch a stick o' dynamite with more accuracy than ol' Bubba. 'Tweren't legal, of course. Even so, ever' time the man tossed one in, darned if he didn' bring up a passel of fish. Yessir, had some of the best fish fries in the county at Bubba's Bar." She uttered a deep sigh. "Anyways, that bar was kinda dingy and darklike, which is good for a bar but not for a church service. So the preacher liked to use candles. Bubba let him keep boxes of 'em in the back room. Weren't his fault he didn't know Bubba's fishin' supplies was in a box right next to the candles. Best any of us can figure, that preacher musta got in a real hurry one Sunday morning and grabbed the dynamite by mistake. My guess is he didn't even look at 'em afore he lit 'em."

Alex almost choked on her water. "Oh, my…"

The waitress nodded. "Yup. Blew the place sky high. That's why I said we *used* to have a bar." She frowned. "Don't think they ever did find all the pieces."

"Of the bar?"

"Of the preacher." Her wide, solemn eyes kept Alex from

laughing out loud. "But they gave what they could find a right decent burial." With that, she held her pen poised above her pad. "Now, what can I get you lovely ladies to eat?"

The meal had been just as promised: home cooked and delicious. Birdy had even admitted the food was "more than passable"—high praise considering her state of mind.

"Well, I'd best find the necessity room before we head on our way," Birdy said, lips pursed as she cast a dubious glance toward the back of the café. She leaned toward Alex. "If I'm not back in five minutes, send the Mounties to find me."

Alex laughed, then leaned her elbows on the table and drained the last drop of her fifth cup of coffee, savoring the rich flavor.

"So how were your meals?"

She looked up to find the waitress smiling down at her. "Excellent. Really. My compliments to the chef."

"Honey, you gotta be one of the nicest little things to come in here in a coon's age, you know that? I *know* you're one of the purtiest." The woman's tone was so warm and her smile so broad it felt as though she had reached out to embrace Alex, like some doting, matronly aunt. Quick tears sprang to Alex's eyes in response, then coursed down her cheeks, taking her completely by surprise.

"Aw, honey chile…" The ample woman landed on the seat next to Alex and engulfed her in a hug, thumping her on the back in what Alex guessed were meant to be comforting pats but in reality nearly dislocated her shoulder.

Choking back both tears and laughter, Alex gently disengaged herself from the woman and sighed. "I'm sorry. I don't know what came over me."

"Sweetie, it's plain as the rose on my face that you're a little girl in trouble." She took Alex's hands in her own. "Listen here, I know a place you can stay."

"Oh, really—"

"Now, chile, don't you argue with ol' Gladys. It's hard enough to stay safe today, and I'm just figurin' the good Lord sent you—" she barely missed a beat as Birdy slid back onto the seat across from them—"and your *personable* friend here for a reason."

Alex bit her lips to keep from laughing at the look on Birdy's face. It wasn't often that anyone got one over on Bertilda, but Gladys had managed it with style.

"So listen good." She reached into her apron and pressed a piece of paper into Alex's hand. "This here is an address. I want you to go there and tell the gentleman in charge that Gladys from Granny's sent you—"

"A sterling reference, I'm sure."

Gladys frowned and glanced around. "You know, I'm gonna have to ask Bubba to come take a look at our ventilation system." Her gaze shifted to pin Birdy to her seat. "There's a powerful lot of *hot air* getting in here, and that just ain't right."

Alex nearly choked at that. Birdy fixed the waitress with a glare, but Alex was fairly certain there was a grudging admiration in her friend's eyes.

"So, my good woman, I don't suppose you could direct us to a lodging place?"

Gladys nodded. "Matter of fact, I was just telling your pretty little friend here about it when you interrupted us." She pointed at the paper. "Nothin' fancy, mind you. In fact, it's what they call a halfway house."

Birdy looked up sharply. "A halfway house?"

"Now, don't go getting your fancy knickers in a knot. It's a place for them what hit a hard place and needs to start again. And the fella in charge, why, he's one of God's best."

"Would ye care to mention the paragon's name, perhaps? So we know whom we are seeking?"

Gladys nodded, clearly warming to her subject. "Evan. Mr. Evan Noland."

Birdy leaned back in her seat with a slow nod. "A good, strong name."

"For a good, strong man," Gladys agreed. "His place is called Heaven's Corner—" she beamed at Alex—"ain't that nice? Heaven's Corner? Anyhow, the rooms are clean enough; you could do a lot worse for a place to stay. 'Sides, as I was saying earlier, Evan needs some help. You know, someone to do some cookin' and cleanin', and I'm thinkin' you two would just fit the bill."

With that, Gladys stood up. Clearly, in her mind, it was all settled.

"Cooking and cleani—"

Alex cut Birdy's indignation short by stomping on her foot. She clutched the piece of paper in her hand and looked up at Gladys. "Thank you. This is an answer to prayer."

Gladys shot Birdy a smile that could only be described as triumphant. "Well, of course it is! Now, off you go."

Alex reached for her purse. "How much do we—"

"Not a dime." The woman cut off Alex's protest with a wave of one broad hand. "Don't you argue with ol' Gladys, child." Humor glimmered in her eyes like sparkles of light in a finely cut diamond. "Ain't you learned nothing from your friend here? When it comes to takin' on Gladys, you jest cain't win.

Three

W hen night fell in the remote regions of Oregon, it *fell!*

With a vengeance.

Who knew night could be so dark? Alex shook her head as she looked out the side window of the car, scarcely able to see the trees surrounding them. She supposed her amazement at the inky blackness came from living in the city all her life. She'd never realized how impenetrable nighttime could be when there were no streetlights, no lights from nearby buildings, no city lights on the horizon.

Well, she'd wanted remote, and that's what she had. From what she could see in the swatch of visibility her headlights cut, there was nothing outside but black, inky and dark. A lot of it.

She squinted down at the directions on the paper in her hand. She couldn't read a thing. What's worse, she had no idea where they were. She'd thought she was doing fine, turning first down one country road then another. She'd even managed to ignore Birdy's increasingly dire comments about "falling off the edge of the earth into oblivion." But as daylight had waned and they still hadn't found their destination, Alex had begun to feel a bit nervous herself.

The final straw came when they'd bumped along a gravel road for what had to be a half hour. Birdy had inched forward with each passing minute until she was perched on the edge of her seat; nose all but pressed to the windshield.

Alex had just maneuvered a tight corner, then turned to tell the woman to relax when Birdy emitted an ear-splitting shriek.

"*Stop!* Fer the love of heaven, child, stop!"

Alex slammed on the brakes, barely managing to control the big car's resulting fishtail on the gravel road. When at last they came to a halt in a cloud of choking dust, she spun to glare at Birdy.

"What on earth—"

"I told you we'd plummet from the earth!" She pointed out the windshield, and Alex followed her bony finger…then swallowed the cold wave of fright that slammed into her.

They were, indeed, on the edge—not of the world, but of what appeared to be a massive pit.

Thank heaven she'd responded to Birdy's cry as quickly as she had. Another few feet and they would have gone over the edge. Alex tried to steady her trembling hand as she reached down to shut off the engine.

After a few moments to calm herself, she'd pulled the directions from her purse to study them again. For all the good it did her.

"Birdy, I can't believe you don't have a map light in this car—"

"If you wanted the modern fandangles, you should have taken your own car."

"But you don't even have a dome light."

Birdy lifted her chin. "I have one. It just happens to be burned out."

At Alex's exasperated glare, Birdy shrugged. "I never go out at night. What do I need with a dome light?"

"Fine. Great. Just…*peachy*." It felt good to spit the words through her clenched teeth as she opened the car door and stepped outside.

Whoa...

She stopped cold, staring in wonder. True, all around them was a dense, murky darkness, but above them—Alex had no idea there were that many stars in the sky.

It looked as though someone had sprinkled an onyx blanket with a million tiny dots of twinkling light. Everywhere she looked, stars winked and blinked, as though laughing at her awe. Cutting down the center of the sky was a thick river of white dots, far denser than the rest of the sky.

Alex felt her eyes widen as realization hit her: The Milky Way. So that was what it looked like...wonder at God's stunning creation swept over her.

"Of course, ye wouldn't need a light—" Birdy's terse comment broke into her study of the sky—"if ye hadn't spent so long at the stores."

Alex gritted her teeth. So much for her moment of wonder. She leaned down and planted her arms on the window frame of the car door. "I couldn't very well show up asking for a job dressed in a wedding gown, now could I? Or without even a toothbrush? And how did I know it would take us nearly an hour to find a decent store to buy clothes? Besides, I'm not the only one who took her time—"

"I can't help it if I'm hard to fit, now can I? They don't make clothes nowadays for real women. Infants, that's who they make them for. Anorexic infants with no taste whatsoever."

Shaking her head, Alex stomped toward the front of the car. In the beam of the headlights she got a clear view of what had almost been her final resting place: a garbage pit. A *huge* garbage pit.

Half the county must dump their trash here, she thought, taking in pile after pile of refuse. And that was just what the headlights illuminated. No telling how large this valley of yuck really was. *No, make that the* whole *county. And half of the county next to it!*

With a shudder, she leaned down to read the directions in the beam of the headlights. The faster they got away from this stink-hole, the better.

She was jolted from her task by another shriek from Birdy.

"Ye miserable creature! Get *back* here!"

Oh, that was too much! A creature, was she? Well, it was about time she let the good Miss Bertilda Hiffenstone know exactly what she thought of her!

Alex spun—and just caught a glimpse of a small, brown, furry mass as it catapulted out of the open car door.

Oh…no, no, no…

Dusty!

Alex ran to grab the tiny dog. Unfortunately, Birdy had launched herself out of the car and was trying to do the same thing. The two women ran into each other full-tilt and went flying.

Dusty, on the other hand, deftly danced past their flailing hands and made a mad dash into the night.

"*Dusty!*"

The dog didn't even break stride. Her tiny legs scrambled double-time as she bolted around the car and over the edge of the pit, disappearing into the dense darkness like a will-o'-the-wisp. The only evidence she still existed was the sound of her rapid-fire yips floating back to Alex on the night air, like the sharp blasts of a trumpet heralding an attack.

Birdy jumped to her feet, vengeful determination etched in her angular features. "I'll get the little beastie!"

Alex surged to her feet. "No!"

Birdy froze and looked at her. "But Alexandr—"

She shook her head. "Birdy, she won't come to you. She never does, and you know it."

"Further evidence of the creature's lack of breeding and sense."

Alex crossed her arms and glared at her friend. "Dusty has *plenty* of breeding and you know it. As for sense, she won't come to you because she knows you don't like her. And the last thing we need is for you to chase her even further into this…this…" She peered into the darkness. "This stupid black hole! Now, you stay with the car and keep the headlights aimed. I'll get her."

Birdy's only reply was a loud *harrumph* as she stomped her way back to the car.

Brushing the dirt from her jeans with far more force than necessary, Alex turned and walked to the edge of the garbage pit. Standing as close as she dared, she leaned forward and called.

"Dusty, come here, sweet girl."

A snort sounded from behind her and she spun to glare in Birdy's direction. "Hush! She'll hear you."

"Oh, heaven forbid," came the muffled reply, "that the ridiculous creature, who's probably going to get us killed by trash-mongerers or mauled by a bear, should hear me."

"Birdy!"

"Fine. Fine. I'm hushing."

Turning back to the dump, Alex scanned the scene before her. Upon closer inspection, she saw it wasn't as bad as she'd thought.

It was far worse.

Mound after putrefying mound of discarded items loomed before her. Everything from food to clothes to furniture to heaven knew *what* else was piled all around her. As for the fragrances wafting toward her on the night breeze, well….a string of descriptives flew through Alex's horrified mind: malodorous, fetid, reeking, rank, foul, vile, disgusting…

No. They were all too good for what she was smelling.

Get used to it, she told herself dourly. That's *exactly how you're going to smell after you go down there.* The thought was far from encouraging.

A sound from within the pit, off to her left, made her jump.

"What?" Birdy's question was shrill and full of concern. "What's wrong?"

Alex waved her off. "Nothing. I'm fine." She turned back to the pit, then inched her way over the edge, seeking a solid foothold in the loose dirt. The sound of something metallic dropping and rolling made her freeze in her tracks.

Her pulse pounded in her ears, and her heart beat a reggae rhythm in her chest as she forced a harsh whisper out into the darkness. "Is...is anyone there?"

No reply.

She stepped down again, easing her way to the bottom of the pit, stepping over trash and decaying piles, keeping her ears attuned to any sound.

Relax. It was probably just the piles shifting. Don't piles of things do that? Shift around?

Sure, came the reply from her all-too-accommodating imagination, *especially if someone...or something...is digging in them.*

She grimaced. *Don't be silly. Who on earth would be digging in a trash dump?* She closed her eyes. *No, wait! Forget I asked that.*

Too late. The answers came flying through her mind.

Rats...

Her steps slowed.

Stray dogs...

She hesitated.

Bears.

She froze.

Her resolve wavered. Maybe she should go back to the car and have Birdy call the police on her cell pho—

The cowardly thought was pushed away by a sudden eruption of excited, high-pitched barking. It was a sound Alex recognized all too well. Dusty had found something—and she was going to take it on.

Alex ran into the pit, visions of vicious, snarling bears nipping at her heels. "Dusty!"

The dog's excited barking increased—which made it a perfect match with Alex's pulse rate. The light from the headlights was overhead now, so it did little to illumine the darkness in front of her. She peered, squinting her eyes, struggling to make the bulging forms come into clearer focus.

Thankfully her eyes were adjusting somewhat to the night, and by squinting just right, she finally discerned that the large mound in front of her was in fact a pile of what seemed to be rotting food. As relieved as she was to be able to see something, her heart sank as she pondered what terrible, disease-ridden piece of garbage her dog had most likely found—

She froze. A silent scream tore at her, clawed its way into her throat, and lodged there, almost choking her as she took in the horrifying sight before her.

There, looming in the darkness, moving toward her, was the hulking form of…of…what?

Alex moved backward as surreptitiously as she could, praying she'd escape the thing's notice, taking in the large shoulders, the massive arms…until horrified clarity shot through her.

A bear. She was being attacked by a *bear!*

Don't run. No, run downhill! Wait! Drop and play dead.

She knew that last thought was good advice. After all, she'd read it in a book on surviving in the wilderness. But this wasn't the wilderness. This was a garbage dump, for crying out loud! Obviously this particular bear *liked* dead things.

Backpedaling frantically, Alex spun about, ready to run for her life—but her traitorous foot sank into the rotting layer beneath her, and the next thing she knew, she was lurching forward, face-first, into the muck. The impact with the ground drove the wind from her lungs, and she lay there, panting helplessly, as the hulking form approached her.

Play dead! her terrified mind screeched again, and she curled into a ball. *Why not?* she thought with a hysterical, tear-filled gulp of laughter. *May as well get used to it.*

She pulled her jacket up over her head, praying it would shield her from the animal's slashing claws, wishing with all her panicked heart that she'd bought a jacket made of stainless steel rather than nylon.

And as she prepared to meet the Creator she'd loved for so long, one overriding thought filled her mind: *Lord, let me at least give the critter indigestion!*

Four

Alex lay as still as the long-dead refuse beneath her, waiting for the first strike.

And waited.

And waited...

What is the beast doing, for cryin' out loud? Saying grace?

A nervous giggle escaped her at the thought, and she tensed, sure she'd given herself away...that she'd feel the claws tearing at her any second now...

But nothing happened. After a few seconds, she peeked out from under the collar of her jacket, grateful her eyes were adjusting to the dim light enough to make out...what? What *was* that?

The form was still there, standing a few feet away from her, waving its arms and muttering in a low, furious growl.

Muttering?

Alex frowned and sat up. Then pushed to her hands and knees, crawling close enough to get a good look at her assailant. Her eyes widened when she realized it was covered in a long, oversized coat of some sort. There were...*things*...dangling from the coat, top to bottom. Standing slowly, Alex took a step closer until she could make out some of the shapes.

Large, wilted lettuce leaves. A blackened and decidedly over-ripe banana peel. Pieces of paper and even some foil were stuck here and there. And other things—things Alex didn't dare try to identify if she had any hope of keeping her dinner down—stained and smeared the figure's coat with abandon.

But none of that was as bad as the stench that assaulted Alex anew as the apparition stood there. Though whether the smell emanated from the garment or from the person, she couldn't discern.

Nor did she care to.

"What are you staring at?"

The voice was deep and rich, with well-modulated tones that Alex found startling, coming, as they did, from the most disgusting excuse for a man she had ever seen.

"I asked what you were staring at." He took a menacing step toward her.

On the heels of the man's growled question came another sound, one that set Alex's senses on full alert: Dusty. Snarling. Clearly displeased.

Before Alex could utter a warning, a flash of brown darted at the man and attached itself to one despicable coat sleeve.

Oh…yuck! Alex cringed at the thought of Dusty putting the filthy material in her mouth. She'd have to find a vet tomorrow. Surely the dog would need some kind of fortifying, cleansing shot.

"Hey!" The man jumped back, shaking his arm up and down rigorously, doing his best to dislodge the furiously fastened terrier.

Without thinking, Alex ran forward, batting at the man with her fists. "Don't you *dare* hurt my dog!"

"Hurt your—*umpf!*"

The surge of satisfaction that filled her when she felt her fist connect with his midsection was short lived. It quickly morphed into a jolt of panic when he reached around her with one very solid arm and clamped her against his refuse-smattered chest, pinning her arms between their bodies, pressing her face into his shirtfront.

Fine. Not only did the man tower over her, he was obviously three times as strong as well.

"Oh! Let me go, you…you—"

"Let you *go?*" The words were as furious as the look he directed down at her. "Why? So you can sucker punch me again? Not on your life, lady. As for hurting your dog—"

He held out his free arm. Dusty dangled from the coat sleeve, legs spiraling, teeth clenched like a Northern Pike refusing to give up the hook without first taking off the fisherman's arm. "You gotta be kidding me."

Alex opened her mouth to reply, but nothing came out. Admittedly, the coat was as vile as she'd feared, but the man… well, up close and personal like this, he didn't look like a bum. Nor did he feel like one.

Not by a long shot.

No, what she felt beneath her imprisoned fingers wasn't a body emaciated by living on the streets, but a lean, taut, muscled strength. The iron band around her shoulders spoke of power and, oddly enough, restraint. The material of the shirt she clutched in one hand wasn't the least bit grimy or worn. Instead, it felt soft and fine, and the fragrance that assaulted her nose, which was smashed against the fabric of the shirt at the moment, was that of soap and softener.

She pushed back with all her might, determined to ask the man who he was and what on earth he was doing here—and immediately regretted the action. If she'd had half a brain, she never would have let her gaze come into full—and far too close—contact with the man's eyes.

She'd never seen such eyes. Eyes the color of rich, velvety chocolate…the kind you let melt on your tongue as you close your eyes in ecstasy. Eyes that held a wealth of emotion and depth. Eyes that seemed to speak of laughter and wisdom, resolve and determination…and something more. Something indefinably, irrefutably male.

Oh…my…

On the heels of that thought came another. And this one almost buckled Alex's knees: *Awaken, my love, and come away.*

Shock ripped through her, leaving her nerves raw and sensitized. Awaken? *Awaken?* She stared at the man, her breath catching in her throat, one thought overcoming all else: *God, You've got to be kidding!*

Awaken? *Now?* In a garbage dump, with a man she didn't even know? A man wearing a coat that smelled like last week's blue-plate special?

Please tell me You're kidding!

Awaken, beloved. The time has come.

Hysterical laughter clawed at her throat even as tears of frustration burned at her eyes. It took every ounce of self-control not to throw her hands up and run screaming from the man before her.

This was a dream. It had to be a dream. Things like this simply didn't happen in real life…did they?

Alex stared up into his eyes, searching, probing…and froze. Her mouth fell slightly open as a soft *"Oh!"* whispered past her lips into the night air. The man's forehead creased, and those brown eyes shifted, studying her carefully…questioningly—as though he'd suddenly grown aware of something that caught him entirely by surprise.

Alarm swept through her and Alex clamped her mouth shut. Biting her lip, she schooled her features to reveal nothing, hoping it wasn't too late…that he hadn't already read how deeply he'd affected her…that she could retain at least a shred of dignity…

No such luck. Her hopes did a prompt crash-and-burn when her captor's brow cleared, his eyes softened, and his lips eased into a quizzical, almost bemused smile.

"Well, well…"

The two, softly murmured words danced across her ragged nerves, sending her senses into maximum overdrive. Alex felt the arm clamped about her relax slightly, and the man lowered his chin, an enigmatic light coming into his eyes. His face was so close to hers that she could feel the gentle warmth of his breath on her cheek, and she shivered, wondering what it would be like to reach out, to let her curious fingers discover if his neatly trimmed hair was as thick and soft as it appeared—

"*Freeze* where ye stand, ye scoundrel! Or prepare to meet yer Maker!"

The man stiffened so abruptly that he smashed Alex's face into his chest, nearly crushing the breath from her in the process. He spun, Alex still clamped against him, to stare in the direction of Birdy's querulous voice. Turning her head to peer over his arm, Alex caught a glimpse of her friend—and couldn't believe her eyes.

Birdy was the image of an avenging angel—albeit a scrawny one—standing there, feet planted firmly, arms stretched out in front of her as she brandished…

Alex blinked. It couldn't be. She looked again, focusing carefully, and her eyes widened.

Merciful heaven…

Bertilda Hiffenstone was packin' heat!

Five

*I*t couldn't be real, could it?

That couldn't *possibly* be a real gun in Birdy's clawlike hand.

Alex risked a glance up at the man's face. Apparently the weapon looked real enough to him, for he stood there, eyes fixed on Birdy, and did as commanded. He froze. Completely. Utterly. Alex felt his muscles tense, his breathing shift gear.

Birdy took a few quick steps toward them, then jerked to a halt. In the moonlight Alex saw an odd expression flit across her friend's face. The arm holding Alex tightened again, and she looked up to see a similar expression on her captor's face.

Then he smiled. "Okay, lady, let's just relax here. How 'bout you put down the gun?"

The calm, rational tone surprised Alex. He sounded totally in charge.

"First ye let the girl and her dog go." Birdy's tone brooked no argument. "Now, buster!"

Buster? Alex was certain she was dreaming now. Near-hysterical laughter bubbled up inside her. Birdy had never called anyone "buster" in her life!

She must have been convincing, though, because the man's arm relaxed about Alex's shoulders, and she was able to ease away from him. Almost. He let her step back, but as she did so he slid his fingers along one arm to capture her hand in a gentle grip.

He glanced down at her, and when their gazes connected, she went still.

She wasn't sure what she'd expected to see in his eyes—fear, maybe, or anger. After all, he'd been assaulted by her, chewed on by her dog, and had a gun pulled on him by Birdy! But she saw neither. Instead, what she read there looked for all the world to be a grudging sort of respect. Even admiration.

And not a little amusement.

Alex blinked. He thought this was funny?

"I've let the girl go…" His words were directed to Birdy, but his gaze rested on Alex in a manner that brought quick heat to her face and made her grateful for the darkness. Bad enough to be overcome with a schoolgirlish blush, at least she was spared the humiliation of having him see the effect he was having on her!

"But as for the dog, you'll have to talk to him about letting go." He held out his arm, and Alex gave a choked sound. Darned if Dusty wasn't still attached to the sleeve of the man's coat.

Trust a terrier to bring a whole new meaning to the term *tenacity*.

A smile twitching at his lips, the man gave his arm a small jerk, bouncing Dusty so that all four of her short, little legs started pinwheeling and her you'd-better-watch-yourself-buddy-'cuz-*I'm*-in-control-here growl raised a notch.

The man lowered his voice, speaking to Alex now. "I'm afraid I'll hurt the little guy if I make him let go." He dipped his head slightly in a gesture that was utterly charming and alarmingly disturbing. "So what do you say, miss…care to pull the…uh, thorn from my paw, so to speak?"

"Okay," Alex croaked through a throat gone suddenly dry. She didn't know who this man was, but one thing was becoming glaringly, desperately clear in her mind: If she knew what was good for her, she'd get her dog and get out of Dodge. Now.

If not sooner.

Stiffening her spine, Alex reached for Dusty, determined to do exactly that. She would have made it too, if only she hadn't looked at the man again. Hadn't let her gaze lock with his.

Oh, help...

"You have ravished my heart." The words flitted through her mind with an almost perverse glee. *"I am overcome by one glance of your eyes..."*

She clenched her teeth. *Stop it, stop it!* How *dare* those verses, which had so often brought her such comfort and hope, come back now? In this ridiculous place. This man was *not* her beloved. He was a garbage scrounger, for heaven's sake!

A garbage scrounger whose eyes flicker with gentle amusement... who looks at you as though he knows you. Really knows you...

She pressed her lips together mutinously. *So what?* She crossed her arms and lifted her chin, fixing him with a glare. So the man had been careful and gentle with Dusty, despite the fact that she'd turned his sleeve into shredded wheat. So what? So his smile held the most inexplicable tenderness she'd had ever seen in her life. So wha—

"Please?"

Never had one word had such a devastating effect on Alex. It was as though she melted from the inside out. Her resolve, her determination to escape, her ability to form a coherent sentence— it all dissolved, right then and there, into a little puddle at the man's feet.

"I...you...your sleeve...but...I mean..." She closed her eyes. *Take me now, Lord. Just let the ground open and swallow me whole.* "He's a she. That is...she's a—"

She shook her head. *Now is definitely good for me, Lord.* "Never mind."

Taking a firm grip around Dusty's furry middle, Alex tugged on her diminutive defender. "Release, Dusty."

The dog gave one final *R-r-r-ruff!* of defiance and—to Alex's utter amazement—let go, turning to snuggle against Alex as though grateful she'd been relieved of her post. Cradling the trembling terrier to her chest, Alex watched as the man inspected his sleeve, then flexed his hand, as though ensuring himself all fingers were still intact.

Seemingly reassured, he combed a hand through his chestnut hair, then his gaze moved to Birdy.

"Okay, I let them go. Happy?"

"Rapturous," came Birdy's almost playful reply.

His lips twitched again. "Well then, how 'bout lowering the squirt gun?"

Mouth dropping open, Alex spun to stare at Birdy. "*Squirt* gun?"

Birdy gave a sheepish grin and shrugged. "Well, it was worth a try. And I had to do somethin'." She moved to stand beside Alex. "I knew there had to be trouble when you didn't come back for so long." Her attention turned to the man standing beside them. "And if there's one thing ye've always been, boy, it's trouble."

With that, Birdy stepped past Alex and threw her arms around the man's neck. He broke into hearty laughter, hugged Birdy tightly, and planted a kiss squarely on her sharp nose.

"Aunt Bert! As I live and breathe! Why didn't you tell me you were coming?"

"*Aunt* Bert." Alex stared at the two. She opened her mouth, then closed it again. Fitting Dusty into the crook of one arm, she planted her free hand on her hip and waited while the two chattered away.

And waited. And waited…

Finally, she could stand it no longer. "Excuse me." They didn't even look at her. She took a step closer. "Ex*cuse* me."

Birdy and the man started guiltily. Birdy smiled at Alex, then stepped back, keeping a grip on the man's greasy coat sleeve. "Alexandria, my dove, come meet Evan—" she directed an adoring glance to the man who towered over the two of them—"my dear, sweet nephew."

Six

Evan Noland rubbed his eyes, giving in to a weary, bone-deep sigh as he shut off his light and slid between the sheets of his warm bed.

He needed sleep. Desperately. He knew it and was determined to get it.

Too bad determination didn't stop the flow of images racing through his mind—or the grin that kept sprouting on his face.

Aunt Bert. Whoda thunk it? He hadn't seen her for two, maybe three years. Not since he'd moved to Oregon. He'd sure never expected to find her on his doorstep—or, to be more accurate, in his garbage dump—in the middle of the night.

And then there was Alexandria Wingate…Alex. He'd heard about Alex, even seen pictures of her, for as long as he could remember. Aunt Bert loved that girl; thought the sun rose and set on her. He'd always been a bit jealous of that. Until now.

Now he understood.

Alexandria Wingate was something special. And not just because she was easy on the eyes. Which she definitely was. What with her thick, auburn hair and lovely features, she looked like she belonged on the cover of a magazine or something. And those eyes…green as eyes could be, with a color—he'd discovered tonight—that only grew deeper and richer when she got worked up.

Yup. She was a pretty woman, all right. But he was much

more impressed—and surprised—by what seemed to be beneath the packaging.

She was nice. Feisty—he grinned—but really nice. That was clear in the way she treated Aunt Bert, in the respect and love that showed as she spoke to the older woman.

Once she got over her indignant sputtering, of course.

He grinned again at the memory of her blazing eyes, her jutted chin… She might be a petite little thing, but she could be quite a force.

Why on earth had Aunt Bert brought Alex here? Especially without telling her what she was up to? He'd fought the urge to pull his aunt aside and ask her. He learned a long time ago that his spinster aunt didn't do things without good reason. Usually *very* good reason. So he'd just have to bide his time and let her fill him in when she was good and ready.

Until then, hey, let them stay at Heaven's Corner. With the housekeeper leaving so abruptly last week—another casualty of the Matty Express—he could use them. True, they didn't have many residents right now, but he hadn't relished the thought of taking on the cooking and cleaning chores along with everything else.

Why not? You seem to think you can do it all on your own. What's a few more responsibilities on Superman's shoulders?

He rolled over, ignoring the snide inner comment. He wasn't Superman. He knew that. He was just…determined. God had given him a task to do with Heaven's Corner, and he'd be darned if he wasn't going to do it.

As for doing it on his own…well, other people just hadn't proven too dependable in his life. Seemed as though nearly every time he'd start to rely on someone, they'd walk away. Which was why he'd made sure there was more than one ministry supporting

Heaven's Corner. Safety in numbers, wasn't that how the saying went?

So why do you stay so isolated? Why not let someone help? Even better, let someone care about you?

He shook his head against the silent questions. He didn't have *time* for relationships. Oh, sure, he'd tried love. Had even been serious about it once or twice in his thirty-four years. But it had never worked out. And that was fine. Now his focus was this place and helping the people God brought his way. That was enough for any man.

"It's not good for man to be alone…"

"I'm *not* alone."

Evan almost jumped at the sound of his own voice in the darkness. He rubbed the bridge of his nose, willing his mind to be still. What was with all these questions, anyway? He'd been perfectly content for years to be on his own. What was all this letting someone in about?

The image of Alex's face came clear and strong in his mind—the way she'd stared up at him when they met…the sound of that soft exclamation that had whispered past her open lips…and the sudden sledgehammer of awareness that had smacked him right between the eyes as he watched her.

"Forget it." He spoke more quietly this time but no less forcefully. Alexandria Wingate was a wealthy young woman. Her future was more than likely already settled, and there was no way it had anything to do with Heaven's Corner or with Evan Noland.

No way at all.

So why can't you get her off your mind?

He muttered something as dark as the night around him and turned to punch his pillow into submission, determined to do the same to his thoughts. Best thing he could do, for Alex and for himself, was keep his distance. Which shouldn't be that hard, not if he kept her busy.

He nodded, the plan forming in his mind. When it came right down to it, Aunt Bert's surprise appearance was a godsend. Evan didn't kid himself that Alex would be a great deal of practical use—he'd heard about her mansion, her cook, her servants. Stood to reason a woman like that wouldn't have much know-how when it came to doing for herself or for others. But Aunt Bert, now there was another story. That woman could cook and clean like nobody's business.

Tucker would be thrilled.

Tucker…

At the thought of his resident groundskeeper and handyman, Evan folded his arms behind his head and leaned back against the pillows. Now there was someone he could think of with pleasure. He loved success stories, and Tucker was definitely one of those. Amazing how God could turn a life around when He really got hold of a person's heart and mind. Hadn't been easy for Tucker. Still wasn't; what with getting Penny and Peter to trust him again. But Tucker was tough…he'd make it.

Evan only hoped Peter and Penny made it, as well. Those two were more like walking wounds than kids. True, they'd been through a lot over the last few years—a lot more than any kid should have to face. Tucker was doing his best to make up for his past mistakes, but Peter didn't seem to be softening even a little to his dad. Penny, on the other hand…

Well, Penny was a little girl who needed her daddy as much as he needed her. She just didn't know how to deal with that. 'Course, how many six-year-olds could deal with Penny's life?

Evan's lips pressed together. Not many. If not for Peter, Penny could well have been yet another casualty of the system. Peter was her life preserver. Peter and Snufflebunny.

A muffled chuckle escaped Evan at the thought of the stuffed rabbit. It was Snufflebunny's fault that Evan had been buried to his elbows in rotting refuse tonight. Penny didn't go anywhere without that toy clutched in a hand or hanging from the crook of an elbow. But somehow, earlier tonight, Snufflebunny had made an unplanned detour. By way of a trash can.

Evan had his suspicions. Peter was constantly trying to break his little sister of her dependence on the stuffed animal. It was entirely possible the boy tossed the rabbit out in a misguided attempt to help Penny grow up.

Whatever the cause, when Snufflebunny's absence was discovered right after the evening chores were done, chaos ensued. Penny's panic had been complete, and the child had practically been in hysterics as they combed the house, then the grounds, looking for the stuffed critter.

When they'd made the search one last time, it was Matty who had the brilliant thought that someone may have thrown Snufflebunny out. "You know—" he said with a too-casual shrug—"accidental like."

Evan had looked from Matty to Peter, but neither boy's expression had given anything away. It didn't matter. If there was any chance the rabbit was in the trash, Evan knew what he needed to do.

It was just an added blessing when Peter informed Evan that the trash had already gone to the dump.

"Your dad took it already?" He'd stared at Peter. "He *never* takes it this early."

Peter shrugged again. "He was ahead of schedule today." The boy's sullen reply made Evan pause. He put a gentle but firm hand on Peter's shoulder.

"Pete, you don't know how Snufflebunny got into the trash, do you?" The dull red that traveled up Peter's cheekbones confirmed Evan's suspicions and he sighed. He considered telling Tucker, letting him take care of the mess, but something in Peter's eyes just wouldn't let him do it. "Did you go to the dump with your dad?"

Peter nodded.

"S'pose you can show me where he dumped the bags?"

Another nod, then Peter's eyes came up to meet Evan's. The boy's features were even more pinched than usual and pink tinged his cheeks. But it was the uncharacteristic gleam of gratitude in his eyes that grabbed Evan's heart. "Thanks."

Evan nodded this time, and they went to his car. Once Peter pointed out the general location of the trash, Evan took him back home and told him to let his father know Evan would be back as soon as he could. The boy slid from Evan's car, and the relief on Peter's young face told Evan more clearly than any words could that he was doing the right thing.

He was even more certain of that now. If he hadn't been at the dump, heaven only knew how long it would have taken Aunt Bert and Alex to find Heaven's Corner. It was a bit hard to find in the daylight. After dark, without directions…well, unless you could maneuver with a compass or by the North Star, it was a bear.

Besides, the whole dump incident had given Evan a chance to see what Alex was made of. And he'd liked what he'd seen. She'd no sooner found out why Evan was there than she was pulling back her sleeves and digging through the muck with him.

It took about another half hour, but Alex had finally given an excited yelp. Evan looked up to see her holding out one once-white, long-eared, fuzzy stuffed rabbit.

"Snufflebunny, I presume?" Her face, though smudged with grime, had been glowing.

"Way to go, Sherlock." He resisted the urge to sweep her into a congratulatory hug. Something about this woman just begged to be hugged. He settled for going to take the rabbit from where it dangled between Alex's thumb and finger and wrap it in a hand-towel he'd brought. "A little detergent, a little brushing…"

"A little fumigation…" Alex added with warm humor.

"And this little guy will be good as new."

"Lovely," Aunt Bert had said coming up behind them. "If only we could be as fortunate." She held out her muck-covered hands and gave Evan a pleading look. "Please tell me you have baths in the rooms, m'boy."

"And plenty of hot water," he'd assured her as they made their way up the side of the pit, back to solid, nonrotting ground.

Alex hadn't even seemed bothered by the ordeal. In fact, Evan would bet dollars to donuts she'd *enjoyed* it. He closed his eyes, picturing the way her face glowed in the moonlight…

Knock it off, Noland!

He jerked himself from the memory—and from the emotions surging through him. Okay, so Alexandria Wingate was something special. Made sense. God only brought people here with a purpose. So all Evan had to do was keep his focus on God and what He wanted for Alex while she was here.

What does she need, Father? What can we do for her?

When no real answer came, Evan shrugged in the darkness. Maybe he'd put her to work with Tucker. They'd seemed to hit it off right away. Tucker had been waiting for Evan when he and the women got back to the house. When the older man caught sight of Snufflebunny in Aunt Bert's arms, he'd whooped and grabbed her up in a hug. Much to Evan's amazement, Aunt Bert had taken it all in stride—in fact, she looked for all the world as though she enjoyed Tucker's gratitude. Not to mention the hug.

They had all been too jazzed to go to bed, so they ended up sitting in the living room, holding steaming mugs of hot chocolate and talking. It might be summer, but the evenings up here got cool, and hot chocolate was always welcome.

Tucker had told Alex and Aunt Bert his story, about how he and his wife had married late in life, when both were near forty. They'd had two children, Peter and Penny, making their happy family complete.

Then three years ago, after just seven years of marriage, Tucker's wife was killed in a car crash. Sick with grief, terrified at the thought of raising two kids on his own when he was nearly fifty, Tucker Telford had started drinking. Within a year he lost his job, then their home.

The final blow came when his children were taken away by the state.

"I lost everything," he said, his gaze even and unflinching. "Thanks to fear and cowardice."

Aunt Bert looked as though she were going to burst into tears. Evan didn't think he'd ever seen her so moved before. She clutched her hands together in front of her. "How terrible for you! And for those poor, wee children."

"It was hardest on them, that's for sure. But God gave it back. He gave me my life back. Brought me to a good church with people who cared. They got me into a recovery program. Then when I got done with that, they sent me here."

Evan lifted his mug, holding it between his hands. "Didn't take me long to realize Tucker was just what we needed to keep this place running smoothly. Took me a few months, but I finally convinced him to hire on full time."

Tucker nodded. "Evan spoke up for me in family court, and 'bout six months ago they finally let my kids come live with me again. I'm on probation, but I'm not worried. With friends like Evan—"

"And with God on yer side," Aunt Bert added, and Tucker paused, looking at her. Evan couldn't be sure, but he thought he'd seen more warmth in Tucker's smile than he'd seen in a long time. As for Aunt Bert, Evan could have sworn the woman actually blushed!

"Now you're talkin', Miz Hiffenstone, and right as rain. With God on my side, we're gonna make it. I'm sure of it."

Evan chuckled. Tucker and Aunt Bert…now there were some interesting possibilities. Well, tomorrow he'd have to ask Alex if she wanted to work with Tucker outside or help Aunt Bert in the kitchen. Everyone who stayed at Heaven's Corner worked. It was the rule.

It was a good rule, too. It had helped more than one person gain—or regain—a sense of confidence, of making a difference. It had been a saving grace for Tucker and others like him. If only…

Evan grimaced. If only the work—or something—could get through to everyone who came to Heaven's Corner. But there were those who didn't seem to respond to anything. Like Matty.

A heavy sigh escaped Evan. He'd never had a kid at the ranch who was quite as hard to reach as this one. Matty seemed so…what? Protected? Walled in? Detached? Yes, that was it…detached. Matteo Navarro was fifteen years old going on ninety. He was here as a last-ditch effort to keep him from ending up in prison. Or worse. The kid was tough, streetwise, and blessed with an abundance of attitude. Not that there wasn't good reason for that. He was lucky he'd lived to fifteen. If not for his sister Teresa, he might not have. She was only thirteen, but she mothered Matty like nobody's business. She was the only one who got through that shell of his. The two of them had survived for each other. If only Evan could help them see that there was more to life than just survival.

Matty, Teresa, Penny, Peter, Tucker…they all needed so much. Most of all, they needed to know they weren't alone. That someone was there for them.

That God was there for them.

But as hard as Evan had tried, it didn't seem to be working. He didn't seem to be able to get through to Matty or Peter or Penny…

He turned over and punched his pillow once, twice, then a third time for good measure. The action did little to ease his frustration. He needed help, but answers weren't easy to come by. And so, as he'd done every night for the past three years, ever since the doors of Heaven's Corner had opened, Evan buried his face in his pillow and took his concerns to the only One that could help.

To God.

Seven

It was an ungodly sound. A screeching, undulating, nightmarish yowl that assaulted Alex's unconsciousness and wrenched her from slumber.

Someone was being murdered!

Alex scrambled to sit bolt upright in the bed, grabbing the covers and pulling them to her chest, almost flipping Birdy into the air in the process.

"What—? What's wrong?" Birdy asked, hands grappling for the covers as she threw herself spread-eagle on the bed to keep from ending up on the floor.

"Did you *hear* that?"

Birdy's forehead creased. "Hear what?"

The screech came again. *"That!"* She turned to Birdy. "Something's being mauled! Murdered, even!"

The expression on Birdy's face was one of pained restraint. "That, my dear gel, is a rooster."

"A…" Alex lowered her protective covers and stared out the bedroom window. "Well, for cryin' out loud, what's it doing outside our window?"

Birdy jerked at the covers, lying down and pulling them up to her chin as she closed her eyes. "What all roosters do at the break of day. Crowing."

Alex fell back against her pillow. *"Every* day?"

"Without fail," came the smug reply. Birdy cracked one beady eye open to peer at Alex. "You're in the country, m'dear, remember? Fresh air, hard work, animals—" she rolled onto her side— "living, as they say, the good life."

"Good for whom?" She nudged Birdy with her elbow. "Masochists?"

A muffled laugh was her only response.

Sitting next to the open window, watching the sunrise tinge the sky with vivid hues of orange and rose, Alex let loose a sigh.

Late last night, as they lay in the dark of their room, Birdy had explained that coming to Heaven's Corner had occurred to her in a flash of genius.

"I knew, from Evan's letters, that it was remote in location and distant from your home. Both good things. And I knew it would be a safe and welcoming place. A place you can get yer hands dirty…do something physical. A place to give you the time you need to think."

From what Alex had seen last night and this morning, Birdy was right. The buildings included the two-story ranch house; a narrow, two-car garage that Evan explained was more a shop than a garage; a small barn, a wooden structure that Birdy explained was a chicken coop; and a shed in the back. Evan had said they had five acres of land altogether.

"Just enough to give us space, but not so much we can't manage it."

"We" being Evan and the residents. He'd explained that people could only come to Heaven's Corner on the recommendation of a selected list of pastors, priests, social workers, and others familiar with both the struggle of those whose lives had gone out of control and with the principles on which Heaven's Corner had been built.

"It started as a ministry outreach with one small, country church," Evan told them as they sat drinking hot chocolate late into the night. "The program had such an impact that several of the churches in the county decided to support it. We don't take in a lot of folks at one time—we want to be sure we can give the attention and help needed to those God brings our way. And we're not plush in the pocket, that's for sure, but at least we're keeping our heads above water."

"So, people come here to start over?" Alex liked the idea.

"Right. We give them a place to stay for six months or so—sometimes longer—helping them in whatever way they need. Sometimes that means helping them find jobs. Sometimes it means just giving them the tools to stay even emotionally. All we ask from them in return is compliance with our rules and an honest day's work here on the ranch until they find jobs. We offer prayer time together, but it's optional. We don't force faith into their lives, but we do let them know the door's always open."

Alex leaned her head back against the chair, studying the room that was to be her and Birdy's home for...how long?

She didn't know.

Don't worry about it. You don't have to have all the answers now. Wait, remember? That's what you've been told to do. Wait.

The room was neat and clean, with simple, homey furnishings. Though a far cry from the elegance she was used to, there was a feel about the place that she liked. A warmth...a welcome.

Her gaze fell on a sampler on the wall: "Surely the presence of the Lord is in this place."

She had to agree. And that was what she needed—a place where God was...a place to listen and think and learn what she was supposed to do. Where she was supposed to go.

A place to figure out if what I heard last night was for real.

She closed her eyes. Could it be…? Could this place be some part of the answer to her prayers? What if this was what God was calling her to—to help in the work here? But what on earth did she have to offer a place like Heaven's Corner?

Or a man like Evan Noland?

Alex had few illusions about herself. She knew that, when it came right down to it, she lacked any viable skills beyond living up to her social station. She clenched her teeth against the frustration nudging at her heart.

What if Daddy was right? What if I'm asking for too much? Maybe marriage to someone like Shelton is the most I can ask for…to be a supportive, compliant, silent decoration on Shelton's arm at parties and social functions—

"Poppycock!"

Alex started and turned to find Birdy scowling at the radio on the dresser. The older woman reached out to turn off the radio with an impatient flick.

"W-what?"

Birdy turned to her. "Oh, sorry, m'dear. I let my tongue get away with me, I'm afraid." She picked up her work gloves from the dresser. "Radio psychologists. They drive me to the edge of madness, they do."

Alex's lips twitched. "That's hardly a drive, Birdy. More like a short putt."

Birdy swatted at Alex with her gloves. "Scamp. But ye must confess, it gets tiring, all that mumbo jumbo about comin' to peace with yer inner self." She slapped her gloves against one palm. "Seems to me if folks would just get their focus off of themselves and onto God, they'd have far fewer problems. 'Seek ye first the kingdom of God, and then all these things shall be added unto you.' That's what the Good Book says, plain and simple."

Alex grinned. "I'll go along with plain, Birdy, but simple? I'm not so sure."

"I said it before, I'll say it again: poppycock! It's people who make it hard, gel. Not God. He makes it simple as can be. Read the Word, be still before the Creator, listen more than ye speak, then do what He calls ye to do with all yer heart."

Birdy reached down to take Alex's hand and pull her from the chair. Looping elbows, she marched them toward the door. "Listen for the Master's voice, m'dear. And then obey. That's been the path to peace and joy for me for many a year." She gave Alex a sideways grin. "And though it pains me to admit it, it's not because I'm so verra special or favored that it works so well." She held out her free hand. "Now, don't argue with me."

"I wouldn't dare," Alex managed around the laughter. Oh, but it felt good to laugh.

Birdy gave Alex a playful bump with her shoulder. "See there, gel? You're showing remarkable wisdom already. Ye're learning. Slow, but sure. Ye're learnin'."

Alex leaned against her friend, torn between laughter and the sudden prickle of tears that she didn't quite understand. "I hope so, Birdy. Oh, I hope so."

"Well, here we are, wide awake and ready to be put to work."

Evan looked up. Sure enough, Aunt Bert and Alex stood there, decked out in fresh, white T-shirts, new leather work gloves, blue jeans, and…what did they have on their feet?

He stood up and went for a closer look. Boots. They were wearing huge, bright yellow, rubber boots. They looked like a couple of malformed mallards.

He couldn't have held back his grin to save his life. "Where did you get those things?"

"Don't ask," Alex replied with a grimace.

"Now, don't be such a snob, Alexandria. It was a perfectly good store—"

"With a giant, fiberglass crow in the parking lot," came the dry rejoinder, "complete with a huge, floppy fishing hat and fishing pole. Oh, indeed, *totally* respectable."

"Black Bird," Evan supplied. "It's not a store, it's an adventure."

"You wanted me, Mr. Noland?"

Evan and the women turned. Matty stood there, the picture of relaxed insolence. Incorrigible, his last foster home had labeled him; Matty was more than happy to look the part. His handsome features were often drawn into a scowl. His midnight black hair was cut close to the scalp. A dragon tattoo stretched around the back of his lean, well-muscled neck. Evan had seen more than one person stare askance at the beast's savage head and the raised, blood-soaked claw, both of which curved along the right side of Matty's neck. It was a fierce sight, to say the least.

Which fit Matty perfectly. The boy exuded a fierce kind of power, a fearlessness, a lawlessness. Here, his stance, his burning eyes seemed to say something is wild and, if need be, savage. So steer clear. Evan knew the image was just a cloak, a form of protection, and he'd been working hard to get past it, to get to the kid inside. So far, he hadn't had much luck. But he wasn't about to give up.

"Yeah, come on in, Matty."

The boy sauntered toward them, and Evan wanted to cuff him for the way his dark eyes moved over the two women in the room. But to Birdy's and Alex's credit, they didn't even flinch. Evan moved to stand between the two women, sliding an arm around Aunt Bert's shoulders.

"Matty, this is my aunt, Miss Hiffenstone, and her friend, Miss Wingate. Ladies, meet Matty. He and his sister, Teresa, are two of the residents staying with us now."

"Yeah, residents." Matty smirked. "Nice word for prisoners."

"Personally, I like slaves much better." Evan crossed his arms. "Speaking of which, I thought I'd have Matty help you two out today."

Matty's gaze went to the women's boots, and he scowled at Evan. "You expect me to be seen with those things in public? Man, where'd they get those things? On the ugly truck?"

Evan grinned. "As a matter of fact, yes. And they got a pair for you, too, pal."

The boy snorted. "Don't do me no favors, *hijo.*"

"I never do," Evan retorted. Then he turned to his aunt. "I told you last night that our cook-cum-housekeeper left—"

"No great loss."

He ignored Matty's muttered comment. "So I was hoping you could take over some of her work while you're here. There aren't many of us right now, so it won't be too much work, I don't think."

"Certainly, m'boy," Aunt Bert chirped.

"What about me?"

Evan turned to Alex, his gaze roving over her, taking in the brightness of her eyes, the sincerity in her smile. Unless he missed his guess, she really did want to help. He was surprised how much that warmed his heart.

"Your choice. You can work outside with Tucker, or go help Aunt Bert and Matty in the kitchen."

"The kitchen? Oh, man, I don't do no kitchen work. That's for women—"

"Don't tell me yer afraid of a little hard work, m'boy?" Aunt Bert moved toward Matty, who crossed his arms and stood his ground with a lift of his chin.

"I ain't afraid of nothin', old woman."

Evan almost intervened at that, but Aunt Bert didn't give him a chance. She just directed a bright smile at Matty and clapped her hands.

"Exactly! I *knew* you weren't. Not a big, strapping lad like yourself. Why, I was just thinkin' how fortunate we are to have such an able young man to assist us in our endeavors."

Matty frowned, as though trying to determine if he'd just been insulted or not, when Aunt Bert reached out to lay a hand on Matty's arm.

At the contact, Matty went stiff, and Evan caught his breath. Leave it to Aunt Bert to plow right into forbidden territory. Nobody touched this kid. Evan watched, poised to jump in if need be, as Matty looked down at Aunt Bert's hand where it rested on his arm, then slowly directed a narrow-eyed glare to her face.

The message in those dark eyes was clear: *Don't touch!*

Obviously Alex understood. Evan felt her stiffen beside him and start to move. Without thinking, his fingers closed around hers, holding her beside him, squeezing a gentle warning. She looked up at him, then frowned when he shook his head. Thankfully, she chose to trust him and remain where she was.

Evan looked away from Alex in time to see that not only did Aunt Bert not remove her hand, she actually dug her fingers into Matty's arm and tugged him closer.

If Evan hadn't been so acutely aware of the undertones in the room, he would have laughed out loud at the stunned expression on Matty's lean face.

Aunt Bert let the boy go just long enough to clap her hands in

delight. "Well, now! Look at what's peekin' out at me here." She took
hold of Matty's chin, turned his astonished face to the side, and
peered at the tattoo. Before the boy could react, she released his chin
and gave his chest a quick pat. "What a *fine* specimen of a dragon.
Why, he's the spittin' image of Draconigus himself. Ye must tell me
where ye found him, boy. He's a work of art, pure 'n' simple."

Evan almost choked on a bark of laughter at the dazed look
Matty gave the small woman standing before him. "I...spittin'
image of *what?*"

"Of Draconigus, lad. Oh, surely you've heard of him. Never
did a fiercer beast ever live. Isn't that so, Evan?"

Evan started. Uh-oh. *Now* what? He'd never heard of the creature. Alex's wide eyes and slight shrug told him she was as unin-
formed as he and would be no help whatsoever. "Um, well—"

"Oh, never mind him, lad." Aunt Bert dismissed Evan with a
wave of her hand, then leaned close to Matty. "He never did listen," she said in a stage whisper, "even as a boy."

Matty's dark gaze was smugly amused as he peered back at
Evan over Aunt Bert's head.

"But you, now—" Aunt Bert's voice was full of admiration as she
linked arms with Matty—"I can tell you're a bright one. Why, I'll
wager it won't take but one tellin' for you to learn all there is to know
about old Draconigus. He was born for evil, you know. But one man
of courage and honor won the beast's heart to the side of good."

Matty didn't even resist as Aunt Bert tugged him along, heading toward the kitchen. "Now *there's* a tale to be told, m'boy.
Bloodcurdling, to be sure." She eyed him carefully. "But I'm
thinkin' ye can take it. Now, then, it's down this hallway to the
kitchen, isn't it? There's a good lad. Show me the way."

Evan watched in amazement as Matty complied, leaning his
dark head down to catch every word as Aunt Bert launched into

312

the tale of dragons and knights and honor restored.

It was a full two minutes before either Alex or Evan moved.

"So, may I please have my hand back?"

At Alex's bemused question, Evan looked down, surprised to find he was, indeed, still gripping her hand. It had felt so natural, so…*right,* to have her hand cradled in his, to feel her leaning against his shoulder as they stood there.

He lifted their hands, studying them, fascinated at the way their fingers fit so well together. Almost as though they were parts of a puzzle that had just found each other…

"Are you going to let me go?"

"No."

"I…what?"

At Alex's startled question, he looked up and realized what he'd said. So much for keeping his distance! He dropped her hand and stepped back. "Uh, problem. No *problem.*" He inclined his head toward her hand. "You know, letting you go. I mean, like you said, it's your hand and you can have it back. No problem."

Good grief, Nolan, shut up. You sound like an idiot.

"So, anyway…lunch." He took a step back, toward the doorway. "You and Aunt Bert are going to fix it, right?"

"Evan…"

"Good. Great." Two more steps back.

"Evan, what…?" She took a step toward him, and he reacted without thinking. He turned and bolted. It was only pure force of will that stopped him at the doorway.

What are you doing? Turn around and face her like a man.

Slowly, he turned. She stood there, astonishment painting her pale features. Silence filled the space between them, and Evan gripped the doorway. *Come on, man! Say something!*

"Alex…I…"

Anything!

"I…look, don't put any milk products in lunch, okay? I'm allergic."

And with that, he made good his escape.

Birdy and Matty looked positively chummy when Alex finally entered the kitchen. They were leaning together over a cookbook, arguing in good-natured tones.

Is there anyone Birdy couldn't work magic on? Alex doubted it.

Birdy waved at Alex as she came to stand at the table beside them. "So, come to join us, have you? Well, have a seat. We were just trying to decide what masterpiece to concoct."

"Say what?" Matty stared at Birdy, torn between confusion and laughter. "Lady, when you gonna start speakin' English?"

Birdy swatted the sinewy arm next to her. "Get on with you, boy. I'm speaking the King's English. And you will be, too, before we're done with ye."

"Dream on, old woman. Dream on."

"That's *Miss* Old Woman, to you, ye rascal."

Alex half heard the lively exchange, but she didn't take part. She was too busy trying to figure out what had just happened with Evan. The man had looked positively terrified, but of what?

You.

She crossed her arms against the reply but had to admit it was the only logical answer. Evan Noland was afraid of her. Why? She hadn't done anything. He was the one who'd grabbed her hand, for heaven's sake. Practically squeezed the blood out of it with those long, lean fingers of his.

"Alex?"

And he had the *nerve* to turn tail and run for the door. Just toss off that ridiculous comment about lunch and then run like the devil was nipping at his heels!

"Miss Wingate?"

Well! Of all the insulting—

"Alexandria!"

"*What?*" She bit her lip at the surprise on Birdy's and Matty's faces. "Oh, I'm sorry. I was…"

"Rude."

She opened her mouth to dispute Matty's succinct assessment, then clamped it shut. The kid was right. She let her frustration out in a huff. "Absolutely right, Matty. I was rude." The boy blinked at her. Clearly this wasn't the response he'd expected. But Alex wasn't finished. "I wasn't listening, and I should have been." She folded her hands in her lap. "What were you saying?"

He stared at her for a beat, until Birdy poked his arm. "Now *yer* bein' rude, boy. Out with it."

Matty shook his head. "Women. Go figure." With a shrug he pointed at the cookbooks in front of them. "It's a toss-up for lunch. Miss Birdy wants chicken."

Alex leaned her elbows on the table and rested her chin in her hands. "And what do you want, Matty?"

He pushed the cookbook toward her, and she glanced down at it. A smile sidled past her anger, lifting her lips and her heart. Oh, this was too perfect… "I side with Matty."

Birdy nodded. "So be it. Deep dish pizza, it is."

Alex's grin widened. "Not just deep dish. Stuffed. With extra cheese."

"*Hoo*-ah! I knew you was a sharp lady when I laid eyes on you!" Matty crowed. "This is gonna be great!"

"You have no idea," Alex replied as she walked to the fridge. "You have no idea."

Eight

*A*lex had just finished setting the table for lunch when she became aware she wasn't alone in the dining room.

Turning around, she discovered she had an audience. A young boy and an even younger little girl stood watching her. Alex smiled when she caught sight of Snufflebunny, the rabbit they'd rescued from the garbage dump, being squeezed in the crook of the girl's elbow.

"Well, hello there."

Neither child answered Alex. Instead, the boy took the little girl's hand and tugged her to the table. "What's for lunch? It better not be sandwiches. I'm sick of sandwiches. Almost as sick as I am of cereal for breakfast."

The boy's tone was low and just this side of hostile. Alex leaned on the back of one of the chairs. "How's pizza sound?" Her lips twitched. "With extra cheese."

His somber young eyes lit up at that, but he caught himself before he gave voice to his evident pleasure. Instead, he shoved his free hand into a pocket and shrugged. "Okay, I guess."

Alex straightened and held out her hand. "I'm Alex."

"I know."

She tilted her head at that.

Another shrug. "I heard Mr. Noland introduce you to Matty. And I know it's not polite to eavesdrop and I don't care."

What on earth had happened to make such a young boy so hostile? "And you are…?" She wasn't sure he was going to answer, then he jerked a chair away from the table and directed the little girl onto it.

"Peter," he mumbled. "Peter Telford. I live here."

Understanding swept Alex. So these were Tucker's children. She knelt down next to the little girl's chair. "I take it this little angel is your sister?"

Peter fixed her with a withering glare. "Penny's my sister, but she's not an angel. You hafta be dead to be an angel." He pulled out another chair and took his seat. "The only dead person in our family is my mom."

The comment was delivered with such a dearth of emotion that Alex found herself unable to speak for a moment. It took a lot of energy to keep emotions that tightly in rein—energy…and pain.

"Hi, Penny," Alex finally managed around her too-tight throat. "I'm Alex." She touched one of the now-clean stuffed rabbit's ears. "This happy fellow I've already met. Snufflebunny, right?"

The wide, somber eyes that turned her way held a depth of emotion that made Alex's heart want to break. Penny nodded solemnly, putting both arms around the rabbit and hugging it even harder.

"She doesn't talk to anyone but me."

Alex looked at Peter, frowning. "What about your father?"

Peter's face hardened. "Just me."

A sudden yap drew their attention. Dusty, who'd been sleeping quietly in the other room, apparently had awakened and decided someone should be paying homage.

"Here, girl," Alex called, and the little dog came skittering into the room, vaulting into her arms. Alex laughed, then turned to find Penny staring at Dusty, her eyes wide. The little girl's gaze shifted from the dog to Alex's face for a moment, then, Snufflebunny clutched to her chest, she reached out to lay a small, soft hand on Dusty's head. Alex stiffened, waiting for Dusty to snap or snarl—her usual reaction to a strange touch—but the little dog just tipped her head, inviting Penny to scratch an ear or two.

Before Alex could say anything, Penny slid from her chair and went to tug on her brother's shirt. He leaned down and she whispered in his ear.

He glanced at the ceiling, pushing her away. "No. Don't be stupid! Go sit down."

Alex stood. "What did she say?"

His mouth tightened, and he shrugged. "She wants to know if that's her kitten."

"Her kitten?"

"It's stupid, okay? Mr. Noland's been telling Penny how great prayer is, how God really hears and answers and stuff, so she's been praying for a kitten." He looked away. "She'll see, though. She'll see it's all a bunch of garbage."

Penny's small fist shot out and punched her brother in the arm.

"Hey! Knock it off. That's not a kitten, it's some kind of shrunken dog, okay?" He raised his hand as though to hit Penny back, and Alex let Dusty go and moved to catch Peter's fist midstrike. The look he directed at Alex was one of fury. "Don't touch me!"

"You shouldn't hit your sister." Alex was amazed at how calm her voice was.

Peter jerked away from her. "What do you know about it? She's *my* sister, not yours. I wish you'd leave us alone. I wish everyone would just leave us alone and quit pretending they care!"

Alex took a step toward him, her heart breaking for the despair in Peter's young voice. "They're not pretending, Peter. Not Mr. Noland or your daddy, anyway. They really do care—"

Peter all but vaulted out of his chair, grabbing Penny's hand and hauling her back with him. "Sure. My dad cares. That's why he let us go. That's why he let them take us to live in those crummy places."

Tears ran down his face, but Alex was fairly certain he didn't realize it. "Oh, Peter. I'm so sorry…"

His voice was choked now. "Everyone's sorry. But that doesn't change anything, does it? We still lived in those places. And there's still no such thing as God." He glared down at Penny. "And there's sure as heck not going to be any kittens showing up, no matter how much you say your stupid prayers."

With that, he stomped out of the room, dragging Penny behind him. But as he did so, the little girl turned and looked over her shoulder at Alex…and giving her a small, shy smile, she waved good-bye.

Lunch was more than just a meal. It was a study in behavioral psychology.

Tucker did his best to interact with his kids, but Peter was having none of it. From what Alex could see, Penny watched her father with a longing in her eyes…as though she wanted to be close to him but was afraid of upsetting Peter if she did so. What a burden for a little girl.

Matty and Teresa were something else altogether. Like her brother, Teresa was a strikingly attractive teenager. Unlike her brother, she smiled easily and laughed often. Her dark eyes were reminiscent of her brother's in color and form, but the similarity ended there. Where Matty's eyes gleamed with sullen detachment, Teresa's eyes danced with unbridled glee. She teased Matty unmercifully throughout the meal. Amazingly, Matty's only reaction was an indulgent smile and an occasional swat in his younger sister's general direction.

Clearly, Teresa was the apple of her brother's eye.

It was Teresa who erupted into giggles at the look on Evan's face when he came to the table and sat down, looked at his plate—and turned what Alex thought was a particularly interesting shade of green.

He lifted the plate with both hands, holding the edge between his thumbs and forefingers, and demanded, "What is this?"

Teresa laughed. "Come on, Mr. Noland. You've seen pizza before, haven't you?"

Alex allowed herself a small smile as she made a show of studying the monstrous slice of pizza on Evan's plate. Cheese oozed from on top of and between the layers of crust, flowing to the edges of the plate like lava from a volcano with overactive glands.

Evan's gaze met hers as he pushed the plate away, and she made her smile as sweet as her face could stand. "Not hungry, Mr. Noland?"

"Not hardly, Miss Wingate," came the dry response.

"But she made it special for you, Mr. Noland." Matty gave the older man a scolding look. "Least you could do, man, is taste it."

Evan's gaze remained on Alex, and his eyes narrowed a fraction. "Made it special for me, did you?"

Alex inclined her head in mock graciousness. "I thought you deserved it—"

"You want me to fix you a sandwich, Mr. Noland? *I* know the kind you like."

Evan and Alex started at the intrusion into their little duel, and both turned to look at Teresa. The girl was watching them carefully, and her eyes, as she looked at Evan, were filled with concern. But when she shot a glare at Alex, there was something more in those dark depths.

Jealousy.

"*Thank* you, Teresa." Evan directed a smile at the girl sitting opposite him. "That would be great. It's nice to have someone who *really* cares about me."

Alex knew his words were directed more at her than at Teresa, but she couldn't miss how they impacted the young girl. A hint of red flowed into Teresa's exquisite cheeks, and her dark eyes shone. She rose from her chair, pausing only to toss a triumphant smile Alex's way.

Oh, my... Alex looked from Evan to the girl and back again. *Now there's a problem waiting to happen.*

"So, Alex, you up to tackling a tough job this afternoon?"

She turned her attention back to Evan, lifting her chin at the challenge in his eyes. "Of course."

His smile was pure smug. "Great. I'd like for you to gather the eggs from the henhouse."

A sudden silence fell over the room, and Alex looked at the others. They were staring at her, odd expressions on their faces. What on earth was wrong with them?

"Sure. No problem."

"Evan, I'm not so sure that's a good idea..." Tucker's face was slightly pinched with uncertainty. "You know how testy those birds can be."

"Nonsense, Tucker. I'm sure Alex will be more than able to handle them. Unless—" Evan's gaze came back to Alex, the picture of courtly concern—"you think it might be too much for you? In which case, I'm sure we could find something for you to do." He waved his hand. "Sweeping, cleaning the bathrooms…"

"I'll take the chickens, thank you."

At her dry comment, Peter angled her a look. "Um, you ever been around chickens before?" His tone made it clear he had no more confidence in her than his father had. For heaven's sake! What could be so hard about gathering a bunch of eggs?

"Dozens of times. My family and chickens go way back." Well, in a way it was true. Her father owned several fast-food chicken restaurants.

Birdy opened her mouth, most likely to give Alex away, so she delivered a swift kick under the table.

At Birdy's yelp, Evan arched a brow, but Alex plunged on. "So, how many eggs do you want?"

Amusement danced in Evan's eyes and at the corners of his mouth. "As many as have been laid."

"Oh." Alex digested that. "Of course. I knew that."

Teresa came back in then, setting Evan's sandwich in front of him. "No cheese," she said, and Evan gave her a warm smile.

"Just the way I like it, Teresa. Thanks."

The girl was positively glowing as she went to sit down. Alex's heart hurt for her. She remembered the first serious crush she'd had on an older man. It had led to her first broken heart. She only hoped Teresa wouldn't end up in the same place.

But with a man as clueless as Evan evidently was, Alex was afraid that was exactly what was going to happen. Maybe she should say something to Evan, warn him before—

"This is great, Teresa," Evan said, dabbing at his mouth with a paper napkin with exaggerated pleasure. "Best sandwich I've ever had. Obviously *you* know what you're doing in the kitchen."

His implication was clear, and Alex gave him her best glare.

Then again, maybe she wouldn't say a word to Evan. She crumpled her napkin and plopped it on her now-empty plate. Far be it from her to interfere. He probably wouldn't even listen to her.

Besides, if ever someone deserved whatever trouble he got himself into, it was Evan Noland.

Nine

"Heeeere, chicky, chicky, chicky…"

Alex tried to make the call bold and confident, but her quavering heart betrayed her and her words sounded fearful even to her own ears. She couldn't believe it. She was afraid of a bunch of scrawny, knobby-kneed birds!

Of course, she'd never been this close to chickens before. At least, not live ones. There were quite a few of them, too, all scampering and squawking about. Then there was the fact that several of them had run at her, flapping their wings and making determined jabs at her legs with those rotten little beaks.

Why hadn't anyone ever told her chickens were mean-spirited little twerps?

Of course, it hadn't helped that Dusty had raced into the enclosure with her, snapping and yapping with glee as she caromed after the birds. It had taken Alex several frantic minutes to corral her dog and take the wriggling little hunter back inside. She'd closed Dusty into her room, then marched back out to face the chicken music.

But not even her fear of those feathered kamikazes would make her ask Evan for help. She'd considered asking Birdy to come along, but darned if her good friend hadn't disappeared this afternoon. Alex had hunted high and low for her, only to have Peter almost scare the living daylights out of her when he came up behind her and asked what she was looking for.

"Birdy," she replied.

"You mean Miss Hiffen-whatsit?"

"Hiffenstone," she corrected automatically. "Yes."

"She went to town."

Alex wondered absently what Peter's face would look like without a scowl.

"With my dad."

So much for calling in the cavalry.

"They went together."

Alex cocked her head, but Peter wasn't done.

"Laughing."

Fighting the ripple of mirth that was sparked by his dour proclamation, Alex forced her tone to be neutral. "Together, huh? And laughing? Hmm—" she wiggled her brows—"could be serious."

His baleful glare just before he stomped from the room was almost her undoing. Clearly Peter was less than pleased that Birdy was spending time with his dad. Well, she's wasn't overly thrilled about it herself. Not at the moment, anyway. How could Birdy go gallivanting about just when Alex needed her?

Gallivanting? Her grin broke free at that. Since when did Birdy *gallivant?*

Still chuckling, she went to retrieve a basket from the pantry area. Well, Birdy or no Birdy, she had a job to do.

Straightening her back, Alex marched outside, right to the chicken enclosure. She hesitated only a moment at the sight of all the little feathered bodies doing the herky-jerky in the enclosure. *These are helpless, little chickens,* she encouraged herself. *They'll probably just run away.*

With that, she opened the gate and stepped inside—only to find herself the target of poultry posturing as a particularly large bird flew at her with a shriek that had to have come straight from the mouth of Hades.

It was only Alex's ability to high-step and scramble that saved her hide.

"That's the rooster."

At the quiet, maddeningly smug words, Alex peeked out from her hiding place—behind the coop. Peter was standing there, watching her. He jerked his chin toward the large bird that had launched itself at Alex.

"The rooster," the boy repeated.

The rooster! Well! Apparently the little monster wasn't content with just ruining her sleep more mornings than she cared to count. Now he was trying to kill her. "What's he got against me?"

Peter shrugged. "He's protecting his clutch."

"Well, bully for him," she muttered, fixing a glare on the large, reddish creature. "Can you say drop-kick, Mr. Rooster?"

Peter actually giggled at that, and Alex gave him a quick smile, hoping her surprise didn't show. His expression as he studied her was pensive. Then he opened the gate and eased into the enclosure. "Let me distract him. Then you can go into the coop and get the eggs."

Alex peered around the coop, looking inside. What eggs? She didn't see any eggs. Just a bunch of birds sitting around, clucking. She frowned.

"The hens are sitting on the eggs."

She shot another look at Peter and gave him a sheepish grin. "That evident I didn't know, huh?"

He shrugged. "I could tell at lunch that you didn't know nothin' about chickens. Why do you think I came out here?"

"To watch me make a fool of myself?"

"Now you're talkin'," he quipped in a perfect imitation of his father. They both burst into laughter, and Alex didn't know which of them was most surprised.

Moments later, Peter had the rooster backed into a corner and yelled at Alex over his shoulder, "Go for it!"

She scampered inside the coop, noting that the low clucking she'd been hearing since she opened the gate increased in intensity. She paused, holding her breath, and looked from side to side. There looked to be two shelves, each with six or seven hens sitting there, on piles of straw. Their little feathered heads were doing the bob and weave as they fixed Alex with beady-eyed glares.

She had the oddest feeling they were taunting her!

Squaring her shoulders as best she could in the cramped quarters, she stepped to the first hen. "Move."

The bird lowered its head, a low sound gurgling in its throat—and the other hens increased their clucking again. The hairs on the back of Alex's neck rose in response, and she shivered. What was this? Some weirded out Stephen King movie?

Keeping her eye on the hen, she muttered in a low, theatrical tone, "They're small…they're feathered…and they're out for blood. The Chickens. Compared to them, Cujo was a kitten and Christine was a Hyundai. Don't even *think* about stealing their eggs…"

She swallowed a nervous giggle, then reached out to poke a cautious finger under the hen, trying to disturb the creature as little as possible. Her eyes widened. There were eggs underneath; she could feel them.

Biting her lip, she flattened her hand out and tried to slide it under the hen as slowly as she could.

Obviously it wasn't slow enough.

With a sound that was somewhere between a cackle and a

shriek, the hen launched itself at Alex, flapping and pecking like mad.

"Aaaaahhhhhh!" Alex's scream mingled with the sudden cacophony of chicken hysteria as the other hens followed the first bird's lead. Before she could say Shake 'n' Bake, Alex found herself in the middle of a chicken tornado. She swung the basket wildly, felt it connect several times, felt something wet and sticky on her head, but didn't quite stop swinging. She couldn't; the cloud of flailing birds was still coming at her.

Suddenly something grabbed the back of her shirt and gave a mighty tug. With a yelp, she went flying backward, out the door of the coop.

"Alex, calm down! I've got you."

The fight went out of her when she recognized Evan's voice. She went limp, sagging against him, trembling from head to toe. He circled her shoulders with a sheltering arm and led her from the enclosure.

"How…" She had to swallow and try again. "How did you know? That I needed help, I mean?"

He plucked a piece of straw from her hair. "I'm intuitive that way. I hear a bloodcurdling scream, I figure someone needs help. That and the fact that Peter came after me—" he inclined his head, and Alex saw that both Peter and Teresa were standing by the chicken enclosure watching them—"hollering that the hens were ganging up on you."

She managed a choking laugh, and Evan leaned down to peer into her face. She jumped a little when his hand came up to stroke her face; the gentle touch of his fingers trailing down her cheek, along her jaw, was the most disturbing sensation she'd ever had.

"You okay?"

Her wide eyes met his concerned gaze, and she had to try

twice before she could force any words from her suddenly dry throat. "I...I think so—oh!" She looked at the coop. "Oh, did I hurt them?"

Her gaze collided with Teresa's, and Alex stiffened. The girl was staring at her with what could only be called an ice-cold loathing. "Well, you didn't do 'em any good." Her tone was filled with outrage. "Them hens will probably never lay another egg."

"I don't know about that—" Evan said, giving Alex's hand a squeeze—"But I'm betting at least two of them won't be walking a straight line anytime soon."

Alex must have looked as stricken as she felt because he reached out to pluck a piece of straw from her hair, a spark of some indefinable emotion in the eyes that studied her. "But you can sure sign up for my softball team anytime. I think you hit two or three home runs in there."

She moved a still-shaking hand to brush the hair from her face, but Evan caught her fingers in a gentle grip.

"Uh, better not."

A sound from behind them pulled Alex's attention from the sight of Evan's hand covering hers. Peter was alone now. Alex looked around and saw Teresa stomping toward the house.

"I think she's upset about the chickens," Peter offered. "She just kicked the gate and walked away."

"She'll be fine, Peter," Evan said. "Teresa's just got a soft heart, that's all. She hates to see anything injured." He tugged at Alex's hand, and she turned back to him, frowning her question. An easy smile played at his mouth. "Come with me."

Any resistance she'd been feeling melted at the low command. He led her back into the house, to the bathroom just off the porch, then gently placed his hands on her shoulders. "Close your eyes, Alex."

"What?"

He shook his head at her, a teasing light in his eyes. "Trust me. Close your eyes."

She swallowed, then slowly, hesitantly, did as he asked. He applied a gentle pressure, directing her until she stood in front of him.

"Okay, open them."

She hesitated, then let her eyes open and found herself in front of the mirror, staring at…at…

"Ack!"

His fingers tightened on her shoulders. "Steady, now. It's nothing a good shower won't take care of."

"I…but…oh, good grief!" She couldn't believe the sight that met her eyes. Her hair stuck out in all directions, a masterpiece of madness plastered in place by a mishmash of straw, feathers, egg shells, and raw egg. The dripping yolks were making a sticky path from her hair down the sides of her face—which provided an interesting complement to the broken eggs and bird droppings splattered all over her shirt.

"Why don't you hop in the shower?" At least Evan's tone was gentle…at least, she thought it was, beneath all that barely restrained mirth. "I'll send Aunt Bert down with some clean clothes for you."

"But—"

Evan paused in the doorway, brows arched.

Heat filled her cheeks as she held out the empty basket, which was still clutched in her hand. "What about the eggs?"

He nearly choked—on laughter, she was sure—and Peter came to take the basket from her. "I'll get 'em."

Both Alex and Evan looked down at him. He shrugged. "Dad keeps tellin' me he wants us to do things together, so when he and Miss Hiffen-whosit get back, I'll ask him to take me to the store."

Alex smiled her thanks. "Thank you, Peter. That's very nice."

His cheeks went pink. "No big deal. I'm tired of cereal, that's all." With that, he ducked out of the bathroom.

Alex and Evan looked at each other, and a slow grin eased its way across Evan's features. "I think you've got a bit of a fan there."

Her responding smile was warm. "He's a good kid." She turned slightly and caught a glimpse of herself again. "Uh, Evan, about tomorrow?" She faced him with a sigh. "Can I do something that has nothing to do with eggs?"

His grin broadened.

"Or chickens," she added for good measure.

He winked at her, and the only thing that surprised her more was the emotions that playful action stirred up inside her.

"You got it, Alex. I'm sure Tucker will be happy to have you working with him."

"Okay—" she said, trying to throttle the dizzying currents running through her—"great. Whatever."

He hesitated, and she turned quickly to turn on the water in the shower, then gave him a pointed look. "Now, if you don't mind, I'd like to get this gunk out of my hair."

Evan beat a hasty exit, and Alex turned back to the mirror with a low sigh, listening to his deep chuckle as he made his way down the hallway.

Awake, my love…

At the whispered call, she gave a shiver of awareness and leaned her head against the mirror. *I'm awake,* she replied, leaning her cheek against the cool glass. *Oh, boy, am I awake.*

Now if she could just figure out how to turn off the alarm!

Ten

It was late in the afternoon when a soft sound pulled Evan from the paperwork on his desk.

It was an incessant sound...a kind of *plop...plop... plop...*

Frowning, Evan looked up—and his jaw dropped.

Tucker stood in the doorway to Evan's office, brows drawn together, an expression on his face that reminded Evan of a brewing thunderstorm. Which was only appropriate, since Tucker was wet. Not just wet, mind you, but *soaking* wet, from head to toe. As Evan watched, tiny rivers ran from Tucker's hat, cascading to the floor, and Evan realized that was the sound he'd heard.

Evan's gaze traveled from Tucker's drenched, sagging hat, to his shirt—which was now missing a pocket that Evan was sure had been there at lunch—on down to one pant leg, which was hanging in shreds.

Without a word, Tucker moved into the room—a sickly *squii- ish* sounding with each step—and Evan was startled at the man's decided limp.

"Tucker, what—?" he began, rising from his chair, but Tucker held up a gloved hand, in which he clutched something green... something with dirt still clinging to the roots. As Tucker made his way to the desk, little clumps of dirt dropped onto the floor, mixing with the soggy trail Tucker was making.

Slowly, deliberately, Tucker laid his burden on the desk in

front of Evan. He looked down and saw that it was some kind of wilted plant. He brought his gaze up to Tucker's again.

"Know what that is?"

Evan shook his head.

Tucker sighed. "It's what's left of my *Pyrus salicifolia* 'Pendula.'"

"Your…what?"

He closed his eyes, then opened them again, slowly. "My Pacific Coast Iris. The one I transplanted last spring…"

Evan nodded. He remembered it clearly. Tucker received a starter plant from an elderly woman they'd met during a trip to the coast. For some reason, she'd just walked up to him and handed him the plant, all wrapped in a paper towel. She'd told Tucker God had asked her to share it with him, to remind him that it takes care and nurture for things to grow. "And patience," she'd said in that crackly voice, "lots and lots of patience."

Tucker hadn't challenged the woman. He'd taken the gift and held it carefully, nursing it during the drive home. Peter and Penny had helped him, making sure the paper towel was kept damp but not too wet. And they'd planted it together.

Over the past year, Tucker had watched over that plant as if it were one of his kids. Evan looked down, staring at the sad little uprooted thing. How on earth had it ended up like this?

"Alex."

At the one-word answer to his silent question, Evan felt his stomach clench. "Alex?" he asked, meeting Tucker's long-suffering gaze.

"Alex." Tucker's sigh was long and low. "I told her to pull weeds. Guess she didn't know which was weeds and which was plants."

"Ah." Evan eyed Tucker's torn shirt. "And the pocket?"

"She was trying to dig a hole to plant one of the rosebushes we bought last weekend. Apparently the ground was a bit hard, so she jumped up on the shovel with both feet, then hopped up and down on it as hard as she could." He glanced down, rubbing his hand over his forehead. "She lost her balance 'bout the same time I came along. Grabbed at whatever she could to keep from falling." He looked up again. "My pocket was just most handy, I reckon."

Evan's lips twitched. He was not going to laugh. Not with Tucker standing there looking so…abused. He chomped down on the inside of his lips. Hard. "The pants?"

"Weed wacker."

Evan grimaced. "Ouch." He hated to ask, but…"And the limp?"

"Guess I shoulda checked first to see if'n she knew how to drive a wheelbarrow. Ran down two bushes and my shin trying to figger it out."

Evan's gaze peered over the edge of the desk at the water pooling at Tucker's feet. "I take it you had her help you with the sprinklers?"

Tucker took hold of his shirttail, wringing the water from it, watching as it joined the puddle on the floor. "Seemed like a good idea at the time."

Evan looked down, ostensibly to rummage through the papers on his desk, but mostly to control his features before the laughter escaped him. Poor Tucker! "Tell you what, Tuck. If you can spare her, I think we probably need Alex to give Birdy a hand in the kitchen tomorrow. Sound okay?"

Tucker cleared his throat, then nodded. "Sounds fine to me, Mr. Evan."

"Now you're talkin'."

Evan knew that was the closest Tucker would ever come to

asking him to take Alex off his hands. He watched the older man turn with care and head for the doorway. Evan was about to turn back to his papers when Tucker paused.

Evan tilted his head. "Yes?"

Tucker turned to face him. "You know, that young woman 'bout killed me today—"

"Look, Tucker, I'm sor—"

The man shook his head, leaning on the doorjamb. "No need to apologize, 'cuz for all that I may never walk right again, I wouldn't have changed a thing about the day."

"You wouldn't?"

"Nope, 'cuz something happened out there." He angled a look at Evan that told him Tucker was still sorting through it all. "I mean, it was the darndest thing. You know how we can never get Matty to help with the yard work?"

"Yeah…"

"Well, 'bout the second time Miss Alex ran into me with the wheelbarrow, the kid shows up, like outta nowhere. Takes the handles from her and wheels it like a pro right to where we wanted it."

Evan straightened in his chair. "You're kidding."

Tucker gave a slow shake of his head. "Nope. He stuck with her all day, helping her out, digging the holes for her, showing her how to do things right…and the whole time, they was talkin' and laughin' like old pals."

Evan blinked. "Laughing?"

The chuckle that escaped Tucker was low and rich. "I know! Didn't think the kid knew how to laugh until today." Another head shake, and then he pushed away from the doorjamb, hands in his soggy pockets. "Darndest thing I ever did see." He held Evan's gaze. "God did something out there today, Mr. Evan. Ain't no other way to say it. And I'm just glad I was around to see it."

"*I'm* just glad you survived it, Tuck."

A slow grin curled its way across Tucker's mouth. "Yeah, me too, boss. Me too."

"Well, tomorrow we'll see what miracles God wants to work in the kitchen, okay, Tucker?"

The man nodded, but as he left the room, his final words drifted back to Evan. "Just do us all a favor and keep her away from the knives."

Evan pulled Aunt Bert aside right after dinner.

"What say you have Alex help you in the kitchen tomorrow?"

"Has she finished her outside work so quickly, then?"

He bent his head and studied his hands for a moment. "Let's just say she's finished Tucker so quickly."

Aunt Bert's sharp gaze turned back to the doorway through which Tucker had left just after the meal. "Oh, dear. I did notice the dear man was limpin' a bit."

"Look, Aunt Bert, Alex is a great gal…"

She folded her hands in front of her. "She has a heart of purest gold, that girl."

"Yes, ma'am, she does…"

"And two left feet when it comes to doing things of a practical nature."

Evan's sigh gave vent to his relief that his aunt understood. He chuckled. "Yes, ma'am. Exactly so."

Aunt Bert's soft eyes met his, and he saw the entreaty there. "Evan, m'boy, she so wants to help. She's a young woman lookin' for a place to belong."

The words struck his heart with a force he didn't understand.

Lots of the people who came to Heaven's Corner were looking for that, a place to belong. But hearing the words this particular time, about this particular woman...well, it rocked him. And a responding desire welled up within him—a desire dredged from a place deep within him...a place beyond logic and reason.

Suddenly he wanted nothing more than to find Alex, to fold her into his arms and draw her close, to tell her she belonged, all right. And she always would. Right here. With him.

Evan sucked in a breath and planted his hand on the wall, desperate for the feel of something solid.

"Evan?"

He jerked his gaze to meet his aunt's eyes and forced a non-chalance to his voice. "We just need to keep Alex someplace safe, okay?"

Aunt Bert frowned slightly. "Certainly, dear—"

He waved a hand. "Give her something easy to fix for lunch tomorrow. Something simple. Oh—" Tucker's parting words rang in his memory—"and something where she won't have to use anything sharp."

"Sharp?"

"Yeah, you know, like knives or shish kebab sticks or those little corn holders with the spikes or anything like that." He was rambling. He knew it, but he couldn't stop himself. He closed his eyes. He never rambled! At least, he never had until Alex Wingate showed up and, seemingly without even trying, managed to obliterate his ability to think clearly.

Help, Lord... I think I'm going crazy.

It's not good for man to be alone.

Forget alone, Lord. I think I'm goin' nuts!

A gentle touch on his arm opened his eyes, and he met his aunt's worried eyes. "Evan, dear..."

He patted her hand. "I'm okay, Aunt Bert. Just a little tired, but it's nothing a good night's sleep won't fix."

"Are you sure, dear?"

He gave a firm nod. "Positive. Eight hours of shut-eye and I'll be like new." He leaned down and gave her a peck on her lean cheek. "Scout's honor."

"Ye were never a scout, m'boy."

At the wry words, he laughed out loud. "Is there anything you don't know?"

The grin that creased her angular features was decidedly cheeky. "If there is, m'boy, it's simply not worth the knowin'. Now, come take a walk with yer old auntie. I'm thinkin' my bones—and your brain—could use it."

Gratitude washed over him. "Right you are, Auntie."

"Well, of course, dear boy. Of course."

Alex scampered out of sight, dodging from the dining room to the kitchen just as Birdy and Evan came into the room, on their way to the back door.

She plastered herself against the wall, heart palpitating as though she'd just downed ten triple-espressos, until she was certain they were gone and she'd been undetected.

Tears smarted at her eyes and she let herself give the air a vicious kick. Take that, Evan Noland! She hadn't meant to eavesdrop. Really she hadn't. She'd gone in search of Birdy to ask her a quick question but had halted at the sound of Evan's hushed voice. Realizing Birdy and Evan were talking in the hallway, she started to leave. Until she heard Evan say her name.

She'd been less than helpful today, she knew that. As much as she wanted to help Tucker, she'd only ended up getting in his way.

She grimaced. Or worse. When Tucker walked into the dining room this evening still limping, she had felt even more terrible than when she'd run into him with that blasted wheelbarrow. But still…

She almost convinced herself it all had a reason, that God was using even her lack of ability to do things to work miracles—and this afternoon's miracle had come in the form of Matteo Navarro. They'd had such a great time today! She'd been stunned when he came up behind her and stopped her from jumping, yet again, on the shovel. He took the shovel out of her hands, a faint glint of humor in those deep, brown eyes. "You gonna kill yourself, *mija.*"

Mija? He didn't call anyone but Teresa that…

Alex had stood there, mouth agape, as Matty turned around and started digging. He stuck around the rest of the afternoon, digging holes, planting bushes, talking, and teasing Alex in much the same way Teresa usually went after him.

Once, as she and Matty were laughing, Alex caught Tucker's eye. Just that morning he had told her that the two things Matty never did were joke around or get his hands dirty. They grinned at each other over Matty's bent head; each aware that Matty was doing not just one, but *both* of those things even as they watched.

Alex had been so certain that God was moving, and everything inside of her had rejoiced, had felt warm and—dare she admit it?—at home. God had brought her here; she was sure of it. And watching Matty, laughing and talking with him, made her feel, for the first time in her life, as though she had a purpose, a place.

As though she belonged.

But now…

Now her delight in the afternoon with Matty had dimmed. Evan's words slammed around in her head, ricocheting off the walls of her self-worth: "*…she finished Tucker that quickly…keep*

Alex someplace safe… where she won't have to use anything sharp…"

Alex gritted her teeth.

Here she was, struggling with these inexplicable feelings she had for Evan—for a guy she'd just met, for crying out loud—feeling for the first time in her life as though she might actually belong somewhere…and now…now…

He was laughing at her.

Tears stung her eyes, but she didn't give in to them. Instead, she clenched her fists at her sides. She'd show him. She'd show them all. Tomorrow, she'd not only use knives, but she'd use whatever it took to fix these people the best darned meal they'd ever had.

And then—her lips trembled and she pressed them together with fierce determination—she was putting as much distance between herself and Evan Noland as possible.

Eleven

Alex studied the sheet of paper where she'd written down Birdy's recipe for chili.

"It's an easy, tasty meal to fix, m'dear," Birdy had patted her on the arm as she went over the recipe with her. "You'll do grand, I'm sure of it."

So sure, in fact, that when Tucker had stuck his head in the kitchen and asked Birdy if she wanted to go help him pick out rosebushes, she'd scarcely given Alex a second look as she sailed from the room.

Alex sucked on a fingernail. So what if her mentor had abandoned her in favor of a bunch of thorny roses? So what if she'd never cooked a meal by herself in her life? So what? She could handle this by herself.

She focused on the recipe again. She'd copied it down as accurately as possible from Birdy's recitation. She read over each item again, relieved that it all made sense. Well, almost all.

"C powder? What the dink is C powder?" Oh dear. She should have listened more carefully.

"Mr. Noland know you're back in the kitchen?"

At the cool question, Alex turned to find Teresa watching her from the doorway into the dining room. "He knows," she said with a smile. "Don't worry; I'm not going anywhere near the cheese."

Teresa almost laughed at that. Almost. Alex had the definite impression the girl was determined not to like her. She started to say something, to reassure Teresa that she was merely passing through, when the girl moved to peer down at the recipe in Alex's hands.

"Chili?" She crossed her arms, leaning one slim hip against the table. "I make chili all the time."

"Really?" Alex's concerns about the girl vanished at this news. "Then do you have any idea what this ingredient should be?"

Teresa narrowed her eyes, reading, then brought her gaze to meet Alex's. "C powder…"

"I wasn't listening as well as I should have—"

The girl straightened, then went right to a cupboard, pulled it open, and reached inside. She came back to Alex and handed her a small, metal box.

Alex looked down at it. The name of the spice wasn't exactly what she'd written down, still…it started with a "C." And the box was red. Chili was usually red, wasn't it?

She looked up at Teresa. "Are you sure this is right?"

The smile that lifted the girl's beautiful lips was one of utter delight. "Oh, it's right all right. You use that, Miss Alex, just like it says. Four tablespoons. It'll be a chili they never forget. I promise."

Without thinking, Alex reached out and pulled Teresa into a tight hug. "Thanks, sweetie. You're great."

Teresa pulled away, then hesitated. She looked as if she was about to say something, then she shook her head. "I got things to do." With that, she hurried from the kitchen.

With a satisfied sigh, Alex went about following the recipe as carefully as possible, browning the meat—which resulted in only two or three burns from spattering grease before she figured out she shouldn't have the burner on high. Finally, everything was in the pot but the last ingredient. Picking up the small, square metal box, she tapped out the required four tablespoons of powder, dumped it in, stirring. It already smelled great! She put the lid on the pot, a slow grin easing its way across her features as she did so. If she'd known cooking was this easy, she'd have done it long ago.

She clapped her hands together. On to the cornbread!

Evan couldn't believe the tantalizing aroma drifting his way. Mouthwatering. He pushed back his chair and headed for the kitchen.

Peeking around the corner, he found the room empty, but there on the counter were pans of cornbread. A pot was on the stove; the lid bouncing a bit as whatever was inside simmered away. Evan drew in an appreciative sniff of the still-warm cornbread. Alex had made this? He shook his head. Birdy must have helped her. Still…it smelled wonderful.

A quick glance in either direction told him no one was about, and he grabbed a knife, but just before he plunged it in, he paused. It really wouldn't be fair to Alex to cut up her masterpiece before it was time.

His glance slid over to the pot on the stove. No one would be able to tell, though, that he'd snitched a bowl of chili. Grinning, he found a bowl and a ladle, scooping out a generous portion of the rich, meaty concoction. If this was the first meal Alex had ever cooked, she was a natural.

The first spoonful was heaven. The rich spices tantalized his tongue, and there was just enough bite to make him sweat. Perfect. Just the way chili should be.

Keeping an eye on the doorways, he gulped down the rest of the bowl. No sense lingering over it, no matter how good it was.

He didn't want to get caught sneaking an early taste. He smacked his lips, which were tingling now, and lifted the lid on the pot. There was plenty. He could snitch another small bowl and no one would ever know.

It was on the third spoonful that he realized his lips were no longer tingling. They were numb. And the pleasant bite at the back of his throat had become something more.

Like a burn. No, a blaze. His eyes widened and suddenly filled with tears. No, make that an out-of-control, five-alarm, some-body-get-the-*firehose!* inferno.

"What do you think you're doing?"

He couldn't even respond to Alex's indignant exclamation— mostly because he couldn't breathe! Gasping, eyes streaming, stomach suddenly roiling, he made a mad dash for the slop sink in the utility room. He made it in time. Barely.

He turned on the faucet full blast, stuck his face under the cooling stream, and sucked water into his burning mouth and throat.

"Evan, are you all right?"

Apparently Alex had followed him in his mad dash. It was several minutes before he could answer her, but finally he was able to pull his head out of the sink and angle a look her direction.

"What—" His raw throat barely managed a raspy whisper— "what's in that chili?"

She frowned, looking from him to the pot on the stove. "Just the stuff from the recipe, why?"

"What's happening here?"

They both turned to find Birdy standing at the doorway to the utility room. Her eyes widened as she took in Evan's sopping face and soggy shirtfront. Without a word she moved to the shelf above the washing machine, grabbed a towel, and brought it to him.

"Are you saying my chili is what made you sick?"

Alex was clearly affronted, but he just met her look. "That's what I'm saying." He led the way into the kitchen, pulled a glass from the cupboard, and filled it with ice and water. This he set on the counter next to Birdy, then he held the bowl of chili out to her. With an apologetic glance at Alex, she lifted the spoon and took a bite.

"Why, Evan, I think it's quite tasty—"

"Try some more," was all he said.

"Oh, really now!"

He ignored Alex and held the bowl out to Birdy again, who did as he'd requested. After the third bite, her eyes grew as round as saucers, and her hands flew to her mouth. She made a dive for the glass of ice water and downed it in record time. By the third glass of water, she was finally able to talk again.

"Oh my…" She fanned her mouth. "Alexandria, child, where is the recipe you used?"

With a huff, she produced a paper with the recipe scrawled on it. Birdy read it carefully.

"I followed it perfectly," Alex declared, counting off ingredients on her fingers. "Two pounds of ground beef, two cans of kidney beans, one small onion, chopped celery, four tablespoons of cayenne pepper—"

"*What?*"

Birdy and Evan asked the question together, startling Alex from her recitation. She frowned. "*What* what?"

Again, Birdy and Evan spoke together.

"Cayenne pepper?"

"*Four* tablespoons?"

They looked first at each other, then back at Alex, whose utter bewilderment was evident on her face. Birdy looked down at the recipe in her hand again. "Alexandria, where on this sheet do you see cayenne pepper listed?"

There was a hint of red seeping into Alex's cheeks. "Well, it isn't. But I couldn't remember what C powder stood for."

"Four tablespoons of cayenne pepper—" Evan shook his head, then chuckled and shot Birdy a glance—"we're lucky we're alive."

"Would one of you explain what's going on?"

Alex was clearly peeved by now. Birdy stepped forward, circling her protégé's shoulders with a comforting arm. "C powder, m'dear, is *chili* powder. And it's vastly different from cayenne pepper. Four tablespoons of chili powder makes wonderful chili. On the other hand, four tablespoons of cayenne pepper, makes… um…"

Evan figured it was better to show than tell. "Here." He held out a spoonful of the chili to Alex. She hesitated, then, shoulders back, stepped forward and took a bite.

"Hey—" her eyes lit up—"that's pretty good."

Evan's glance met Birdy's over Alex's head, and they grinned. "Have another bite," he said.

"Don't mind if I do." So saying, Alex took the bowl from him and, before he knew what she was up to, ate several more bites.

"Alex, wait!"

"Oh, child—"

She cut them both off with a wave of her spoon, then scooped up the last of the chili from the bowl.

"Alexandria…" But this time it was Evan who stopped Birdy's intervention by putting a restraining hand on her arm. She glanced at him and he shook his head.

Alex ate the last, large spoonful. "I don't know what you two are so worked up about—" she said, licking the spoon—"this stuff is…"

Evan leaned back against the counter in front of the sink, crossing his arms, watching as Alex's words died out and her face began to change color.

"Is...is..." she tried again, blinking rapidly, her cheeks going from pink to red.

He arched his brows. "Yes?"

She clamped her mouth shut, her face white now, and her desperate gaze moved from him to the faucet and back again. The look in her eyes said it all. He turned on the cold water and stepped aside.

"*Hot!*" Alex yelped just before she shoved past him and stuck her face into the sink. "Oh my gosh! *HOT!*"

As Alex coughed and gasped and gulped water, Birdy moved to stand beside Evan.

"Now what?" she asked on a sigh.

He angled a look at her. "Now you fix a new pot of chili. And—" he couldn't hold back the rueful grin—"we find something for Alex to do away from the kitchen."

"Far away, I presume."

His answering nod was as solemn as he could make it around his grin. "Far, far away."

Birdy nodded, watching Alex at the sink. "Yes, well. At least we kept her away from the knives."

Alex sat on the porch swing, her hand on Dusty's head, scratching the dog's ears as she slept. With a deep sigh, Alex lifted her head to stare up at the clear, night sky. She'd been here for several days now, and she still couldn't get over the beauty of the night sky out here.

"You didn't tell Mr. Noland."

She turned with a start; Teresa was standing there.

Alex cocked her head, regarding the girl in silence for a moment. "No, I didn't tell him."

A huff of air escaped the girl and she came to sit on the swing beside Alex, casting a doubtful look at the snoozing Dusty. "That dog don't bite, does it?"

Alex smiled. "Not when she's asleep." At Teresa's pointed look, she shook her head. "Dusty's okay. A little high-strung at times, but then, most of us are like that sometimes."

Teresa settled back against the seat. "So why didn't you tell? I mean, I would have if someone pulled on me what I pulled on you."

Alex leaned back in the swing. "I figured you just made a mistake."

Teresa's sidelong glance told Alex she wasn't buying it, and Alex grinned. She turned to face the girl, reaching out to lay a tentative hand on her arm. "I didn't tell them because I didn't want to get you into any trouble. And no one was really hurt—"

"Mr. Noland looked pretty green." There was a mixture of regret and wry amusement in the girl's tone, and at Alex's raised brow she shrugged. "I was watchin' from the dining room. But you all were so caught up in what you were doin' that you didn't even see me."

Alex grinned. "I don't think you can see the dining room when your face is in the sink."

Teresa chuckled, then grew silent. She started to speak, then closed her mouth.

"It's okay, Teresa. I understand."

The girl gave her a quick look, studying Alex's face.

"Mr. Noland is a good man," Alex went on. "He's caring and honest and he believes in his friends. Like Matty. And Tucker."

Alex offered Teresa a soft smile. "And you."

Teresa's eyes lit up. "You think he considers me a friend?"

Alex nodded. "I'm sure he does."

Another deep sigh escaped the girl, and she settled back into the swing. "Matteo told me I was being stupid." Her eyes shifted toward Alex for a moment, and her tone was grudging as she admitted, "He likes you, you know. My brother." Her grin was lopsided. "He doesn't like many people. Mr. Noland. Mr. Telford, maybe. They're the first people he's liked in a long time. Then you and the bird lady show up—"

Alex's lips twitched. "The...bird lady?"

A glint of humor finally returned to Teresa's beautiful dark eyes. "That's what Matteo calls her, 'the bird lady.' He says she reminds him of those birds you always see delivering babies."

"You mean storks." At Teresa's nod, Alex giggled. "I suppose she does a bit, doesn't she?"

Teresa's answering smile was warm. "Yeah, but he likes her, you know? Says she treats him good, like she thinks he's smart." She drew her knees to her chest and circled them with her arms. "And he likes you, too."

Warmth swept through Alex at that. "I'm glad."

With a sigh, Teresa laid her cheek on her knees, watching Alex as she spoke, reaching out a cautious hand to touch Dusty's fur. A smile broke out on her young face. "She's really soft, isn't she?"

Alex nodded. "You'd be surprised what a nice dog Dusty is if you'd just give her a chance."

Teresa's next words told Alex the girl had understood the underlying meaning in her words. "Matteo told me I shouldn't have treated you the way I did." At Alex's surprised look, she shrugged. "I told him about the chili. I felt real bad, you know? And he could tell. He asked me what was wrong, and...well—"

another small shrug—"I never could keep secrets from him. He told me I was stupid, about you and about Mr. Noland. Said I should be glad you're here. That you're the kind of lady who could be a good friend."

Alex blinked away the tears that sprang to her eyes. "That was nice of him."

"Nah." Teresa's grin was quick. "Matteo's not nice. Just honest, you know? He says what he thinks. And you know what? I think maybe he's right. He said Mr. Noland is too old for me for anything but a friend. That he just sees me as a little girl."

At the slightly wounded tone in Teresa's voice, Alex laid a gentle hand on her arm. "He thinks a great deal of you, Teresa. He wants the best for you."

She rubbed her cheek against her knees, then leaned back. "I know." She fell silent for a moment, then turned to Alex again. "Mr. Noland, he's a nice man."

Alex followed suit and leaned back in the swing, looking up at the sky. "Very nice."

Teresa reached up to gather her thick, black hair in her hands, winding it into a loose knot at the back of her neck. "And he's pretty good looking."

"Very good looking," Alex said without thinking, then bit her lip.

Teresa's eyes sparkled. "*Very* good, eh?" She giggled and Alex laughed, despite the heat filling her cheeks. With a start, Dusty woke up. Casting a baleful glance at both Teresa and Alex, she stood, stretched, then jumped down and trotted off.

Teresa grinned. "Oh, yeah, a real nice little dog. Real friendly, eh?"

Alex lifted her shoulders. "Hey, we all have our moments."

Teresa's gaze followed Dusty. "Just some of us more than others, right?" She shook her head. "Okay, with Mr. Noland, I'll go with *very* good looking. But Matteo, he's pretty smart for a boy. I think he's right. Mr. Noland, he's too old for me, you know? To be anything but my friend."

There was a note of sad resignation in her words, and Alex waited, giving the girl time to process her thoughts, her feelings. They sat in companionable silence, watching the stars twinkle above them.

"I think," Teresa finally said into the darkness, "that being Mr. Noland's friend is a good thing."

"A very good thing," Alex agreed, a smile tugging at her lips.

Teresa turned toward her then, and her answering smile was easy and playful. "*Si*, a very good thing." She reached out to take Alex's hand in hers. "Almost as good as having you for a friend."

Alex squeezed Teresa's hand, unable to do anything but nod. Teresa smiled. "I'll tell you another very good thing, Miss Alex."

"What's that?" The question came out in an emotion-choked whisper.

"The day you came here." Warmth moved through Alex, wrapping around her heart, filling it with a joy she didn't fully understand, but she embraced it all the same. She had to swallow twice before she could speak.

"Thank you."

And then, as though He hadn't already done enough, God took the miracle of Teresa's changed heart one step further when the young girl leaned her head on Alex's shoulder and uttered a happy sigh. "Thank God, eh?" she said, her hand still holding Alex's. "I mean, I think He's the one who brought you here. 'Cuz He knew we needed you."

Almost as much, Alex thought, wonder filling her heart to overflowing, *as I needed you.*

❧

Evan leaned back against the wall, watching the steam rise from the mugs he held in each hand. He hadn't meant to eavesdrop. He'd thought it might be nice to join Alex on the porch, bring her some cocoa.

He'd halted as soon as he heard voices, then started to leave when he realized Alex was talking with Teresa. But then he'd heard his name…and something about the chili…

He blew out a breath he hadn't realized he'd been holding. Teresa had a crush on him? Closing his eyes, he leaned his head back. What a dope! Why hadn't he seen it? He'd sensed she was giving Alex a bit of the cold shoulder, but it never occurred to him that he was the reason.

Relief had swept him as he listened to Teresa sort through her feelings about him; gratitude had filled him as he listened to Alex help the girl do so.

And an emotion he couldn't even begin to understand surged into his veins, burning hot and intense, when he heard Alex's words about him: *He's a good man…very nice…very good looking.*

Who knew so few words could rouse such a powerful response from deep in his gut? It took all his willpower to stand there, not to give in to the urge to walk out on the porch and take Alex's hands in his, to pull her from that swing and…and…

He pushed away from the wall and strode toward the kitchen. He had to get rid of these mugs. They were making him sweat.

Liar. It's not the cocoa and you know it.

He ignored the voice, just as he ignored the fact that the brown liquid he was pouring down the drain was ice cold.

It's not good for man to be alo—

"*No!*" He ripped the word out. "I don't need her. I don't need anyone!" The harsh edge to his whispered cry startled him. What was wrong with him? He'd always prided himself on being even-tempered, able to take things in stride. What had happened to his self-control?

You can't do it on your own, son.

Setting the mugs into the sink with a studied care, he gripped the edge of the counter, bowing his head. *Father...* He swallowed as the truth hit him. *I'm afraid. I'm afraid to care about her. Look at who she is! How can I ask a woman like that to come here...to live in a place like this? To give her life to helping people no one else cares about anymore?*

The image of Alex's face, her laughing eyes, danced in his mind. He heard again the compassion in her voice as she'd talked with Teresa...heard the amazement in Tucker's admission: *"Miss Alex got to Matty. Got right to his heart..."*

He didn't doubt it. How could he? She'd gotten to him, too. Right to his heart. And he knew it was going to tear him apart to let her go. But that's what he had to do.

No matter how much his heart told him otherwise.

Twelve

*I*t was a beautiful day, sunny and warm and perfect for being outside.

If only Alex could find something helpful to do. Birdy had made her swear to stay clear of the kitchen. Tucker had turned pale when Alex asked if he and Matty needed help with the yard work. Peter and Penny had actually burst into laughter when she'd offered to help them feed the chickens, and Teresa had almost finished her cleaning chores by the time Alex found her.

That only left Evan, and Alex had been so desperate to be useful, she'd given in and gone to track him down. She'd found him, perched on a ladder, paintbrush in hand, touching up the window frames.

At her offer of help, he'd glanced down at her. "You? On a ladder?" He hooted. "You've got to be kiddi—"

Her quick hurt must have shown on her face because he stopped, then shook his head. "You ever paint before?"

"Of course," came her quick reply.

When his eyes narrowed and then came to rest on her, she felt heat creep into her cheeks. She crossed her arms and lifted her chin a fraction. "I'll have you know I was the best in my class."

"You took a class on painting houses?"

She had the grace to look down at that, scuffing the toe of one tennis shoe in the grass. "Not exactly…"

He quirked a brow, and she gave a huff. "Okay, so it was finger painting and I was five, but I don't recall any catastrophes!"

"You ever hear of suppressed memories?" Evan muttered as he turned back to his task. At her silence, he looked down at her, a mixture of compassion and impatience in his eyes. "Look, Alex, I appreciate the offer, but this won't take long. I'm sure you can find something els—"

"Evan!"

They both turned. It was Tucker. "Phone call, Evan."

Evan slid down the ladder and took two steps toward Tucker, then stopped. He turned, looking from Alex to the ladder. "Don't—" he enunciated slowly and clearly—"even think about it."

So saying, he walked away.

Alex sighed and moved to rest her elbows on the ladder step. She'd wait until Evan came back and try again. Surely there was something she could…she could…

Hmm.

A quick look around confirmed what Alex already knew: she was alone. There was no one anywhere to be seen. It was just her. And the ladder.

And the can of paint.

What had Evan said? Don't *think* about it, right? Okay then, she wouldn't. She'd just do it! After all, it wasn't as though one needed special skills to paint a house, for heaven's sake! And with all Evan had to do, well, she could at least give him a hand with painting the windows, couldn't she?

Of course she could.

She climbed the ladder carefully, testing the balance on her way up. Dipping the brush in the can of paint, she reached out to stroke it along the window frame. Satisfaction filled her as she watched the clean, bright coat of white cover the worn wood.

Whoever said painting was hard? This was easy! And fun. Imagine Evan worrying about letting her help—

"What are you *doing?*"

The bellow came from right below her, and she jerked around. The sudden move threw her off balance, and a sinking feeling came over her as she realized she was about to go airborne.

Her scream caught in her throat just as strong hands shot out to catch her. Evan. Of course.

He must have made a dive for her because he rammed the ladder as she fell right into his arms. She grabbed his neck as she landed…unfortunately, she still had a death grip on the paintbrush, and it slapped with a wet *thwack* against the side of Evan's head.

"For the love of…" Grimacing, he tightened his hold on Alex, pressing her against his chest.

They stood there for several moments, their ragged breathing the only sound breaking the silence. Alex knew she should apologize, should tell Evan she was fine and he could let her go, but, try as she might, no words would form.

Something about the way he held her, the warmth of his breath fanning her cheek, the feel of his heart hammering beneath her fingers—something about the way the air was suddenly charged with an odd, indefinable current rendered her motionless.

She knew he'd be frustrated with her, even angry. And yet, held as she was, cradled against him, she felt…safe. At home.

Like there was nothing she'd rather do than stay there for a very, very long time.

A sensation of warmth spread from the back of her head, down her neck, down the middle of her back…. She swallowed hard. Could this be…love?

No…she frowned. Not love. Love might be warm, but it wasn't—sticky!

Her eyes widened with a sickening realization. Paint. It was paint. Focusing on Evan, horror ripped through her at what she saw.

The can of paint, which had been sitting so safely on the shelf of the ladder, apparently had taken flight too. And it must have done a perfect one-point landing right on Evan's head. Thick, white paint coated his head and oozed down his face, matting his hair, sliding down to drop off the end of that sculpted, straight nose.

That was what had landed on the back of her head as she'd been pressed against him.

"Oh…" She reached up, scooping at the flow as best she could, trying to keep it out of his eyes. "Oh, Evan…I—you…I mean… Oh, dear."

He didn't say a word. He simply set her down and took a step away from her, then turned and walked back to the house, leaving nothing but a trail of white spatters in his wake—and the sound of his muttering on the breeze.

Thirteen

Alex leaned forward, resting her elbows on the steering wheel of the riding mower, blowing her soggy bangs out of her face.

She was melting. She was sure of it. Who knew it got so hot in Oregon? Wasn't this supposed to be the green state, where everything was cool and fertile?

So why did she feel as though she were in the middle of a desert? She'd even closed Dusty up in her room where it was nice and air-conditioned. Last thing she needed was an overheated terrier staggering around.

"Here, you look like you could use this."

She turned to find Matty holding a glass of iced lemonade out to her. "Oh. You're wonderful!"

He grinned at her as she snatched the glass and drained it. "Yeah, I know."

She made a face at him over the rim of the glass, pulling an earplug from one ear. "You're one funny guy, Matteo." She smiled sweetly. "But, hey, looks aren't everything."

Matty stepped back, grabbing at his chest as though grasping the hilt of a knife that had been plunged there. "Ooooh, the lady makes an insult. I'm cut, man. Cut deep. I may never recov—"

"Stuff it, funny boy."

When Matty laughed this way, head thrown back, eyes alight, he seemed like a carefree young boy. Alex loved seeing him this way, loved feeling as though she were part of the reason he was warming up, letting people in. "Oh, man, Miss Alex. You'd better be careful you don't let Mr. Noland hear you talk like that. He'll wash your mouth out."

"With soap, I suppose."

Matty's grin was so cheeky it was infectious. "Nah, with some of that chili you made!"

During the last few days, Matty had become her shadow. Or, to be more accurate, her guardian angel. Ever since she'd so effectively doused Evan in paint, Matty had been assigned to keep her out of trouble. Oh, no one had said so, but it didn't take a genius to figure it out. Whatever Alex got involved in, he always turned up just as she got started and offered to help.

Today they'd been doing lawn work, something Alex found she was surprisingly proficient at. She'd finished the fenced-in backyard in record time and was now working on what Evan called the "back forty," an expanse of grass and weeds and young trees. It was more challenging than the backyard, which Tucker kept well manicured, but that was okay. Riding the mower was downright fun, and once Matty showed her how it was better to cut the lawn in increasingly smaller circles rather than in a random, criss-cross pattern, she did fine.

She didn't even mind the noise. Matty had shown her how to use earplugs, so it was kind of like being in a world all her own; one that smelled like freshly cut grass and afforded her the opportunity to think through the events of the past week and a half, since she and Birdy had arrived at Heaven's Corner.

As Matty took her empty glass and strolled back toward the house, she put her earplugs back in place and started the mower again. Encased in the roar of the machine, she found her thoughts drifting back to yesterday. She'd finally called her father, just to let him know she was safe and well. He'd surprised her by listening quietly as she talked to him, apologizing for the hurt she'd caused him.

But his response had been too true to form: "Apologies won't fix this, Alexandria. I want you to come home. Immediately. We'll discuss your marriage then."

Sadness had struck her heart, and she didn't try to keep it from her voice. "There's nothing to talk about, Daddy."

The conversation had gone downhill from there, and when Alex hung up she was crying.

A soft touch on her hand drew her attention down. Penny stood there, bright blue eyes filled with concern. She had a thumb in her mouth, and the ever present Snufflebunny clutched in her arm. Alex smiled, but she couldn't keep back a weepy sniff.

At the sound, Penny's lower lip came out and she held Snufflebunny out to Alex, clearly offering the best consolation she could. Alex leaned down to sweep both the little girl and her rabbit into a fierce hug.

Penny snuggled close, and Alex went to sink onto the couch, the little girl cuddled under her chin.

Alex sighed at the memory of how good it had felt to hold Penny, to sit there together like they belonged to each other. *Please, Lord, give Penny her kitten.*

The little girl still asked for one nearly every day, either through Peter or by pointing at pictures. Her father remained adamant: "Unless the good Lord sees fit to drop one out of the sky, you are not getting a cat, young lady! We don't have the money to buy one nor the time to care for it."

Alex had gone to discuss it with Tucker later, but for once the big man wasn't of a mind to talk. He just gave her a firm shake of his head. "Not gonna happen, Miss Alex. I 'ppreciate your concern, but I jus' can't see it. Penny's got enough to deal with—

"But this would make her so happy. And every time I pray about it, I get the strongest feeling that it would make God happy, too."

He'd pinned her with an enigmatic look. "Well, ma'am, I'm not gonna argue on that. Me 'n' God, we don't do a lot of talking."

"Oh." It was the only thing that came to mind, and Tucker's expression was wry as he shrugged.

"Look, I know you're big on God. So are Mr. Noland and Miss Hiffenstone." He let loose a sigh that seemed to come from somewhere around his toes. "Miss Hiffenstone, you know, she's been at me since you two got here to turn everything over to God. 'Rest in Him,' she says, like I know what that means." He met her eyes. "You know what that means, Miss Alex?"

She smiled. "I'm learning…"

"Yeah, well, when you get it figgered out, explain it to me, will ya? I mean, I know God's a good guy, and I believe Jesus was who He says He was. I just…"

He shoved his hands in his pockets and gave a quick jerk of his shoulders. "I just figger I've messed things up so bad, why should God listen to a guy like me?"

"Because He loves you, Tucker."

Her quiet answer hung there in the silence, until he ran a hand through his silvery hair. "Yeah, well, I'm glad you think so. The jury's still out on that for me." He gave her one final look then turned away. "'Scuse me, ma'am, I got work to do."

As the man strode from the room, Alex hugged herself tightly. Tucker had been through so much…. She closed her eyes, asking God to touch the man. To show him in a way he could no longer deny that He loved Tucker, just as he was, weaknesses and mistakes and all.

Remembering the moment, Alex shifted on the hard seat of

the mower and sent another prayer winging heavenward for Tucker. And then, just for good measure, she said a little prayer for Penny's longed-for kitten.

Tucker stood near the shed, watching Alex as she bounced along on the riding mower, cutting the lawn with a precision that rendered him speechless.

She'd finally found something she was good at. Thank God. He hadn't been sure they'd survive her efforts at being helpful.

At a sharp tug on his shirt, Tucker looked down.

Penny stood there, blue eyes wide, her sweet face framed by a halo of blond curls. She looked so much like her mother that it broke his heart.

He took her tiny hand in his, cradling it gently, careful not to squeeze too hard. "You want something, sweetie?"

Talk to me…please, baby, talk to me.

She just kept looking up at him, and he felt the frustration brewing inside. *God, what's it gonna take? All I want to do is hear my baby's voice…*

Penny's tiny fingers curled into the palm of his hand, and she tugged. Took a step. Tugged.

"You want me to go with you?"

The smile that broke out on her face was a blessing that touched his heart, suddenly choking his throat with tears. Unable to speak, he nodded, then followed Penny as she led him across the yard, through the gate, and into the backyard.

Alex turned off the riding mower, then pressed her palms at the low of her back and stretched. Ooooh, those muscles were…

She frowned. What on earth was Matty up to? He was standing there, head cocked, his forehead creased in concentration. Alex pulled out her earplugs, hopped off the mower, and walked over to him.

"Matty, what—"

"Shh!" He grabbed her arm. "Listen."

She did so, tilting her head. Sure enough, she heard something. A high, yowling, pitiful kind of sound. She and Matty looked at each other, and she knew the surprise she saw on his face was mirrored on hers as well.

"It's a cat!"

Matty nodded. "Sure sounds like it." He scanned the tops of the trees around them, then pointed. "There!"

Alex followed Matty's finger, and dismay swept over her. The heartrending cries were coming from an adorable, tiger-striped kitten. Alex longed to pick it up and soothe it. There was only one problem.

It was stuck, roughly fifteen feet above her head, in the top branches of a small, willowy tree.

Tucker halted. *Oh no…*

There, in the middle of the backyard, was a bright pink cat bed. "Where did you get that, sweetie?" He did his best to keep the question light.

Penny tugged her father along until they stood beside the bed. Then, with another wide-eyed, pleading look up at him, Penny knelt on the soft grass.

A sharp pang of apprehension hit Tucker in the midsection. He looked around, hoping against hope to catch a glimpse of Evan, to be able to call him over…

A gentle pull on his pants leg drew his attention down to his daughter. Her gaze said it all.

"You want me to pray with you? For a kitten?"

He knew the answer before she nodded. Swallowing hard, Tucker stood there, staring down at the child who held his heart in her tiny hands. His own agonized words came back to echo in his mind, but he knew they weren't coming from him.

They were coming from his Father.

Talk to me...please, son, talk to me. What's it gonna take...?

Once again, he knew the answer almost before the question had faded.

What would it take? This. Exactly this. His baby girl, on her knees, begging him with those wide baby blues, to join her.

Looking down at her, something inside Tucker shattered... surrendered...and even as his knees gave way, he felt his heart give way as well.

Okay, God. Okay. You win.

"Man, that thing's stuck there for good. Might as well call it crow bait."

Alex glared at Matty. "What a horrid thing to say!"

His astonishment was clearly genuine, and she immediately regretted her harsh tone. "Hey, Miss Alex, I didn't mean nothing bad. I just—"

She held up her hand. "It's okay, Matty. I'm sorry."

He nodded, then turned to study the kitten's predicament again. "You know..."

Alex glanced to see his eyes sparkling. "You have an idea?"

He inclined his head, a slow smile easing across his face. "Maybe." He trotted back to the shed, then returned with a ball of twine and the ladder. He waggled his eyebrows. "The ladder's too short to reach it, but I got an idea."

Alex stepped aside, wavering between curiosity and apprehension as she watched Matty climb the ladder, tie one end of the twine as high up on the slim tree as he could. Tugging to be sure it was secure, he slid back down the ladder and went to kneel beside the riding mower. Once he'd tied off the twine, he hopped on the seat and fired up the machine.

"Matty, what are you—?"

"Check it out!" he crowed.

Alex spun to follow his pointing finger and caught her breath. Slowly but surely, as Matty eased the mower forward, the tree was bending lower.

"Get ready, Miss Alex. You should be able to grab the *gato* any minute now."

She did as he suggested, hands outstretched, hoping the kitten didn't decide to jump before she was ready and make a perfect four-claw landing on her head.

The animal's pitiful cries came closer…closer…

"Just a little more, Ma—"

Her words were abruptly cut off by a terrible sound. The sound of twine snapping. "Oh, no!"

Before Alex could move, the tree whipped upright—and the kitten went flying; its terrified yowl followed closely by Alex's horrified cry. The animal made a perfect arc through the sky, then disappeared over the backyard fence.

"Oh…man," Matty's low, stunned voice came from just behind her. "Now *that's* what I call a catapult."

Fourteen

ucker knelt in the grass, and his heart swelled with emotion when Penny reached to fold one of his fingers between her small hands. She bowed her head, and the trust in that gesture was nearly his undoing.

"God…" Tucker tried, but the words stuck in his emotion-tightened throat. He sucked in a steadying breath and tried again. "God, I don't know what to say here. My little girl wants a kitten. Well, Evan keeps saying You answer prayers. And so does Miss Hiffenstone, and you know how convincing that woman can be. So God, I'm askin'. Fer Penny." He swallowed hard. "For both of us. Please…can You give Penny a kitten?"

The words were barely out of his mouth when he heard a sound…a high-pitched, wailing whine. And it was getting closer.

"What the…" He opened his eyes and jumped to his feet as something hurled out of the sky and landed, with near surgical precision, in the cat bed. Tucker blinked. He stared. And his knees went weak.

It was a kitten. A real, live—albeit seemingly terrified—kitten!

"It worked!"

He spun to stare down at Penny, who was staring at the animal, her face a picture of total joy. She crawled over to take the trembling kitten into her arms, cradling it close…and when she looked up at him, tears were flowing from her sparkling eyes.

"Oh, *Daddy!* Your prayer worked!" Her smile was the most

beautiful thing Tucker had ever seen. He watched, speechless with wonder, as his little girl stood and came to lean against his leg, the tabby kitten cradled in her thin arms. "Thank you, Daddy! I love you."

Overwhelmed, he put his hand on his daughter's head, lifting his face to the heavens. *Thank You, Daddy,* his heart breathed. *I love You. And I'll never doubt You again.*

Alex didn't think she'd ever forget the horrible sight of the kitten, legs splayed, vaulting through the air.

She and Matty had stood there in stunned silence for a full minute or two. Then they ran to the fence. They stared at each other, afraid to look. Then Matty had boosted her up to peek over the fence. She closed her eyes at first, then opened them slowly, looking through slits to find…nothing.

No kitten. No sign of where it had landed.

Nothing.

It was as though the animal had vanished into thin air. Shaking her head, Alex tapped on Matty's head and he lowered her to the ground.

"Well?"

Her mouth hung open and she clamped it shut, then lifted her shoulders. "It's not there."

"Wow. You don't s'pose it flew all the way over the house?"

She took his arm and turned him back toward the mower. "I don't know, but we're going to find out."

They went to gather the ladder and twine remnants, putting them away. As they came back inside the house, Alex wondered whether or not to tell Evan what had happened.

"Petey!"

Alex paused, glancing around. It sounded as though Peter had a little friend over. A little girlfriend. She peeked around the corner of the hallway into the living room and almost fell over. Tucker, a broad grin on his face, was being dragged by an ecstatic Penny into the room to where Peter and Evan were sitting on the couch.

And Penny was talking. No, she was *chattering!*

"Petey, look! God did it. He really *did* it! He answered Daddy's prayer! Just like that!" She held out her hands, and Alex almost fell over.

"Hey!" It was Matty. He'd come up behind Alex and was peering over her shoulder at what Penny was holding out to her brother. "Isn't that—?"

Alex's hand shot back and clamped over his mouth. "Shhh!"

"Hey, get that cat outta my face," Peter said, pushing away the kitten his sister was holding out to him.

"But, Petey, Daddy prayed for a kitty for me, and God *sent* one!"

Peter snorted. "Yeah, right."

"He did so, didn't he, Daddy?"

Tucker shrugged, a bemused smile on his face. His gaze met Evan's, and Alex caught her breath. Tucker looked as excited as Penny. "He sure did, honey."

"How did God do that?" Evan's question was more curious than doubting.

"Daddy asked, and God dropped the kitty right out of the sky. He just flew over the fence and landed right into my cat bed. Just like magic. Like *God's* magic!" She beamed at her brother. "See, Petey? I *told* you God was real. And He does so answer prayers. So *there!*"

Alex pulled back and leaned against the wall, torn between

laughter and tears. Matty was grinning at her like some kind of smug Cheshire cat. "Well, whaddya know? I helped answer somebody's prayer." He shook his head. "Whaddya think about that?"

Laughter won out, and Alex pulled the delighted young man into a hug. "I think it's absolutely perfect," she said. "And I'm not the least bit surprised."

Fifteen

hree days later, Alex was up before anyone else, even Birdy.

She knew she was tempting the fates, but she didn't care. She was going back into the kitchen.

Yes, she'd almost done Evan in with cheesy pizza and killer chili. And yes, she'd outdone herself in proving just how ineffective she was at outside work and saving kittens stranded in trees. But God had promised His mercies were new every morning, and so she was moving forward in confidence.

Today was going to be different. Today she'd cook a meal, and it would actually be edible.

Tiptoeing from her room, she made her way through the house to the kitchen.

Last night Alex had lain awake praying—that and trying to erase the images flitting through her mind…images of chickens' sprawling bodies, Evan's head in the sink, Tucker's poor shin, the kitten hurtling through the air with far less than the greatest of ease. She'd lain there for hours, asking God to show her where she fit in. Surely she was meant to do more than mow lawns?

She'd had little luck with either the image erasing or the prayers. Apparently God didn't have an answer for her.

Well, actually, He did, but she didn't like it. As always, while she begged and pleaded for Him to tell her what to do, she received one, small inner whisper of a reply: *Wait*.

But she'd *been* waiting, and she still struggled inside. She felt so at home in this place. *And with this man,* her heart added. She didn't deny it. All it would take was a word from Evan, a sign that he wanted her to stay here, and she would. Gladly. She'd join him in his work, doing...doing...

What? What could she do? What on earth good was she?

None, came the glum inner response. *None whatsoever.*

She didn't want to believe it, but it was a little hard to argue the point when the signals she got from Evan were that he couldn't wait to see her leave.

Maybe she should give him his wish. Maybe she should just go home and accept Daddy's dictates on her life.

She'd pressed her hands to her head in an effort to still her spinning thoughts. She took a deep breath and replayed the day through her mind, asking God to give her some hint, some inkling of what she was supposed to do. What had come to her hadn't been what she'd expected. It had been the memory of Peter grumbling at breakfast that morning, saying he and Penny, who sang out her agreement—now that she'd started talking, she didn't seem terribly inclined to stop—were tired of cereal. Alex figured Evan and the others probably were as well. So, since God didn't seem to have any bright ideas, she'd come up with one.

She was going to fix breakfast. A good, hot, nutritious breakfast.

After all, how hard could *that* be?

Scrambled eggs, toast, and ham. That beat crummy ol' cereal any day. She'd have the meal all fixed and the table all set by the time the group was up and moving. Now that would make an impression.

On whom?

She made a face at the inner voice. *Birdy. Matty. And the kids, of course.*

Yeah. Right.

She ignored the mocking reply and reached out to grab the alarm, set it, and put it under her pillow so it would wake her and not the softly-snoring Birdy.

Alex entered the kitchen and flicked on the lights. She rummaged around, finding pans and nonstick spray, then went to pull what she needed from the fridge. In minutes she had everything ready but the ham—mainly because there wasn't any to be found. Nor was there any bacon.

Alex bit her lip. Scrambled eggs without ham? Or bacon? Or any kind of meat? That just wouldn't do.

She went to the cupboards and started searching. Surely there was something she could use…

Her eyes landed on several cans, and she frowned. Had she ever had scrambled eggs made with…? Well, even if she hadn't, that didn't mean anything. Besides, what could be more nutritious? She grabbed the cans.

This was going to be great.

"Wow, someone cooked us breakfast!"

At Peter's happy exclamation, Alex stuck her head out of the kitchen and watched. The others came into the dining room, looking with an assortment of grins and pleased expressions at the plates Alex had set out; each filled with several pieces of toast, a cluster of grapes, a slice of orange, and a generous helping of her own special scrambled egg creation.

Let them like it. Oh, please, please, let them like it…

Penny clapped her hands, a huge grin on her face as she slid onto the chair her father held out for her.

"Whaddya know?" Matty picked up his fork. "Toast and grapes and…" He stared at his plate. "And…"

"Hey, there's something wrong with my eggs," Peter said.

"Yeah, mine too," Teresa remarked, pushing them around on her plate with a fork.

"Don't be ridiculous, children," Birdy remarked, picking up her fork and spearing some of the eggs. Alex smiled. Good ol' Birdy. Trust her to stand up for—

Birdy brought the eggs to her mouth, then paused. "Oh, my." She looked at what was on her fork, then bit her lip. "Why…they are a bit…well…"

"Gray?" Evan supplied, peering down at his plate.

"Ewww, what *is* this?"

Alex couldn't take it anymore. She stepped into the room, hands planted on her hips. "It's scrambled eggs, Peter."

"Yeah," Matty held up a forkful, "but how *old* are they?"

"How…?" Alex came to look at his plate. "I just made them!"

"With what?" Evan asked, and Alex could tell he wasn't trying to be difficult. Just curious. And cautious.

She studied the faces around the table and swallowed hard. They all looked…what? Dismayed, at best. Nauseous, at worst. Even Penny's sweet face and little button nose were wrinkled up in a look of barely concealed distaste.

Oh, Lord, what have I done now?

"I…well, I made them with some meat…"

"Gray meat?" Peter howled. "She's tryin' to poison us!"

Tucker put his hand on Peter's arm. "That's enough, son. I'm sure it's just something new to us. Probably some delicacy Miss Alexandria learned to fix when she was just a little girl." He smiled at Alex and took a big bite of the eggs—then froze.

Alex felt a lump form in the bottom of her stomach as she watched the poor man struggle to chew what was in his mouth. Once…twice…then, as though steeling himself for something horrific, he swallowed. His eyes closed, and he sat there for a moment, silent.

Peter took one look at his father's face and pointed at Alex. "You killed him!" Tucker's hand shot out and grabbed Peter's arm again. "That's enough, boy," he managed, but Alex could tell it took an enormous effort for him to speak.

Birdy was up and out of her chair in a heartbeat. "Oh, Tucker, my dear, are you all right?"

Alex stared. *Tucker…my dear?*

"Take a drink, Tuck," Evan suggested, and the older man complied, throwing back his glass of orange juice like a barhop tossing back a shot of whiskey.

Evan's expression was one of strained patience. "Alex, what's in the eggs?"

She bit her lip again, scuffing her toe on the carpet. "I just… well, there was no ham or bacon, so I thought I'd try something… different."

"*How* different?"

If only she could disappear. *Please, God, can't the ground open up and swallow me whole?* But no such luck. "Fish."

The stares that greeted this announcement made her stomach hurt.

"Fish?" Peter grimaced down at his plate. "You ruined scrambled eggs with *fish?*"

"Not fish, exactly. More like…well—" she gave a weak wave of her hand, as though she could erase their incredulous looks from their faces—"tuna." Was it possible to feel any more miserable—not to mention idiotic—than she did right now? Alex didn't think so, and she fervently hoped she'd never have to find out. "I couldn't find any other meat, so I used tuna."

Silence. No one moved for a full three or four seconds. Alex stood rooted to the ground, closing her eyes against the sting of tears in her eyes and the blazing heat rushing to her cheeks.

I can't even make eggs, Lord. I'm useless. Totally, utterly use—

Something soft touched her hand, and she started, then looked down. Penny smiled up at her. "I like gray eggs." Her eyes were wide and sincere. "I think they're pretty."

Birdy chimed in, patting Tucker's shoulder as she did so. "Well, the fruit and juice are excellent, Alexandria."

"Sure beats cold cereal," Tucker added, following Birdy's lead. He nudged his son, but Peter just scowled and looked away.

Birdy moved back to her seat. "And the toast! Well, perfectly browned, if I do say so, my dear. And what magical concoction did you put on it? It's wonderful."

A half sob, half laugh escaped Alex. "B-butter," she managed. "It's j-just butter."

"Yeah," Matty joined in, taking a bite, "but you put just the right amount on."

Teresa nodded. "And you got all the pieces buttered while the bread was still hot. I mean, none of 'em are hard, you know?" She smiled at Alex. "I hate hard toast."

"The eggs still suck," Peter announced, but instead of being hurt, Alex almost burst out laughing because the words were no sooner spoken than everyone at the table shot Peter a glare. He sank low in his chair. "But you done real good pourin' the orange juice," he muttered. "Didn't spill it or nothin'."

Evan laughed then, leaning back in his chair and giving Alex a warm smile. "Alex, thanks for trying. It was a good idea. We've been having cereal way too often around here. We needed something—"

his eyes twinkled—"different." He glanced at the others. "Tell you what, how about we all go to Micky D's for breakfast. My treat!"

"Now you're talkin'," Tucker and Peter said together, then they grinned at each other and Peter gave his dad a high five.

Emotion played across Evan's face as he stood. "Okay then, everyone get ready to go in five minutes. Meet at the front door."

With that, they all jumped up from the table and hurried off. Penny gave Alex's hand one final squeeze and fell in step with Peter as he left the room. In seconds, only Alex and Evan were left in the room.

Evan slowly moved around the table, coming to stand beside her. "Don't worry about cleaning up, Alex. We'll take care of it…when we get home."

She looked at Evan, caught off guard. Not by what he'd said, but by how he'd said it. Gently. Even tenderly. The look in his eyes as he studied her brought a shiver dancing up her spine. There was tenderness there as well. And something more…

"I…" She held out her hands in front of her. "I'm sorry."

At her whispered word, his mouth softened. "Don't be. You did a good thing here."

She gave a short laugh. "What? Disgust everyone?"

His gaze scolded her. "Why, Miss Wingate, weren't you watching? God used you in an amazing way just now."

Alex looked from him to the table, to the plates heaping with her failure, then back at him again. "Were you just in the same room as I was?"

He took her hand, holding it between both of his. "Didn't you see how everyone reacted? How they came together for you?" He looked down at their hands, and then, using one finger, he traced a pattern of warmth on her palm.

The shiver skittered from her spine to her shoulders.

"I've been seeing it happen more and more since you and Aunt Bert came here." His eyes captured hers. "Especially since you came. These people—these hurting, wounded people—have been forgetting about themselves, about their anger and struggles and hurts, and focusing on you." Alex felt her breath catch in her throat as he studied her face. "They care for you, Alex. You may not realize it, but that's a big step for them. A good step. So you did something good here."

He gave her hand a squeeze, then released her—and winked. "Tuna notwithstanding, of course."

Alex's giggled surprised both of them—but it died in her throat when she looked up to meet Evan's gaze.

There was something there....something in the way he was looking at her that suddenly had the air between them crackling with awareness.

"Alex..." His voice was rough...raw. "I..."

She caught her breath, her senses sharpening, honing in like a microscope being dialed to its most minute focus as she stared at Evan. She shivered when, almost as though he couldn't stop himself, he reached out and let his fingers trail the line of her cheek, her jaw...

Ask me. The silent plea came from the depths of her heart. *Ask me to stay. And I will.*

The thought should have startled her, even frightened her. She hardly knew this man. And yet, every sense within her rang with nothing but certainty. She belonged here, with this man, in this place, doing this work. After all this time, all the waiting, it had happened.

She'd found her place. She was home. And she didn't ever want to leave.

Nor did Evan want her to. She could tell from the tremble in his fingers as they cupped her face, from the emotions coloring his face with wonder and realization.

He wanted her to stay.

Ask me...

The words sang through her, filled with a joy she could hardly contain. They rang in her heart, her mind, her spirit—everywhere but in the charged silence between them. And though she didn't voice the request, she knew he could see it clearly in her eyes.

As clearly as he could see her answer.

He opened his mouth again, and she waited, poised on the edge of what she now knew with every fiber of her being was her destiny, when another sound shattered the silence, breaking the connection between her and Evan with a jolt that was as painful as if she'd been physically torn apart.

"Alexandria!"

She spun, staring, disbelieving. It couldn't be! But blinking didn't dispel the apparition standing before her, and the truth slapped her right between the eyes.

It was.

There, against all reason and hope, standing in the doorway like some vengeful, disapproving specter, was her father.

Sixteen

addy."

At Alex's stunned whisper, Evan felt as though someone had sucker punched him. He followed her gaze to the man standing in the doorway to the dining room.

The man standing there was older, but his ramrod posture and clearly expensive suit spoke of power and prestige.

Evan still stood close enough to Alex to feel a tremble pass through her, and without thinking he slid a protective arm around her waist, offering his support. She didn't look at him, but he felt her gratitude in the way she leaned against him.

He knew Alex had come here without her father's knowledge. Aunt Bert had filled him in on their challenges, on the wedding, the trip out the window and down the trellis. And she'd told Evan that Alex was determined to find her own way, to follow God's path rather than her father's.

He'd respected Alex's stand. But now...standing there, feeling her shiver against him, bearing the brunt of Charleston Wingate's disdainful scowl, he began to understand all Alex had faced. And what it had taken for her to do what she did.

"I'll thank you, sir, to release my daughter."

The cold tones slammed into Evan and, almost instinctively, his arm tightened around Alex. Charleston Wingate might be rich and powerful, but this was Evan's home. And Alex was...was...

He swallowed. What? What exactly was Alex to him? His heart offered up a clear answer, but he brushed that aside, unable to ignore one glaring fact.

No matter what he felt about this woman, no matter how much he wanted her with him, he didn't have the right to ask it.

She belonged in a world vastly different from his, one where Evan and his work and the people who mattered most to him—people like Matty and Tucker and the others—would never fit in.

He cared about Alex...deeply. But rather than feeling joy at the thought, all he felt was loss. He cared about her, but there was no way around it: He couldn't have her.

"Evan?"

Her soft voice pulled his attention down to her, and the question he saw in her eyes was like a dagger plunged into his chest. She wanted him to say something, to stand for her.

Instead, he gave into one last impulse, reaching up to touch her face as though he could memorize the feel of her, then he let his arm drop and stepped away.

"Your father is waiting."

The words cost him, but not nearly so much as the shock of hurt that filled her eyes.

God, his heart cried out to the only One who could help him, knowing even as he did so that there was no way around it.

He had to let her go.

Alex stared at Evan, not wanting to believe what had just happened, but there was no way around it: He didn't want her.

Sorrow was a huge, painful knot within her as she turned to face her father. No point asking how he'd found her. She was just surprised it had taken him as long as it had.

Her father's gaze swept the room and came to rest on Evan, his brows raising slightly.

"Mr. Wingate," Evan said, inclining his head. "Welcome to Heaven's Corner."

Alex's cheeks burned when her father didn't even acknowledge Evan. "Alexandria, the car is outside—"

"Mr. Wingate!" They turned at the exclamation. Birdy and Tucker stood staring at them, and Birdy looked ready to faint. "Oh, dear…"

"Bertilda, good. You can help Alexandria pack. I'd like the two of you ready and in the car in ten minutes. We'll send someone after your car later." He gave a dismissive sniff. "Either that, or we'll just replace the thing. It's a piece of junk anyway."

Alex closed her eyes. Nothing had changed. Her father still expected her—and everyone else—to jump at his command. But that wasn't what bothered her most. What bothered her far more than her father's overbearing attitude was Evan's silence.

She turned to him again, searching his expressionless face. "Evan?"

He didn't meet her gaze right away. Instead, he drew in a breath, then let it out slowly. Only then did he lower his eyes to her face—and a tingling of hope raced through her at the intensity she saw in the depths of his gaze. But whatever he planned to say was lost when Matty and Teresa came into the room.

"Hoo-oo, man! You gotta see the car that's sitting outside!"

"It's a for real limousine!"

The two came to a halt when they saw Alex's father. Matty looked from Alex to her dad to Evan, then back again. He put a restraining hand on Teresa's arm, nodding toward Alex and Evan. "Somethin's up, man."

Evan was the first to speak. "Alex is going home, guys. You'd better say a quick good-bye."

So he could dismiss her that easily, could he? Alex felt sick inside. *God, how could I have been so mistaken?*

"Leavin'? You leavin'?" Matty's incredulous question increased the ache inside Alex's heart, and all she could do was look up at Evan. He wouldn't even meet her eyes. Fighting to keep the tears back, she looked at Birdy, then shook her head and turned to run from the room.

Evan stood outside, at the corner of the house, elbows leaning on the fence while he watched the limousine with dread. Any minute now, Alex would come out, suitcase in hand, and walk out of his life forev—

"Man, you a coward, you know that?"

He spun at the sneering words. Matty stood there, arms crossed against his chest, his face a mask of disdain, his eyes burning coals of anger. Teresa was beside him, and she didn't look much friendlier.

Evan narrowed his eyes. "What did you say?"

Matty didn't even hesitate. He stalked up to Evan, and though the boy was several inches shorter than Evan's six-foot-two height, he squared off in front of him. "I said, you a coward. Miss Alex, she's your woman—"

"She is *not* my woman," Evan ground out. "And it's none of your—"

"That's not true and you know it, Mr. Noland!" Teresa's fierce reply took Evan back. He looked from her to Matty, but she didn't give him a chance to reply. She came to poke one slender finger into his chest. "Anybody who sees you two together knows you got somethin'. Somethin' *special*. She cares about you. And you care about her." The raw emotion in the girl's voice struck Evan mute.

"You don't just give up, man. Ain't that what you been tellin' me?" This came from Matty, and Evan wondered if this was what a professional wrestler felt like when his opponents tag-teamed him. "If Miss Alex was mine, you better *believe* I'd fight for her. And not her father, you, or the stinkin' president of the Newnited States would take her away from me!"

Evan started to speak, but Matty cut him off with a vicious wave of his hand. "I don't wanna hear it. All your talk about standin' for what's right, about standin' for each other? It's garbage. Mr. Rich Man walks in and you step aside." He mimicked the action and then, as though there were no other way to express the depth of his disgust, he spit on the ground near Evan's feet.

Fury swept Evan, but he held it inside. Matteo was a boy; he wouldn't understand loving someone enough to let her go—

"The heart is deceitful above all things."

Evan scowled. What on earth did *that* verse have to do with anything?

"You're wrong, Matty."

They all spun around at the sarcastic remark. Peter and Penny were walking toward them. Peter came up beside Matty, then angled a look from him to Evan. "I don't think Mr. Noland is a coward at all."

Evan shot Matty a smug look.

"Nope. I think he's just really stupid."

"Peter, that's not nice!" This came from Penny, who moved to take Evan's hand. "Mr. Evan's not really going to let Miss Alex go. He's just playing a game with us—" Evan's heart sank as those sweet blue eyes came to bear on him with immeasurable trust— "aren't you, Mr. Evan?"

Evan opened his mouth, then closed it again, and Matty snorted.

"I told you, man. He's a coward." He glanced at Peter and shrugged. "Or he's stupid. One or the other."

"I've always said, Matteo, m'boy, that you have an amazing sense of discernment. How very gratifying to see such irrefutable evidence that I was correct."

Evan closed his eyes. He didn't even have to look to see who had joined this little "Let's bash Evan" party. But he looked all the same and his suspicions were confirmed: Aunt Bert and Tucker were both there.

"Another country heard from," Evan muttered, and Aunt Bert simply patted him on the arm.

"Don't fret, dear boy. When one does something this dull witted this publicly, one simply has to expect some commentary."

"Dull witted?" Evan shook his head. He'd thought at least Aunt Bert would understand. "Look—" he ground the words out through clenched teeth—"I did the only thing I could do."

The bland stares that met this proclamation only served to fuel the blaze of frustration growing in his gut. "Just back off! All of you!" He was being childish; he knew that. But it felt remarkably good to yell. "Alex doesn't belong with me any more than a...a..."

"A swan belongs with a toad?" Peter offered.

"A total fox belongs with a total reject?" Matty added.

"A reasonably intelligent woman belongs with a nitwit?" Aunt Bert supplied.

Evan glared at them. "Thanks, but I'll come up with my own comparisons, if you don't mind."

"Comparison, schmarison," Matty shot at him. "What you're saying is Miss Alex doesn't belong with us."

"With me," Evan corrected, but Teresa shook her head.

"With us. It's not just you here, Mr. Noland. It's all of us. And the others like us who will come after we leave."

The thought of Teresa and her brother leaving brought a lump to Evan's throat, cutting off the argument he'd been preparing.

"She does *so* belong here." Peter's expression was mutinous. "She's the one who helped me stop being mad at my dad."

"And she helped Matty stop being mad at everyone." Teresa slipped her hand through her brother's arm.

"Yeah, and she was the one who helped God give Penny a kitten."

At Matty's comment, everyone shot him a confused look, and he just laughed. "I'll tell you all about it later," he promised with a grin.

"She's been instrumental in opening dear Tucker's eyes to how much he needed God again," Aunt Bert put in, and Evan's ears perked at the "dear Tucker" part of the comment. "And she's brought more joy and laughter and reason for trustin' the Lord than any of us have ever seen before." She fixed Evan with a firm look. "Yourself included, I daresay."

He couldn't argue with that. No one had ever sent him to his knees as often as Alex.

Tucker tilted his head, studying Evan for a moment, then seemed to come to a decision. "Evan, I guess it's pretty clear we all think you should ask Alex to stay."

His jaw clenched. "Painfully clear."

Tucker nodded. "But we also know you've always been straightforward and honest with us." He glanced at the others, and Evan felt some measure of vindication when they each had to nod in agreement. Tucker crossed his arms loosely over his chest. "So here's the deal. You want us to get off your back? Fine. Just tell us one thing and we'll go away, and we won't bring this whole thing up again."

The others started to argue, but Tucker just held up his hand and they fell silent.

Evan stood there, studying their faces, and finally sighed. "One thing?"

Tucker inclined his head. "One thing."

Leaning his hip against the fence, he steeled himself. "Okay, what one thing?"

"Do you love Alex?"

The silence that followed Tucker's question was so profound it pounded at Evan's head—and his heart. He started to reply, then gritted his teeth and closed his eyes. It was as though someone had driven a semi onto his shoulders and parked it there, so heavy was the weight of that one, simple question.

When the silence became too much to bear, he opened his eyes, meeting the gazes fixed on him. *Say no. Deny it! Don't say it's tru—*

"Yes."

At the admission, the weight lifted from his shoulders and his spirit. It felt so good, he said it again. Louder. "Yes, I love Alex."

I love Alex. The words echoed over and over again in his heart, his mind, every fiber of his being. *I love Alex…*

As though the giddy feeling sweeping over him were contagious, Penny and Teresa whooped and hugged each other, squealing with abandon. Matty and Peter high-fived each other, and Tucker simply slid an arm around Aunt Bert's shoulders, smiling first at her and then at Evan.

"So—" Tucker's tone was warmer, more affectionate than Evan had ever heard before—"are you still going to let her go?"

The gang watched him, seemingly with a collectively held breath. As though to add to the moment, the inner cry he'd heard so often—and done everything he could to ignore—echoed again: *It's not good for man to be alone.*

He shook his head with a resigned chuckle. *Okay, God, You win.* "No, Tucker, I'm not." More whooping and high-fives erupted, and Evan found himself laughing at the exuberance. Aunt Bert came to place her palm on Evan's chest, and he looked down at her, tenderness washing over him.

"You knew all along, didn't you?"

She didn't even pretend not to understand. "Of course, m'boy. Why do you think I brought her here? I knew the two of you were meant for each other. I knew you'd been alone too long. And I knew God was at work. Fer you—" her gaze drifted to Tucker, and the grin she turned back at Evan was almost girlish—"and, I'm delighted to say, fer me as well."

He reached to cover her hand where it rested, warm and loving, over his heart. "I love you, Aunt Bert."

Tears shone in her eyes. "And I you, dear, dear boy." She sniffled, rubbing at her nose, then waved her hand in the air dismissively. "Now, off with ye. Ye've got a young woman to woo—" her brow arched—"and it won't be easy, with the muddle ye've made of the situation."

He nodded, straightening. "Pray for me."

"I always do," Aunt Bert said, her eyes sparkling. "I always do."

Alex shoved the last of her clothes into her suitcase, then closed the lid with far more force than was necessary. Dusty made a mad dash under the bed.

"Coward!" Alex yelled after her dog's scrambling feet.

Be still...

She gritted her teeth, grabbing the zipper and jerking it closed.

Be still...

With a muffled cry, she slammed both of her fists on top of the suitcase and fell to her knees, pressing her face into the bedspread and letting the tears flow.

He doesn't want me, Lord! He told me as much. How could You let me think he loved me? How could You let me make such a fool of myself?

The voice came again, washing over her, feeling both like a chastisement and a balm to her weary heart.

Be still, child, and know.

Know? She frowned. *Know what? Know that once again I don't belong? Know that I'll go through life loving a man who doesn't want me? Because I will, You know. I won't ever be able to get him out of my heart…*

She choked on a sob, pressing her fist against her mouth. A small, wet touch made her look down. Dusty was there, looking up at her, eyes wide with what Alex was sure was concern. With another sob, she reached down to lift the little dog into her arms, letting Dusty bathe her face in empathetic licks, wiping away Alex's tears.

If only she could wipe the hurt from her heart, too.

Know that I am God.

The words rang through her, bouncing off the walls of her hurt and resentment, ricocheting from one inner protest to another until they all faded away and nothing was left but silence. And that one, irrefutable truth: *Know that I am God.*

She buried her face in Dusty's fur as she surrendered. *But I wanted Evan to love me, Lord.*

Wait on Me.

I wanted him to stand up to my dad for me.

Lean not on your own understanding.

Her lips quivered, and she sat back, absently stroking Dusty's soft, silken ears. *I love him… What am I going to do about that?*

Wait...and I will give you the desires of your heart.

She didn't understand it. Couldn't see how things could possibly work out. But Alex knew, as certainly as she knew her own name, that God was faithful, He was present...and He loved her.

That was enough.

She stood, drew a deep breath, and, holding Dusty in the crook of one arm, lifted her suitcase from the bed. Casting one long, last glance around the room, she turned and walked away. From her heart. From her dreams. From the home she thought she'd found.

And toward the God she didn't understand but trusted with all her heart. When she stepped out of the house, she nearly stumbled when she saw her father wasn't the only one waiting for her at the limousine.

Evan was there as well.

Her steps faltered, then she straightened her back and marched on. She was a Wingate, after all. She could face Evan calmly, never letting him know how much he'd hurt her.

As she walked up, her father motioned his head toward Evan. "Young man, if you'd be so kind as to put my daughter's bag in the trunk—"

Evan stepped forward, took Alex's bag, then faced her father. "I don't think so."

Alex didn't know who was more startled: she or her father.

It was quite clear, on the other hand, who was more peeved. "I *beg* your pardon."

Her father's icy tones seemed lost on Evan. He simply set Alex's bag on the ground, then reached out to take Dusty from her. Surprisingly, the little dog didn't protest. She just licked Evan's hand.

Traitor! Alex's heart cried.

Evan opened the car door, made sure a window was left mostly open, and put Dusty safely inside. Then he closed the door and came to face Alex's father. "I said I don't think so. I'm not putting Alex's bags in the car. She's not leaving. At least, I hope she's not."

The feel of her hand nestled in his sent her poor, overwrought nerves into a tizzy; the sound of calm confidence in his words sent her heart soaring. What was Evan saying? Was he saying what she thought he was saying? If so, what would her father say about what Evan was saying, and did she have any say in any of this?

She closed her eyes as slightly hysterical laughter bubbled into her throat. She was so confused, she couldn't even think straight.

"Do I dare ask why not?"

"You can ask." Evan's reply to her father's challenge was immediate. "But you won't like the answer. Fortunately, what you do and don't like isn't what matters the most. Not when it comes right down to it."

"Evan, I—"

"Alexandria, keep out of this!" Her father's irate tone made her jump. "Get in the car this instant."

She turned to reply, but suddenly Evan was there, in front of her father, nearly touching noses with him.

"You will speak to your daughter with a good deal more respect, sir. If you can't see your way clear to do so, then you can get off my property."

Alex's mouth dropped open—almost as far as her father's did. Before either of them could say another word, Evan turned to her.

"I need to talk with you."

She clamped her mouth shut, refusal on the tip of her tongue, but there was something in his expression that held her silent.

"Please, Alex."

He'd done it again, destroyed her walls and resistance with two simple words. All the hurt and ache within her came rushing forward, and suddenly she was crying, tears streaming down her face, leaving a trail of heat in their wake.

"Oh, Alex…"

The tender regret in Evan's tone made her knees go weak, but it didn't matter, for he was there, arms around her, cradling her against his chest, cheek resting against her hair. The mere touch of his hand sent a warming shiver through her, and she sagged against him, clutching at his shirt, soaking in his nearness, letting the feel of his arms imprint itself on her memory so she would never forget—never forget how it felt to be held by Evan Noland…never forget how it felt to know, for the first and only time in her life, that she was in love.

I love you. I love you…

Her heart repeated the refrain, over and over—but she wasn't alone.

"I love you."

Evan's deep voice washed over her. His words filled her with an inexpressible joy.

"I love you, Alex. Stay. Please. Stay…"

She gave him her answer in the only way she could. She lifted her face and, standing on tiptoe, touched her lips to his. He went still for a heartbeat, and then his arms around her tightened and he responded in kind, telling her more clearly than words could ever express how he felt.

When he finally lifted his head and gazed down at her, she felt transported, as though she were floating somewhere safe and altogether too lovely to ever leave.

"I think she's staying."

The words were brimming with laughter, and Alex rested her cheek against Evan's chest as she looked to the side…laughter bubbling from her when she saw they had an audience. A very happy, grinning-like-goons audience of six wonderful, precious people who were, in Alex's mind and heart, her family.

Slowly, as though it took great restraint for him to do so, Evan set her away from him and turned to face her father. "Alex is staying here." His tone was firm, though respectful.

She met her father's eyes and was surprised to see them soften. He let loose a sigh. "So I see." With that, he turned to Birdy.

"And you, Bertilda? I assume you'll be staying on as a chaperone until the wedding?"

Tucker moved to Birdy's side, slipping his arm around her slim shoulders. "As chaperone, and my fiancée."

Alex and Evan exclaimed as one at that.

"Your—oh, Birdy!"

"Aunt Bert, that's great! Tucker, you sly dog!"

Birdy's smile was broad as she looked from Tucker to the two of them. "God does love His little surprises in life, doesn't He?" She slanted a glance at Alex's father. "And, of course, I'm staying here, Mr. Wingate. I wouldn't dream of leaving these two lovebirds on their own." She wiggled her eyebrows. "Wouldn't be proper, now would it?"

Everyone laughed at that, and Evan took Alex's hand in his. "Matty, why don't you grab Alex's bags and that crazy dog of hers and take 'em back upstairs."

"Oh, sure! Back to being a slave, eh?" But the twinkle in Matty's eyes belied any resentment.

Alex chuckled, then went to her father, laying a hand on his arm. "Will you stay for a while, Daddy? We have a lot to talk about."

He hesitated, looking from her to Evan and back again. He

pursed his lips, then spoke over his shoulder to his driver. "Austin, get my bags out, will you? I believe I'm going to stay here a day or so with my daughter—" his eyes drifted to Evan—"and the scoundrel who thinks he's going to take her away from me."

Evan grinned. "No thinking to it, sir. It's a simple fact."

Alex's father surprised them all by laughing at that. He slapped Evan on the shoulder, then pointed to the house. "Suppose you show me the lay of the land, my boy, and we'll discuss it. You can fill me in on what you're doing here, and I—" a broad grin split his features now—"can warn you exactly what you're getting into."

As the group fell in step and headed to the house, Teresa came to link arms with Alex. She winked at her. "He's a good kisser, eh?"

Alex knew her grin was cheeky, and she didn't care one bit. "*Very* good."

Teresa giggled. "Just think, Miss Alex. You get Mr. Noland *and* all of us. How did you ever get so lucky?"

"I waited a lifetime," Alex replied with a happy laugh. "And believe me, it was worth every second."

Seventeen

ne year later

"Arise, my beloved, my fair one, and come away."

Evan's voice rang out through the elegant, beautifully decorated garden. Alex felt her heart thrill at the words she'd waited so long to hear. Her hands tightened on Evan's, and her gaze was locked with his.

"You are so beautiful, my beloved. So perfect in every way. How sweet is your love, my treasure, my bride."

Happy tears pricked at Alex's eyes and she blinked them away as she responded, "My lover is like the finest apple tree in the orchard. I am seated in his delightful shade, and his fruit is delicious to eat. He brings me to the banquet hall so everyone can see how much he loves me." Emotion choked her voice, but at his tender smile she pressed on. "I am my beloved's, and he is mine."

"As I am my beloved's," Evan echoed, "and she is mine."

Alex breathed a sigh of relief. She'd made it! The vows they'd written and memorized, the vows she'd waited so long to share with this man, had been pledged aloud. Only one thing remained.

The pastor laid his hand over theirs. "Even as Alexandria and Evan, and Bertilda and Tucker, have pledged their love and devotion to each other and to their Lord, so, now, we pledge as their friends and family to support and encourage them in love, in faith, and in truth. Amen and amen."

The pastor stepped back, then smiled first at Alex and Evan, then at Birdy and Tucker, who stood beside them. "Well, gentle-men," the pastor said with a grin. "You may kiss your brides!"

He didn't have to make the offer twice. A current of chuckles and giggles ran through those seated in the garden as Evan and Tucker performed the prescribed task with skill—and enthusiasm.

But when her new husband's lips touched hers, Alex forgot about everything and everyone except the man standing with her, cradling her face with tender hands, pressing a kiss to her lips that melted her soul.

When he released her, she had to hold on to him for support. His laughing eyes told her he knew the effect their kiss had had on her—and his lopsided grin told her he had been as affected as she.

Peeking to the side, she caught Birdy's shining eyes and couldn't hold back the smile. They'd all agreed: a double wedding was the only way to go. And the year of planning and preparation had been filled with laughter and joy and sharing God's goodness. And the wedding had been more perfect than any of them had imagined.

Penny had walked down the aisle, winning hearts right and left as she tossed rose petals from a wicker basket and bestowed angelic smiles on all those gathered. Teresa had been thrilled when Alex asked her to be her maid of honor, and as she handed Alex her bouquet now, her dark eyes shone with joy.

Matty stood tall and handsome beside Evan as his best man; Peter stood beside his father, looking more mature—and hap-pier—than Alex could ever remember.

Which was only fair because Alex was happier than she'd ever been in her life.

I'm my Beloved's, and He is mine.

The pledge sang through Alex, and she couldn't stop the tears of gratitude to the Lover of her soul for all He'd given her. She leaned against Evan's solid shoulder as they turned to face the happy crowd.

"Ladies and gentlemen," the pastor said from behind them. "It is my distinct honor to present to you Mr. and Mrs. Evan Noland, and Mr. and Mrs. Tucker Telford."

As the recessional music filled the air, Alex sought out her father. He was seated in the front row, and his smile told her how happy he was for her. Yes, God had worked miracles.

She stepped out, walking beside Evan with sure steps.

The reception flew by in a joyful blur, and Alex barely had time to catch her breath before it was time for Birdy and Tucker to leave.

Alex fought back tears as her dear friend enveloped her in a hug.

"Now, now, none of that," Birdy scolded, blinking against her own tears. "We're old married women now and must act more circumspectly."

Alex laughed. "Oh, dear, then it's a good thing we'll be living in the same place. I don't think I can manage circumspection without you."

Birdy chortled. "Don't try to fool me, m'gel. You can't manage it *with* me!" She drew down Alex's face and pressed a soft kiss to her cheek. "And that's just one of the reasons I love ye so very much."

Not long afterward, it was Alex's turn to change clothes and get ready to leave. As she came out of the bride's room, suitcase in hand, she found Evan there, waiting for her.

"Hi ya," she said, torn between a sudden shyness and a love that threatened to overwhelm her. His smile was slow and easy.

"Hi ya." He came to take her suitcase from her. "Thanks, Alex."

Her eyes met those of her husband—her *husband*—and she laughed. "For what? Packing light?"

His grin warmed her from head to toes. "For not going out the window and down the trellis this time."

Alex laughed. "Not a chance, buster. I wouldn't have missed this for the world. Besides, Birdy's with Tucker. I would have been on my own this time. And who knows what kind of trouble I would have gotten into then."

"Heaven help us all," came his laughing reply.

"Hey, I didn't do so badly." She gave his arm a playful punch as they headed for their car. "I managed to find you, and I did my best to help you…"

"To cripple me *and* poor Tucker, you mean." He reached his free hand down to capture hers, holding it in a warm, secure clasp.

"…work with you…"

"Nearly drown me in paint…"

Her lips twitched. "…pray for you…"

"Send me to my knees in desperation…"

She lifted his hand, pressing it to her cheek. "And come to love you. More than I ever dreamed it was possible to love a man."

His eyes burned into hers. "You won't ever be sorry, I promise you that."

She believed him. After all, how could she not? She'd been waiting for him all her life. He was the answer to all those years of waiting, of questioning, of wondering. All those years of asking God over and over what she should do…of hearing the same reply time after time

Wait. Wait on Me.

She had. And look where God had led her. To this time, this place, this man.

The desires of her heart, that's what God had promised to give her. And that, Alex knew as her husband slid his arm around her shoulders, was exactly what He'd given her.

And then some.

Dear Readers,

I've discovered, after nearly twenty-one years of marriage (and all to the same man, no less) that there's one thing no married couple can do without: a sense of humor!

The simple fact that Don and I survived our first years is a miracle. Well, okay, the fact that *Don* survived is a miracle. Not that I was trying to kill him off. I mean, I was kinda fond of the guy. But somewhere along the way, I missed those courses on how to do the things you need to do as a new wife. You know, like fix edible meals and not blow up things in the kitchen.

You know how writers are always being told, "Write what you know?" Well, much of what poor Alex did in "Bride on the Run" came from real-life experience. One of the first meals I made as a new bride was chili. Don raved about his mom's chili, and she was kind enough to give me the recipe. Happily, it was simple, easy to follow. If only someone had *told* me cayenne pepper wasn't the same as chili powder! Hey, they're both red, both powders, both start with the letter 'c'... And it's not *my* fault the recipe called for four tablespoons of the stuff.

Yes, you read it right. *Four tablespoons.*

Of course, like many new wives, I was on a diet. So I didn't eat the chili. Too fattening. But I sure spooned up a big bowl of it for my sweetie. And said sweetie, being a good new husband, managed to eat two bowls of that blazing brew before he had to make a mad dash for the restroom. When he came out, he was slightly green around the gills. But all he said was, "Hon, I think I've had enough dinner." What a guy.

Thankfully, I now know the difference between cayenne pepper and chili powder. Just as I now know you should never... repeat *never*...fix an omelette with tuna. (Trust me on this one. It's not pretty.) And as I know you do *not* put Pyrex bowls on the burner to boil water. They explode. Into tiny shards of glass. (By God's grace, both Don and I were out of the room when the explosion came. We must have picked glass out of the plaster for years...) I also have discovered that turkeys come with two, count 'em, two holes. You really don't have to cram all that stuffing into the tiny cavity at the back end and *streeeeetch* the skin over the large lump. There's another nice, huge cavity on the opposite side, where it all fits in nicely. (What can I say? My Thanksgiving job as a child was always opening the cans of olives, okay?)

As you can imagine, I've been eternally grateful that God not only brought me a husband with a great sense of humor, but with an inordinate amount of patience (not to mention considerable skill as a handyman and cook). It used to really bug me that Don and I seemed so opposite, but after all these years, God has helped me see we balance each other out. Don is the solid anchor that keeps my flighty, daydreaming side from floating off into the ozone. Sure, we have conflicts. But we've discovered over the years that God is bigger than our differences, and what matters most isn't who's right, but who you love. The answer for us is each other. And God.

And that, my friends, is really what marriage is all about.

I pray you have found a combination of laughter and truth in "Bride on the Run." And I pray that the One who designed us male and female, who declared it isn't good for man to be alone, will bind you with cords of kindness and passion to the one you love. May your marriages abound with differences and laughter, and may you find wonder in each other on a daily basis.

As always, feel free to drop me a note through Multnomah, or on my e-mail at kbeditorial@aol.com. I love to hear from you!

God's best blessings—

Karen M. Ball

OUR WEDDING DAY

TODAY

Mom Ball's Killer Chili

If there's one thing my mother-in-law can do, it's cook! This chili is wonderfully flavorful and delightfully easy to fix. A great meal for a cool night, especially when served with cornbread or a loaf of a nice, dense bread. What's best, though, is if you follow the directions and let the chili simmer until it's nice and thick, your house will smell positively scrumptious!

Ingredients:

1 pound ground beef
4 cans each kidney beans and stewed tomatoes
1/4 cup dehydrated onion
2 Tablespoons parsley
1/3 cup chopped celery
4 Tablespoons chili powder (NOT cayenne pepper!!)

Brown ground beef. Drain, then place beef and rest of the ingredients in a pan on the stovetop. Cover and cook on medium until hot, then simmer on low until it cooks down to the desired thickness—anywhere from several hours to most of the day. Stir periodically.

Multnomah Publishers ®

The publisher and author would love to hear your
comments about this book. *Please contact us at:*
www.multnomah.net/threeweddings

More Fabulous Fiction
from Liz Curtis Higgs

Bookends

Dr. Emilie Getz is into saving historical relics; Jonas Fielding into saving souls. Imagine what happens when these two "bookend" land on the same shelf, filed betw *strongwilled* and *stubborn*. A romant comedy bestseller!

ISBN 1-57673-611-3

Mixed Signals

D.J. Belle O'Brien is weary of looking for happiness, "town to town, up and down the dial." A phone call from smooth-talking Patrick Reese sends her packing once more. The on-air cast of characters provides an entertaining backdrop for Belle's search for joy and her reluctant hero's own journey toward grace. Award-winning romance!

ISBN 1-57673-401-3

Bookends

Liz Curtis Higgs

Home.

The slightest shiver of expectation ran down her neck.

Emilie Getz noted with a smile of satisfaction that the old Moravian Congregational Store, circa 1762, hadn't been altered one iota except for the addition of dormers in the roof. There were laws about remodeling such buildings. "Remuddling is more like it," she murmured to no one in particular as she neared the corner and turned right onto Moravian Church Square.

In the chilly night, her heart skipped one beat, then two.

It was all there. The trombone choir, their elegant brass slides pointed toward the sanctuary doors, sounded a hymn as recognizable as her own name. The snow-dusted sidewalks guided visitors to the *Putz*—the church's annual diorama of Bethlehem of old. And hanging from every porch ceiling on the square were Moravian stars dancing in the wind, their ivory glow dispelling the darkness.

Nothing had changed. *Nothing.*

And that pleased Emilie immensely. From her wavy brown hair to her sensible leather boots, she was a woman who understood the importance of tradition. This was her hometown, after all. Her home congregation. Her "people," as her Winston-Salem friends would say. The last thing she wanted was to find everything she valued—everything she loved—tossed aside in the name of progress.

Slipping through the door with a nod to the greeter, she made a beeline for her favorite seat near the front, blinking hard as her senses were overwhelmed with awakened memories. The lump in her throat felt like an orange stuffed in a Christmas stocking. She sank onto a much-worn padded pew and tucked her small purse beside her, careful not to disturb the couple to her left as she made a nest for herself with her cashmere dress coat.

It seemed that every minute of eighteen years had passed since she'd sat in that exact spot.

Not true. It seemed like yesterday.

Letting her eyelids drift shut, Emilie drew in a quiet breath, savoring the spirit of Christmas past that hovered around her. The lingering scent of beeswax candles—snuffed at the close of the earlier vigil service—still tinged the air. *Home.*

Eyes still at half-mast, her ears tuned to the faintest traces of Pennsylvania German in the voices murmuring around her, Emilie didn't see the man preparing to sit down next to her until he landed with a jarring *thump*, flattening one side of her cashmere nest.

Good heavens. Didn't he realize he was sitting entirely too close?

She shifted to the left and whispered "Pardon me" while she tugged at her coat sleeve. The black jeans plastered on top of it were the sorriest excuse for Christmas Eve attire she'd ever witnessed. *Obviously not a Lititz man.*

When his response wasn't immediate, she turned her whisper up two notches. "Sir, if you would, please. You're sitting on my—"

"Really? No kidding."

His full-volume growl sounded like a muffler headed for a repair shop. Young and old in a three-pew circumference turned to see who was disturbing the peace. When Emilie's gaze joined theirs, she found herself face-to-face with something even more disturbing.

The man—and he was definitely that—had impossibly short hair, enormous eyes with brows covering half his face, and a five-o'clock shadow that darkened his chin line to a slovenly shade of black.

Before she could stop herself, Emilie grimaced.

Ick.

A lazy smile stretched across the field of dark stubble, at which point his narrow top lip disappeared completely. "Sorry, miss." He leaned slightly away from her, keeping his eyes trained on hers as he released her coat. "My mistake."

She snatched back her sleeve, chagrined to feel the crush marks in the fabric and the warmth of his body captured in the cloth. *Men!* Flustered, she fussed with her coat, trying to rearrange it just so without brushing against those tasteless black jeans of his. The ones that matched his black T-shirt and a black sports coat, which, Emilie couldn't help noticing, displayed an unseemly number of blond hairs.

A masculine hand thrust into view and the muffler rumbled again. "So. I'm Jonas Fielding. And you are…?"

Blushing is what you are, Em!

She swallowed, hoping it might stop the heat from rising up her too-long neck, and offered her hand for the briefest shake. He was so…so *not* like her professorial peers at Salem College. This man was…goodness, what was the word for it? Earthy. Masculine. *Something.* Whatever it was, it unnerved her.

Still, she really ought to be polite. They *did* have an audience, and it *was* Christmas Eve.

Pale fingers outstretched, she nodded curtly. "Dr. Emilie Getz."

He didn't shake her hand—he captured it. "New in town, Dr. Getz?"

The oldest line in the book! And he couldn't have been more wrong. She jumped at the chance to tell him so as she slipped her fingers back through his grasp and stuffed them in her skirt pocket.

"Not new at all. I was born and raised in Lititz. Graduated from Warwick High School, in fact." *Valedictorian, in fact.* She didn't mean to jerk her chin up, it merely went that way all by itself. "I've been…ah, gone for a few years."

His gaze traveled over her longer than necessary before his eyes returned to meet hers. "I'd say more than a few years, Emilie."

"Why…I…!" She was sputtering. *Sputtering!* The warmth in her neck shot north, filling her face with an unwelcome flush even as a sly grin filled his own devilish countenance.

An arpeggio from the pipe organ provided a blessed means of escape from his boyish wink and the chuckle that followed. *Heavens, what an ego he has!* With his dark features and all-male charm, he was undoubtedly the sort of fellow other women found drop-dead hand-some. Emilie hoped he would simply drop dead. Or, at the very least, vanish at the end of the service, never to sit on her coat—or step on her toes—again.

"More than a few years"? Humph!

An out-of-towner, no doubt. The borough of Lititz, nestled as it was in the heart of Amish country, swelled with visitors over the holidays. Clearly Jonah belonged among their number.

Calm down, Em. It's Christmas Eve.

An organ prelude by Pachelbel soon softened the corners of her mouth into a tenuous smile. For historians, a Moravian vigil service approached heaven on earth.

Though at age thirty-six, Emilie herself was anything but historic. Wasn't that so?

"More than a few years…"

The echo of his words tightened her smile. *The nerve.* How old was *he*, then? Reaching for a hymnal, she stole a furtive glance at the stranger on her right. The man was easily her age. Older, judging by the hint of silver in his close-cropped hair. Granted, only two hairs were gray, but they *were* gray. Definitely.

His eyes shifted toward hers before she realized she'd lingered too long. "Counting my gray hairs, Emilie?"

"No! I mean, yes, but that's not what I was looking for." She sat up straight and pointed her chin toward the pulpit. "Never mind."

He leaned closer. "In case you're wondering—and you apparently are—I was born in the sixties. And another thing: you can skip the hymnal. All the words are in this program." He waved it under her nose, clearly enjoying himself. "Didn't you get one?"

"It's not a program, it's an ode. And I don't need one, thank you. I was born Moravian. I know all these hymns by heart, including the German ones."

"More than a few years, Emilie…"

That infernal man and his insinuations! He was at least as old as she was, she'd quickly calculated. Probably the very same age. It was quite obviously the *only* thing they had in common.

She'd seen his type all her life: athletic, popular, big man on campus, strutting around with a pretty airhead on each arm. The sort who wouldn't give a sober, studious girl such as her the time of day.

When the congregation stood to sing "All Glory to Immanuel's Name," Emilie was amazed to hear a tolerably pleasant bass voice booming from the broad chest next to her. He also seemed to know the tune, even without printed music. Had he been here in years past?

Curiosity overruled her good sense. In the sparse moment of silence before the pastoral prayer, she whispered in his general direction, "Have you attended our Christmas vigil before?"

"Five years in a row. I'm Moravian too."

Her jaw dropped before she could catch it.

"Not *born* Moravian, like you," he chided softly. "You'll have to explain that one to me later."

Later? As in after the prayer? After the service? Later over tea in her cozy kitchen on Main Street? *Surely he isn't suggesting such a thing!* Surely not. Disgusted with the mere notion of brewing a pot of Darjeeling for a Neanderthal, she fixed her gaze on the enormous Moravian star hanging above the pulpit, spinning ever so slightly in the rising heat, and composed her features into an attitude of worship, even if her mind wasn't cooperating.

The man is not your type. At all. Another quick glance at the blond hairs on his jacket assured her of that. Still, his comment taunted her. Explain *what* to him later? Explain why she was back in Lititz after all these years? Explain why her whole academic career depended on what she might uncover less than a mile away?

Wrong. No explanations needed, not when there wouldn't be anything happening *later* with Jonah-something-or-other.

Coming June 2003 from
KAREN BALL
THE BREAKING POINT

ISBN 1-59052-033-5

"*The Breaking Point* goes beyond superb and engrossing—which it most certainly is—and enters the realm of heart-changing, life-altering fiction. Karen Ball has penned a modern classic and given us two unforgettable characters to root for. This is an author to watch!"

ROBIN LEE HATCHER, bestselling author of
Firstborn and *Promised to Me*

Gabe and Renee Roman are on the edge—relationally and spiritually. Both consider themselves Christians. But after years of struggling in their marriage, their greatest test comes in the most unexpected of forms: a blizzard in the Oregon mountains. Their truck hurtles over the side of a mountain, and each encounters the realities of suffering, sacrifice, and service in Christ's name. It isn't until they surrender their last defenses that their surface understandings are torn away and all that's left is truth: Only through obedience to God's call can they find true joy.

December 19, 1:15 P.M.

Dark.

Cold.

Pain.

Each sensation whispered over Renee...drawing her into awareness, away from the stillness.

"No..."

Had she spoken the word or just thought it? Either way, it seemed to echo through her, a sound as brittle and frightened as any she'd ever known.

Slowly her eyelids lifted, and she blinked against the brightness, battling the fog that seemed to fill her mind as well as her vision. But what she saw when things came into focus didn't make any sense.

White. Everything was bathed in white. There was a suffocating blanket of it outside the truck, where snow blew and swirled, cloaking the world around them. And inside the truck...the white was there, too. On the windshield...in the air...

As Renee's dazed eyes focused, she saw the reason why. Snow was piled on the dashboard, on her lap, and every time she exhaled, a white puff filled the air in front of her face. She drew a deep breath, but as the frigid air flowed into her lungs, she was seized by a fit of coughing that wracked her body.

It was then, as she struggled to breathe, that she realized how cold she was. So cold she couldn't stop shivering. "G...Gabe?"

A flash of red and white came into view, and she pulled back just as Bo vaulted the seat backs and landed half in her lap, half on the floor. The dog's frantic tongue bathed her face, and Renee grabbed at his front paws as they raked her shoulders.

"Bo, no! Down!"

True to his training, the Siberian scrambled back and landed on the floorboard, sitting with a thump at Renee's feet. But he leaned into her, his two-colored gaze fixed on her like a child seeking comfort after waking from a terrifying nightmare. Renee dug her cold hands into his fur, scratching his neck, trying to comfort him even as she struggled to understand what had happened.

Her gaze roamed the cab of the truck...and realization seeped in. They'd gone over the edge of the road. The momentum of their spin had slammed them right through the wall of snow and ice at the road's edge. They must have plummeted down the mountainside...

As the reality of their situation hit her, she turned with a jerk. Sweet relief made her weak when she saw Gabe. Though he was unconscious, puffs of white hanging in the air near his mouth bore blessed testimony to the fact that he was breathing.

"Gabe...?" She reached for him, then halted when punishing pain stabbed through her, sucking the air from her lungs, making everything go faint and faded. She drew in shallow gulps of oxygen, fighting to stay conscious. *God...help me...*

She reached again, frustrated with how sluggish her motions seemed, as though she were trapped in some slow-motion segment of a movie. She crept her fingers along until they found Gabe's wrist and searched, pressed...

Yes! There was a pulse. When she felt it pound, strong and steady, against her fingertips, she let herself cry.

Thank God...thank God...

She leaned her head back against her seat, staring up at the truck ceiling, then looked down at Bo while she felt the ceiling. "It's not crushed or caved in at all... We must not have rolled. Well, that's a blessing anyway." She shifted her gaze and grimaced. The front of the truck was another story. It looked as if it had been put in some gigantic trash compactor.

From the look of it, they must have slid down the side of the mountain, taking out some of the small trees in their path. The front of the truck was accordioned back to the cab—but not into it, thank heavens, or she and Gabe might well have been crushed. Their legs surely would have been.

She glanced at Bo again and nudged him off her feet and flexed her toes, her ankles, and then her knees. No injuries, at least not that she could feel. Just then a gust of wind blasted the side of her face, and she shivered as she frowned. Where was that coming from? She turned, searching...and stared. The window in the passenger's door was gone; jagged remnants were all that remained. The wind and snow were taking full advantage of the opening.

"No wonder I'm so cold!"

Bo cocked his head, his ears pricked, as though agreeing with her wholeheartedly. A small chuckle escaped her, and she laid her hand on the dog's broad head.

"I'm glad you're okay, boy, and that you're awake—" Emotion clutched at her throat, choking her. She fought back tears and leaned down to press her forehead to the top of Bo's head. "It helps to have someone to talk to."

He rewarded her whispered admission with a quick lick. She rubbed his soft head, then straightened, looking at the shattered window. "I've got to cover that up. Which means I need to move."

This wasn't going to feel good, and she knew it. She forced her aching body into action, though the response was far slower than usual. Her fingers groped for the release on the seatbelt, but it eluded her. Muttering her irritation, she shifted—then gasped at the pain that jabbed through her. She grabbed at her side, groaning, pressing her hands to her ribs. They must have been bruised by the seatbelt when the truck hit bottom.

At least she hoped they were only bruised.

One thing was for sure, she needed more room to maneuver. She nudged Bo with her foot. "C'mon, boy, into the backseat." He resisted for a moment, then hopped across the wide console between the seats and moved to his blanket.

Renee inched her hand along the seatbelt and fingered the catch, trying to stir up as little pain as possible. She let out a relieved breath when she pressed the release, and the seatbelt snapped free. She pushed it aside and leaned toward Gabe, grimacing at the ugly gash on the side of his forehead. Blood trickled down his pale, still face.

"Jesus...Jesus..."

Even as the prayer escaped her frantic heart and flew skyward, she felt her shaking increase, as though whatever inner dam had been restraining the tremors had finally given way. Blinding panic sparked to life somewhere deep in her gut, jumping and growing like flames in a stack of tinder-dry wood.

411

Suddenly the cab of the truck felt like it was closing in on her, and a chilling, wailing scream was filling her mind. She sat back, pressing her spine into the back of her seat, forcing herself to take deep, even breaths of the cold, wintry air. With each puff of white as she exhaled, she repeated one, fierce word over and over: "Calm…calm…calm…"

She wasn't sure how long it took until her pulse resumed a more or less normal beat, but she let her relief out with a slow breath when it finally happened. If only she could stop shaking. She knew it was partly nerves, partly the aching cold that seemed imbedded in her very bones.

And shock…it could be shock…

She pushed the grim thought aside, then swiveled to kneel on the seat and then reach into the back. Amazingly, though he never took his eyes off of her, Bo stayed where he was. She grabbed the strap of the canvas duffle bag Gabe always insisted they take along when they traveled in the winter.

Renee remembered how she'd reacted to his precautions. She'd cast her gaze to the ceiling, making no effort to hide her disdain when he told her to pack extra clothes and food. Though she hadn't voiced her complaints, her mind had overflowed with caustic comments: He was, as usual, being overly cautious, hyper-vigilant. Why on earth couldn't the man just relax and have a good time?

Now…

She glanced at her unmoving husband and felt her throat catch. She swallowed back the wave of tears struggling to take over. Steady, Renee. Don't fall apart now. You need to stay focused. She looked at Bo. "Thank heaven he ignored me and listened to his instincts, eh, boy? He sure was right about this."

The husky's steady gaze never wavered. "I know, I know… it's too bad he isn't awake to hear me say that." She turned back to the bag. "Wouldn't he just love to hear me admit I was wrong."

Heaven knew he seldom ever heard those words from her. In fact, Renee thought, allowing herself a small smile, hearing her admit she was wrong might even make their nosedive down a mountainside worthwhile. For Gabe, anyway.

She reached out to stroke the back of her husband's hand where it lay, so very still, on the console. "I'll tell you when you're conscious, Gabe. I promise."

Turning back to her task, she grabbed the bag and tugged it free until it landed in her lap with a thud. The increasing tremor in her hands made it a struggle to jerk the zipper open, but she finally managed to do so. She pulled out gloves, a scarf, a hat, snow pants, each item making her feel like a giddy child on Christmas morning.

At the bottom of the bag were a blanket, an assortment of imperishables—chocolate bars, protein bars, dried fruit, nuts, water—and a large baggie with a dozen or so pocket heat packs.

Her numb fingers fumbled with the extra clothing, but she finally managed to pull the snow pants and a long-sleeved fleece top over her clothes. That done, she stuffed a few of the heat packs into her pockets, placing the rest back in the bag. As cold as it was now, it would only get colder when the sun went down. Better to save the heat packs until they really needed them.

Thankfully, warmth was coming back into her body. Amazing what an extra layer of clothing could accomplish. With a fortifying breath, she reached under her seat for the small first-aid kit they stored there. Within minutes she had Gabe's wound cleaned and dressed. She was careful not to move his head, in case there was any kind of neck injury. She felt a whisper of relief when the bleeding on his forehead seemed to have stopped. As carefully as she could, she eased a knit cap over his thick hair.

A blast of cold air and spitting snow hit her, and she glanced at her window. "I've got to find a way to block that wind, boy."

The tip of Bo's tail wagged. Obviously he agreed. Too bad he didn't have any ideas to offer. She peered into the backseat, then grabbed a ragged towel and Gabe's ever-present roll of gray tape.

Duct tape, she heard his longsuffering voice correct her in her mind. He hated it when she called it gray tape, though she'd explained time and again that that was what her dad had called it, so it only made sense she'd call it that as well. After all, the stuff was gray...

A scene flashed through her mind. She and Gabe couldn't have been married more than a few weeks when she'd first called it gray tape. He'd looked at her, eyes wide, mouth open, as though she'd just spit in his mother's soup or something equally unforgivable.

"It's called duct tape, Renee."

She wrinkled her nose, peering at the roll of tape in her hand. "Doesn't look like a duck to me."

He stared at her, then a wry smile lifted his lips. "Duct tape, with a t."

"Oh, of course, that makes so much more sense."

He'd laughed then, and she joined him, throwing her arms around his waist and snuggling close. His eyes as he looked down at her had shone with such tenderness, and he'd ended the debate as they always did back then...back when things were so much simpler, so much easier to understand...by enfolding her in his arms and silencing her with a kiss.

Renee bit her lip. *We used to have so much fun...*

Shaking off the melancholy creeping over her, she turned to the window and got to work. It took longer than she liked to get it covered, but the band of pain that had taken up residence around her midsection wouldn't let her work more than a few seconds at a shot. When she finally finished, she could feel a thin sheen of perspiration on her face. She was shaking again, and the thought she'd been avoiding forced its way into her mind.

Shock...I could be going into shock...

As though sensing her anxiety, Bo moved then, stretching out on top of the console and pressing his side into her. She leaned against him, grateful for the dog's warmth, and rubbed her hands up and down her arms, fighting the tears that burned at the back of her eyes. *Don't cry...it just makes it* harder to breathe. Besides, you can't afford to lose the moisture.

Renee gave a small laugh. None of this was the least bit funny, but she couldn't help it. That last thought had sounded so much like Gabe, in all his oh-so-practical glory. He was definitely rubbing off on her. And for once, she admitted, that was a good thing.

Pillowing her head on Bo's soft back, she angled a look at her husband, then reached over to lay a hand on his shoulder, struggling to draw encouragement and strength from the steady rhythm of his breathing.

And yet, as they lay there in the shrouded silence of the truck cab, she couldn't help but wonder...

Is this where it ends, Father?

Renee pressed her burning eyes against her arm, refusing to surrender to the grief that hung at the back of her heart. Grief for all that could have been...all that should have been.

But most of all, grief for the loss of all those wonderful hopes and dreams born long ago in the purity of childish innocence.